The Toll

The Toll

Loren Schechter

Merrimack Media
Boston, Massachusetts

Library of Congress Control Number:

ISBN: print: 978-1-945756-19-1

Published by Merrimack Media, Boston, Massachusetts

Contents

This novel is dedicated to all who try to improve the quality of life for the mentally ill and/or disadvantaged.

Author's Note

This novel is the first one I started, but it has taken me forty years to finish. As my children grew up, my career progressed, and I wrote three lighter novels, I kept drafts of the The Toll tucked away in a drawer, and later in a computer file. This novel was the hardest to write because the topic of mental illness is serious, and because this story is the most personal in terms of my feelings and observations.

I never was young Doctor Daniels, nor were any of my patients or their caretakers the other characters in this book. What I took from real life were some of the situations I experienced or heard about, but I used my imagination in creating the characters that encountered those difficulties. Their physical appearance, thoughts, feelings and actions are all my own invention. Any flaws in their portrayal are entirely my responsibility.

As a fiction writer, the question "what if?" haunts me, and effective dramatic scenes seduce and challenge me. As a doctor, I often imagine worst case scenarios that I refrain from sharing unless specifically asked. That combination of "what if?" and "worst case" impels me to embroider drama from a factual remnant of life. Were my wife and children actually threatened by a madman I treated? Yes. Was he like the character in this novel, and did he go after them? No… But "what if?"

I hope a reality that does come through to readers of this fiction is my great debt, not only to the psychiatrists, but to all the mental health clinicians and patients who taught me how to be a more understanding human being and a better psychiatrist.

Whenever I pulled this manuscript out of a drawer to work on it, I would share my latest chapter with family members or with whatever writing group I was in at the time. My children grew up hearing about George Elton Cruber and wondering how their father could have someone so wicked in his head. So I thank Amy, Julie and Nathan for their love and patience, their suggestions and enthusiasm, all of which helped me finish this novel.

In the 1980s, I benefited greatly from a writing group in Wellesley, Massachusetts that was led by a great teacher of writing, Art Edelstein, and his talented wife, Tima Smith. I was helped with filling out the background and language of my Greek character, Petro, by Vangie Gallow Tzellas Boule. Any mistakes made thirty years later in my use of Greek are mine alone.

More recently, I've been fortunate enough to participate in two writing groups whose members have helped with the final rewrite of my novel. My longest and finest association has been with a writing group in Newton, Massachusetts. Without the constructive criticism and suggestions generously given by Laurie Nordman, Holly Raynes, Karen Halil and Megan Connelly, my novel would have been a much poorer product. The same can be said of my more recent associates, Jenny Pivor, Diane Sharpe, Mary Baures and Linda Malcolm, members of a writing group sponsored by my publisher, Merrimack Media. Jenny Pivor,, the owner of that enterprise, has gracefully guided me through the publication of this and two other novels, for which I sincerely thank her.

Last, but certainly not least, I thank my editor, muse and true love, Susan Wetherall. I am very fortunate to have married all three.

Important Characters

IMPORTANT CHARACTERS

Starred names represent characters who have some importance but do not appear in person.

Eric Bergstrom, M.D. – Professor of Psychiatry at University Hospital

Nancy Brill – a 14 year-old girl suffering from schizophrenia

    Joseph (Joe) Brill – Nancy's father, a state senator

    Nan Brill – Nancy's mother

George Cruber – a 38 year-old toll collector and meat cutter

    Denise Cruber – his 32 year-old wife

    Carol — their 4 year-old daughter

    George, junior — their 2 year-old son

Raymond Daniels, M.D. – a 28 year-old, third year resident in psychiatry

    Lisa Daniels – his wife

    Julie – their 3 year-old daughter

    *Ethan – Raymond's younger brother, killed in Vietnam

    *Sarah – Raymond and Ethan's younger sister

Anita DeSimone – Executive Secretary, Dept. of Psychiatry, University Hospital

Gail Eggers – Chief Nurse on the Adult Psychiatry Unit, University Hospital

IMPORTANT CHARACTERS

T.J. Fremmer – Acting Chief of Security, University Hospital

Laurence Kroft, Ph.D. – Superintendent of the area's state hospital

Mary Margaret (Maggie) Saxe – a suicidal, 20 year-old university student

  John – Maggie's mysterious boyfriend

  *Franklin Dexter (F. Dexter) Saxe – Maggie's father

  *Wanda Saxe – Maggie's mother

  *Patricia (Tricia) Saxe – Maggie's older sister, died from an overdose of heroin

  *Maurice Hermann Saxe – Maggie's younger brother

 *Roberta (Bobbi) Stowell — former Chief Nurse on the Adult Psychiatry Unit

Harrison Taylor, M.D. – Chairman of University Hospital's Department of Psychiatry

Petro Tsourakis – owner of Peter's Place, the pub in which Maggie works

Leroy White , M.D. – Assistant Professor of Psychiatry at University Hospital

PART I

MAY 1969

1

City Hospital

Two steps into the brightly lit treatment room, Doctor Raymond Daniels stopped short. The angry glare from the scantily-clad young woman sitting on the examining table warned him not to step closer. Joanne! he thought. No, not Joanne, but this woman's dark hair, green eyes and unspoken command were so like those of the girlfriend he'd loved and lost. Raymond backed up against a tile wall, crossed his arms and let his shoulders sag within his white jacket, shrinking his six-foot frame to appear less threatening.

Kevin Brailey, the scrub-suited intern, was wrapping gauze around the woman's wrist. A used suture pack and bloody gauze pads lay on the instrument stand. On the other side of it, a middle-aged nurse handed him a strip of adhesive tape. Her nametag identified her as Alicia Howell, R.N. She looked at Raymond and shook her head.

The woman still won't speak, thought Raymond. Brailey had groused about that when he'd telephoned the on-call room for a psychiatry resident. "She spoke a few words at registration, but the guy who brought her to the ER took off and she hasn't said a word since. I'll sew up her wrists, but then she's yours. I've got truly sick people to attend to."

Well, what overworked doctor wouldn't be annoyed by willful mutism at 4 a.m.? thought Raymond. It was a piss-poor time for anything but sleep. He felt exhausted, too. This stint at City Hospital had given him plenty of experience with street people, but never a decent night's sleep. Only one more week, then back to University Hospital and a saner schedule.

The young woman bowed her head toward the wrist being wrapped, but there was no forgetting those green eyes, that hostile face. Twisted in a French braid, her black hair glistened beneath the operating light. A small crucifix on a thin, silver necklace was her only piece of jewelry. His gaze dropped to her scarlet toenails and worn sandals, then inched up her long legs to the surgical gauze that disappeared beneath her cut-offs. Her midriff was bare; a black halter scarcely contained her breasts. Probably in her early twenties, he thought. Not many years between us.

The intern finished taping gauze around the patient's wrist and glanced up. "Ms. Saxe, this is Doctor Daniels, the psychiatrist I mentioned. Doctor Daniels, this is Mary Saxe."

She gave no indication that she'd heard. Except for her measured breathing, Mary Saxe was a forbidding statue balanced on the edge of the examining table, a well-thumbed magazine by her side.

"Hello," said Raymond, his tone polite, a bit warm, not overly friendly.

She didn't respond.

The intern lowered Saxe's outstretched hand onto her bandaged thigh. "There you are," he said. "Not quite as good as new, but a pretty close approximation." He turned away and moved toward the sink.

Give them time to clean up and get out, thought Raymond. He watched the nurse as she cleared the instruments and surgical gloves, dumped paper wrappings and bloodstained gauze into the appropriate buckets. Every now and then, he glanced at his patient. Mary Saxe kept her eyes downcast, her hands on her thighs, apparently awaiting whatever came next. Was she a hooker? Not unusual at City Hospital. But in denim cut-offs and without make-up? But why else would a man desert her in the middle of the night? If he was a boyfriend, he'd given her a tough good-bye.

As the nurse sprayed the instrument tray with disinfectant and wiped it clean, the intern washed his hands in the sink. Brailey used an elbow to shut the tap, a wet hand to snap paper towels from the dispenser. "I put nine sutures in her left wrist, seven in her right," he said. "The surgical resident didn't see any nerve or tendon damage. The cuts on her thighs just needed to be cleaned and bandaged." Brailey tossed the soggy towels in the waste bucket, then turned back to his patient. "Those stitches should come out in seven to ten days, not before. Understand? Please don't mess up my good work – or God's, for that matter."

Mary Saxe's head inched upward, but the intern ignored her movement. Raymond wondered what her response meant. Was it acknowledgement or defiance, "thank you" or "fuck you" – a twinge of guilt or only an easing of tension?

"Do you want Mrs. Howell to stay?" Brailey asked him.

Raymond rubbed the back of his neck. The intern was worried that this female time-bomb might explode or cry "rape." Her tears and attorneys could be more damaging than violence. On the other hand, she'd be less likely to confide in him with someone else listening. "No, thank you," he said. "Leave the door open."

The intern nodded. "If you need something, just call."

"Will do." Raymond watched the nurse follow Brailey out. My move, he thought. Keep it low key, aim for a climate of safety.

He retrieved a metal stool from the far corner of the room and placed it halfway between Saxe and the open door. He sat down, started to cross his legs, then thought better of it – he might have to move quickly. Toes on the floor, hands on his knees, palms drying on the soft corduroy – he was ready to begin.

"My name is Raymond Daniels. I'm a resident in psychiatry. I'd like to be of help if I can."

With the grace of a dancer and without lifting her head, Mary Saxe swung her legs up and pivoted away from him. She crossed her legs and tucked her feet under her bandaged thighs. His view of her back was obstructed only by the tapered strap of her halter and the bow of black ribbon at the base of her neck. Yup, he thought, Lisa would kill for a figure like that, especially since their daughter Julie was born.

"I gather you're less than enthusiastic about seeing me," he said. "I don't take it personally. And I won't do you any harm."

Mary Saxe didn't move a muscle.

"I don't know what your silence means, but my guess is you're scared. Are you?" He let the question hang in the air until all hope for a response evaporated.

"Whatever you're feeling, it would probably help to get it off your chest." Remembering her ample breasts and skimpy halter, he wished he'd said "mind," not "chest." Not that anything he said seemed to matter to her. And not many clues to go on. She was alert and very much in control, so certainly not drunk and probably not stoned. Her pivot had been easy and graceful, and she'd spoken at the reception desk, so the diagnosis of catatonia didn't fit. Didn't her scanty attire and wrist-cutting suggest an hysterical personality? Well, whatever else she was, she was undoubtedly pissed off.

"I suppose," he ventured, "that you're pretty angry that your boyfriend took off from the reception desk."

This time, her lack of response puzzled him. No ring on either hand; father or husband unlikely to leave her after she cut herself; and good Samaritans rare after 3 a.m. It had to be a boyfriend, lover or customer.

"It was a rotten thing for him to do — unless, of course, he left you the keys to the car or taxi-fare home. You do have a way home, don't you?"

Mary Saxe reached for the magazine. Placing it on her lap, she turned page after page, as if scanning each one for an article worthy of her attention.

"Maybe he didn't leave you a way home because he was worried about you and felt you needed to be admitted to our psychiatric unit. On the other hand, maybe he just took one look at this building and mistook it for the city dump."

"Fuck you!" she snapped.

Got you talking, he thought. He swallowed his satisfaction. This was not Little Mary Sunshine. "I don't think you really want to. You hardly know me."

"I know you're a prick."

He blinked, reminded of the insults he endured as a Jewish kid raised in Bensonhurst's Little Italy. His smile was bittersweet. "That may be largely true."

"Don't flatter yourself. You're a puny prick. That's why they call you 'shrink'."

"Am I really so scary you have to put me down?"

"Schiz – o – phre – ni – a," she said, stretching each syllable like Eliza Dolittle practicing vowels.

"Are you worried you have it, or that you might get it?"

"You're the shrink."

"But not a mindreader."

"Just a mindfucker."

"Not that either. What do you want to know about schizophrenia?"

Saxe tossed the magazine aside, uncrossed her legs and pushed down with her hands, wincing with pain but rising until she stood on the examining table. Angrily triumphant, she towered over him like a warrior taunting a vanquished foe. "What makes Doctor Jekyll become Mister Hyde?"

His hands came up to explain, to protect. He lifted his gaze quickly past her pale thighs and breasts to her face. "That wasn't schizophrenia. It was a fictional case of dual personality."

"You may read books, but you don't understand me." She seethed with contempt. "You don't understand me at all. What makes Doctor Jekyll become Mister Hyde?"

Was she speaking of herself? Others? How had she become the interrogator? His muscles tensed, but only her words leaped at him.

"Louder, asshole. I don't hear your answer."

He glanced toward the door. Were they hearing her mocking tone and defiance, his inept silence? Focus! She'd remained mute in fear and rage – now she was trying to turn the tables. "Why don't you sit down, and we'll talk about your riddle."

"Do you have the vaguest notion of what I mean?"

"I think so. You're asking about me, or your boyfriend – or perhaps all men." He hardened his tone. "Now please sit down."

"I like standing."

"Fine. Stand on the floor."

"Why? Are you getting nervous?"

"No." He'd gone beyond and back. "I'm getting a stiff neck looking up."

"Grandma told me to watch out for stiff-necked boys. She said they usually had limp pricks."

Raymond's lips tightened. Yes, provocation was her weapon, reversal her defense – or at least one of them. And her fears? About madness and powerlessness. Better to focus on the now. "What did Grandma tell you about standing on the furniture?"

"To take off my shoes before I did it." Saxe balanced on her right foot and removed her left sandal. She flipped it directly at him. He caught it before it hit him in the face. The right sandal followed the flight of its mate. "I'll bet you never did it with your shoes on," she taunted.

He dropped the sandals and stood up. "Look, this is no game. Unless you sit down, I'm going to call in as many nurses as are needed to sit you down and strap you to that table. Maybe then we can talk like reasonable people about why you cut yourself up. And if you won't do that, I'll have no choice but to sign a detention order and admit you to the psychiatric ward."

"And I'll have no choice but to sue your ass." Saxe laughed and jumped lightly from the table. She winced as her bare feet hit the floor, but she turned her landing into a curtsey, then rose almost to his height with a mischievous smile. "How do you do, Doctor Jekyll. I'm Mary Margaret Saxe. My friends call me Maggie. I'm less than delighted to make your acquaintance." Her smile disappeared. "May I ask you something?" Her manner suddenly became shy. "It's a bit personal."

"Sure. What?"

Moving close enough so he could smell her lavender scent, she whispered, "I've got to take a leak. Do you know a John I can piss on?"

Raymond blinked. Piss on? Not in? "There are bathrooms at the rear of the emergency suite. I'll call for Mrs. Howell to go with you."

"I don't need any help."

"I'm concerned about your safety. Will you go and come back without hurting yourself?"

"You're concerned about not getting blamed if I do something." She bent down for a sandal and rose slowly enough to give him a good view of her breasts before she slipped the sandal onto her foot. "Don't worry. I just have to use the toilet." She repeated her slow-motion performance with the other sandal. "If I fall in, I'll try to tread water. You going to jump in and save me?"

He pursed his lips and wrinkled his brow as if considering the pros and cons. "Before or after you pee?" he asked.

"Very funny." But her tone said it wasn't. She tilted her jaw upward, pinned him with her eyes. "I'm telling you it can get very messy. You going to jump in?"

Jump into what? Next week he'd be out of here, on vacation, then back to University Hospital. "I'm here with you now," he said. "Do you have to keep testing me?"

She backhanded the air. "I don't have to do anything. Just be careful I don't drag you under without really trying."

"I'll be careful. But are you going to hurt yourself in the bathroom, or run away, or do anything else to endanger yourself in the next ten minutes?"

"I don't know. Who looks that far ahead?"

He let out a sigh. "I'm trying to. Please join me."

"It's hard to resist when you say please, especially with those brown, puppy eyes. Okay, Doctor Jekyll, I'll go pee like a Girl Scout."

"Then this way." Without looking to see if she followed, he led the way up the central corridor of the emergency suite. Two other examining rooms were in use, with the beeps of a cardiac monitor coming from one of them. Seeing no lock on the door of the ladies' room, he felt more comfortable about letting her go in alone. He stepped aside and folded his arms across his chest.

"Are you the shrink or the bathroom monitor?" she asked.

He tilted his head toward the bathroom door. "Why don't you just leave all the crap in there."

Saxe pushed the door half open. "I may have misjudged you," she said.

"In what way?"

"You may be a smarter bastard than I thought."

He watched the door close behind her. What was with this woman? Would Professor Bergstrom accept "Bitch, Grade A, chronic and severe" as a diagnosis? Who would treat her? Even if her provocative behavior was the result of trauma, her anger a defense against fear or depression, who in his right mind would want to put up with her abuse? It wasn't as if she were psychotic; Maggie Saxe knew what she was doing.

A ripple of laughter floated down the corridor from the nurses' station, accentuating the silence from the ladies' room. The minutes passed slowly, each one dragging a train of worries through his brain. Could she have removed the screen and squeezed through the small window? Perhaps she'd broken the mirror and cut herself again. Was she lying on the floor within, life oozing away, while he stood outside like a fool? Stupid to have trusted her. He strode to the door. "Ms. Saxe, are you okay?"

No answer.

He sprang forward and was inside before her head jerked around. She was kneeling on the white tile floor, hands clasped, tears in her eyes. Her lips formed an unspoken word. He felt astonished, flustered, embarrassed. She'd been praying.

"I'm sorry," he mumbled. "I didn't know."

She looked away, examining the frosted windowpane. Her hands separated and formed fists. "I forgive your ignorance. I doubt I'll forget your bad manners."

What hypocrisy! She'd been anything but well-mannered. Yet her pain was real enough, perhaps her prayers were, too. She'd not wanted him to see her tears or her piety — or had she? "I was concerned. I called. You didn't answer."

"I don't answer to your call. I answer to His."

God's? Was she serious? "I apologize for intruding. I'll wait for you outside."

As he turned to go, he heard her voice, softer, almost mellow. "Daniels – "

He looked back. She still faced away. "What?"

"I'll meet you back in that room when I'm done. And I won't forget your concern."

"Yeah – well, maybe you can put in a few good words for both of us then."

He eased the door closed behind him.

2

George

George found a suitable woman curled up on flattened cardboard in the back doorway of a Greek restaurant, not far from the dumpster which probably had provided her a midnight supper. Watching her sleep, he put on a pair of extra-large medical gloves, then scuffed his sneakers against the pavement close to her feet. The beam of his flashlight caught her startled look as she pushed back a thin blanket and sat up, one hand reaching for the large knapsack, the other for either a bottle or a weapon inside her coat. He wondered if she'd already taken on the alley's stink of garbage and stale urine. If so, he'd have to clean her up before he called a doctor.

"You look like you need help," he said. "Do you want to come with me to a shelter?"

Under a fringe of stringy gray hair, her eyes narrowed. "Leave me the fuck alone." She pulled out a butcher knife and pointed it up at him.

"No need for that." George flashed his beam up and the down the alley. No one. He clicked off the flashlight. "I'll just leave you a better blanket." He eased the plaid blanket he'd taken from his mother's closet out of a plastic bag. "How tall are you?" he asked, stepping toward her.

"Don't come any closer." She let go of the knapsack and scrambled to her knees. She thrust the knife a few inches forward.

Holding one edge of the blanket, he let the bulk of it spill from his hand. "You remind me of my mother before she got cancer. I think this will fit you."

"I don't want your dead mother's blanket."

George almost smiled. "She's not dead. Not yet." He dropped the blanket onto the knife, grabbed the woman's wrist and slammed the flashlight into the side of her head. As she fell, he threw himself on her, twisting her wrist until she cried out and dropped the knife. He beat her until she stopped struggling, then pulled the plastic bag over her head and gathered it tight. Her thrashing was as futile as her efforts to breathe. When it was over, he wrapped her in the blanket, positioned her as if she were sleeping, and went for his car.

3

Maggie

Exiting the ladies' room, Raymond glanced about self-consciously. He ran a hand through his unruly hair. Was he right to barge in there? To leave her now? So easy to crash when you're flying blind. Maybe Mary Saxe's registration form could provide useful information.

He strode up the corridor toward the nurses' station. Behind the white counter, Mrs. Howell was sitting and chatting with an obese male attendant. As Raymond approached, the nurse greeted him with raised eyebrows.

"Our patient is in the ladies' room, praying," he said.

"Is that a joke?" asked the attendant.

"If it is, it's on me. I need her registration sheet. Is it here or does Doctor Brailey have it?"

"It's here," said Mrs. Howell. She reached for a clipboard holding a sheet of paper. "Doctor Brailey said I should tell you he and the charge nurse are in treatment room 4 if you need them. They're with an asthmatic."

"Thanks." Raymond took the clipboard. "If the coffee pot's going," he told the attendant, "I need two coffees stat – one black, one light, and some sugar on the side."

"Sure, Doc." The attendant's belly sagged over an invisible belt as he struggled to his feet and headed into the small office behind the nurses' station.

Raymond scanned the registration form. Born in September, 1948 – Mary Saxe was twenty; she wouldn't be twenty-one for four months. Her address, 27A North Howard, was a stone's throw from the University's main campus. With University Hospital so close to home, why had she come all the way across town to City Hospital after three in the morning? Had she stayed the night at her boyfriend's pad? That might account for her shorts and halter — fine for a sunny afternoon in May, but scant protection against the night air. And why was the word "NONE" typed into the box specifying next of kin? Were all her relatives dead? More likely that Saxe and her lover wanted everything kept secret.

Back in the treatment room, he placed both cups of coffee and the sugar on the stainless steel counter next to the sink. He moved the stool closer to the door and sat down.

Would she keep her word and come back? If she did, would she be the mute, the temptress, the penitent? Beneath each mask there was another. Would the real Mary Saxe show her face?

The tread of sandals coming up the hall alerted him. He took in a deep breath and exhaled slowly. Mary Saxe appeared in the doorway and hesitated. She'd straightened her French braid and washed away her tears, but her green eyes and tight facial muscles expressed wariness and defiance. It was a strong face, with high cheekbones, straight nose, prominent jaw, and full lips drawn tight with determination.

Don't get up! thought Raymond. Get up, she'll bolt. He offered her a smile and a hand which rolled lazily toward the counter top. "I thought you might like a cup of coffee."

"I can get a better one at home."

"I'm sure you could. How do you take it?"

"Black." She took a step into the room.

"It's the cup on the left." He watched her move to the sink.

"Do you serve coffee to all your patients?"

He offered a small smile. "Perhaps we ought to drink it before it gets cold." He got up and moved slowly toward the sink, anticipating that she'd take her cup and move aside. She stood her ground, picked up the cup on the right and extended it to him. His fingers closed on the cup, but she wouldn't let it go.

"Why me?" she demanded. Her eyes pierced his; her fingers didn't withdraw.

"How do you mean?"

"Why are you giving me coffee – going out of your way? What do you want from me?"

Oh, brother. "Does everybody who offers you something want something in return?"

"In spades. So what do you want?"

He shook his head. "You're hurting, and I'm trying to be of some help. It's as simple as that. Only I don't know enough about you to be helpful, and you're too afraid and angry to guide me."

She let go of the cup and turned away. "Why should I? I didn't ask for your help. I don't need it. I don't have the faintest idea why you give a damn."

"I know that you didn't ask for help with words. But you demanded it with a knife or a razor blade. Maybe you asked for help in your prayers...And why do I give a damn?" He rubbed the back of his neck. "I guess because, if I were feeling desperate enough to slice myself up, I sure hope someone would try to help me."

"You finished?" said Saxe. "Your coffee is probably cold by now." She picked up her cup, took one sip, twisted her lips downward, and poured the coffee into the sink.

"It's that bad?"

"Now I know why people die in the hospital."

Like hell she did. His mother had died of cancer, not coffee. He pushed away the memory of her ashen face and emaciated body on the hospital bed, the pain of a helpless twelve year-old that had made him a doctor and brought him here, to help this woman and others. "Did you want to die tonight?"

Saxe turned to inspect the supply cabinets above the sink. He allowed the silence to build.

"Yes," she finally said.

"Why don't you sit down and tell me what happened."

"I don't want to sit." She glanced at the door. "I want to go home."

Raymond took a sip of coffee. She could easily walk around him if she was determined to leave. Yet she didn't want to look at the events of the night, and she'd avoided looking at him. Shame? How to say that without provoking her to deny, clam up or leave? "I hope you don't mind if I sit, then," he stalled. He got the stool, moved it toward her, and plopped down on it with a small sigh. "It's very painful to feel ashamed."

"Then don't feel it," she snapped.

"I have, and I'm sure I will again. I don't understand how some people can believe that feelings are turned on and off like water faucets."

"You don't understand much."

The Toll

"Then help me understand more. Tell me about tonight." He set his cup of coffee down on the floor.

"Then you'll let me go home?"

"No promises. But the chances are better."

She sighed, then walked to the examining table, lifted herself onto the far edge and sat facing away. "It's an old bedtime story. I went to bed with a guy. We had a fight. I wanted to die."

"What was the fight about?"

"His wife."

"You found out he was married?"

She snorted. "You're as big an ass as he is," she said as if speaking to the wall. "He wears a wedding band, just like you do. I haven't decided whether all big asses become husbands or all husbands grow into big asses — not that it really matters — the result is the same. He moved out on his wife and in with me a couple of weeks ago. Tonight he was very passionate in bed. He told me how much he loves me, that he'll always love me, how very special I am — and that he's going back to his wife. End of story."

"Did he say why he was going back?"

"The kids, his parents, his conscience – nothing about his wife. He's the fruitcake that needs to be here."

"Why didn't he stay here for you?"

"I can't tell you anything more about him. I told him I wouldn't."

"He doesn't seem to return your loyalty. Do you still feel that you want to die?"

"No."

Sincere? So hard to tell. "How about turning around and looking at me?"

Her back stiffened. "How about sending me home?"

"I'm not sure it's safe. Have you ever tried to kill yourself before?"

29

Grudgingly, she catalogued her past attempts: an overdose of her mother's sleeping pills at age 10, another overdose in 9th grade, wrist-cutting twice during her high school years, once more in college. She refused to give explanations. No, she'd never received counseling. She'd refused to go and her parents were convinced she was "only looking for attention." Her father "didn't believe in psychiatry, anyway." Time after time, she refused to give any details about important issues – childhood, family, sexuality – nor would she say why she needed to keep those parts of her life hidden. Twice, he deliberately persisted with a line of questions she blocked, and on both occasions, she lapsed into silence. Bit by bit, he learned that she was born in Baltimore, baptized Roman Catholic, went to parochial schools through 8th grade, then to a public high school, where she relished the comparative freedom.

"What did you like to do with more freedom?" he asked.

"I didn't go wild, if that's what you're driving at. I graduated with an A average. I liked to read and there were a lot of books in the library that I couldn't read at home or in parochial school. Anything that kept me away from home was good — school plays, tutoring a kid after school, that sort of thing."

"You tutored kids?"

"Only one — a younger girl had trouble reading and was getting picked on. But what does that have to do with me going home?"

"Did you use drugs in high school?"

"Sure – but I never shot up. I hate taking needles. But getting high is something else. Weed, acid, mushrooms — on a really good trip, I feel at one with the harmony of the universe. Did you ever feel like that?"

Had he? Surely he came closest to complete harmony when he made love with Lisa, but then he only felt at one with her and didn't give a damn about the universe. At other times? No, he was too busy, and life was too transient and fragile. If the early death of his parents hadn't proved that, then the illnesses he'd seen and the autopsies he'd helped with as a pathologist's assistant certainly had. The world was a battlefield — always dangerous, rarely rewarding. Perhaps the dead were in harmony with the universe, dust mixing with dust, the result of some vast incomprehensible accident.

"You falling asleep?" asked Mary Saxe.

She'd turned and caught him gazing at his lap, adrift in his reverie. He jerked his shoulders back. "I'm sorry. I was thinking about your question."

A smile of understanding softened her facial expression. "Then I won't ask you anything difficult. You'd probably sleep on it for years." Her tone was mocking, but there was a twinkle in her eye.

"Forgive me. We were talking about drugs. What have you been using recently?"

She told him she averaged three joints a day, used cocaine to party and Ludes when she needed to sleep. In response to his questions, she said she was a junior at the University, taking courses in literature, art, philosophy and geology, with no particular goal in mind. She had some money saved for tuition and waitressed three nights a week at Peter's Place, a local pub.

Two details nagged at him more than the rest. Asked about her parents and siblings, she didn't confirm that they were dead, only insisted "It doesn't matter – I won't talk about them." Her restroom prayer was the other incongruity, even odder because she hadn't attended church for years. Asked why, she said, "I can pray on my own, when I need to."

"What about going to Confession and taking Communion?"

She sucked in her lips for a moment, then said, "Jesus will understand."

"Would you share with me why you were praying in the ladies' room?"

Saxe wrinkled her brow and stared at him. Apparently, he stood the test of her scrutiny. Her voice was soft but clear. *"'But thou, when thou shalt pray, enter into thy chamber and having shut the door, pray to thy Father in secret; and thy Father who seeth in secret will repay thee'."*

"New Testament?" he asked.

"Ignoramus," she said mildly. "That's Matthew 6:6."

"You have quite a memory."

"Memory is the venom that seeps relentlessly from old wounds," she recited.

"Shakespeare?"

She emitted a puff of air through her lips. "You really do have a shrink-sized brain. It's amazing that you're able to help anybody."

Raymond suppressed a smile. She'd become almost affectionate in disparaging him, in proving her superiority. "Who did write it?"

"Maggie Saxe." Pride pervaded her tone.

"So you write."

"Just poetry."

"Nice that you do that…Would you share what your prayers were about?"

"No. Do you want to share your prayers with me?"

Raymond rubbed his jaw. Where to, now? he thought. There was something she'd said…"When you asked me about the bathroom, you asked if I knew a John you could piss on. Not 'in,' but 'on.' Am I correct that your lover — "

Saxe's head jerked up, her cheeks flushed with anger. Like coiled springs suddenly released, her limbs flew up and out and she catapulted from examining table to floor.

"You're not as smart as you think," she shouted. "I didn't mean anything."

"Okay. Take it easy," he soothed. "I'm sorry I upset you."

Saxe advanced and pointed an accusing finger between his eyes. "You don't upset me, Mr. Hyde. You disgust me!"

Her forefinger whirled and her body followed. She ran out the door and raced down the corridor. Raymond reeled in her wake as he came off the stool and into the hallway. He saw her sprint past a dumbfounded Brailey and barrel through the emergency suite's swinging doors.

Raymond followed slowly. He was confused, ashamed and angry, excruciatingly aware that he had blundered. He'd lost his patient. She might still be suicidal.

Brailey was grinning as Raymond reached him. "You sure know how to liven up a dull evening, Doctor D. Prayer meetings in the john and track practice in the hall. The Space Utilization Committee will love it."

Raymond didn't bother to respond. He'd have to call the police. He strode past the intern, pushed his way through the doors and passed by the reception desk, the waiting room, and the cubicle in which a security guard dozed in his chair. Raymond hit the exterior doors hard. He felt the sting on his hands and the cool air on his face as he stepped onto the street. In the faint glow of dawn, he thought he saw a figure moving rapidly away. He stood there gazing at distant shadows, biting down on his lip as self-recrimination gnawed from within.

LOREN SCHECHTER

4

Daisies

He let himself into his mother's apartment at 5 a.m.

"It's George," he announced so as not to alarm the aide on duty. He walked down the narrow hallway, screwing up his face in response to the stench of human waste that lurked below the odors of Lysol, bleach and rubbing alcohol. Bringing his mother home from the hospital to die in her own bed had its drawbacks. Only a week or two to live, the doctor had said. But the doctor didn't have to put up with her shit.

The aide emerged from the bedroom holding a finger to her lips. Her wrinkled dress and the bags under her eyes told of a long nine hours. "Your mother's asleep," she whispered. She motioned that he follow her into the small living room.

It took him only ten minutes to convince her that, as he couldn't sleep and would stay until morning, she could leave a progress note for the daytime nurse and go home early. Paying her for the full twelve hours smoothed her way out the door. As he locked it behind her and went to his mother's bedroom, he congratulated himself on hiring two women who didn't know each other rather than using an agency.

His mother was sleeping peacefully despite the hiss of oxygen flowing into her mask. A dark brown comforter covered her body, but her hair was little more than post-radiation stubble, her cheeks were hollow, and her nose seemed flattened under the mask. She certainly looked frailer than she had two days before, after the ambulance had brought her home. It was as if she'd been buoyed up by returning to her own bed, only to have the glow wear off as she struggled to hang on. George reached out to touch her, then stayed his hand.

Too late now, he thought. Her long black hair and her daisies were gone. She'd put a fresh daisy in her hair every time a new man came to the apartment. How many times had he watched her pin that white flower above her ear? A hundred? A thousand? In the mirror of her second-hand vanity table, she would wink and smile at him through patches of green eye-shadow and a smear of red lipstick.

"A white daisy, Georgie," she would say, "that's the perfect touch of class. It's soft and pretty and pure – it's like wearing another lovely smile on your head."

He'd thought so, too. Yet when he'd stretched out his hand, she'd rise up out of reach. "No, you mustn't touch. That would ruin it."

Maybe he should bury some daisies with her. Touching the daisies, then burying them might feel good. Probably not as satisfying as refusing Ma's demands to be cremated, but no pleasant feeling had ever lasted more than a minute or two — not even as a kid. The door buzzer would interrupt and she'd shoo him off to his tiny room. "Go to sleep, now. And I don't want you comin' out for a pee and look-see, you hear? Grown-ups need their privacy."

"Who's coming?" he'd ask.

"Doesn't matter to you. He's coming to see me, and he doesn't want two more eyes lookin' at him."

Men never wanted kids around. That's why his father drove off and never came back – or so she'd said. There came a time when he stopped believing her. He never could find a wedding photo or a marriage certificate. But as a kid, he didn't know any better; he just knew he didn't want to get whacked around again, so he went quietly to his room. And had trouble falling asleep. No door could shield him from her drunken laughter or arguments, her shrieks of pleasure or of pain. Sure, the daisies had to be buried. Along with his memories.

George left the apartment as quietly as he could and went to his car. He scanned the windows of the apartment houses on both sides of the street, then looked up and down the street to make sure there were no joggers or dog walkers out so early. Convinced he was not going to be observed, he opened the trunk, removed the body wrapped in his mother's blanket and carried it up the three flights of stairs to her apartment. Still, he was breathing as easily as his mother was when he unwrapped the body and put it in the bed beside her. He caressed his mother's head to wake her. She didn't stir, so he prodded her shoulder.

"Ma, wake up," he said. "I want you to meet a friend."

5

Nancy

Nancy heard the Devil tap on her window. She sat up in bed and switched on her lamp. The light shone on the closed window shades and pink curtains, on her flowered wallpaper, maple dresser and desk.

Better not look outside, she thought. There'd only be darkness. The wind. And the Devil.

She heard one slow tap after another. Daddy said her fears were crap. Claptrap. If there was a Devil, he'd burn killers and drunks, drug addicts and punks. Those were the facts, acts, pacts. Fourteen-year-old girls shouldn't fear the Devil. Or hear Him, or see Him. Mommy said fourteen should be a happy age.

Maybe her parents had made a mistake about her age. They were always correcting each other about other things. And she'd always been the smallest in her class. Her brothers were much — Stop it! Joe Brill said it was crap. He'd also said the squeaks and the creaks meant the house was settling. He would've gotten angry had she asked "settling what?" It didn't take much to get him angry. He didn't understand how she thought. Mommy tried — tried and cried. It was all the Devil's fault, the squeaks and creaks, the hurrying, scurrying, worrying noises in the walls. No one else understood, or maybe they were too afraid to admit it — the Devil was torturing the house. Until it would give her to Him.

Yes, at night, all things were clearer, nearer. Her parents didn't know, because they slept soundly. In twin beds. Yet they weren't at all alike. Mommy said she was different, too. Told people, "She's just not the same Nancy. She was so adorable as a little girl." Daddy said that was a lot of crap. "Stop babying her, she'll do fine," he kept telling Mommy. If she was a baby, how could she be fourteen? Maybe, baby, she wasn't the same Nancy. Was there another Nancy Veronica Brill? A twin? This was a twin bed. Maybe that's why she hardly slept any more — she was in the wrong bed. The wrong body? Yes, certainly confusing. She had to spend so many hours sorting these things out. Maybe she really was going crazy. Except, if she was, she wouldn't think that, would she? Maybe Reverend McBirney could figure it out.

Please stop tapping! My Daddy, Senator Joe Brill, said You don't exist. Maybe Daddy could make that a law. The Devil does not exist and therefore is prohibited from tapping on windows – no, torturing houses. That would be a fine law, saw, floor. Yes, she should sleep on the floor. Would her bag of odd things, rings, strings be safe under her pillow? No, move the bag, the pillow and blankets to the floor. She'd better leave the light on, keep the darkness outside.

There, that's better. Now maybe she could fall asleep…

Oh, rats! Why won't the Devil obey the law?

6

John

The turn of the doorknob and click of the latch became part of Maggie's dream. Mr. Hyde snapped the lock of her secret room; she was praying and could not rise. Serum oozed from Hyde's eyeless sockets down blistered and blackened skin. As he groped his way toward her, she tried to scream but was smothered by the stink of burned flesh. He reached down for her, but she ducked and twisted away, then tried to crawl. Hyde growled, reached down and grabbed her by the neck, shattering her nightmare.

Maggie blinked against the rays of sunlight that pushed around the venetian blinds of her bedroom. Her mouth felt parched, her tongue thick. The pungent odor of last night's marijuana lingered. She worked her lips and gums to produce some saliva. The sheet had bunched up under her nude body. From beneath the bandages on her limbs, aching pain surfaced as the residue of yesterday.

Mother of God, another day to endure. Only the white satin comforter felt cool and forgiving, so she rolled onto it and closed her eyes.

"I'm sorry I woke you," said John. His voice was soft, his tone concerned.

A lot less sure of himself here than in class, she thought. She heard him hang his jacket on the back of the rocker, then move to the dresser to empty his trouser pockets.

"Mr. Hyde woke me," she said. Would those nightmares ever stop? No, some sins couldn't be forgiven. She rolled off the comforter and pulled it over her back and head. "What time is it?"

"One thirty. It's really nice out."

She felt the bed sag as he sat, heard the rub of a foot leaving its shoe, then another. The mattress gave a small bounce as he rose to take off his shirt and trousers.

Maggie grit her teeth. Take this off, put that on, take that off, put this on – John changed women just as readily. Her feelings didn't count for shit. He was just like her father – insensitive, self-centered and cruel. Francis Dexter Saxe, Knight of Columbus, Hospital Trustee, member of the Million Dollar Round Table – what a hypocrite. Why had she thought John was different?

"Was it the same nightmare?" John asked.

"Yes." Awful — like life itself, she thought. So end it soon.

"There must be something you can do about it," John said.

She poked her head out from beneath the comforter and blinked rapidly as her eyes adjusted to the light. "Like what?" she asked. Without a joint or a few shots before sleep and John next to her in bed, she'd have Mr. Hyde in her dreams every night.

"You could see a doctor."

"I saw more than enough doctors last night." She was a fool for telling John about her nightmares. Now he'd walk out with some of her secrets – nothing big, but didn't any secret give him some power? Like the power she finally had over her father.

"I didn't hear you come in, this morning." John opened the closet and hung his trousers and jacket away. He took a deep breath before turning back to her. "Why didn't you call me to pick you up? I told you I would." There was more than a trace of annoyance in his tone.

Big deal, she thought. If he'd cared, he wouldn't have run off from the hospital. He could've made up a name; no one would've recognized him in the middle of the night. "I didn't have a dime for the phone."

"You're still angry with me," he said.

"Angry? I'm not angry. Try enraged, or furious, or fucked over – or check answer D, teacher, for all of the above."

"How did you get home?"

She burrowed her head into her pillow. "It was a terrible night. I don't want to think about it."

"How did you get home, Maggie?" He closed the closet door with a thud.

Conscience bothering him? Too little, too late. "Get off my case."

"I wish you would have called."

Rolling onto her side, she saw his patrician nose profiled between light brown hair and short beard. He was concentrating on getting his Levi's on. Men never wanted to fight with their pants off. She sat up, fluffed her pillow against the headboard, and placed his pillow in front of hers. The down pillows yielded graciously as she leaned back and kicked off the comforter. Let him see what he'd be without.

"You should have called," he persisted. But his blue eyes widened as they took in her nude pose.

"You needed a few hours sleep before class," she said. "You're a bore when you're tired." And she was a shrew. Better to move forward from yesterday. "Did your class go alright?"

He zipped his fly and sat carefully on the bed. "Even the fly on

43

my desk was dozing." He extended his long legs down his side of the bed. The headboard creaked as he leaned back. "I'm glad you weren't there to see me in such poor form."

"Don't worry. Every woman in class admires your form. Too bad the content doesn't live up to it."

"Ouch. You are pissed off. But I really did miss you, today."

"I bet."

"I did. You don't realize how painful this will be for me, too – how hard it'll be to see you in class and then have to go home to Roberta."

"That hard?" Men were fuck-and-flee animals. "Well, life is tough for everyone...I'll bet you even marked me absent, today."

"It doesn't matter — you're allowed three cuts. What's the point of keeping records inaccurately?" He placed his hand on her knee. "You never even stirred when the alarm went off. I didn't want to wake you. I thought you'd feel better after a good sleep."

Maggie laughed; the sound was sharp and hard. "John, just for the accuracy of your records, I didn't try to kill myself because I was overtired."

He withdrew his hand. "Don't you think I know that? You were furious about my decision. Not that you said anything. You just sat and braided your hair, doing your damnedest to ignore me. Then you went calmly off to your bath and tried to check out before I did."

"What more could I say? You want to go back to Roberta, go! You want me to beg you not to? As I see it, I was doing us both a favor."

"A favor!" Above his beard, his cheeks flushed with anger. "That was no favor to me. Did you want me ruined by scandal and hung up with guilt for the rest of my life? Or were you only trying to trade a pint of blood for a repentant lover? Which one was it, Maggie?"

She looked down at her thighs. "You're wrong. I didn't plan it... I don't even remember getting the razor blade. I was in the bath, but

I didn't feel the water, didn't even feel the pain. I was off somewhere looking down at me." She hunched over, crossed her forearms on her chest and dug her long fingernails into her arms. She needed to feel pain, wanted to feel alive. "It was like I was dead – no thoughts, no pain – just dead."

"I'm sorry." John placed his hand on her arm. "I really am sorry. I worry about you... I never thought I'd say this, but maybe you ought to see a psychiatrist."

"I saw one last night. Now it's your turn again. Go back for another three years."

"Maybe I should. Maybe I'd get more out of it than when I was a kid. But that won't help you, Maggie. You need help for yourself."

"How fucking kind of you to let me know. Your sensitivity is beyond belief."

"Putting me down won't stop your nightmares, or change the fact you tried to kill yourself." John extended his palms in appeal. "Can't you admit there's something twisting your insides?"

"How can I put down an underachiever? You even let my insults pass over your head." She touched her forehead, feigned sudden insight. "Hey! No wonder therapy never helped you much. You underachieved with your shrink. Rather similar to your marriage, if you ask me."

John's face and tone hardened. "I didn't ask you. The shrink was my father's choice, not mine. My wife is a diff — " He shook his head. "My real fight was with my father. I was the only person in his life that he couldn't control or cast aside."

"I see the resemblance."

"Look, get off my back. I know I have problems, but I never wanted to kill myself. What was the name of the psychiatrist you saw last night?"

"Daniels. You know him?"

John's thin eyebrows converged momentarily. "I don't think so. What does he look like?"

"Like he needs to be dry cleaned and pressed."

"Please, Maggie." John's tone was impatient, not at all gentle. She knew that tone all too well. Telling her to shape up, give him what he wanted; otherwise, he'd become enraged. Her fucking father, F. Dexter, all over again.

With a sigh of concession, she leaned back against the pillows and closed her eyes. "He's three or four inches shorter than you, probably close to six feet. He has dark, curly hair that hasn't been brushed, over a long face. His nose has a bump on the bridge, like it was broken and never set right, and he has sad brown eyes — puppy eyes, I called them. Appealing face, if you like the mournful puppy look. You satisfied?"

"He must be one of the residents," said John, caressing the skin above her bandage. "I can find out about him."

Her eyelids flicked open. "Don't bother. I won't be seeing him again."

"You should see someone." His fingers moved up along the inside of her thigh.

Maggie reached down, grasped his hand firmly and set it upon the bed. "I'll be fine once you get out of my life. When will that be?"

"I'm not sure."

"You're not a lot of things. Give me an answer."

"Tomorrow's Saturday. I'll go by the house, see the kids, and finalize the thing with Roberta about coming back."

That bitch would take him back, too. He'd agree to all of her conditions. "Take all your clothes and books so you won't have to make another trip."

"Maggie, you know that I really care about you. I'm not one of those guys who sleeps with every pretty girl who comes along. You're very special to me. But I can't walk out on my kids, my wife, my parents – "

"Especially your parents," she interjected

" – without an all-out effort to make my marriage work."

"What do you know about all-out effort?" She rose to her knees and glared at him. "You've always gotten everything you've wanted without really trying. And you just throw it all away. That's what you did to your wife, that's what you're doing with your job, and that's what you're trying to do to me. Well, pack up and fuck off! You can make an all-out effort at that."

He shook his head. "I'm not throwing you away. You're too valuable a person."

"My value to you is what I do for you in bed."

"You're more than that. Shit! It's a pity you cut yourself up that way. If I hadn't gotten up to see why you were taking so long, you might've died."

Isn't he the noble one? she thought. Trust a Judas and not only does he betray you, but he acts as if he's the Savior. "Your only concerns last night were to get your rocks off and then to tell me good-bye without a big scene. That's why you suggested getting stoned. Now you want a medal for barging in to take a leak — all of a sudden, you see your piss as my salvation. Well, I don't need you, John. I don't need your pecker or your pity. Give them to your frigid wife; she's the one who needs them."

The back of his hand whipped across her cheek, jolting her head and body.

Maggie grabbed the headboard for support. She tasted blood, felt her lip swell, her cheek ache. She didn't mind the pain. She was glad her words wounded him; she wasn't going to be the only one to bleed. He looked pale, his eyes remorseful. Good! She forced a smile. "Not bad for a philosophy instructor. Was that a lesson in ethics or in values?"

He got out of bed and faced her. "You bring out the worst in people, don't you, Maggie. You certainly do in me. I give you an A for effort." He began removing his Levi's, but his gaze didn't leave her face. "You need me a lot more than you're willing to admit. You were the one who sought me out, remember? Coming up after class with questions, bumping into me 'accidentally' on campus, trying to get me to — "

"Bullshit! You encouraged me. You wanted me."

He shed his shorts and socks. "You made it happen. You pursued me 'til you caught me, hook line and sinker. And you still want me." He lifted his tee shirt over his head and stood nude before her.

Mother of God, don't let him. "I don't want you. I don't need you. You're an emotional dwarf. You disown responsibility for everything. I'll bet you even blame the wrong prick when you masturbate. Well, I don't need either prick, John, the little one – " She glanced down and then at his face. " – or the big one."

"We'll see, Maggie. I'm certain that your great experience with pricks has taught you how to put each and every one in its proper place."

Maggie sat up, yanked the glass lamp from her night table and heaved it high and hard at the bedroom door. The white shade sailed off on a tangent, but the bulb rode the potbellied missile into orbit, the cord whipping the air behind. John jumped for the safety of the bed as the lamp hit the door with a loud crash and a shower of white and gray splinters.

"Jesus! You're crazy, Maggie."

48

"If you can't shut your mouth, you're going to eat more than your words." She tried to reach around him to the lamp on his night table, but he caught her wrist and pushed her back against the pillows. She winced as he forced her bandaged wrist down to her side. Her breathing was ragged; her body trembled. Only her eyes were unwavering.

John eased his grip, but he didn't let go.

He doesn't trust me, she thought. Doesn't know me. Didn't he have eyes? She'd thrown the lamp at the door, not at his head. If she harmed anyone, it'd be herself — didn't he know that?

John lowered his head to hers and touched her swelling cheek with his lips, a silent apology. The touch of his lips and brush of his beard were distractions from the pain. No, not this time! Maybe he could ignore the suffering he created, but she was stuck with the pain. She closed her eyes and watched his hand come round and strike her cheek again. She magnified the blow, the ache, the swell and the sting. She savored the taste of her blood. Pain would keep her from giving in.

His hands moved up to cradle her head. His lips came to hers, seeking tenderness, finding none. She pushed her injured cheek against his chin, relishing the pain.

Rebuffed, his mouth moved to her neck, then to a breast, on to its twin and back again. His lips parted and nibbled, his tongue came out to play. His hands stroked her hair, then worked their way down her back. She felt helpless and small, unable to move. No, thought Maggie, not now, not like this. He'd hurt her more than enough. She'd give him nothing. He could pack up his prick and go home. She was finished with men.

Even as defiance poured from her brain, she was jolted by her body's weakness, betrayed by the erection of her nipples. Do something! she told herself. Bite him! Poke at his eyes! Cut off his cock! Anything – but don't give in.

He pulled her down on the sheet and spread her limbs as if they belonged to a manikin. He stroked her body lightly, patiently. His fingers circled her nipples, spread out across her belly, roamed through her pubic hair and down the inside of her thighs.

She stared at the ceiling, followed the lines and whirls and arcs in the white plaster, doing all she could to ignore any thought, fight back any feeling. She couldn't block out enough. His brush and tongue probed everywhere, ultimately finding where she was most vulnerable…staying there. She felt sickened by her growing excitement. Just like before, she thought. Before and again. Again and again. Her fucking father, F. Dexter, was right, God damn him.

She had to feel, had to move, had to moan and respond. As she did, she began to cry.

7

Spells

The crows wouldn't let him sleep. Their hoarse, insistent caws called him to the back window. George raised the shade and looked out over the sunlit yard. A loudmouth crow cawed from the tree. Another barked back from the grass. They were black as Ma's heart and ugly as her life. A couple of rounds from one of his rifles would blow them apart. No, the yard was too small, the neighbors too close. He'd have to find another way to kill the suckers. Then he would touch them and bury them, just as he'd bury Ma.

Once she was six feet under, perhaps he could sleep in peace and wake revitalized. The end of her life would be the real beginning of his. Maybe he could finally break through his thick, dead shell into a life where he could feel and taste and enjoy. But even though he'd sent Denise and the kids over to his in-laws for the afternoon, the crows hadn't let him sleep. Were they there to tell him something? Why else hadn't they let him rest? Those grubsuckers were asking to die.

A shower and shave did not help his mood. Sure, his mother had awakened to see her fate, and she'd died slowly enough in his hands.

Her blanketed body was now in his trunk, and the funeral director had the other one. The prostitute playing his grieving sister had tearfully backed up his statement that the woman in the bed was their mother. And as the doctor summoned to his mother's apartment had never seen her before, he accepted everything said by her grieving relatives and hospital discharge summary. A formal death certificate would be forthcoming.

Still he had nagging thoughts that something would go wrong, that nothing would change, or that whatever he was missing couldn't be obtained. He should be feeling better about his life. He was physically strong and handsome enough; he had a wife, two kids, a small house in the suburbs, an old Plymouth Fury and a Harley Sportster. Two jobs and generous in-laws made it all possible; yet nothing and no one made it worthwhile. He stayed because it was easier than leaving. He worked day and night because it was less difficult than thinking – and it kept him away from Denise.

He opened the medicine closet, took Denise's diet capsules from the top shelf and poured several into a small vial. Instead of doing this evening's shift, he could have called in and explained that his mother had died. But then he'd have had to accept clingy condolences from Denise and put up with the kids' whining. Better to work. The amphetamines would help him get through.

Four years ago, when Denise brought Carol home from the hospital, she insisted that all medication be moved to the top shelves of the linen closet. He thought Denise was crazy — the baby wasn't strong enough to spit up – but he silently followed Denise's instructions and transferred her collection of preventatives, antidotes and restoratives to the closet. Then she bitched until he put a lock up top. Denise seemed to have a pill for every disease except two: cancer and emptiness. His mother had one; he lived with the other. It had been bearable until the spells began.

George took the vial of pills to the bedroom and began to dress. Had the amphetamines made his spells worse? Not likely. Nothing he ate or did changed what happened. It was what others said or did. He was okay as long as no one bothered him. It didn't matter who, didn't matter why. In one second, he'd get tight as a drum; in the next, he'd go ripshit. The only good thing was that no one else could see it happen. It was so real to him, so very real. He'd go berserk with a cleaver and chop Denise into bloody pieces; he'd crush Carol's skull between his hands and mangle little George. Then he'd come back to his senses and hear Denise ask, "Did you hear what I said, George?" He was always amazed that she was still alive. Denise never knew that he said "I'm sorry" for killing her, not for ignoring her. She didn't have the faintest idea of how far he tuned out, of the violence he envisioned. And he didn't know when some of the visions would become real. Only two things were certain: he had no control over the spells, and they were getting worse. He'd convinced Denise, the police and Protective Services that shooting four year-old Carol had been an accident, that he'd dropped the gun, didn't know it was loaded. Lucky for him Carol just had a flesh wound. But it was a wake-up call that he had to get some help before something worse happened.

Dressed in the green uniform that Denise had pressed, he packed a pair of jeans and a blue shirt in a canvas bag. Bag in hand, pills in his pocket, he went to the kitchen and stuffed the sandwiches she'd prepared into his lunch pail. Closing the black box, he was reminded of the coffin he'd selected for a stranger, of the fear in her eyes, and the hatred in his mother's.

He felt a sudden stab of terror. What if the spells meant he had a brain tumor like his mother's? He wasn't afraid of death. But a brain tumor! From beyond the grave, he heard his mother laughing at him, saw her reaching out to stick it to him again. He was stuck with her genes. There was nothing he could do – nothing. He was fucked by the twisted genes she gave her bastard son.

8

Lisa

With his overnight bag in hand, Raymond exited from a side door of City Hospital. He blinked rapidly to adapt to the afternoon sun. After thirty-four hours on duty, he felt like a prisoner tossed from a fortress Into the confusion of pedestrians hurrying home, the fits and fumes of rush hour traffic. A car horn honked twice. He looked down the street. Lisa was behind the wheel of their green Valiant. He threaded his way toward the car, opened the passenger door and tossed his bag onto the back seat. *Aquarius/Let The Sunshine In* blared from the radio.

"Want to make a house call, doctor?" Lisa turned off the radio.

"That's the best offer I've had all day." He plopped into the seat and leaned over to kiss her. Her hazel eyes closed, her lips were tender; he was sorry when she pulled back.

"Pretty good for a pregnant old bird," he said. Her obstetrician had told them she was "no spring chicken." Typical Lisa, she'd hit back with a smile, telling her doctor she wasn't the only one in the room who could lay an egg.

Now she wrinkled her nose. "Nonsense. I'm still young and fantastic."

"You certainly are." What with her diabetes under control and twelve weeks pregnant, she seemed to glow with health, her red hair framing rosy cheeks and a wide smile. "God, I missed you."

"I missed you, too." She gave his hand a squeeze, smoothed her denim skirt beneath her, and started the car. As she drove away from the curb, a black car beeped from behind. "Okay, okay, I'm going."

"Everybody wants to get home yesterday," he said. "How's our Julie-jewel?"

"Fine. She's discovered ants." Lisa grimaced. "This afternoon, she was picking them up and bringing them to me to admire. I hope she's not bringing ants to Helen. Good neighbors are hard to find."

Lisa slowed the car. A pair of teen jaywalkers were crossing the street as if they owned it. Raymond shook his head, then looked out the side window at the row of dingy tenements. The alcoholic in delirium he'd admitted yesterday came from this neighborhood. Ragtag children on the sidewalk, litter on the street, men hanging out on the corner. People shouldn't have to live in poverty, he thought. There were too many shouldn'ts without solutions. Even in his own family, middle-class as they come, Mom and Dad shouldn't have been taken by illness and violence; his brother Ethan shouldn't have been killed in Vietnam. Senseless, all senseless.

The tenements gave way to a row of small stores: luncheonette, laundromat, liquor store and barber shop. Across the street, the ubiquitous Chinese restaurant. Pedestrians seemed to walk with purpose. A young woman in a yellow sundress carried an armful of books.

College? Grad school? He remembered arguing with his sister Sarah when she informed him she was dropping out of grad school to marry an unemployed actor. Well, she was an adult; she didn't have to listen to her big brother's advice any more than Ethan had. Had Ethan not enlisted and died in Vietnam, would Sarah have jumped into a relationship? What's done is done. Much better now that they speak on the telephone once a week. Still have to work on not being judgmental, not being overprotective. Easier with patients than with family.

Raymond sighed. "What's for supper?"

"Besides ants? Fish, rice and salad. I baked a cake for dessert. You hungry?"

"Starved. It's been a long day. Started at 4 a.m."

"The emergency room?"

"Yeah. Some co-ed had boyfriend problems and tried to kill herself. It was a bad night for both of us."

"Is she – Stupid man!" Lisa stepped on the brake, honked the horn. "Did you see that black car cut in?"

"A Porsche, no less."

"Is the girl okay?"

"I hope so." He massaged his forehead. "Something I said freaked her out and she ran off. I had to call the police."

"I doubt they'll do much. They're too busy. There was another protest last night. The students have taken over the University's admin building."

"I'm not surprised. Bombing Cambodia is bad enough. Now Kent State — where does it stop?"

Their car bumped its way over old trolley tracks. "What did you say that made her run off?" asked Lisa.

"The girl? I made a bad mistake. I tried to get her to identify her boyfriend even though she'd told me she wouldn't."

"Everyone makes mistakes, Ray."

He shook his head. "It's not the same with someone who's suicidal."

"Don't be so hard on yourself. You can't be responsible for what other people choose to do."

"I know that in my head. Still, it bothers the hell out of me. I wonder if I'll ever be a really capable psychiatrist."

"I worry about you. You take on some of the pain of every patient you see. How are you going to last without getting depressed yourself?"

Good question, he thought, what with his family's history of manic-depressive disorder. "Don't worry. I talk to Doctor Korline about this stuff." About bottling up his own pain at the loss of both parents in order to be a peacemaker between ten year-old Ethan, grief-stricken and furious, and their bipolar Uncle Jack, who took the three of them in but often threatened to send one or all of them to an orphanage. If not for Aunt Rachel, Ethan might well have been sent.

"I'll work it out," he told Lisa. Poor Ethan had fought it out, at home, in school, in the Army, and it had cost him his life.

"Psychoanalysis isn't a cure-all. You've said that yourself." Lisa eased the Valiant to a standstill at a red light. "That girl must've been in a lot of pain."

"She was. There was so much fear and hurt and rage in her face that it frightened me for a minute or two. Once I realized what she was communicating, the going got a bit easier — until the end."

"I'm sorry you had such a bad night." Lisa gave him a worried glance, then got the car moving again.

"I just hope the police follow up, especially with this student sit-in happening."

"They've had sit-ins before," she said. "It shouldn't tie up the whole police force."

He patted her thigh. "Eight-ten years ago, you probably would've been right in the middle of it."

"Vietnam wasn't an issue then. And I wasn't that daring… Here we go." She stepped on the gas pedal and the car moved up the curving ramp toward the tollbooths. "It didn't take daring to join thousands of people at a demo. You have any change? I used mine on the way down."

"No, but I have a single." He reached for his wallet.

She steered the Plymouth into line behind a red Firebird convertible and took the dollar from his hand.

The young man driving the Firebird handed the toll keeper a bill. They seemed to be exchanging angry words as well as currency.

"What's happening there?" said Lisa.

"I don't know."

Tires squealed as the Firebird roared out of the tollgate. Lisa moved the Plymouth up to the booth and extended the dollar to the uniformed collector. The big man's gaze was riveted on the fast-disappearing Pontiac.

"Did that driver give you some trouble?" asked Lisa. Getting no response, she spoke louder. "What did he do?"

Raymond leaned toward her to hear the toll collector's answer.

The big man's shoulder moved in a half-shrug, half-twitch. His head shook rapidly, as if negating unpleasantness that came from both sides. When he turned, Raymond was surprised by the humorless smile that seemed pasted on the wide face. The wave of black hair that curled onto his forehead, the turned up nose, smooth complexion and dimpled chin made him appear boyish despite his bulk, gentle despite his odd smile. His voice was low, his tone conciliatory. "I'm sorry, ma'am. I was thinking. What did you ask?" Cold eyes stared and appraised.

"I wondered if that man in the red car gave you some trouble."

The toll collector's smile neither waxed nor waned as he plucked the dollar from Lisa's hand. "No, ma'am. He was a garbage-mouth. But no, no trouble at all." He retreated into the booth, leaned out again and planted the coins in her palm. As he did, they saw the name on his jacket, which seemed a size too small.

"Take care," said Cruber.

"Thank you." Lisa thrust the coins at Raymond. As soon as he took them, she stepped hard on the accelerator, jerking Raymond back in his seat.

"Creepy guy," she said.

"Yup, but not our problem. Maybe you can drive a little slower. You have a baby on board."

9

Hands

He watched hands come at him, one by one. White, black, brown, yellow. Tough and calloused, bony or tender. Hands wrinkled and hairless, veins and fingers twisted by age. Trembling hands, with nicotine-stained digits, nailbeds bitten half-bare. Bearers, clingers, graspers, takers: they came, they reached out and he touched them.

As a child, he'd learned that words deceived and silences concealed, faces were false, hearts not visible; what was left to watch but hands? So he'd memorized the lines of his mother's palms as her hands fended him off. He'd studied the hands of his "uncles" as they pinched and fondled, then knotted, battered and bloodied her. Only to hate his own hands, small and soft, clumsy in striking, feeble in defense, earning him a rough palm in his face or a hairy backhand across his tearless cheek.

Now hands reached and offered. And he always took more than he gave. A look, a touch, and their secrets became his. The lonely hand sought friendship in a crowd of rings, while the show-off demanded attention with gaudy gems and polish. The guilt-ridden were indicted by skin scrubbed raw, the fearful avoided his touch. He poked at the pampered, for whom other hands labored, yet was gentle with the mourner, from whom a member was missing. He brushed aside the ordinary, was careful with the clumsy. Above all, he despised the alienated, the emotionless, the empty – he knew those hands best. They were his, the hands of George Elton Cruber.

The hand that extended a folded two-dollar bill from the red Firebird was tattooed on the backs of the fingers. From forefinger to pinky, the four letter word was "LOVE," each letter isolated on a separate finger, an inch below the knuckle. From his tollbooth, George looked down upon the offering. Love was a balloon – an empty shell given form and energy by hot air. When had he ever gotten a balloon he could keep? If it hadn't escaped his grasp and flown away, it had ended up deflated, killed quickly with a prick or slowly by time. No hand could hold on to love; the tattoo was a futile gesture.

"I haven't seen one of those for a long time," George said to the hand.

"Don't give me a hard time, man – I'm in a hurry. Just give me the fucking change. The deuce is okay."

George looked at the driver, noting the large pupils, hollow cheeks and jackal's sneer. A hop-head, a punk, thought George, squeezing out the ghost of a smile.

"I know the deuce isn't queer. I was talking about the tattoo." George eased the two-dollar bill from the driver's hand. "You've got 'LOVE' on your left hand, is 'HATE' on the right?"

"None of your business, motherfucker."

George's eyes narrowed; dimples appeared as he bared his teeth. "I don't think you realize what a big mistake it is to say that to me."

"You're the big mistake, man – and your mother made it — but you're not so fucking big that I can't cut you down to size. Give me my fucking change!"

George put the bill on the narrow shelf of the validator, the box-like machine that registered tolls. Ignoring the neatly stacked piles of coins on the counter-top, he slowly selected six quarters and a dime from his top drawer. He pushed the validator button to ring up the sale, transmitting date, axle class, toll, and his key number onto tape in the administration building. Then he leaned out of the booth so his words wouldn't be picked up by the intercom.

"This isn't the only kind of change I can make for you." He jabbed the coins into the driver's palm. "You'd better move on."

"Who the fuck do you think you are? A friggin' pig? I'll tell you the same thing I tell them, motherfucker. You want me, you come for me — your mother did, so you can, too."

The Firebird roared forward, tires squealing in pain as they left part of their life on the pavement. George stared after the Pontiac. The smell of burnt rubber assaulted his nostrils; his muscles screamed to strike. He focused on the license plate number – 992-36E. He repeated it over and over in his head. He'd never forget it. There'd have to be a bigger toll.

PART II

July 1969

10

A Touching Gesture

Listening to the rain beat down on his Plymouth Fury, George Elton Cruber waited in the dark. His body felt cramped and the stink of sweat crept from beneath his poncho. Opening the window a crack had not helped. Moisture beaded on his brow and fogged the glass. When necessary, he wiped the windshield with a rag. He wanted his gloves to stay dry.

A car coming around the corner onto the one way street passed with a splash of water. A Buick. He slouched down in his seat, told himself to relax. The rain and the lateness of the hour minimized the chance of being seen. Street walkers would stay in; street watchers could see little. He'd unscrewed the bulb in his overhead light and, except for their hall lights, the apartment houses on both sides of the street were almost entirely dark. Unless Garbage Mouth parked his Firebird in a garage somewhere, he'd bring it home eventually. It had taken time to get Garbage Mouth's address, but it wasn't that hard. All it took was an empty billfold, a condom, and five minutes alone in his supervisor's office. Buying the used billfold at a Sunday flea market meant it was untraceable, and the condom added the right touch. On Monday, after the rush hour traffic had come through, he'd recorded the billfold and its contents, along with a description of the Firebird and its plate number, on his Unusual Occurrence Report. At the end of that shift, he'd turned the billfold over to his supervisor.

"This fell out of a guy's pocket during rush hour, Mike. I told him not to open the door – I'd get the bill he dropped. But no, he had to do it himself. I saw the billfold on the ground after he drove off."

Mike's booze-ripened face frowned at the unwanted responsibility. He fingered the worn leather, then searched every pocket. "A fucking Trojan, but no ID. The idiot may be driving without a license. No money in it, George?"

"No." If money had been in it, Mike would have turned it over to the State Police. Lost property only rated a letter. "I got his registration number. Maybe you can get the billfold back to him before he needs the condom."

"Yeah, I'll tell him to come in and try it on for size."

If Garbage Mouth came in and wanted the billfold, it would become his going away present; if he said it wasn't his, so what? An honest mistake. It must have fallen from another car — who could keep track at rush hour? It didn't matter what the slimebag did; a copy of that letter was in Mike's files. And seeing it was easy enough because Mike was famous for spending a long time in the can. Constipation, he called it. More like old age setting in. In the end, all bodies betrayed.

To get what he needed, he sat in the lunchroom during his breaks and at lunch, ignoring the chatter about last winter's bowling league and the latest snafu in Vietnam as he leafed through an old issue of Cycle World and waited for Mike to go down the hall with his newspaper. In Mike's office, the letter was filed under Personal

Property, Found. Five seconds to memorize Vincent C. Korstezian's address, then back to the lunchroom to write it down.

And so he'd come to Marmion Street, scouting it after leaving the meatpacking plant at eleven, or early in the morning, before he punched in to collect tolls. He almost always found the red Firebird parked nearby in the morning; it was never there before midnight.

Bright lights…a Mustang. George found it hard to sit still. His body was revved up like the time he took too many diet pills — each car was like another speedball going down. He touched the sheathed cleaver that lay next to him on the seat. He'd hook that to his belt when it was time. Come on, Garbage Mouth, bring yourself home.

George took the tire iron from the floor, put it on his lap and massaged it, feeling its strength and rigidity, thinking how it would feel to beat Vinnie with it, to use the power, to ram it home. Bright lights…Firebird!

No, no sound. Leave the door open a crack. No light and no sound other than rain drumming on his poncho, on the street and parked cars. Park yours, Vinnie. No meter to feed tonight — tonight all you pay is a toll. "Love" and "hate" are on your hands, Vinnie. I prefer gloves. You should have worn gloves and kept your mouth shut like I do. Bare anything, people tear into it, peck it apart. People, Vinnie. Grubsucking crows that can't fly.

The Firebird's engine stopped, the headlights went out; the overhead light blinked on, then off as the man closed the door.

"Vinnie?" whispered George.

Korstezian spun around. "Yeah. Who – "

The light trapped his eyes. The tire iron whooshed through the dark. George felt the shock shoot up his arm as Korstezian's head shattered like a ripe melon dropped on concrete. Bloody flesh and splintered bone fell from the light. Vinnie's body crumpled to the street.

Dead, Vinnie? Don't die on me yet – here's one for mother! And this is for the crows. Where's your Garbage Mouth now?

George flicked off the light, put down the tire iron and dragged Vinnie's body between the Firebird and the car parked in front of it.

He searched Vinnie's pockets, taking the wallet and a bag of weed. Then he went for the wristwatch. Let it look like a robbery. But he couldn't leave the body like that – the hands weren't right. Those hands started it all. He grabbed Vinnie's right hand and flashed the light on it for an instant. The tattoo spelled HATE, a letter on each of four fingers. George put down the light, took the cleaver from its sheath and chopped down. Vinnie's wrist bones crunched, blood leaked from the wound. Another cut and George held the severed hand in his own. He put it down on the Firebird's hood while he sheathed the cleaver, retrieved his flashlight and tire iron. Smashing the driver's window, he tossed the hand on top of the dashboard. Then he walked back to his Plymouth, got in, and carefully put his tools and gloves into a plastic bag. He'd get rid of this stuff and everything would be okay. It had all gone so well. He'd even permitted Garbage Mouth to keep the hand that said LOVE. Yes, a touching gesture.

11

Doctor White

She returned to consciousness with a throbbing head, a tube down her throat and an IV needle taped into her arm.

Shit! Still alive, thought Maggie. Where had she gone wrong? She'd swallowed as many pills as she could without puking. Now she looked at the bottle of fluid that hung upside down from a chrome IV stand. A drop formed, hesitated, then surrendered to gravity, falling into the plastic tube. Horrendous coughs from the next bed distracted her, but her view was cut off by a blue curtain encircling her bed. The other sounds were no better: a pump motor clicking on and off as it sucked gunk from the tube up her nose, moans from a woman across the room, and electronic beeps from a cardiac monitor.

Maggie winced as she tried to swallow. She reached under the sheet, tugged the hospital gown lower and smoothed it out across her thighs. What horny bastard had shoved that tube up her peehole? What else had they done to her while she was unconscious? No wimp tears now, be strong. Tricia had said that before running away. Last whisper in the dark. Last will and testament for her little sister. God, why did You take Patricia and leave me to live? Life is just a tube of piss, a descending spiral of waste twisting down to a body bag. No wimp tears now, sister, be strong!

An ebony hand dragged the curtain back enough to admit a portly man in a white coat. His smile was broad and engaging. "Good morning," he said. "I'm glad you're awake."

"I'm not." Her voice was raspy, her throat felt raw. "Where the fuck am I?"

"University Hospital. I'm Doctor White."

"White?" She wasn't sure he was serious. With his styled Afro and carefully trimmed mustache, mint green shirt and yellow tie, she thought he looked more like a pimp or a peacock than a doctor.

His mustache twitched into another smile. "Leroy White. With a capital W. Makes it easy to remember." His voice was deep, his tone reassuring.

"Are you the S.O.B. who stuck these tubes in me?"

"No. I take it you're very uncomfortable."

She coughed, then tried to swallow and grimaced. "What's your form of torture?"

"I'm not into torture, okay? I try to help people."

"You a shrink?"

He nodded. "What's hurting the most right now?"

"I've got a porcupine in my throat. How about getting me a drink?"

"Sure."

Maggie watched him belly up to the night table. Too much rich living, she thought. Probably wears the Afro to make him look taller. He'd pour her a cupful of water, expecting her to pour out her guts in return. No way! She struggled to a sitting position, received the paper cup from his thick fingers. Sweet Jesus, water never tasted so good.

"Thank you." She held the empty cup out for more.

White refilled the cup twice for her. She drank slowly, trying to prolong the relief, delay the questioning.

"Your throat feel a little better?" he asked.

"Not much."

"Tough porcupine. I can appreciate that, okay? But your insides might hurt less if you shared some of your pain with me."

"You want my tube up your you-know-what? Look, it's not personal. I don't like shrinks."

"How many psychiatrists have you met before?"

"One. That was more than enough."

"Where was that?"

"City Hospital."

"After a suicide attempt?"

Maggie didn't answer.

"How did that psychiatrist offend you??"

"He asked too many stupid questions. Can you get someone to take these tubes out?"

"I'll see what I can do about that, okay? And I'd like your permission to get your medical record from City. Were you admitted there?"

She blew a puff of air through her lips. "Do as you please – you will anyway. It won't tell you anything. Neither will I."

"I don't see how silence helps your situation, but that's for you to think about. Meanwhile, I need to figure out if you're still determined to kill yourself."

"Would you believe me if I said no?"

White smiled. "That sounds like a 'yes.' I'll see what I can do about the tubes, okay? The nurse will bring you a form to sign so we can get your record." He moved to the gap in the curtains, then turned back to face her. "After they take out those tubes, they'll bring you some soft food. Even though it hurts to swallow, try to eat, okay? Hunger never helps one's mood." He pushed through the curtain and was gone.

By that afternoon, the catheter and nasogastric tubes had been removed and she'd been transferred to a private room. The intravenous drip had been left in her arm and a volunteer sitter had been brought in to make sure that she stayed behind the bedrails. She'd needed only thirty seconds to determine that the graying, bespectacled woman craved conversation and hoped for gratitude, so she'd told the woman she didn't need a babysitter and ordered the prissy woman to leave. The sitter got flustered and hid her beak behind a magazine. After that, there was only silence. Which was why seeing Doctor White again started out as a relief. She was pleased that he asked the sitter to leave the room while they talked.

As he came to her bedside, Maggie sat up against the pillows. "I want to get out of here."

"I think you should, too," said White.

"Good. When can I go?"

White rested a hand on her bedrail. "Very soon. The real question is 'where'?"

"What do you mean? I'm going home to my apartment."

"But you still feel suicidal."

She shook her head. "I didn't say that."

"Did your feelings change from this morning? They were the same eight weeks ago. I had a medical records supervisor read me the note Doctor Daniels wrote after he saw you in the emergency room. She'll mail me a copy as soon as she gets the form you signed. I couldn't wait for the postman."

"I said I'm going home." Her tone was steely.

"I know you want to, okay? But I think it makes sense for you to come into our psychiatric unit for a few days before you go home."

She raised her voice. "I don't care what you think. I'm going home."

"Not right away. Let me give it to you straight. You can sign in to the psychiatric ward here or I'll sign a paper saying you're dangerous to yourself, which you've already proven, and the police will escort you to the state hospital. Think it over. Here you can sign yourself in and, after a few days, sign yourself out. The state hospital means temporary commitment."

"You bastard! You really mean it." Her face became hot, her muscles taut.

He nodded. "You bet your sweet sassafras."

Maggie reached over with her right hand and jerked the tube from the needle in her vein. She tore at the tape that bound her left forearm to the board on which it rested.

"Nurse! Nurse!" shouted White, reaching over the bedrail to restrain her. Maggie fended him off with the armboard and yanked the I.V. tube. The stand and bottle crashed on the floor. Blood dripped from the needle in her vein. White lowered the bedrail. Maggie rolled to the other side of the bed and grabbed the water pitcher from the nightstand. She flung the water at White, then the pitcher at the window.

"Shit!" said White as the water hit his face, splashed his clothes. Reaching for the bedpan, Maggie heard the window shatter and splatter glass, then an "Oh my God!" from a nurse and a "What's going on?" from an attendant and then she was struggling to throw the bedpan with lots of hands grabbing at her and White's weight forcing her down onto the bloodstained sheet until she felt crushed and yelled "Get the fuck off me, you black tub of lard!"

White's belly began to shake and press her deeper into the bed. He couldn't restrain his laughter. Maggie was dumbfounded. She stopped struggling and tried to comprehend what was funny. The belly laughs diminished as White clumsily raised himself off her, leaving other hands to pin her limbs to the bed. He staggered to his feet, pulled a monogrammed handkerchief from his pocket and mopped his face.

"Did I tickle your little funnybone?" she asked.

"'Black tub of lard,'" he said. "That's exactly what my sister called me whenever we fought. I haven't heard that for more than thirty years." He grinned at the assortment of frowns and stares on the faces of nurses and attendants who'd come running. "Thank you. It's all over, I think. I appreciate your help. But now Miss Saxe needs to decide which hospital she'll grace with her presence. What do you say, Miss Saxe?"

"To you it's a big joke, isn't it? You can laugh because you won. But my time will come; believe me, you won't laugh then."

"It's no joke, Miss Saxe. And we're not on opposing teams, okay? Which hospital do you choose?"

"Choose? Is that a joke? What can I choose? Can I choose that these idiots take their grubby paws off me? Especially this ham-handed nurse pressing the needle into my arm. Get the hands off, the needle out and a Band-Aid on. Then I'll sign your fucking paper – this room's a mess, anyway."

12

The Chairman

"Okay, Anita, tell me what I'm in for this time," said Raymond.

Anita DeSimone, Executive Secretary of University Hospital's Department of Psychiatry, didn't look up from her steno pad as her fingers danced on an electric typewriter. Iron-gray hair formed a helmet protecting her ears; granny glasses straddled the arch of her nose. From plump cheeks down to the top of her white polyester sundress, Anita's skin was flushed and glistening. A mole on her neck and a vaccination scar on her shoulder were islands in a sun-drenched sea.

"Come in and close the door, Raymond." Her voice was sharp with annoyance. "Close it all the way – my air conditioner has emphysema. The Chief's on the phone; he'll be with you in a few minutes."

Raymond pushed the glass-paneled door shut, then pulled a handkerchief from his hip pocket and wiped his forehead. Beneath the noose of his tie, the collar of his white shirt felt glued to his neck. All four windows in the office were closed, with their venetian blinds tightly drawn against the sun. One blind was half raised, its gathered slats trembling atop the overwrought air conditioner. The machine wheezed and rattled, smothered by the heaviness in the air.

"Did you have a nice vacation?" Anita glanced up from her typewriter without slowing her fingers.

"It was great to be at the lake in this heat wave — especially because I was between assignments and didn't have any patients to worry about. But Adult Outpatient here should be a much easier rotation than my two months at City Hospital... Do you know why the Chief called me away from the clinic before I even got started?"

"Doctor Taylor does his own talking. Just relax and take a seat. I have work to do."

He tucked his handkerchief away and sat down next to a coffee table with magazines. Anita typed on, arms bare, fingers flying, lips tight with determination. Raymond glanced at the closed door to his boss's office. He didn't need the gold letters to tell him that Harrison Bryce Taylor, MD, Chairman, sat in judgment behind it. Shrugging off the memory of their last meeting, he reached for the closest magazine. From the cover of *Life*, the face of a dead soldier stared back at him. The caption was "American Dead in Vietnam, One Week's Toll."

Two hundred forty-two in a week? Raymond grit his teeth. Sixteen months, four days, and the Pentagon still hadn't come through with information about how his brother Ethan had died. Now all these families were going through their own grief, getting their own bureaucratic runarounds. He swallowed hard. Yes, there were things far worse than getting chewed out by the boss. Still, if Taylor refused his request for a fellowship, he'd have to honor his contract with the Army next July. It certainly didn't look like the Vietnam war would be over by then. Did they deploy psychiatrists to Vietnam?

He dropped the magazine onto the table. "I think that air conditioner is dead. Why don't you pull the plug and put it out of its misery?"

Anita's lips hinted at a smile. "The Chief is against euthanasia."

"I'm not surprised. The last time I was in there, he didn't show any mercy."

"My understanding is that you embarrassed him at Grand Rounds, in front of the entire staff." She plucked a Kleenex from the box on her desk.

Was she saying that he'd deserved Taylor's diatribe? Raymond watched her dab at the perspiration on her neck. Married only to her job, Anita mothered everyone in the Department, her boss most of all. Even if Doctor Taylor had said nothing, she would have been told about the incident repeatedly in the last four months. Anita was empathic but discreet, a natural sponge for organizational leakage. She would have heard about the Grand Rounds confrontation both from Taylor loyalists, who would've denounced "that wise-ass Daniels" and the depths to which the residency program had fallen, and from departmental dissidents, who would've joked about Taylor's embarrassment.

Anita looked up and saw him staring at her. "It is true, isn't it?" she asked.

He lifted his hands chest-high and let them fall back to his lap. "What's true is that Doctor Taylor presented a research paper submitted to the American Journal of Psychiatry which listed him as the senior author. Was I supposed to know that he didn't have anything more to do with it than approve the project and use his clout to get it funded? Anyway, after he presented the paper, I asked a question. He was vague, so I pressed him." Raymond shook his head. "God, I was stupid. Hammelstein had done the research, and he wasn't there to bail Doctor Taylor out."

"Doctor Hammelstein called in sick that day."

"Maybe he was. But all I knew was that Doctor Taylor was hedging, so I asked him why. It was a naïve question; I wasn't looking to embarrass him."

Anita smiled as if she knew better. "No one took you for being stupid or naïve. If they had, you never would have been accepted for our residency program."

"Everyone makes mistakes. Maybe they should have looked at my principles, not just my grades." He looked away, surveying the room. "Why don't you open a window? You'd get a better breeze if a bird flew by."

"I have too many allergies." She saw the light on the telephone disappear. "The Chief's off the phone. Listen, for your sake, maybe this time you shouldn't ask him why — about anything, okay?"

"Sounds like good advice." Raymond heard a door open behind him. He put on a smile and stood up to face his boss.

Calm, cool and connected, thought Raymond. Still tennis trim and posture perfect, with white hair styled to minimize the losses up front, Harrison Taylor seemed unruffled by the heat, his busy schedule, or his sixty-three years. Wire-rimmed glasses failed to conceal the lines around his blue eyes. What Taylor lacked in youth and height, he made up for in poise and polish. His beige suit was flecked with gold thread, untouched by a wrinkle. His shirt was pale gold, his tie a strip of sand upon which ghostly owls eyed the onlooker.

"It's good to have you back, Raymond. I hope you had a restful vacation."

Raymond managed to hold his smile. Oh, it was "Raymond" now, was it? What happened to "impertinent fool," "attention-seeking asshole" and the other insults that Taylor had peppered him with, four months ago? "Yes, thank you," he said. "I'm glad to be back."

"Please come in." The Chairman moved aside to let him pass into the office. "Anita, no calls, please. Except from Senator Brill."

"Yes, Doctor Taylor."

Raymond paused inside the door, unsure whether to sit or stand. The air was cool, the overhead light subdued by a dimmer. Taylor's mahogany desk and a set of leather chairs were at the far end of the rectangular room, with light filtering in between closed venetian blinds on corner windows, one of which harbored a humming air conditioner. Overcrowded bookcases under framed diplomas and citations occupied one long wall; an analyst's couch, wooden chair, floor lamp and file cabinet took up the other.

The Chairman shut the door, strode to his desk and sat down. "Please," he said, indicating the leather chairs in front of his desk.

Raymond settled himself in the nearest chair and eyed the desktop, bare but for the telephone, a stapler, and a green personnel file stacked atop a manila folder and a blue loose-leaf binder of a patient's medical chart. No need for Taylor to tell him whose personnel file that was. What did the Chairman have in store for him? What was so important that Taylor had summoned him the instant he came back to work?

"You look a bit apprehensive, Raymond." Taylor's deep voice reached for fatherly concern.

"I suppose I am, a little. First day back, not knowing why you wanted to see me. And waiting out in that hot office didn't help. I don't know how Anita copes with that heat."

The Chairman nodded. "She needs a new air conditioner. Unfortunately, the Purchasing Department moves slowly." Taylor extended his right hand, palm up and open. "But let's see if we can get the elephant in this room out of the way. I apologize for what I said in our last meeting. I don't usually lose my temper like that. I reacted poorly to embarrassment. I should have realized you made an honest mistake. This time, I'm sure we can have a more pleasant chat."

"Thank you, sir. I apologize for what I did, too."

"Water under the bridge." Taylor's manicured hand flicked the past away and came to rest on the green folder. "I have your personnel file here." He picked it up and slowly leafed through the pages. "Your supervisors think very highly of you. Still, there's always room for improvement. Let's see…you've spent seven months on the Adult Inpatient wards, a month in Neurology, six each on the Children's Unit and the Adolescent Service, two at the State Hospital and then two at City. You've really covered the territory."

"There are a lot of opportunities here. I wanted to experience as many as possible."

Taylor looked up. "Including psychoanalysis?" It was barely a question.

Raymond's muscles tightened. How did Taylor know? "Yes, I've started. It's not a training analysis. It's a personal analysis."

"Doctor Korline is very good," said Taylor.

Raymond's throat constricted. Had Korline told him? No, that would be unethical. So who did? One of last year's supervisors? Raymond cleared his throat. "That's why I went to him."

"Indeed… How was your rotation at City Hospital? Not many residents have chosen that option."

"It was interesting. I got what I wanted, experience with emergencies and with patients off the street."

"Mmm. And now you're going to be working in our Adult Outpatient Service?"

"Yes." Raymond felt pressure on his fingers and realized he was squeezing them. Why didn't Taylor get to the point?

Taylor placed the green file on his desktop. "I want to be clear, Raymond, I called you over this morning to make you an offer. Feel free to refuse if you don't like it. Believe me, I'll think none the less of you if you refuse." His fingers gave the file a single tap. "That's clear, isn't it?"

Clear but false, thought Raymond. "Yes."

"Good. I want you to understand the situation. Because of my consultations in Washington and throughout this state, people in high status places come to me with their personal or family problems. Most often, such people want everything kept off the record. Their jobs or family considerations may depend not only on complete confidentiality, but also the absence of a paper trail. Most of the time, I refer such patients to colleagues in private practice who are extremely discreet, but occasionally someone in an influential family needs hospitalization." The corners of Taylor's lips turned down. "Regardless of how we may feel, the stigma of psychiatric hospitalization is very much alive, so the family asks me to admit the patient to a private room here, but in the medical wing. I try to persuade them that a private psychiatric hospital can be very helpful and much more private, but some insist that admission to any psychiatric unit is out of the question. It's an unfortunate dilemma, but getting the patient hospitalized and treated is more important than having my way about it. You understand?"

Raymond nodded. Taylor's concern for the patient might be real, but so was his desire to have influential people and their checks in his pocket. "Yes. You admit a few V.I.P.s to private rooms in the medical wing and treat them there as your private patients."

Taylor straightened in his chair. "I don't make a dime from it,

Raymond. The hospital collects for all services rendered, including my fee, and that's credited to our department, not to me."

Had he judged Taylor too harshly? "Does such a patient get a psychiatric diagnosis in the medical record?"

"If there's any medical problem at all, that condition will be listed as the primary diagnosis," said Taylor. "For example, alcoholics will often be discharged with a diagnosis of acute gastritis. If the psychiatric diagnosis might be embarrassing, or if the patient has no physical problem at all, I use the most benign psychiatric diagnosis that indicates something of the patient's condition. That's clear, isn't it?"

Sure, the procedure was, but the ethics weren't, thought Raymond. Why should a poor man's alcoholism be a wealthy man's gastritis? Was pleasing the patient or hiding information from the insurance company more important than honesty? But this wasn't the time to ask. "That was my only question."

"Good. Now here's my problem." The Chairman settled his glasses higher on his nose as if to better focus his blue eyes on Raymond. "Because I've many commitments to professional groups and government agencies, I'm often required to go out of town. Even when I'm here, I have so many duties that I can't be available enough to hospitalized patients. So each year, I select a resident on the Adult Outpatient Service, one who's not burdened with the usual load of hospitalized patients, to work with me on those private cases I mentioned. Under my supervision, of course. When I'm away, the resident follows through on our treatment plan, bringing any problems that arise to a designated senior professor. This year, I've chosen to ask you to assist me." Taylor rubbed his lips as if he were sorry his last words had escaped. "It's extra work, and there's no extra pay for it. Not for me, not for you – is that clear? It's for the good of our department. And sometimes I've shown my appreciation for good service in other ways – an excellent reference, an introduction here and there – it never hurts to know the right people. I understand you're thinking about applying for a fourth year fellowship in our Institute."

"Yes, I'm very interested in joining Doctor Corrigan in his research on Manic-Depressive Disorders."

"And why is that?"

Confide as little as possible, thought Raymond, pushing aside the image of his uncle vegetating on a couch. "It runs in my extended family," he said.

"You might be a good addition to Doctor Corrigan's team." Taylor raised a cautioning hand. "I make no promises, mind you. It all depends on how things go. So with that understanding, do you want the assignment?"

Raymond was dumbfounded. He'd expected a lecture with stern warnings about his future conduct. Instead, he was being given a full pardon, a vote of confidence, a flattering plum. Was he way off base about Taylor? The offer sounded so good; was anything wrong with it? Think it over, talk to people. No need to get hurried into it.

"Doctor Taylor, I'm truly flattered by your offer. I hope you don't take offense if I ask for some time to think about it before I give you an answer."

The Chairman offered a smile that bespoke understanding. "No offense at all. Under other circumstances, I'd gladly give you several days, even a week. Unfortunately, I already have one patient in the hospital and I just received a call at home yesterday about someone else who will probably be admitted today. I only get six or seven of these people a year, but here I am with two of them and I'm scheduled to fly to Washington at the end of this week. Federal funding for the Community Mental Health Centers Act is being threatened again and I've been asked to testify. So if you can't give me an unqualified 'yes,' I really must ask someone else. I'm sure you understand."

Sounds plausible, thought Raymond. But why did Taylor pick him in the first place? "May I ask one more question, sir? In view of what happened at Grand Rounds, why would you choose me rather than any of the other residents on the Adult Outpatient Service?"

"Didn't I make that clear? You're in your third year, you've had a variety of good experiences and you come well recommended by your supervisors. In fact, Doctor Markowitz told me personally how well you handled that very difficult deaf girl they thought was schizophrenic and wanted to send off to the state hospital. So you seem to be the right man in the right place at the right time. And I'm not one to hold a mistake against a person if they learn from it." Taylor's eyebrows arched above his glasses. "And I trust you have learned from it and will be more tactful in the future. Am I right?"

Raymond nodded. "You needn't have any worries about that." Getting a few answers certainly made it easier to give one, he thought. Taylor was buying his cooperation while showing all factions in the department that the Chairman could be fair and forgiving. And it wasn't as if Taylor owned him. He could always resign from this assignment. What if the Grand Rounds incident hadn't happened? Wouldn't he have received the Chairman's offer with pride instead of suspicion? Raymond breathed a sigh of decision. "Thank you again, sir. I accept."

"Wonderful. I'm delighted." Chairman Taylor's tone and smile were the warmest Raymond had ever received from the man, yet they were reminiscent of a stern father congratulating his son for passing an important test.

"You know," said Taylor without missing a beat, "I thought you'd decide to do this, so I've dictated a memo to the Chairman of the Department of Internal Medicine with copies to the service chiefs in my department – letting them all know you're assisting me and may need to ask for things in my behalf. Naturally, I haven't sent those memos yet. It's just best to be prepared."

God! The Chairman had been two steps ahead of him. Well, Taylor might think two steps ahead, but he certainly wasn't a good chess player. No tournament player he'd faced across a chessboard would ever boast that a pawn was only a pawn, not when it could advance and become a powerful queen. Even unchanged, a pawn could help checkmate the king.

Taylor looked at his wristwatch. "I have to leave in five minutes for a meeting, so let me brief you on these two cases. You can read what records I have — which brings up another point. Please be careful that no highly personal details appear on the official record. Keep your notes separate and don't write the patient's real name or initials on them. Destroy them when the patient is discharged. You understand?"

"Yes."

"Then first there's this girl I expect to admit today. Her name is Nancy Brill. She'll turn fifteen next week. Her father is a state senator – on the Senate Appropriations Committee, no less. I haven't met the girl, but apparently she's been quietly psychotic for some time. Her father called me yesterday. Most of what he told me is in this file." Taylor offered up the manila folder from his stack of files. Raymond came out of his chair to receive it, then sat down again.

"Apparently the girl was seen for a while by their minister because she had delusions about the Devil. Her father thought the girl had seen too many horror movies. Then the girl started saying that the Devil was talking to her, but the clergyman gave the parents some religious explanation. I'm sure if the girl had said she'd been talking to Martians, the Senator wouldn't have sent her to N.A.S.A." Taylor flicked his hand through the air. "In any case, her condition worsened. She stopped going to school in March and was tutored at home. This past week, she said that the Devil was ordering her to kill herself. Two days ago, she set her waste basket on fire. That finally got her parents to take her to a psychiatrist out in the western part of the state. He considered the suicide risk substantial and strongly recommended immediate hospitalization. But the Senator didn't want her in a local hospital – or in any psychiatric hospital." Taylor glanced at the telephone on his desk. "He's supposed to call me again this morning, to confirm that they'll bring the girl in today. I insisted that both parents bring her."

"Considering the delusions and fire-setting, shouldn't she be on our Adolescent Unit rather than a medical floor?"

"Of course. But the Senator is up for re-election this fall and doesn't want the voters thinking that he drove his daughter crazy. Until we get the girl thoroughly evaluated, you'd better arrange for sitters around the clock."

Raymond ran a hand through his hair. "Do we talk to the Senator about his priorities?"

"Let me do that," said Taylor.

Would he? Why hadn't he already? No, don't be naïve. "What about the second patient?"

"Another suicidal young woman – came in two days ago after an overdose of barbiturates. She was in Intensive Care for a day, then was moved to a private room with a sitter. She was transferred to the locked psychiatric ward yesterday."

"She's not going to be in the medical wing?"

"No. This is a different situation. It's not political. It's just a favor to – another father, an old friend. Because of the social ties, I don't want to be involved, either as therapist or supervisor. An occasional progress report will do. Doctor Bergstrom will supervise, but you'll be the patient's therapist and will make whatever decisions are necessary. All the details are in this chart." He pointed to the loose-leaf binder.

Raymond nodded. The Chairman was trusting him, on a limited basis to be sure, with the evaluation and treatment of the daughter of a state senator, and with almost the entire responsibility for the daughter of Taylor's good friend. Truly a vote of confidence from his boss. "What's the name of the second patient?"

The Chairman extended the blue binder across the desk. As Raymond got up and reached for it, Taylor said "Mary Margaret Saxe."

Raymond managed to keep his hand from faltering, but his eyebrows jumped and his eyes darted to the Chairman's face. Taylor's expression was one of curiosity. The man was observing him, waiting for his reaction. Well Taylor wasn't the only one who could play close to the vest. Raymond sat down again, settled the binder on top of the manila folder on his lap, and opened the blue cover as if he intended to read every word. If Taylor wanted to get to his meeting, he'd have to speak first.

"Doctor White said that you met her at City Hospital, two months ago. Do you remember her?"

"She would be hard to forget." Judging by her serum barbiturate level in the ER this time, she was lucky to have survived.

"I asked Doctor White to see her yesterday. He called City Hospital and convinced a supervisor to read your note over the phone to him. Did Mary Saxe tell you any more than you put into the record about the man who brought her to the hospital?"

"She wouldn't say anything about him. Did he show up when she was admitted here?"

"No. The police brought her in after receiving an anonymous call."

"If she gives us permission to contact her family – assuming she has a family – maybe they'll know the identity of her lover."

Taylor waved his hand impatiently. "It seems she keeps the details of her personal life quite secret. The important thing is that she's still depressed and suicidal. I doubt that the specific identity of her lover matters much. But talk to the girl, her family, anyone you like – as long as she gives permission. She's your patient and you're responsible for her care. I don't want to be involved." Taylor raised a forefinger. "One more thing. Once the insurance runs out on these two girls, we'll pick up the expenses under one of our clinical research grants."

"You want me to see if they qualify for — "

"Don't worry about qualifications. I'll take care of that. They're both to have whatever duration of hospital care they need. That's clear, isn't it?" Without waiting for an answer, Taylor pushed his chair back from his desk.

Raymond closed the binder and stood up. "I assure you I'll do my best." He headed for the door. Taylor's voice turned him around.

"I know you will. For your sake and the sake of those two women, I sincerely hope your best will prove satisfactory."

The Chairman's doubt was obvious, his threat unmistakable. Raymond's lips tightened. What game was Taylor playing? No, whatever it was, it wasn't a game.

13

You Don't Know Me

Raymond walked rapidly through the hospital corridor, body on automatic pilot, head floating in anticipation of meeting the state senator. Senate Ways and Means, Anita had said — budget and appropriations. That's where real power lay. He came to the door of room 417 and knocked gently.

"Come in," said Doctor Taylor.

Raymond entered and sensed the tension. Nancy, her parents, and Doctor Taylor appeared stiff and uncomfortable, like strangers waiting for an overdue bus, eager for it to take them away. Indeed, the room offered little comfort, dominated as it was by the white-sheeted hospital bed, the wall fittings for oxygen and electricity, and a disconnected cardiac monitor. On the near side of the bed, Mrs. Brill, a petite brunette in a tailored pink suit, perched on a plastic chair. She clutched her purse with one hand, sodden tissues with the other. A television set, a whiteboard with nursing staff names, and a picture of a field of wildflowers were mounted on the powder blue walls.

"Ah, Doctor Daniels," announced the Chairman from his

professional stance at the foot of the bed. "I'd like you to meet Senator and Mrs. Brill and their daughter Nancy."

Mrs. Brill looked up with tearful brown eyes and a bird-like face streaked by mascara.

The Senator turned reluctantly from the double window on the far side of the room. He was average in height and couldn't hide a pot belly beneath his grey suit, but his salt and pepper hair, large dark eyes, and generous mouth were a handsome combination. "Hi, Doc," he said, offering a meet-and-greet smile. He started to make his way around the foot of the bed toward Raymond.

"Pleased to meet you all," said Raymond.

Nancy Brill sat on the edge of the bed, her thin arms locked protectively across her chest as she rocked slowly back and forth. She looked frail, remote, almost alien — and very vulnerable. Almost fifteen, she looked twelve, with brown hair cut pixie style and her small frame lost in the ruffles of a juvenile yellow dress.

Raymond offered her a reassuring smile. "Hello, Nancy."

She didn't respond.

The Senator shook Raymond's hand. "You don't know how glad we are to be here. Harry here has been saying some very nice things about you. I know you two will do everything you can to help our daughter."

"We certainly will, sir," said Raymond, noting the Senator's firm grip, his engaging smile – yes, the tools of his trade. Some warmth, some sincerity, yet more from habit than desire. "How are you doing, Mrs. Brill?"

"We're very relieved to be here, doctor. I'm sorry to look so awful. You don't know how – Nancy, say 'hello' to the doctor."

Nancy gazed off to a distant space. "Hello, yellow jello," she said in a singsong tone.

"See what I mean, Harry," said Senator Brill.

Harry? thought Raymond. Senior staff psychiatrists called his boss Harrison and residents privately labeled him "Old Hair-Ass," but Raymond had never heard anyone call him Harry.

"The Senator and Mrs. Brill are going with me to my office," said Taylor. "Doctor Daniels, will you be kind enough to stay here with Nancy until her parents return?"

"Of course."

Mrs. Brill rose and gave Nancy a peck on the cheek. "We won't be long, dear."

"We won't be long, dear," parroted Nancy.

Raymond saw Mrs. Brill wince. He felt a twinge of pity. Her make-up couldn't hide the tautness of her skin, the hollows beneath her eyes and the worry lines across her forehead. "We won't be long," she said to Raymond as she squeezed by him and followed her husband and Taylor out the door.

Raymond sat down in the chair that Mrs. Brill had vacated. He watched Nancy rock to and fro. "I'm Doctor Daniels."

"Doctor Daniels." Nancy cocked her head but didn't make eye contact. "Did the Devil send you?"

He suppressed a smile. "No. Are you afraid that he did?"

"Are you afraid that he did?" she echoed.

"No. I'm not afraid of the Devil."

Nancy rocked harder. "Then He will punish you worse." Her voice was flat, her tone certain. "Do you know Melissa Tolliver?"

"No. Who is she?"

Nancy giggled. It was an abrupt, mechanical sound. "Do you know Valerie Murphy?"

"Are these friends of yours?"

"Are these friends of yours?" She giggled again.

He felt his innards sink. Nancy's strange affect, concreteness of thought, echoing and rhyming and delusions about the Devil were suggestive of schizophrenia. God, what a waste, he thought. What might she have been had she drawn a different set of chromosomes or experiences in life's lottery? "Is finding out who I know a way of trying to get to know me?"

Her rocking slowed. "You have a nice voice. You have to be punished."

"Why?"

"What makes you bleed? Bleed, seed, the seed bleeds." Her tone became a shrill singsong. "When blood will run, it won't be fun; won't be fun – not for none."

"Nancy, look at me." His command was firm, yet gentle.

"I can't. Did He send you?"

"The Devil did not send me. Now I would like you to stop rocking and sit quietly, so we can talk."

Her rocking slowed, stuttered, stopped. "Who sent you, then?" She looked over her shoulder, then down at her lap.

"Your parents and Doctor Taylor asked me to look after you."

"Look after?" She glanced over her shoulder again. "What about before? Who'll look before me?"

"I'll do everything I can to see that no one hurts you. I'm going to try my best to help you get well."

"A well is a hole in the ground." She pulled on her ears as if to lift herself out of her chair.

"Why did your parents bring you here, Nancy?"

She looked nervously about. "Where are they? Did the Devil take them away?"

"No, they went with Doctor Taylor. They'll be back soon." He sighed. "You're very worried about the Devil. Have you seen Him?"

"Yes. Hasn't everyone?"

"No, most people don't see him. What does He look like?"

"He told me not to tell anybody or He'll burn me in hellfire." She shuddered.

"In the hospital, we can keep you safe."

"A safe is a hole in the wall." She pulled up on her ears again.

"Do you see the Devil as three dimensional, or like on a movie screen or like a ghost?"

"Six dimensional."

"Six?"

She aimlessly waved a pointed finger. "Up, down, inside and out, now and then."

"Do you hear him talking to you?"

"Can't you hear him? He's been talking since I stopped rocking. Can I rock some more, now?"

"Only if you get very frightened. What is the Devil saying?"

Nancy looked toward the door. "Can I tell the doctor?" she said to thin air. "He does have a nice voice... Just one thing?" She began to rock. "He says I have to die."

Raymond's abdomen went tight, a breath stopped in his throat, but his face remained impassive. "Why?"

"Why die? Why try? Sigh, cry and cry, my, oh my, die..."

"Nancy! Why must you die?"

"Because I'm bad."

"What's bad about you?"

"What isn't?"

Raymond shook his head. "Your Devil judges you too harshly. You judge yourself too harshly. Nancy, I think you're a better person than you believe."

Nancy giggled. "That's because you don't know me."

LOREN SCHECHTER

14

Why Not to Us?

Raymond asked an LPN to stay with Nancy until the hospital could supply the first of many sitters she would need. Sitting at a desk in the nurses' station, he wrote admission orders in Nancy's chart and then called Lisa to tell her he'd be late for dinner.

"But it's your first day back from vacation," she protested. "You said that Adult Outpatient was going to be the easiest service of all."

"I don't have time to explain the whole thing now, but Doctor Taylor asked me to help him with two of his hospitalized patients." Raymond fingered a pile of lab slips on the desk. Had he ordered everything Taylor wanted?

"Do you get extra pay for that?"

"It's considered an honor to be chosen."

"Oh, Ray. You have such trouble saying no. You realize Taylor's exploiting you, don't you?"

"I hope not," he said, but he knew she was right. Well, it was part of the system — to get to the top, you paid your dues; once there, you collected from others who wanted to move up. "I'll be home before eight. Kiss Julie for me."

"God! I left her in the tub!"

He heard a loud click; the line went dead.

Shit! Was Julie okay? Drowned? Call back? No, that would be ridiculous; it would be giving in to his fears. If there were an emergency, Lisa would get back to him fast. He shook his head and put the receiver back in its cradle. Would they be as apprehensive about the risks to their second child? At least Lisa's first trimester had passed uneventfully. Still, the more experience he gained in medicine, the more he realized how much could go wrong. Disease could sabotage any pregnancy, cut down any child, no matter how beautiful, no matter how small. No doubt they could prevent their children from drowning in a bathtub, but what could they do to prevent them from becoming a Nancy Brill? The girl's concrete thinking, clang rhyming, delusions and hallucinations probably meant she had schizophrenia. No one knew how to prevent that. No one knew what caused it, or even if it was one disease or several that looked similar. But whatever it was, it was also a family tragedy.

He tried to keep that thought in mind as he met in private with Nancy's parents. It wasn't easy. The windowless conference room adjoining the nurses' station seemed to shrink before the onslaught of Mrs. Brill's anxiety and shrill voice. With her fists clenched on the table, she leaned forward in her plastic chair and flooded him with fears, memories, wishes, and disappointments she'd collected during the life of her daughter. He tried to acknowledge her pain and worries while trying to get her to give a coherent history of Nancy's illness. For his part, Senator Brill slouched in his chair, smoked one cigarette after another and, when questioned, deferred to his wife.

"Do you understand her change, Doctor?" demanded Mrs. Brill. "No, I'm sure you can't, not without having known Nancy before. What's happened to her boggles the mind. Doesn't it, Joe?" She blinked hard and rubbed her eyes. "Please, Joe, do you have to smoke another? My eyes can't take all the smoke."

"Sorry. Last puff." The Senator's words were clipped, his expression sullen.

Mrs. Brill granted him a nod before refocusing on Raymond. "I mean Nancy used to love going to school. She had a perfect attendance record in the second grade. Her teacher that year told me that Nancy was the most cooperative little girl she ever had the privilege to teach." Mrs. Brill touched her chest. "I was so excited, I went right home and woke Nancy up and hugged her and told her what Mrs. McFadden said. Do you remember that, Joe?"

"Yes." The Senator stubbed his cigarette out in a glass ashtray. "She asked you what 'privilege' meant and you spent thirty minutes telling her."

Pain flickered in Mrs. Brill's eyes. "It couldn't've been more than five," she said. "Nancy understood things so easily in those days."

Senator Brill raised his hand. "Let's not dwell on those days, okay? I'm sure the doctor has other people he needs to see today. And I have a campaign to run."

Sure, thought Raymond. You're running for power and away from your family. No, that wasn't fair. Maybe the Senator was just as deeply concerned about Nancy, but avoidance was his defense against pain. "Tell me, Senator, when did you first suspect that something was the matter with Nancy?"

Senator Brill straightened his tie. "It's hard to know. I've worried about her lack of friends for years. She was always a timid girl — "

"Sensitive," said Mrs. Brill.

The Senator glared at her. "Babied too much, if you ask me." He turned to Raymond. "Naturally, I was very upset when she started up with this Devil nonsense, but I remember being concerned at the beginning of last year, when her grades went down so badly. I spoke to her about it, but she wouldn't say much, except that she'd try harder." He fingered his cigarette lighter. "She did, too, because she spent more time in her room studying and she ended up passing everything."

"But she wasn't herself," said Mrs. Brill. "She got so quiet. I thought she was worried about school and not having friends and not being as physically well-developed as the other girls." Mrs. Brill turned to Raymond. "Those worries aren't abnormal for a teen-age girl, are they? No, of course not." Mrs. Brill shook her head. "If only her first time was easier, poor baby."

"First time?" Raymond prompted.

"Time-of-the-month."

"She's talking about Nancy's period," Senator Brill said. "My wife feels it's crude to use words like 'period' or 'pregnant'. She only mentions sex to give fiends and maniacs a bad name."

Mrs. Brill's cheeks reddened. She bent over to retrieve her straw handbag. The Senator got up and went to the sink for a Dixie cup of water.

"What happened when Nancy had her first period?" asked Raymond.

Mrs. Brill placed her handbag on the table and extracted some clean tissues. "I can't tell you how embarrassing it was for her, Doctor. As soon as she told me she had a male teacher for French, I had a feeling something awful would happen. And it did, in French class, in her very first week of seventh grade." Mrs. Brill glanced at her husband. "May I have some water, too, Joe?" She lowered her voice. "That poor girl didn't even have a cramp before she suddenly felt her undergarments — well, you know, they were suddenly wet and sticky." Mrs. Brill leaned forward. "Of course, Nancy realized what was happening because I'd given her two pamphlets when she turned eleven; but she didn't know what to do when it came in French. She just sat there in absolute dread, trying to hide her shame." Tears welled up in Mrs. Brill's eyes. "Finally — finally, she got up the courage to ask to leave the room, but her teacher was more insensitive than most men — and he's not even French. Why they let him teach children at all is a mystery to me." She rapped the tabletop. "He had the nerve to tell her that the bell was going to ring in five minutes and that she could wait until it did. And when she told him she couldn't, he asked her 'why not'?"

Her husband handed her a paper cup of water. "Thank you, Joe." She set it down without drinking. "'I can't wait'," Nancy kept saying, but that bully wouldn't believe her, so she started to cry. That stupid man told her to be quiet. 'But I'm bleeding!' our poor baby said." Mrs. Brill thrust out her hand. "You don't have to be very bright to imagine what that did to her, what with all those smirking little eyes, those whispers and giggles. When she told me, I cried as much as she did. We just couldn't bear the pain." She lifted the cup for a sip of water.

"I'm sure it was very painful," said Raymond. "What happened after that?"

"I raised holy hell with the principal and the School Board," growled Senator Brill. He pulled back his chair and plopped into it. "That son-of-a-bitch teacher didn't get another contract."

Mrs. Brill set down the paper cup. "Nancy didn't go back to that school for two weeks. I never wanted to send her back at all, and she didn't want to go. It was Joe —" She emphasized his name as if to indict him. " — Joe and her guidance counselor — they insisted that Nancy had to go back. There were some nasty boys who teased her unmercifully. They don't humiliate girls who dilly-dally with them;

they only pick on the innocent, sensitive children who aren't able to defend themselves." She shook her head. "There's something wrong with the younger generation."

"Kids are given too much nowadays," said Senator Brill. "I had to work for everything I got. The only thing my father gave me was a kick in the ass. And if I cried, he gave me another." The Senator reached for his cigarettes. "I never felt sorry for myself, and I didn't want Nancy pitying herself, either. Everyone has embarrassing experiences. You can't let yourself dwell on them. You have to pick yourself up and go about your business. That's what I told Nancy and that's what she did." He took a cigarette from the pack.

"You never understood how difficult it was for her," said Mrs. Brill.

"Of course I understood — but I wasn't going to let her be defeated. Neither of her brothers have failed anything and I couldn't let Nancy fail." The Senator pointed the unlit cigarette at his wife. "All you did was cry and feel sorry for her. I got her back to school. And when she didn't pull up her grades by mid-year, I was the one who took away her privileges and made her stay in her room until she showed us her completed assignments. That's what got her to pass the seventh grade." He reached for his lighter.

"No," said Mrs. Brill.

The Senator cocked his head. "No?"

"That wasn't why she passed," his wife said. "She was allowed to withdraw from French, and she got C's and D's in everything else because the teachers felt sorry for her."

"But I saw her homework. It was good." He looked at her for confirmation.

Mrs. Brill avoided her husband's gaze. "I helped her."

"You what?" He was incredulous.

"I'm sorry, Joe. I knew you'd be upset. But she's so frightened of your anger. She couldn't concentrate on the work, and she couldn't face you without it. I tried to tell you, but you wouldn't listen."

He slammed the lighter against the tabletop. Mr. Brill flinched. Raymond cleared his throat.

"The hell I wouldn't!" Senator Brill's face was flushed, his eyes wide and accusing. "You never told me!"

"That's not true. I did tell you."

"No, you didn't."

"Wait!" said Raymond. "Each of you remembers the past from a different viewpoint. I know it hurts to recall some of these things, but try to put your hurt and anger aside for the moment. We need to get a clear picture of how Nancy's illness began; that's what we're here for."

"You're right," said the Senator, but he continued to glare at his wife.

"This year has been like a nightmare," said Mrs. Brill. "I keep thinking I'll wake up and Nancy will be fine. Even after all the conferences at school and with our minister and family doctor — now even putting her in the hospital — it still feels like a bad dream, like Nancy's drowning and I can't reach her. She's become so withdrawn and forgetful that I have to remind her to do everything. She sits in front of a piece of toast for half an hour, trying to decide whether to put butter or jelly on it. If I don't butter if for her and tell her to eat it, that toast would sit there until it turned to stone."

"You've always told the poor girl how to chew and when to swallow. That's why she never learned to make a decision." Senator Brill lit another cigarette. He eyed his wife as if waiting for her to object and ready to defy her.

"It's much more than that," said Raymond. "Nancy's illness jumbles her thinking in many ways, including decision-making."

"I know I've made mistakes, Joe." Mrs. Brill's eyes watered, her voice quavered. "I pray to God night and day to make her well again, and to forgive me if I've caused her to be like this. I just wish you had helped more and criticized less." She swallowed hard. "When Andrew — that's our middle child — was young, he used to ask: 'How can Daddy love me if he thinks I never do anything right?' I told him you did love him — I've always said that to all three children. But deep inside, I've had the very same question."

The Senator exhaled. Smoke filled the air. "Then why didn't you ask it?" he demanded. "In the thirty years we've been married, I've never known you to be at a loss for words. Lord knows you've come running to me with every other imaginable question." His hand and cigarette jerked upward. "You know I've never held back an opinion. Not that I ever wanted to hurt you or the kids. It's because I love you that I've been so direct. I don't have to like everything you do to love you, but I do have to be honest. I'll be damned if I'm going to be a politician in my own home."

"I've never asked you to be a politician," said Mrs. Brill. "I asked you to be home more and to take a greater interest in the children."

They've lost sight of Nancy, thought Raymond. "Mrs. Brill, when did Nancy start talking about the Devil?"

"When?... In the spring. At first she didn't mention him directly, just that 'he' didn't want her to do this or that." Mrs. Brill shrugged. "I just assumed Nancy was talking about Joe. Even when I found out she meant the Devil, I didn't take it literally. I thought she was fighting temptation, like all of us do. It wasn't until she took my sewing scissors and cut off her beautiful long hair — that was the day before Mother's Day — that we took her to our minister."

Raymond scratched the back of his hand. "Didn't anyone suggest that you take her to a psychiatrist?"

"Well, I suppose the school people did." Mrs. Brill shifted uneasily in her chair. "We were afraid that seeing a psychiatrist would make her feel even worse about herself."

"That wasn't it," said the Senator. "Let's tell it like it is. I don't have much faith in psychiatrists. Your boss probably told you that already. But it was more than that — we just didn't want to recognize that Nancy is crazy."

"Joe! That's a terrible thing to say." Mrs. Brill's jaw trembled.

"Face it — it's true. Isn't it, Doc?"

"If by 'crazy' you mean that her thinking right now is very disorganized and she's hallucinating, then yes, that's true. But that's right now."

"It's her silly rhyming that drives me up a wall," said the Senator.

"She's associating words by sound rather than by meaning," explained Raymond. "They're called 'clang associations'."

"Why?" said Mrs. Brill.

"It's a symptom of her thought disorder," said Raymond.

Mrs. Brill shook her head. "I don't mean that."

"Then what's your question?" demanded the Senator.

Mrs. Brill opened her mouth to answer. Choking back a sob, she brought her hands to her face. Her body seemed to fold in on itself as she let loose her tears.

Raymond looked half at her, half away, searching for something appropriate to say. Senator Brill carefully stubbed out his cigarette in the ashtray, got up and came around behind his wife. He offered her his handkerchief. Once she took it, he placed his hands on her shoulders. "There, there, Nan. Try and grab hold."

The Senator's action startled Raymond even more than the realization that Mrs. Brill's given name was Nancy. It was the first indication he had that the Senator loved his wife.

Mrs. Brill used the handkerchief with one hand, took hold of her husband's fingers with the other. She swallowed hard, then looked up at Raymond. "Why did this happen to our Nancy?"

"I don't know, Mrs. Brill. We're going to do a lot of talking and run a lot of tests to try to find out."

The Senator shook his head from side to side. "Psychiatrists don't have answers — just more questions."

"But I want an answer," said Mrs. Brill. "Why did this happen to us?"

The Senator blinked back his tears. "It's the wrong question, Nan. We're all human: one brain, four limbs and an ass that gets kicked. The real question is — why not to us?"

15

Stuck With Me

Maggie strode up and down the hospital corridor as if momentum could leave memory behind. Head down, shoulders forward, her bare feet and legs flew across the brown carpet until she was turned back by the end of the hall.

They might keep her locked in the loony bin, she thought, but no one could keep her alive. From the large dayroom on her right, a TV blared forth a game show's hilarity.

Maggie grit her teeth, hiked up her shorts and turned back. For the moment, she had the corridor to herself. She'd watched the other patients being led down a back staircase like sheep. "Morning activities," the attendant had called, rounding up the herd. Let the jocks play volleyball, the jerks paint by the numbers. She had to get a call through to John. Damn him for leaving! Why hadn't he called? Didn't he care if she was alive? Don't think – walk!

She could be most alone speed-walking the hallway, aloof but conspicuously alive. No knocks on her door, no people peering around corners, no questioning if she was alright. As long as she walked fast and said nothing, patients stayed out of her way; nurses who tried to talk with her ran out of breath. Only their eyes could keep up with her. Even now, passing the open door to the dining room on her right and the glass enclosed nurses' station on her left, she felt eyes light on her like insects, felt them crawl over her skin and burrow into her head to lay bare her secrets. No way. Fuck them all.

She raced past the staff room, small offices and bedrooms, then the gray metal door of the seclusion suite. What would it be like inside? Worse than the basement at home? Were there rats here, too? Please, God, don't punish me like that – don't leave me a slobbering idiot in an isolation cell.

At the end of the hall, she stopped to catch her breath and look out the window. Heavy security grates fragmented her view of the sunlit university buildings in which she had moved so freely. No, she wasn't going anywhere, not there and not here where the exits were locked and the windows were as good as barred. Like a child locked in the basement, given only a Bible to dull the pain and the blame, and fend off the rats. And for what? Her body tightened and drew inward as if once again compressed by his weight, to be pierced and defiled in the darkness of her bedroom, a rough hand silencing her screams. Shuddering, she spread her palm on the thick pane of glass. "I hurt," she whispered. But not enough.. Her hand drew back, her fingers closed, and her fist shot forward against the pane, then bounced back aching with rage.

"Let me out!" she screamed. "I can't stand it!" She hit the window a second time. Shatter proof. She swung wildly. Pain shot up her arm. A rush of footsteps, a jingle of keys. She spun around, her back to the wall.

A tall, skinny brunette was in the lead. White blouse, green skirt, loafers that slowed to a walk. Behind her, a young blonde stopped a dozen steps back, but the gaunt one kept coming, the keys on her lanyard belt swaying with authority. Maggie took a deep breath. Nurse Slenderella and the keys to her kingdom, she thought. Which key opened the front door?

"You must be Mary Saxe." Slenderella's voice squeezed through a pinched nose and thin lips, emerging high-pitched and nasal. "I'm Mrs. Eggers, the Head Nurse. I was off when you were admitted yesterday. Is there something I can do to help you?"

Maggie scrutinized the nurse's pageboy for a hair out of place, searched for warmth in the wide gray eyes. A lean, mean bitch, thought Maggie. She nodded.

"What?" asked the nurse.

"Get out of my way."

"Oh, is that how it is. Well, before I step aside, there are a few things you need to know. First, if you're feeling upset, you can talk with someone or work it off in the gym, or you can go to your room. We will not tolerate your banging on windows and screaming, or doing anything else that upsets other patients. You understand that?"

Maggie didn't answer. She looked down at the carpet but instead saw the polished oak floor of Sister Alfreda's office, once again stood trembling with fear as the nun shouted "No more lies, Mary Margaret Saxe. We will not tolerate evil thoughts and lies. Even God will not forgive you unless you tell the truth. Do you understand that? Not even God."

"You understand that?" Eggers repeated. Maggie tried to find her way back from age eleven. The nurse didn't know how to wait. "I think you do," Eggers said. "The second thing is that you can't go walking around barefoot. There are health and safety reasons for that rule and I will be glad to explain them if you ask. But from now on,

I expect to see you in shoes or slippers. If you have any problem with that rule, let me know now."

The sound of the door buzzer pulled the nurse's attention up the hall. She nodded at her companion, who went to open the door.

Maggie studied her bare feet. "I have a problem with it," she mumbled. Her toes wiggled in approbation.

"What is your problem?"

Maggie looked up. "That rule sucks. It's a fucking joke."

Eggers sniffed sharply. Maggie hoped her nose would cave in. "We certainly don't need or want your obscenities," the nurse said. "I'm sure you have enough decent words in your vocabulary to express your objection."

Bitch! Obscenities aren't words. They're deeds – uncaring, selfish or cruel. Maggie shook her head. "You wouldn't understand."

"Perhaps I can. What's your objection to shoes?"

"It's my toes – they have to feel free."

The nurse's glance flitted from Maggie's feet to her own ring of keys, then back to Maggie's face. "I understand your point, but health and safety have to come first."

"Why?"

"That's an issue you can discuss with your doctor – which brings me to another thing. Your doctor called a few minutes ago. He's coming down to see you. After you get some slippers or shoes on, go to — "

"Son-of-a-bitch," Maggie muttered, recognizing Daniels as he rounded the entryway, a step ahead of the blonde nurse.

Eggers glanced over her shoulder. "You know Doctor Daniels?"

"What's he doing here?" demanded Maggie. Why wasn't he at City Hospital? Had he followed her on purpose? She continued to stare. Daniels looked suntanned and rested. His blue pants were baggy, his figure leaner, his long face more pleasant than she'd remembered.

"That's what I was telling you," said the nurse. "He's come to see you. He's going to be your psychiatrist."

That couldn't be a coincidence. Was it John's doing? Was she being set up?

Eggers stepped aside as Daniels joined them. "Hi," he said, acknowledging them both. "It's been a long time."

Maggie's lips tightened. Doctor Smug and his pasty-faced bitch, she thought. Let them smile. She'd show them nothing. Daniels wasn't going to see her surprise and confusion. And it would be a cold day in Hell before she'd tell him anything that mattered. "Not long enough," she said icily. "Couldn't you manage to stay away?"

"I suppose I could have, but then I would never have known."

"Known what?"

"Why don't we find an office where we can talk."

"You can use Miss Lowe's office," said Eggers. "She's at a social worker's meeting until noon."

"Thanks," said Daniels. He started up the corridor.

Should she follow him? What did she have to lose? Prolonging the confrontation with Eggers wasn't appealing. She sauntered up the hall, Eggers close behind.

By the time Maggie reached the social worker's office, the blonde nurse had unlocked the door and Daniels had entered. Why doesn't he have keys? thought Maggie as she followed him into the small office. She flopped into a tan plastic chair near the door.

Eggers reached for the doorknob to pull the door shut. "Don't forget to put your shoes on after your meeting."

"Chuck you, Farley," said Maggie. "Without obscenities."

It took a second for Eggers to figure it out. Maggie heard Eggers sniff, then the door snapped closed. She turned back to Daniels. Instead of going behind the desk, he'd sat in front of it in a chair like hers.

Was he crowding her on purpose, testing to see how she'd react? Fuck him, she wouldn't move back — that would block the door. She lifted her feet onto her chair, wrapped her arms about her knees and tried to ignore the pain throbbing up from her swollen hand. Up close, Daniels didn't look comfortable either. His hair was tousled, his eyes were still sad, and now there were red blotches above his white collar. Did he, too, feel the walls closing in, devils pushing them closer?

"You got a cigarette?" she asked.

"I don't smoke."

"Figures." She'd have to bum another one from that junkie Debbie. "So what wouldn't you have known?" she demanded.

"What?" A vertical furrow separated his probing brown eyes.

"Did your brain short circuit or is it just browning out? You said you couldn't stay away because you wouldn't have known something."

"Oh." The furrow disappeared. "I didn't say I couldn't. I said that if I had stayed away, I wouldn't have known. And I meant a few things, not one. For example, what got you so mad at me in the Emergency Room?"

"What difference does it make? It's over and done with." Like her father, foxy Francis Dexter. "I don't like people asking me questions." F. Dexter had asked questions over and over, beginning with "Who do you love best, Mary Margaret? Who do you love best?" A very different catechism from the one she'd learned from the nuns. Fucking F. Dexter and Whiney Wanda never should've been parents. "So don't expect any answers," she told Daniels.

"You may not believe this, but the answers are more for you than for me. The more you're able to uncover and understand about yourself, the more likely it is that you'll act in your own best interests instead of trying to self-destruct."

"Bullshit." She knew herself better than he ever would. Hadn't she tried understanding? Hadn't she tried prayer, and penance, crying, drinking, running? Nothing helped. Nothing. "Spilling my guts to you won't help." Her pain was too strong, her faith too weak. There was only one way to get rid of her devils for good. "I want out of this snake pit."

"You just got here yesterday. Why not give us all some time?"

Maggie rose to her feet. "Look, I want out!"

"You signed an agreement." His tone was matter-of-fact.

"I changed my mind." Damn him. The angrier she got, the calmer he seemed.

"Didn't they give you a list of patients' rights after you came on the ward?"

"So?" She'd been too upset to read them. "Are you telling me I don't have the right to change my mind?"

"Of course you do." His hand rose from his lap, reached a few inches toward her, then retreated. "As a voluntary patient, you have the right to leave against medical advice. But you have to give us a written request to leave, seventy-two hours before you're discharged."

Warily, she moved behind the desk. "I only need two minutes to pack. Why the hell do I have to wait three days?"

"To give us time to seek your commitment on the grounds you're suicidal."

Commitment? Maggie dug her fingernails into the padded back of the desk chair. "It's my life. I have the right to live it like I want – and end it when I want."

His facial muscles tightened. Two vertical lines appeared between his brows. "Show me where that's written."

"It'll be written with my blood. I can kill myself here, too. You can't keep the knives and the belts and the glass away from me forever."

"I know." A sad earnestness colored his tone. "You don't have to try to prove it to me. I'd much rather that you work with me voluntarily."

Her hands jumped and clawed the air. "Voluntarily? The doors are locked and I don't have the keys. I can write a letter to get out, but no one will open the door for three days, meanwhile you'll go to Court to commit me. You call that voluntary?"

"I call that necessary. You do have the right to call a lawyer. There'll be a hearing in which you and your attorney can present your views. Your civil rights will be protected."

"Civil rights? The only civil right I have here is the right to call you a schmuck — I assume free speech is still allowed. But once you get finished testifying in Court, only a crazy judge would believe that I'm sane."

"You also have the right to be examined by another psychiatrist."

"Shut up! Just shut up!" The words spewed out of her. "I don't need you to tell me my rights. I don't need you for anything. And I don't want another psychiatrist to examine me. If I'm stuck with you, then you're sure as hell stuck with me. And I'm going to make your life as miserable as mine until the day I die. You're going to wish you never met me. Now unlock this fucking door!"

He shook his head as if it hurt. "It's not locked. The nurse left it unlocked. I don't have any keys yet."

Maggie had her hand on the doorknob when Daniels spoke again. "I think I got the message."

"I hope the fuck you have!" She yanked the door open and rushed out without looking back. She heard him raise his voice for the first time. His words followed her up the corridor.

"Don't forget your shoes. The honeymoon is over."

16

Something Unusual

Raymond put a red bookmark across the "DOCTORS' ORDERS" page, closed Mary Saxe's medical chart and pushed it back on the countertop. Pocketing his pen, he sat back on a stool and looked through the tempered glass panels of the nurses' station. Both the main corridor and the vestibule leading to the locked double doors were empty.

"All done with your orders?" asked Gail Eggers.

Raymond pivoted on the stool. Gail was at the sink, paper cup in hand. Her face looked taut and pale. "For now," he said. "Where is everybody?"

Gail turned on the tap. "Most of the patients are in the gym. The two that stayed up here are in the dining room having coffee. I have Donna Richards keeping an eye on them." She closed the tap, popped two pills into her mouth and downed them with a swig of water.

"You okay?" he asked.

"My sinuses are terrible. This air conditioning doesn't help any. I think two little green men are tunneling through my forehead with corkscrews." She dumped the rest of the water into the stainless steel sink, crumpled the cup and tossed it into a waste basket. "You want to hand me those orders?"

"Sure." He gave her Saxe's chart. "I've continued all the suicide precautions. I don't want her going off the ward for any reason."

Eggers scanned the orders he'd written. "Diazepam PRN for agitation? What if she won't take it orally?"

"No shots unless she consents or there's imminent physical danger. The State Supreme Court has been very specific on that."

"The judges should come and work on the ward for a day," said Eggers.

"I don't think Maggie's dangerous to anyone but herself. If she starts banging her hand again or makes any kind of suicide gesture, just sit on her until she behaves."

"Easy for you to say. She's a strong girl. It'll probably take four of us to hold her down." Eggers flipped the chart closed and set it down on the desk.

"You've handled customers who were a lot tougher."

"I work at it, Raymond, but when I get anxious out there, I'm a tight-assed bitch. At least that's what the patients say. I don't like myself that way – but it's the only way I can maintain control." She looked above his head at the clock on the wall. "If your girl doesn't come out of her room with her shoes on in three minutes, I'm going to have to go see why. So don't go away. Donna is new and I may need back-up."

"Where's the attendant?"

"He had to accompany a patient to the EEG lab. And Celia called in sick, so I'm ward clerk as well as Head Nurse."

Raymond glanced at his wristwatch. "I can't stay long. This is my first day on the Outpatient Service and I barely had time say 'hello' over there before I was called to Doctor Taylor's office about Maggie Saxe."

Eggers looked down the corridor toward Saxe's room. "Why didn't he ask one of the residents or supervising psychiatrists over here to treat her? Not that I don't enjoy working with you again, but you've already been through this mill."

"She's a special case because she's related to a friend of Taylor's, so he didn't want a first year resident to treat her. I don't know why he didn't ask one of the faculty. It's possible he asked me because I saw her once before, during my rotation at City Hospital."

"Why was she there?"

Raymond pantomimed cutting his wrist. "Razor blade – wrists and thighs. After losing a boyfriend. Hey, if you think you tighten up when you're anxious, you should've seen me when I walked into the ER and saw her face. There's no shame in feeling up-tight or afraid at times with some of these folks."

Eggers shook her head. "I'm not talking about what I feel. I'm talking about how I act. You should have seen Bobbi Stowell, when she was Head Nurse. She was a natural – bright, intuitive, smooth as silk. Bobbi never got flustered. She always seemed to have herself and everything else under control – and everyone liked her. As her assistant, I did a good job. As her replacement, uh-uh."

"Look, in the seven months I was here, you taught me more about handling disturbed patients than most of my supervisors did."

"You were willing to listen to a nurse. Not many doctors are. They think that they are – "

Raymond saw her face register amazement an instant before she gasped "Holy damn!" and lunged for the door. He spun about to look through the glass panels. Mary Saxe had come out of her room and was walking calmly up the corridor. She was wearing brown platform shoes. Nothing else.

Oh God! His breath caught in his throat. He sat transfixed, stifling impulses to smile, frown, turn away, leap to his feet and rush out to her. Don't move, don't smile, he told himself. She's looking for a reaction — do anything and she's won. Gotten paid for the show, proven she's in control. Look away? That would be backing down. If he went out there, she'd struggle and love the contact. It would be too damn gratifying for both of them. He clenched his teeth and allowed only his eyes to move down over her breasts and curves. Very stiffly, he forced his jaw into a yawn. His gaze and his penis were both rising when Eggers' willowy figure suddenly blocked Saxe's path and Raymond's view.

The two women halted inches apart, toe to toe, will challenging will. Raymond couldn't hear what was being said, but he saw the nurse's back stiffen and her hand come up to point toward Saxe's room. Saxe didn't move. The nurse's hand remained in mid-air. Raymond was about to get up to go help Eggers when Donna Richards came out of the dining room. She did a double take at Saxe's nudity, then moved in to back up her boss. Saxe stepped to the side of the corridor so she could make eye contact with Raymond. She flashed a provocative, self-satisfied smile, then turned and sauntered down the hall to her room. Both nurses followed her in.

Eggers was the first one back to the nurse's station. She let the door slam behind her, looked at Raymond and sniffed sharply. "You can stop leering. The show's over. Donna will stay with her until she's dressed."

"It's not a leer, it's a smile – and I held it in until Saxe was back in her room. What did you say to her?"

Eggers sat down on her desk-chair, closed her eyes and squeezed the bridge of her nose between her thumb and forefinger. "That she obeyed one rule while breaking others, jeopardizing her reputation if not her self-respect. That went over like a lead balloon. So I told her she'd won this round but she'd better get her big tits and little ass into her room before I became too envious and pinned a medal on one or the other."

"Really? That was great."

Eggers opened her eyes. "I think it was the word 'tits' that commanded respect. I saw in her face that she couldn't believe I'd say such a thing. She had me pegged as a total prude."

"So much for first impressions."

"As for impressions," said Eggers, "I didn't notice you doing much."

"I was holding in my leer. Actually, I felt that the situation could be handled better by a woman."

"What can't be? Listen, Raymond – " Eggers pointed to the corridor. " — Lady Godiva out there is as seductive as they come. Frankly, I think she'd be a lot better off with a female doc."

"Probably. But there are problems with that, too."

"What problems? This girl is no amateur, Raymond. I'll bet she twists men into pretzels and pours salt on their broken places."

Raymond ran a hand through his hair. "I assume Taylor assigned her to me for a reason, and only he can take me off the case." His hand descended to quell any objection before it left Eggers' lips. "I'll speak to him about it – I promise – although, in all honesty, I'd hate to give her up. She's bright, challenging – and you saw the obvious. But the biggest problem in terms of switching therapists is that she's picked me out – and I think she'd react badly to losing me."

"Picked you?" Eggers' tone was skeptical.

"Yes. When we were in Sally Lowe's office, Saxe got really upset with me for informing her of her rights. She not only rejected legal counsel, she rejected the idea of seeing another psychiatrist. She said she was stuck with me and I with her 'til death do us part – although those weren't her exact words and she presented it as a threat rather than a hope or a promise."

"So?"

He took a deep breath and plunged on. "So maybe I'm the crazy one, but I believe that Mary Margaret Saxe and I got engaged – emotionally, that is – when we met at City Hospital, and that she moved our relationship along today to some sort of marriage – a bad one surely, because that's probably all she's ever seen. I didn't put it all together until I found myself making a stupid remark when she walked out on me."

"What did you say?"

"I told her she should put on her shoes, that the honeymoon was over." He saw Eggers frown. "I know, I know, it was stupid. But what do you think of my theory?"

"It's on a par with your jokes — not very funny, but usually there's a point to them." Eggers sniffed. "I'm not the right person to ask about your theory. If I understood the chemistry of emotional attraction, I might've saved myself a lot of trouble." Eggers nodded her head toward the glass panels. Donna Richards was walking up the hall. She entered the nurses' station with a bemused smile on her oval face.

"Is she dressed?" asked Eggers.

"If you call bikini panties, shorts and a tee shirt dressed." Richards closed the door. "She's really got her nose out of joint now, because whoever packed her clothes didn't throw in her halter tops."

"She didn't pack her own clothing?" Eggers asked.

"No," said Richards. "When she came over from Medicine, she

was in a hospital gown and had her own nightgown in a paper sack." Richards pulled a chrome stool from under the work counter. "Nothing else was listed on the personal property form."

"Who brought her clothes?" asked Raymond.

"I don't know." Richards sat down. "We received a call yesterday morning from the information desk in the lobby to come pick up a suitcase that was left there for her. And when Joe – do you know Mr. Mills?"

Raymond nodded.

"When Joe brought it up here, the tag on the suitcase said 'Mary Saxe, Palmer 3,' but we didn't have a patient by that name. I called the volunteer at the desk and she said the man who'd left the suitcase had been very specific, that Mary Saxe was going to be transferred from 2 South to Palmer 3." Richards shrugged. "And maybe an hour later, Doctor White called to ask whether we had a female bed available for a transfer from 2 South. Sure enough, it turned out to be Mary Saxe."

Raymond rubbed his forehead as if ironing out the wrinkles of his frown. "You mean someone sent her clothing to Palmer 3 before Doctor White even asked about a bed?"

"Yes," said Richards. "It is a little weird."

"You inspected the contents of the suitcase?" asked Raymond.

"Well, yes – we do that with every patient."

"That policy hasn't changed," Eggers told him. She looked at Richards. "What was in the suitcase?"

"Just a mix of clothes and toiletries. Doctor White told us she was to be on suicide precautions, so we kept her belts and mirror and transferred tiny amounts of her cologne and perfume into soft plastic bottles."

"Anything else?" asked Raymond.

"Nothing dangerous."

"I mean anything unusual?"

"I don't know," said the young nurse. "Do you consider the Holy Bible unusual?"

17

The Arena

Leaning forward in his chair, Raymond paused in his narrative for a comment, a question, even a change in facial expression from his new supervisor. But seated at his cluttered desk, Doctor Erik Tulving Bergstrom seemed focused on unbending the paper clip he held above his lap. Bergstrom's compulsive destruction of paper clips and penchant for bow ties were nothing new. The standing joke was that the professor's habits were the first examples of psychopathology that new residents witnessed in his course on that subject. Still, no resident left Bergstrom's course without a working knowledge of mental illnesses and an appreciation of the agile brain that lay beneath his bald head and quirky habits. So Bergstrom's impassiveness about the Maggie Saxe case was disconcerting. Did the professor resent being given this assignment by Chairman Taylor? No, thought Raymond, Bergstrom would never admit to that. Best to press on.

"The Bible in her suitcase reminded me of her secretly praying in the bathroom at City Hospital. She certainly doesn't come across as the religious type."

"What is the religious type?" Bergstrom's tone was mild,

deceptively bland, like the impressionist landscape that decorated the wall opposite the bookcases, or the faint scent of pipe tobacco with no pipe visible.

Raymond's face became warm. "I see – I'm stereotyping." At least Bergstrom had said something. Raymond paused, hoping for more.

Bergstrom tossed the straightened bit of wire on top of the pile in his ceramic ashtray and took a new paper clip from the box on his desk. He cocked his head as if expecting to hear Raymond's observations without sharing his own.

"Despite that Jekyll and Hyde stuff," said Raymond, "Maggie doesn't lose time, so she doesn't have a multiple personality disorder. And she certainly doesn't have the disordered thinking of schizophrenia. She's very bright — more literate and more cynical than most young adults I've met — but she's extremely hurt and angry."

"A challenging patient," said Bergstrom.

Was the professor doubting his competence? "I've done okay with challenges. But right now, I am a bit puzzled. Apparently, someone packed her suitcase and sent it to Palmer 3 before Doctor White decided to admit her. I asked at the information desk. One of the volunteers remembered that the suitcase was delivered by a man – perhaps in his thirties, but taller and heavier than I am. She described him as having straight brown hair, a mustache and beard. My guess is that he's the boyfriend who abandoned her at City Hospital."

Bergstrom looked up. "You've wondered how he might have anticipated her admission to Palmer 3?"

"Yes. My first idea was that she telephoned her boyfriend. But Doctor White told me Saxe had no access to a telephone either in the ICU or in her room on the medical floor. She didn't have visitors and she had a sitter who didn't leave her bedside because of the suicide risk. Doctor White said that Saxe didn't even know she was going to be admitted to the psych unit until the last minute. She only consented because Doctor White threatened to send her to the state hospital. But there's a second logical explanation — "

The professor seemed intent on deforming yet another paper clip.

Raymond sighed. "It could be that Saxe's boyfriend is a doctor here in University Hospital. Saxe lives in this neighborhood, but he took her to City Hospital rather than be recognized here. Now the second time she attempted suicide, the risk of her dying was greater, or maybe the boyfriend wasn't around, so the ambulance took her here. When the boyfriend found out, he assumed she'd be transferred to Palmer 3 and left her bag with a volunteer he'd never seen before. That makes sense — doesn't it?"

Bergstrom shrugged. "Before you comb the medical center for brown beards, Raymond, you might wonder why any hospital employee would risk stirring up questions by delivering the bag prematurely. An insider could easily find out when she was transferred. And he'd know that we provide hospital gowns and robes when necessary."

Raymond sank back in his chair. "I didn't think of that."

"Even if you knew the identity of this friend, do you believe it would make a significant difference in the treatment process?"

"No. I just don't understand why she's protecting a man who's abandoned her. If I figure out who he is, maybe she'll allow one of the walls she's put up against therapy to disappear."

"A very questionable theory," said Bergstrom.

"Well, whatever she and I are engaged in now, it's certainly not psychotherapy."

"I don't doubt it." The professor looked up, his pale blue eyes and the creases around them magnified by thick spectacles. "Much of what is called psychotherapy is really a preparation for therapy: two people learning to trust each other and the ethics and procedures that govern their special relationship. For all her bravado, Mary Saxe is wounded and very vulnerable. She has little trust in anyone." Bergstrom inclined his paper clip toward Raymond. "If you're right, then Ms. Saxe's lover abandoned her when she was hurting most. That can only increase her rage and bitterness. And you say that she's impulsive, so she's likely to have great difficulty learning to substitute introspection and talk for the immediate tension reduction of action. Her preparation for psychotherapy may take a long time."

Bergstrom took in a breath and let it out sharply. "There aren't any short cuts, Raymond. Try to break down one defense and she'll put a stronger one in its place. She'll only come out from behind her walls a half step at a time — when she's ready, not before." Bergstrom tossed the clip into the center drawer, turned to Raymond and leaned forward. "My immediate concern is not her vulnerability — it's yours."

"What? How do you mean?"

"To put it bluntly, Raymond, Mary Margaret Saxe is a cock-tease. She gives you a show and leads you on, but she will try to keep you from touching her — " Bergstrom's hand became a stop signal. "— maybe not physically, but emotionally. A man less principled and disciplined might have trouble treating her because he'd yield to his impulses. Your troubles will come from your enthusiasm and inexperience, from those very caring and protective feelings which make you so much want to help her. Your good intentions are likely to be mocked and spurned as you try to save her from an early death or a sordid life. It's likely she'll frustrate and anger you to the point you'll want to abandon her, as other people undoubtedly have. If you do, you'll feel terribly guilty; if you don't, she may create havoc with your life."

Raymond was stunned. Abandon her? Not a chance. Where was Bergstrom coming from? "You predict a grim future."

"I'm not an oracle." Bergstrom scratched the back of his hand. "I'm an all-too-fallible human being. But I've struggled for and with people like Mary Margaret Saxe before. Their treatment can become a three ring circus, with an aerial act in each ring." He pointed upward. "You get so involved observing the patient courting and defying death on the high wire in ring one and trying to catch hold of the trapeze that's swinging back and forth between you in ring two, that you forget to keep your own internal balance." He pointed to his chest. "That's ring three, Raymond. Always stay aware that you're both in the arena, and the arena is in both of you."

Raymond nodded. "I feel it." Bergstrom had, too. Maybe the professor's pessimism about Mary Saxe was some deja vu thing. Had Bergstrom once lost his balance with someone quite similar? "I'll do my best," he said.

"Your best will be fine, now that you're forewarned. Don't hesitate to ask for help if you need it." The professor reached into the drawer, selected the deformed clip, and leaned back in his chair.

"I trust you're experienced at holding the net," said Raymond.

"From both sides." Bergstrom frowned. "Tell me, did Doctor Taylor say why he wanted me to supervise you on this case?"

"No. I just assumed it was because we knew each other from your seminar and your office is here in the Outpatient Clinic. Was there some other reason?"

"Not that I know of. Do you have any specific questions on the Saxe case?"

Plenty, thought Raymond. "None at the moment," he said. What made Bergstrom question the Chairman's motives? And what about his fall from the high wire? No, he couldn't ask about those things any more than he could ask the man why he always wore bow ties or why he deformed paper clips. "You've given me plenty to think about."

"Good. Are you settling in comfortably here?"

"To tell you the truth, I've been so wrapped up in this Saxe case that I've had very little time to get oriented. I did report in, and Doctor White showed me my office and gave me a list of outpatients I'm inheriting from the residents who left at the end of June."

"Was I the supervisor for any of those?"

"No. Doctor White did most of them, so I'll just continue with him about those folks. I only got one new case. Arnie Sheflin did the intake in June, just before he left. I'd be pleased if you could help on that one."

"Certainly. What's the individual's name?"

Raymond pulled a pink file card from his pocket. "George Elton Cruber. He's thirty-eight, married, and has two young kids. He was sent over from Neurology with a chief complaint of 'I'm having spells.' The neurologists did a complete workup — waking and sleeping EEGs, NP leads, the whole bit. Cruber even wore a monitor for a day. The tracings showed minor irregularities, but no seizure focus, so they sent him here. Arnie thought they were anxiety attacks. Seems they've been interfering with this guy's work as a toll collector. I suspect he's in a dead-end job."

PART III

September 1969

18

What Matters

Dying matters, nothing else. Sitting on the sofa, Maggie's thoughts came unbidden, debris on a tide of despair. She'd been used and discarded – this time John, last time Mark. Suicide would end it all.

"What does matter to you?" repeated Daniels.

Maggie took a final drag on her cigarette and jabbed the butt into the plastic ashtray on her lap. "Nothing," she said. "Nothing matters." Daniels certainly didn't matter. No need to look at him. She knew he was in that wing chair, trying to keep frustration off his face, fake empathy in his puppy eyes.

"Not even how you're treated by other people?"

"Tell me about it," she muttered.

"Why won't *you* tell me about it?"

How he twisted her words around. "I don't know."

"I think you do."

"Think what you want." Drawing her bare feet onto the sofa, she leaned back against one upholstered arm; her toes prodded the nubby brown fabric of the other. It was so much better not to look at him. Daniels was a robot, programmed to ensnare. For fifty minutes, he could act concerned, then his switch clicked off. "Our time is up," he would say. Her time was up when John walked out. "You can't help me. Just leave me alone."

"I can't help if you won't let me. Why do you push me away?"

Damn him. He was the pushy one, hounding her with questions, punishing her with silence. He accused her of giving too little when it was he who wanted too much.

"You're a man." She made it sound despicable.

"What about that?"

She looked over her shoulder, searched him for malice, turned away unsure. This Doctor Jekyll hid Mister Hyde so well. He certainly wasn't like John, stiff and meticulous, but with a body that turned her on. Daniels was shorter and less muscular, not unattractive, but he didn't have any flair. That awful striped tie and button-down collar —

"What about me being a man?"

"I used the term loosely."

"No, really! What about it?"

She shook her head. "Men don't feel things the way women do."

"In what way?"

"In every way."

"Do any two people feel things the same? And are any two — are the two of us so different?"

Idiot. Maybe he didn't want to understand what she meant, but there was no way he could win this argument. He'd have to admit his position was hopeless. "Can you feel what it's like to be raped?"

"Can you tell me?"

"No!" She bolted upright, swung her feet to the carpet, and looked at the door. "Don't give me a question as an answer. Can you feel what it's like to be raped?"

He said nothing.

She glanced at him. His head was bowed; he was rubbing the back of his neck. His defeat filled her with triumph and despair.

He raised his head. "What does it feel like? Overwhelmed by shock, by fear — by pain and helplessness. Left with humiliation and helpless rage — and guilt, irrational but excruciating guilt."

She glared at him. He had the words, but he could never know the feelings. "You want to know how we're different? I've felt things — lived through a lot — but never blabbed about them. You've gone through school, have read the books and have all the words, but inside you feel nothing."

"How can you be so certain?"

"Prove to me that I'm wrong."

"It seems you need to put me in that position — proving myself to you, understanding your riddles, passing or flunking your tests. That way, you're in control. Are you aware you do that?"

The bastard was changing the subject. "I don't know what you're talking about. Prove to me I'm wrong."

"I don't think I can."

Her back straightened and she smiled for the first time in days.

"Even if I pass this test you'll quickly find another. Sooner or later, you'll flunk me. Do you do that to other people, too?"

Bullshit. She'd given him his chance and he'd blown it. She rose to her feet. "You keep trying to turn things around. You'd blame me for all sorts of shit rather than admit I'm right and you're wrong. Just like my fucking father." She glanced down at Daniels. He was rubbing his forehead. Was she giving him a headache? Good. "You and I are from different worlds, we're on different wavelengths. You can't understand how I feel."

"Sit down," he said.

"I'm leaving."

"Please. Sit down." It was half order, half plea.

Damn him. She sat, not knowing why.

"When I was eight, I walked across a vacant lot." His words were little more than a whisper. "It was a short-cut to the library a few blocks away. An older boy — maybe fifteen or sixteen — it doesn't matter, he was huge to me — stopped me and asked the time." Daniels looked down at his wrist. "I was very proud of the new watch I had — a birthday present. I didn't suspect a thing. When I raised my arm, he slipped handcuffs on, cuffed my wrist to his. He said he'd never let me go. I was frightened and started to cry. Then he said he would let me go, but only if I sucked his — prick. That's the word he used. If I didn't, he'd cut mine off. He showed me his knife. You know, it may seem strange to you, but I didn't know what he meant by 'prick.' He showed me. He also took my watch. I said I lost it — got punished, too. I never told anyone for years."

"Did you suck his cock?"

Daniels laughed with a wrenching sound. "Did you ever consider surgery as a career? I believe we were discussing whether I can understand your feelings about being raped. I've answered the best that I could."

The sorry bastard. He had no inkling of why she'd asked. He must judge her a tactless, foul-mouthed bitch. Well, there was no way she was going to tell him more if that's what he thought. "You did okay — but I still don't think it's the same."

He rubbed his mouth and glanced away, came back stronger than before. "Look — a person can feel happy or sad, frightened or mad, anxious, guilty — yes, and embarrassed or ashamed. Every feeling is a variation or a combination of those basic ones. Sure, I've never lived in your skin — experienced the same events or felt the same way you have. If that's what you mean, you're right, okay?" He ran his hand through his hair. "I don't know that I'm the best therapist for you. Like I told you, maybe a woman would be better."

"I never said — "

His palm sprang forward to stop her. "Let me finish. I'm not dumping you or even suggesting a change. All I'm trying to say is that any match is an approximation. You have to decide whether it's close enough." He sat back. "I don't know — maybe you'd be scared if I got too close. Anyway, those basic feelings — our basic feelings — offer us a beginning, a potential. After that, we can help each other learn."

"Are you finished?"

"Yes."

She got up and started for the door.

"Wait, where are you going?"

She didn't pause. "I'll think about what you said. Our time is up for today."

"But we still have more time." He sounded perplexed.

"No. That's what I have to decide."

19

Supervision

Bergstrom looked up from the paper clip, blue eyes rising above his spectacles. "What was your intention in sharing your childhood trauma with Ms. Saxe?"

Raymond leaned back in the pine rocker, fought its natural urge to regress. How could he explain it? His mistake was obvious, yet the reasons he made it were obscure. "I can't say I made a deliberate choice to tell her. It just felt right at the time."

"Oh?"

"I don't usually get into personal revelations." Wasn't that what was making his analysis with Doctor Korline so difficult? he thought. "God knows, that one was especially hard to share. But I felt she'd opened the door a crack with her question about being raped – and then she was into that challenging routine she gets into – like the 'what makes Doctor Jekyll become Mr. Hyde' bit."

Bergstrom nodded, but he was hard at work on the paper clip.

"Nothing I said was reaching her. She'd gotten up and was going to walk out. I didn't want to lose her that way again."

"Lose her?" asked Bergstrom.

"Like at City Hospital. Out the door and gone."

The professor raised his head. He scratched his chin with the paper clip. "You felt it quite the same?"

"She's an inpatient now; she really can't run off. But yes, it felt very much the same." He wiped his palms against his corduroy trousers

"Why?"

Why? Raymond allowed the chair to rock back. "Well, she was running away emotionally – she was going to close that door behind her and I felt she wasn't going to give me another chance, she wasn't coming – " Like Joanne! The thought sealed his lips, hardened his face.

"What?" Bergstrom asked softly.

"I remembered something – someone — a girlfriend. We lived together for most of my senior year in college. When she left, I felt lost. I mean that was a hundred times worse than Maggie Saxe walking out." He shook his head. "I certainly didn't feel that way about Maggie."

"What way?"

"In love." He looked at the papers and stack of journals scattered across Bergstrom's desk, the ceramic ashtray half-full with dead wire. Weren't love and hate ever spent? "Back then, I felt rejected and abandoned – Joanne found a swimmer more attractive than a plodder. She told me one afternoon, packed her things and left. I was stunned. Something must have been wrong with me that I never saw it coming. Anyway, I thought I'd put out the torch long ago."

"You thought?"

Damn! This was worse than the couch. Raymond bowed his head. "I must have. Christ, I'm married five years." He looked up. "Happily married."

Bergstrom dropped the remains of his clip into the ashtray. "But the experience with your girlfriend was a factor in your sense of urgency with Ms. Saxe?"

"Yes." Was the paper clip better off for all Bergstrom's straightening? "I know Maggie Saxe stirred a lot of stuff up in me. I never thought I'd get so caught up in counter-transference. From the very first, Maggie saw me as someone in her past that was Jekyll and Hyde. And I looked at her and saw Joanne."

"That's something you should mention to your analyst."

"I've talked a lot about Joanne, and will again. But for some reason, I never connected her to Maggie." No, only to Mom. Losing her to cancer, then Joanne to someone else — could he ever make peace with being left by the women he loved?

"How separate are they for you now?" asked Bergstrom.

"Joanne and Maggie?" Raymond's hands parted like magnets that repelled each other. "They're very different. Joanne was methodical. She liked Bach and was a competitive swimmer. Maggie is tease and temptation; she has the body of a stripper and gets off on pot and rock groups like the Rolling Stones and the Grateful Dead... " Had Bergstrom heard of the Grateful Dead? Did Bergstrom even care? He was so busy deforming that paper clip. Maybe it was therapy for arthritis.

"Is it – Oh." Bergstrom grabbed for the clip he'd fumbled. Raymond saw it hit the carpet near the professor's chair. Bergstrom's bald head bent in pursuit.

"To the right," said Raymond.

"Yes, thank you." Bergstrom retrieved the clip, then readjusted his spectacles. "Unfortunate habit. I'm sorry. Where were we?"

"Do you mind me asking what you do with those things?"

"What? Oh, the wires?" He glanced at the one he held and tossed it onto his desk blotter. "I give them away... I believe you said Ms.

Saxe walked out on you. Was it, in fact, 'on you'? Did you say or do something to provoke it?"

Raymond bit his lip. Give the straightened clips away? To whom? "Maggie plays by rules she hasn't shared. I don't think I've done anything outlandish with her since I charged into the Ladies' Room. That was dumb, but it didn't set her off. Neither did my telling her of being accosted as a child, but I can see where that was wrong, too."

"Wrong?"

"Yes. Isn't that what you implied?"

"I hope not. There's nothing wrong in being human, in sharing a personal part of yourself, so long as you maintain ethical boundaries. In terms of technique, it wasn't sound, because it may influence what she's willing to tell and how she'll tell it. It may cause her to change attitudes and feelings she might otherwise have projected onto you, so that the transference may offer fewer clues, become a less reliable tool." Bergstrom shifted his weight, sagged deeper into his chair. "On the other hand, technique isn't everything in therapy – intuition is important, too."

Raymond smiled. "I hope so. Seems I have more intuition than technique. Oh, speaking of intuition, that guy Cruber came back to see me. Neurology can't find any organic cause for his spells. Maybe Sheflin was right about anxiety causing them, but I think he really underestimated this guy's pathology."

"How so?"

"It's not what's there; it's what's absent. Cruber says he has spells where he feels like he's going to jump out of his skin, but then he freezes and goes mentally blank. If they're anxiety attacks, not seizures, why doesn't he ever have a thought he can remember?"

"You think he's malingering?"

Raymond shrugged. "I don't see what he has to gain by lying.

He's not looking to get out of work or a legal case. He says he just wants to get rid of his spells. But what bothers me more than his mental absences is his lack of affect. The guy's as bland as Pablum. He says he's grieving his mother's death, but he doesn't blink an eye when he talks of her. He spouts words without feeling, smiles without humor. He reminds me of a mortician who's just come up from the basement."

Bergstrom removed his spectacles, closed his eyes and squeezed the bridge of his nose. "Have you read *The Stranger?*"

"What?"

"*The Stranger*, by Albert Camus."

"No."

Bergstrom opened his eyes. "How about Hervey Cleckley's *The Mask of Sanity?*"

"No."

"Weren't they on the reading list I gave out in my seminar?"

Raymond tried to keep his annoyance from showing. "There were 110 titles on that list – not to mention the textbook."

"It's difficult to condense a professional education, Raymond. Read those two books – and then the others you missed – but those two to see if they come close to Mr. Cruber."

"Oh!" How could he have forgotten? "There's one other thing – something Cruber told me yesterday, something he'd never mentioned before. It seems that ever since his mother died, George Cruber's been obsessed by crows."

"Really?" Bergstrom reached for another paper clip. "How so?"

20

Crows

He had tried to poison the crows. They wouldn't die. They came each morning to wake him, cawing out their victory, spurning the seeds he'd laced with rat poison. Two robins had died, a cardinal and a jay, but not the crows. They strutted across his grass, pawing and pecking at grubs in the ground. How many times had he glared at them from the bedroom windows, knocked on a pane to chase them away? Today, he'd gone out waving a broom. The crows retreated grudgingly, voicing their anger from the white fence and gray sky. Back inside, he had spied on them from a basement window. No need to get the wife upset. But they came back like unwanted memories, nagging, scolding, disturbing his peace. The black Harpies acted as if they owned his tree. They shit all over his yard.

So he sat upstairs on his bed, shoes off, football game on, resting against the pillows, trying to get all that crow shit off his mind. Not that the game was important. He never cared who won. Ballgames were a way to get by on Sundays at home, and they made talk easy at work. Denise and her folks kept the kids downstairs. No one dared bother him during a game. Only the crows.

He'd thought they would leave him alone once he'd buried Ma. But neither the burial nor the funeral had ended it. Two women, strangers, had showed up at the cemetery. One was a stoop-shouldered black prune; the other a gray and bony hag with fish eyes magnified by lenses that seemed half an inch thick. Tight-lipped and tearless, they'd stood back from the grave, their black dresses making them look too much like a pair of crows. Probably old bags that had nothing better to do than attend funerals – not worth his time or attention. Yet why had they taken the trouble to drive out to the cemetery? Barroom friends? It shouldn't have mattered. The only consolation he'd needed was in burying Ma instead of cremating her like she'd wanted. Now she could lie there for all of eternity without any consolation at all. No men, no bourbon, no excuses.

Was old Fish-Eyes a relative? No, she'd have introduced herself. And the black one? Made no sense. Except for Denise and the two little ones they'd left at home with her parents, there were no other living Crubers. Even if his father were still alive, the bastard was a deserter. No doubt he'd gone on to screw other women; probably left other little bastards behind. Stupid to have thought he might show up at the funeral. Everything had gone smoother without him. No hypocrites to cry or lie about the departed, no mourners at all, not even a pang of grief. He couldn't remember ever feeling sad. What was the point?

He'd told Daniels that, and about the crows, about his troubles with nerves and with sleep. He'd blamed it all on his mother's alcoholism and cancerous death, portrayed himself as the dutiful son. He'd described his spells as just blanking out for less than a minute. And that grubsucker believed every word. Odd that his hands looked familiar. Small for his body, nice moons on the nails — otherwise nothing special. Was it the gold wedding band with the cross-hatch design? The scratched face of the Timex watch? Hell, he'd seen plenty of Timex watches before. They were as common and durable as — crows. Shoot! What was with his mind that it always came back to crows? Maybe if he got out his shotgun and blew them away, that would end it once and for all. The day Daniels told him all the x-rays and brain wave tests hadn't showed cancer or brain rot, he'd made it a point to go into the yard to tell the crows they had failed. No tumor was growing inside his head, and no crows would drive him insane. He'd just done what he needed to even the score. Maybe chopping off Garbage Mouth's hand wasn't smart, for it made the punk's death into news. But the gloves, rags and tire iron were at the bottom of the river and the flashlight and cleaver shone like new. In a lifetime, you expect a few mistakes... Like Denise. She took care of the kids okay, but she'd let herself get fat. He had to be careful what he said to her, not to act different at home. Denise understood little, but she yakety-yakked a lot; she told everything to her mother. Good thing the old lady'd kept her mouth shut.

Hit the quarterback, you suckers. What pussies! Maybe he should turn the tube off. Except if Denise didn't hear it, she'd find some excuse to get him downstairs. She'd yak up a storm until he either walked out or told her to shut up. At least she did what he told her. Finding another woman would be like flipping channels on the tube: more interesting for about five minutes, then the same crap all over again. Denise was dumb, but not so dumb she'd ever turn him in. She'd miss his tongue too much. Who else would get her juices flowing, turn her on like a three-way bulb? Bet she didn't tell her mother about that. Didn't need to — the old lady had her turn. No, his tongue never got him into trouble that way, but with the shrink, it could. Maybe he shouldn't go back, now that the tumor scare was gone. But not the crows – and not the spells.

Daniels had to be told enough to help get rid of the spells, but not a word more. Psychiatrists were supposed to be smart or crazy, sometimes both. So far, Daniels didn't come across as either. But then, he hadn't said very much. It would be a mistake to misread Daniels' silence. That's what fools did with him, too. They figured because he was quiet and never went to college, he had rocks in his head. Shoot. He could read and think with the best of them, and he had the advantage of surprise. Given the start that a guy like Daniels had and some encouragement along the way, he could have placed in any race, won fat purses instead of fat — crows. Grubsuckers! If he didn't see a shrink, they'd drive him insane. Already he half-believed the black grubsuckers were sent by his mother, her curse from a restless grave. If he flipped out entirely, he'd never get back, he'd end up cawing and flapping in a cage. Yes, he had to go see Daniels again. Garbage Mouth must never be mentioned, nor the rat poison, the guns in the basement, shooting little Carol — not even his wish to shoot all the crows. It shouldn't be hard. All his life, he'd fooled other people. He could fool Daniels, too. The only real problem was finding a way to kill those crows.

21

That Girl

She wasn't herself, wasn't Nancy Veronica Brill anymore. This schizo-fitso thing was happening to someone else. Yes, that was it. That Girl was a mental case, out of place in this hospital room of gloom, lying in this railed bed — better off dead — taking pills the Devil told her not to swallow. But the nurses made That Girl drink water and stick out her sick, thick tongue, made her swallow hollow and talk with no saliva, try to eat with trembling hands and restless feet, wanting to jump out of her skin.

True, blue, the Devil's voice is fainter, but He's still here, listening, watching, waiting to sink his claws into That Girl. Not into Nancy Veronica Brill, but That Girl who gets headaches and dizzy, whose mind is foggy, leap-froggy, and whose breasts have grown bigger and leaked milk. That Girl is ashamed, blamed and debrained. She is crazy and lazy. No wonder the Devil wants her to die.

"I stopped your medication," said Doctor Daniels, standing by her bed, his white coat unbuttoned, koala bears on his tie. "The side effects will disappear in a few days, and then we'll try something else."

"Her bosom will go back to normal? The leakage will stop?" said That Girl's mother from a chair on the other side of the bed.

"Yes, and the restlessness and dry mouth, and most likely the tremor," said the doctor.

"I told you how sensitive Nancy is to medication," said That Girl's mother. "This is the third one you've tried. Why can't you and Doctor Taylor figure out which one will work?"

The mother's voice was tinny and shrill in That Girl's ears, like the whistle of a tea kettle whose water was boiling away.

"Add water," said Nancy. Her hand trembled as she turned on an imaginary tap.

"You want water?" the mother asked.

"I want to go home. I'm well, swell, tell you That Girl is sick."

"I know," said Doctor Daniels. "But you — I mean That Girl needs medication to get better. Unfortunately, there's no way to predict which one will work without trying them."

"Try, try, cry and die."

"Don't talk like that," said the mother. "You're going to get better. Don't let yourself think such thoughts."

"You're going to die," said the Devil.

Nancy shook her head on the pillow. "No, That Girl is."

"That Girl is what?" asked Dr. Daniels.

"The sick one."

"What sick one?" said the mother.

Dr. Daniels leaned over the bed railing to look at her face. "What about the sick girl?" His tone was gentle.

Nancy turned her head away. "What about the sick girl?" she echoed.

"I'm going to prescribe another medication for her. I hope it will help her think more clearly but have fewer side effects. I'll explain all of them to That Girl and her parents — and to you, once your father gets here."

"*Don't listen to him. He's lying. He's poisoning you,*" whispered the Devil.

"Are you poisoning That Girl?" asked Nancy.

"No, never. The kind of medicines That Girl is taking, the phenothiazines, can really make her better – "

"Better than what?" Nancy interjected.

"Able to think more clearly, not to hear voices of people who aren't really there."

"They're not working," said the mother.

"We've kept the doses tiny because of her sensitivity," said Dr. Daniels. "There are only a limited number of these medications. We have to find one she can tolerate. They're the best treatment we have for this illness."

"Best isn't always good," said the mother.

"That Girl doesn't hear people." Nancy stared at the ceiling. "She hears the Devil. If she doesn't listen, he'll truth-proof her in fire."

"The medicine can take that fear away," said the doctor.

"It hasn't," said the mother.

"It won't," said Nancy. "That Girl's fear is here, then there — then near and clear. Fear never goes away."

22

Petro

"*Yiassou*, Maritsa." His arms drew her in and squeezed her against him until she felt smothered by the black jacket and cardigan that softened his bony frame. Maggie came up for air, got a kiss on each cheek, a breath of ouzo with a "Ha!" from his throat.

"*Yiassou, Theo Petro.*" Maggie smiled into his craggy face. Uncle Peter. If only he were.

His warm hands found her shoulders, pushed her a step back for inspection with his dark, heavy-lidded eyes. At seventy-nine, he was still going strong, still very much the boss. The only boss she'd ever cared about. He'd be pleased she wore a skirt, not jeans, and that she'd let down her hair. The way everyone on the ward reacted, you'd think it was the Second Coming.

Petro's eyebrows converged into one white line. "Too pale, Maritsa. They not let you out for sun?"

"No."

"How you feel?"

"Glad to see you, *Theo Petro*." She tugged her sweatshirt sleeves down over her wrists to hide the scars.

"Locked up. No sun." Petro's hands spread wide. "How they expect people get well? You look thin. They feed you good?"

"They feed me fine." A small fib was okay if it saved him a worry. This wasn't home, where she'd ached in silence rather than agree to the lies or suffer for truth.

She went back to close the visiting room door. Sure enough, Eggers was outside, snooping again. Shutting the door wouldn't keep the nurse out; she'd peek through its plastic panel.

"How many pounds you lose?" asked Petro.

"What?" Maggie's hand flicked the edge of the door as she turned. The door slammed; the plastic rattled. "Four pounds, maybe five."

"See. You no eat good. The cook, he can't be Greek."

She laughed. There was no pressure now that she'd made the decision to die. And it was good to see Petro again. "Come, let's sit down and talk." She indicated the sofa to his right, but he turned left and away. He limped slightly as he walked toward the small piano. His pants must have come from fatter years, years when his wife was alive.

"You know, Maritsa, this place looks like jail. You write in letter, but I see now myself. They look through bag I bring you." Beyond the spinet, he stopped, stooped over, came up with a supermarket bag. "First thing, they take retsina — so we must make party with no wine." He held the bag with one hand, waved the other at the door Maggie guarded. "Bastards like to want retsina for themself. I tell them, 'you be sure it not get lost. If Maritsa not have wine, I no give it to goats — I take it when I leave'." Clutching the bag, he turned away again and limped past the green wing chairs to the window.

Maggie walked toward him. "Did they take the stone, *Theo Petro?*"

"Ha! No worry so much. *Papou*'s not stupid."

Maggie smiled. *Papou* – grandfather – was great, not stupid. He'd smuggled the stone in.

"This all sun you get this window?"

"There's more in the morning."

"Screen holes too big to keep out flies. They no want people jump, they should let people out in sun." He bent over and poked a finger into the rubber tree's pot. "Too dry. It die with no water, no sun." He wiped his finger on his slacks, straightened up, then turned to Maggie. "You go ask for a pitcher of water — no ice — two cups. I have bread, cheese, and big grapes." He offered the bag with a wink. "We have one damn good party."

"Too bad they took the wine." She accepted the bag; the paper crackled. Odd shapes and a loaf of bread — but too light — where was the stone? "I'll ask for the wine back." She set the bag on the end table.

"No, no. You get water." He touched a leaf and chuckled with delight. "Tree come to party, too."

She left him unpacking his bag of treats. Eggers wasn't in the hall. Worse luck — Debbie and Arnold looking for a handout, eager for trouble. The teen-age pimples of Palmer 3.

"Who's your visitor, Maggie? Did he bring any dope?" asked Debbie, touching a hand to her tight red curls. Maggie wrinkled her nose at the stench of cheap perfume and passed Debbie without a word. Arnold pushed his spider-like body off the wall and matched Maggie stride for stride. From the corner of her eye, she glimpsed stringy brown hair and a grin on his pimpled face.

"Miss Stuck-It-Up finally got a visitor," he said. "Is that your grandpa or your old man?"

"Don't walk so close, Arnold. I might spit in your ear and drown your brain." Should she tell him that Petro was her boss? Why reveal anything to an ugly mind? "Bug off!" She knocked on the door of the nurses' station while Arnold hung back, still grinning. Eggers didn't look up from the notes she was writing.

Blue ink, blue paper, blue people — the story of Palmer 3, thought Maggie. She glanced down the hall. Debbie was peeping through the plastic panel to see what besides Petro's attention she could lay claim to. Maggie knocked harder. Eggers looked up, sighed and came to the door.

"My boss was kind enough to bring me a picnic lunch. He asked if we could just share a glass of wine. He's Greek and wine is very important in their culture."

Eggers shook her head. "Absolutely not. You know we don't allow alcohol or drugs on the ward."

"They get here anyway, don't they?"

"You know of someone who has contraband here?" Eggers' tone was sharp, her gaze probing.

"How about a pitcher of water? Is that a problem?"

The nurse gave her a hard look, then exhaled audibly and lowered her shoulders. "Not if it's plastic. I'll ask Ms. Richards to get you one from the kitchen."

"I can get it."

"You're still on suicide precautions. Remember that glass ashtray you shattered?"

"That was a week ago. This is now."

Eggers sniffed. ""Your behavior hasn't been that—"

"Look! I don't need a lecture. All I asked for is water. One fucking pitcher of water and two copulating cups."

"I'll get them," said Arnold.

Eggers' scowl whipped across Maggie to Arnold. "Don't you have anything better to do than to butt into other people's business? Why don't you find something constructive to do?"

What was the creep after? Maggie's eyes narrowed as she searched his pock-marked face. "Yes, Arnold. Go find a microscope and look for your erection."

Arnold bristled; his face turned red. "Fuck you, you cock-sucking bitch."

Eggers went ape, dropped her shit on them both. Why didn't Eggers shut her trap? And why didn't Arnold bug off like she'd said. It was too much like fights with her brother Maury at home. The brat would be starting college this month.

"Do you understand that?" Nurse Ape was getting the monkeys in line.

"Yeah." Arnold was grudging, but he walked away.

"Yes," said Maggie. "May I have that pitcher, now?"

Eggers locked the office, accompanied Maggie to the kitchen. The pitcher came with another lecture. Ten minutes to get a pitcher of water — no ice — two paper cups. Why was everything in life such a struggle?

The feast was spread out on the end table, which Petro had moved to the center of the room. Greek bread, kasseri and feta cheeses. Two bunches of plump red grapes, even yellow napkins and paper plates. The table was flanked by the green wing chairs. Petro had dragged the rubber tree over, too. Cigarette in hand, he sat on the sofa, his smile anticipating her pleasure.

"How lovely," she said. "*Signomi* for taking so long." She kicked the door shut behind her.

"No worry so much. I have time more than money." He waved at the table with his cigarette, ignoring the fallout of ash. "You like what I do?"

"I love it." Maggie put the pitcher down on a napkin, set a cup behind each plate, then walked to the sofa and touched her lips gently to Petro's cheek. "I can't thank you enough for all you've done."

"You make an old heart young." He stubbed out his cigarette in the plastic ashtray and took her hands between his. "Please Maritsa, no hide from me again."

"It wasn't from you, Theo Petro. I wrote. I tried to explain — it wasn't from you at all."

He shook his head. "Only last letter say you here. Ha! No worry so much." He released her hand, pushed himself to his feet. "First we have party; later, we talk. Bring glasses to bartender first."

She wrinkled her nose at him. He was teasing, recalling her first-day goof at the tavern. She'd gone to the kitchen and lugged out two trays of glasses, when all Stavros needed behind the bar was his specs. She didn't think it was all that funny, but Stavros'd looked at her bug-eyed through a pair of tumblers and Petro had laughed at her confusion and said, "No worry so much — you be a lot smarter after you learn Greek."

Maggie held the paper cups while Petro, his back to the visiting room door, poured ouzo from a thin metal flask. "God makes trees to drink water, Greeks to drink ouzo," he said. Taking a cup from her, he touched it to the one she still held. "*Sigian!*" He gulped it down.

"*Sigian.*" Liquid licorice scorched her throat. Red-faced, she choked back a cough.

Petro filled their cups again. He set his cup on the table, hiked up the back of his jacket and tucked the flask away.

"Where did you hide the stone?"

"I show you." He moved to the wing chair that faced away from the door. "Go see no big nose outside."

"You saw that girl who peeked in?" Maggie looked through the panel, didn't see anyone.

"No girl," he said. "Only big nose."

What was he doing? If she couldn't see, how could anyone from outside? She walked back to the side of his chair. One trouser leg was above his knee. He was removing clips from an Ace bandage on his leg. The swelling on his shin — it had to be the stone.

He put the two clips on the table. "In Greece, I hide things from Germans many times, but never rocks. Greek who hides *petres* belongs in place like this."

"They'd be afraid I would throw it or hit someone with it. I wouldn't, but they'd take it away." Take away my way out of this life, she thought.

He started unwinding the bandage. "They think you do that? They *trelli* – crazy – not you." He stopped, looked up. "Why you want it, Maritsa?"

To kill myself, she thought. "It's a present for my doctor. The crystals inside are pretty." That spur is sharp as a knife.

"Rock is present for doctor?" He went back to unwrapping his leg. "You *trelli*, too."

She laughed. "Of course, *Theo Petro*. Why else am I here? Haven't you been calling me crazy since I went with John?"

"*O Kathigitis,*" growled Petro. She heard his scorn. *O Kathigitis* — the professor — referring to John with a mock promotion that denoted Petro's contempt for any instructor who bedded a student. "Where is *O Kathigitis* now?" asked Petro.

Tears came to her eyes. Shit! Why was such pain still there? John had thrown her away, packed her suitcase and sent her to Hell. "Have you — " Holy Mother, it was difficult to ask. "Have you seen him since I've been here?"

"No. He not come to *taverna*. He not come here?"

She looked down at the flesh-colored bandage barely concealing the stone. "There are reasons he can't — won't visit me here." But the bastard could have written. He didn't need to change his number, get it unlisted. Wasn't she worth a good-bye?

"Stupid goat also grows beard, but alone never finds his way home," said Petro. "So! Here is your *petra*."

He plunked the stone hemisphere into her palm as if it were half an orange to squeeze. The volcanic crust felt cool but rough; her fingers found indentations. She turned completely away from the door and looked at the geode's gaping mouth of amethyst crystals — the lips, grey and white agate bands. The jagged spur was as sharp as she remembered.

"Thank you, *Theo Petro*." For my stone, my *petra*, she thought. *And I say to thee: That thou art Peter, and upon this rock I will build my church.* Except her pain was too great, her faith too weak — so now her church would be her grave.

"See, *Papou* not stupid." He was rolling up the bandage.

"I know." She put down her cup and wrapped the stone in a napkin.

Petro pocketed the bandage. "I give tree water. Then we eat."

A short grace in Greek, old hands breaking bread. Sweet Jesus! A penknife to cut the cheese. He had a knife in his pocket and no one thought to ask him? Would he leave it? Even if he did, she couldn't use it. He'd feel enough guilt about the stone. Well, she couldn't help that; there was no one else to trust.

"Try bread with kasseri cheese, Maritsa."

What a fool she'd been to trust John, a man who cheated on his wife. Yet what man didn't?

"Something wrong, Maritsa?"

"Oh, no. Not at all."

As they ate, Petro told her he'd completed what she'd asked in her letters. Her apartment was vacant, the keys restored to the manager, her possessions were safely stored. The security deposit paid the last two months rent and his brother Stavros' sons did all the moving. No, she hadn't asked for that, but why throw money away. Everything was moved to his own house, anyway; who knew the way better than his nephews?

"But I asked you to put it into storage," she said.

"Too much money." He spit grape seeds onto his plate. "I have rooms more than you have money."

He hadn't looked at her bankbook, then. He wouldn't spit at six thousand dollars. Unless John had it. "Did you find my bankbook? My checkbook?"

"You think *Papou* stupid? You think I bring only rock?" He reached into a breast pocket, came out with an envelope. She saw that it was sealed.

"No. Please keep them for me. They wouldn't be safe up here. But I didn't mean to impose with my things — I mean the bedroom set alone, and the books and the rocks — "

"No worry so much. This way, you need something, I bring."

She thanked him and let it go. To argue would be futile, ungrateful. In a day or two, it wouldn't matter. So she asked him about Stavros and his practical jokes.

Petro said Stavros hadn't been up to playing tricks this summer. He was talking all the time about retiring to Tarpon Springs, that his bones were too old for winter. Yes, he'd said such things before, but now he wanted Petro to agree.

"Do you?" asked Maggie.

Petro sighed. "For Stavros, Tarpon Springs is good. He has Eleni to make a new home and their children and grandchildren will come to visit. But that life is not for me. It's no good to retire alone."

"But you're his brother, part of his family." She saw he didn't agree. A shrug of his shoulders, a twitch of his lips. Without words, they said, "I am and I'm not." He offered her a cigarette, lit them both, dragged heavily on his. Damn. She hadn't meant to get him down. "Do you want to see my room?"

"No. First we talk." She'd shifted him to low and now he was stuck. She watched and listened as he labored uphill. He said yes, he and Stavros had each other — one brother where once there were five. Sometimes, it was a curse to be the youngest, to watch them go, one by one. If only his blessed Penelope had lived, or he was the one God took first. How he missed her. No use for a man to try to understand God. They'd had forty-two years together and she'd given him so much joy. So many happy memories. From Pentalofos to America, a goat herder's hut to a three bedroom home. Happy memories were his children. What was wrong with that? Memories didn't waste his money, didn't get into trouble, wouldn't throw him out when he was old. It was God's will their baby was stillborn. He always said that to Penelope when she grew sad. He even said it with her on her deathbed, when she worried he'd be all alone. The baby and Penelope walked with God in *Parathisos*; he'd join them if it was God's will.

She noticed her cigarette turning to ashes. Had Petro told her he'd had a child? No, she would have remembered. "I'm very sorry they died. Really."

Tears came to Petro's eyes. "God has His plan. I light many candles."

She didn't doubt that God had His plans. But why was Petro's baby denied life and parents who loved it while she was given a Hell on Earth? "Things like a baby's death don't make sense," she said.

"Cord tight around baby's neck. If boy, would have been Georgios, the name of my father; a girl, Maria, after my mother. Both, they died in the war."

"I didn't know."

He shrugged. "No worry. My father and mother, so long ago. Much more I miss Penelope and baby Maritsa."

23

Where Will She Go?

Nancy Brill was missing. Raymond charged up the stairs three at a time, his doctor's coat flaring outward with each thrust of a knee.

Where was the stupid sitter? he thought. Were the nurses deaf, dumb and blind? Psychotic kid — find her before she kills herself. Senseless, tragic death. And they'd all be up shit's creek, even Taylor. Senator Brill would have their balls.

He threw his weight against the fire door, lunged through the doorway and ran down the corridor. He dodged a blood bank technician with her basket of tubes, passed two startled nurses brown-bagging it to lunch. Where the hell would Nancy Brill go? Would Security get their asses into gear? How much time 'til they had to call the police? Damn Taylor for being out of town. Maybe now he'd agree Nancy needed a locked psychiatric ward.

Slow down! Next left was 4 South. There'd be uproar enough without bursting in. The nurses would be frantic; they'd be turning the ward inside out.

A stainless steel food cart and two dietician's helpers dominated the ward's center hall. The rooms that fed off both sides of the hall were surrendering back soiled trays. Not a patient visible, no search underway – only a uniformed nurse entering a room, two pink-smocked aides carrying trays.

Nancy must have come back. He paused to catch his breath. Beyond the counter of the nurses' station, Miss Royer, the charge nurse, was a peach gone sour – no fuzzy-cheeked smile today. Jesus Christ! Nancy's not back. Towering over the nurse, a grizzled ramrod of a man was talking down to her cap. Brown suit, tan shirt, string tie; in his left hand, a walkie-talkie; in his right, a cigarette.

At least one tight ass is in gear, thought Raymond. Not enough, with his own on the line. He hurried toward them, beating Miss Royer's feeble attempts at introduction.

"I'm Raymond Daniels. Nancy Brill's my patient."

"Fremmer. Acting Director, Security."

Raymond's lips tightened. What's with this guy? Last name and rank, no hand. The cigarette wasn't even lit. Raymond turned to the nurse. "Why isn't the ward being searched?"

"You want to do my job?" asked Fremmer.

Oh shit, a temperamental S.O.B., thought Raymond.

Royer shook her blonde curls as if to say "no" and looked between the two men to the hall. "It's been searched. She's not here – my staff's looked in every bathroom and closet and under every bed. The patients must think we're crazy, but we're sure Nancy's not here." Royer's eyes met Raymond's, then darted away. "I'm sorry."

"Me, too," said Raymond. Sorry Nancy had been put on a medical floor, sorry she hadn't responded to anti-psychotic medication. "And worried." If only Taylor had allowed him to try tiny doses or other drugs, but no, Taylor needed complete control. "She believes the Devil wants her to kill herself," he told Fremmer. "How the heck did she get away from the sitter?"

"Walked," said Fremmer. He put the cigarette between his lips. It added droop to his frown.

"We had a new woman today," said Royer, "an L.P.N. moonlighting on her day off. I told her to stay with Nancy, to ask for relief when she wanted a break. She didn't understand I meant every moment. She used Nancy's bathroom for a couple of minutes and when she came out – maybe I wasn't clear enough. I'm sorry." Royer used her thumbnail to scratch her forearm, where a pink blotch was spreading on her skin.

"I know," said Raymond. No sense for Royer to dig at herself. "Don't blame yourself. Nancy should have been on a psychiatric ward. How long has it been since she took off?"

"Twenty-minutes," said Royer.

Fremmer glanced at his watch. "Twenty-four."

"And what is Security doing besides keeping track of the time, Mr. Fremmer?"

The Acting Chief of Security removed the cigarette from his lips as if time no longer mattered. "Searching the building. Except for me. Fact is, I've been waiting for you."

Raymond bristled. "Then why wasn't I paged sooner?"

Miss Royer coughed; they both looked at her. She scratched the blotch on her skin. "I called Security first, then tried to get to Doctor Taylor – well, he is the attending physician. He didn't answer his pager and his phone was busy. When I got through, his secretary told me he was out of town."

"Where do you think she'll go, Doc?" asked Fremmer.

"I don't know. She lives half-way across the state." He'd have to call her parents. He frowned at Fremmer. "How did she get off the ward?"

"Rear staircase. Free access up or down."

"Does it go to the roof?"

"Yes, but the roof is fenced and the door activates an alarm. I sent a man up, anyhow."

Raymond glanced over his shoulder as the food cart rattled by, a helper in white at each end. "Are all the exits covered?"

Fremmer's tongue made a sharp clucking sound; his head waggled from side to side. "Not counting the medical center bridges, there are eleven exits she could have reached within five minutes. I sent some ward staff down and called men over from the next building. I even have one man out circling in a car. Not that we have any legal standing out there, but he could follow her while we called the police. Still, if she beat us to an exit, she's long gone. Where will she go, Doc?"

Home? Too far. Did she have any friends? "I wish I knew. Was she dressed? Did she say anything to the sitter?"

Royer was eager to help. "She's wearing a white blouse and navy jumper. Blue and white saddle shoes – and probably Mrs. Boone's white sweater – "

"With Boone's nametag," interjected Fremmer.

" – that's several sizes too big for Nancy. Mrs. Boone left her sweater on the back of the chair when she went in to the bathroom."

"More of Nancy's collecting?" asked Raymond.

"Collecting?" Fremmer stuck the cigarette in his mouth, then used both hands to clip the walkie-talkie to his belt.

Royer shrugged. "Maybe she just wanted to be warm outside."

"Part of her illness," said Raymond. "Bits of paper, buttons, coins – she hides it all. Where's Mrs. Boone? I'd like to talk with her."

Fremmer took the cigarette from his mouth. "Waste of time. She doesn't know a cow from a sow. The kid asked her a few times if the Devil sent her, then clammed up and rocked in a chair." He withdrew a thin silver case from his breast pocket. "The tutor was there for an hour, nurses in and out a couple of times, but the kid was a zero 'til the woman went to the can." Fremmer snapped open the empty case and inserted the cigarette, then noticed Royer staring. "If you only pack one, you can only smoke one, right? Anyway, the kid never mentioned going anywhere." He snapped the case shut and slipped it into his pocket.

"I still want to talk with the sitter," said Raymond.

Fremmer clucked his tongue. "Then you'll have to go down to the main lobby. She's a spotter for one of my men. Fact is, I sent her to get her out of the way – she kept asking who'd pay for her sweater. Cries too damn much, too."

"Excuse me," said Royer. "I have to get my staff moving." Her head inclined toward a cluster of nurses and aides eyeing them from down the hall. "I'll be back in a minute." Her body seemed to firm up as she moved away. "Let's go, ladies! There's plenty to do."

Fremmer rubbed a forefinger across his lips as if he was tempted to smoke it. "So where will she go, Doc?"

The man's a pain in the ass, thought Raymond. "She's told me that she's going to Hell, Mr. Fremmer. Maybe you can tell me where that is."

Fremmer's lips eased into a mocking smile. "For me, Hell is in an open bottle. I don't know where it is for you or the kid. You want me to notify the police?"

"I'll have to call my supervisor on that one. Nancy's father is a state senator. He's up for re-election in less than sixty days. If the police put her name out over the radio and some busybody with a scanner links her name to his, the shit will hit the fan."

Fremmer nodded. "C.Y.A." He started to walk away but turned back at Raymond's "what?"

"Military," said Fremmer, "for 'cover your ass.' Here we're more refined. We say 'call your administrator.' Where will she go, Doc?"

"Christ! You don't give up easily."

"If I did, my bones would be rotting in Korea."

Royer's voice heralded the return of the nursing staff. " – so check the I.V. in 407. Then you and Janet better go down and turn Mrs. Bates again."

"The boiler room!" said Raymond. All motion stopped; all eyes focused on him. Was it that loud? "I'm sorry." He moved toward Fremmer. "Nancy's very concrete in her thinking. It's a symptom of – of her illness. She believes Hell is a pit with fire, and she must think it's down below. I'll bet she's headed to the boiler room."

Fremmer was trying to restrain a grin. "This building doesn't have a boiler room. Steam's piped in from the central power plant across the street." His face hardened. "Would the kid know that?"

"I don't think so. But you'd better check it out. Anyway, my guess is that she'll go down to the basement, whatever's there."

The walkie-talkie was in Fremmer's hand. Raymond expected static; there was none. "Wally! Check the power plant. The kid may be there. Alert Gino and get over there double-time. You read me?"

The static arrived a second before Wally's, "Got it — will do," then disappeared with Fremmer's voice. "Connor! Forget three. Start at the east end of the basement and proceed west. I repeat: start at the east end of the basement and proceed west until you meet me. Acknowledge!"

The static returned. "Roger that, T.J."

Fremmer looked at Raymond. "Your bet. You want to come?"

"I do, but I can't. I have to make these calls. But get back to me, even if you don't find her. If I'm not here, page me."

Fremmer clipped the walkie-talkie to his belt. "Will do. If you hear more of her, beep me through the hospital operator. Miss Royer!" He beckoned her with his hand. Royer came to his side, but Fremmer spoke to Raymond. "We're clear that you're going to make the decisions about if and when to call the police?"

"Yes."

Fremmer turned to the nurse. "You heard that?"

"Yes."

"Good. Then I can go." As he did, he winked at Raymond. "C.Y.A., Doc. C.Y. A."

24

Die, Nancy, Die

Yes, the basement. Abasement. This is the way. Hear the screech of power from a saw. And louder, deeper, more powerful, the Devil's voice.

"Nan, see! You must die. Your insides are rotting away."

Basement, abasement. He must be obeyed. Big hissing pipes overhead point the way. Walk along the wall and the pipes won't fall. They hiss His song along belong to His organ of steam, of fire. Pyre, glowing hot, flowing clot, Rot, shot, what kills will not. Hot, too hot. Yes, this sweater must come off.

Oh! It's arm is dirty, not white, not bright. Dirt from the wall. Bad Nancy. Filthy Nancy, bleeding down there. Dirty inside and out. Now you've ruined the lady's sweater.

"You'll be punished for that, brat."

It was You, the Devil! You made Nancy take it.

"Liar! Liar! You'll be truthed in fire."

Sorry, sorry, don't be mad. Please. Your voice gets so loud.

"Thief! You'll be punished, then you won't steal any more. Whore!"

Yes, punished for her own good. Take your medicine, dead of sin, dear.

"Nan, see."

Yes, the Devil's voice. It rattles the pipes, makes the power saw cry. Hold on to the bricks, they're trembling.

"Nan, see! Ahead are machines. Their slaves will catch you, lock you away. They'll poison you with pills, make you a machine. Go back to the room with the boxes and shelves. There you can be safe to die."

Sure, that way – hurry. Where? There! Her room, her doom room. Yes, Daddy, she'll go to her room and try, cry, cry and die.

"Close the door! Find a place to hide."

Hide, lied, cried and cried. Don't you have any pride? Yes, Daddy. No, Daddy. Mommy doesn't want her to grow, Daddy.

"Nan! See! That big box — what's inside?"

Inside died. Rotted and died. Open wide. Plastic foam inside.

"Push the box far from the door. More – I said more, whore! Dump the foam on the floor."

It'll make a mess.

"Couldn't care less. Dump it all out. Get the matches before you climb inside."

Inside cried. Rotted and died. Pull down her undies right here?

"Yes. Get the matches from the napkin right now…That's right."

It's stained, but Mommy explained, not my fault, not my fault.

"Liar! Clean everything with fire. Not the safety pin, not the pills. Leave the dirty dollar in the Kotex, too. No sex for you. Just the matchbook, trust the matchbook."

Only two matches left.

"Two will do. Pull up your undies. Everything in the box. Get everything in."

In. Sin. How to climb in?

"Use that stool, fool."

Yes, look, she's tall, tall. Over the wall – oh – ouch! Inside! Tried, tried, inside rotted and died. Tried to do better. Forgive and forget her, Mommy. Sorry, she's sorry.

"Light the match. Strike it! Again!"

This match's no good. It's the match's fault, not hers. Wait! Flame! No blame, no shame, just flame.

"Touch the flame to the box. Die, Nancy, die! "

Yes, die, Nancy die…

25

A Match

The green plastic chairs of the conference room on 4 South had been left in disarray. A newspaper lay abandoned on one, the board eraser was on another. A chalk diagram of an impaired heart remained on the blackboard. Raymond closed the door, dropped Nancy Brill's chart on the table and used the wall telephone to call Taylor's office. Anita DeSimone told him Doctor Taylor was staying at the Washington Hilton; he'd had a morning appointment at the National Institute of Mental Health in Rockville, but she didn't know his plans for the afternoon. Raymond left messages marked 'Urgent' for Taylor to call him, then dialed the Outpatient Clinic. Professor Bergstrom was en route to the V.A. Hospital for his Tuesday afternoon seminar. Doctor White? Yes, he was free.

Leroy White had not heard of Nancy Brill. Raymond briefed him, got back an "uh-huh" and a "hmm." Nancy's bad reactions to medications elicited a more sympathetic "Mmm." Her disappearance brought forth a soft, "Oh, shit."

"Security's searching the building right now," said Raymond.

"Have you notified her parents?"

"Not yet. I'm worried that Senator Brill might tell me not to call the police. He's in a tough fight for re-election."

"And Momma?"

"She'll get panicky, but I think she'll end up asking her husband what to do. She talks a lot, but he makes the decisions." Raymond fingered the downward spiral of black telephone cord. "I bet he'll rationalize that Nancy will come through better for having run off – after he chews me out, that is. The man's got a lot of anger to vent. He'll probably tell me again that he ran away as a kid and how that wasn't so bad because it made him grow up in a hurry. The thing is, what if – I mean unconsciously now – what if he's more afraid of losing his position and power than he is of losing his mentally ill daughter?"

"So you want to call the police first..." White's voice deepened, his words came slower. "Present him with a fait accompli. And you're checking with me because Doctor Taylor may deep fry your hide."

You got it, thought Raymond. "I know it puts you in a difficult situation."

"Difficult?" White emitted a strangled chuckle. "Do you know how many Blacks are on the faculty of this enlightened department? One. Want to guess why? Tell me about difficult situations, my friend."

"I'm sorry. I didn't realize – "

"What? That I like my job? That tokenism exists here? That I'm the affirmative action alligator on the Man's lily white shirt? Well, realize that the Chairman wants a decorative alligator; he doesn't want one that nips his tit."

Raymond rubbed his forehead. "Look, you don't have to get involved. I can call someone else."

"Don't spit in my pie, Raymond. Even with an appetite as big as mine, there's a limit to what I'll swallow, okay? Look, even though you suspect the Senator may value his position more than his daughter, don't you think he'd be worse off if she killed herself? With the press and the voters, I mean."

"I think he'd win on sympathy votes. The dead get a lot more respect than the mentally ill."

"Save it for the Sunday sermon. Exactly what is it that you want to do?"

"Call the police, then the parents." Anticipating a veto, he spoke faster. "I'll tell them Nancy's missing and that I was extremely concerned about the risk of suicide – which I am – so I notified the police. I also want to press them again to admit her to a psychiatric ward. She needs a structured psychiatric program, not this babysitting crap we've got going on 4 South."

White was silent. Raymond took in a deep breath, then exhaled slowly. He'd been on overdrive since Royer had paged him. He'd presented the case as accurately as he could. Now it was up to White.

"I'll tell you the truth," White said. "I don't know whether to cheer 'Right on!' or to commit you for delusions of grandeur. You're talking about screwing the Senator, the Chairman, our state appropriation – worst of all, me – all with one phone call. Raymond, I swear your balls must be black."

Raymond grinned. "Does that mean you agree?"

"It means what I said, okay? It's a judgment call. Is the girl that suicidal? Is the father such a cold fish? All I have to go on is what you've said. I can't – Shit! You have to do what's best for the girl. That's the bottom line. Just don't do more than you said without checking with me first, okay?"

"Thanks. I appreciate it, especially in view of the dif – "

"Bullshit!" said White. "Call the police."

*   *   *

"What do you mean you called the police?" Senator Brill bellowed.

Raymond moved the telephone receiver away from his ear, but the Senator's irate tone pursued him.

"Why in God's name did you call the police?"

"Because I'm concerned Nancy might try to kill herself." His tone was firm.

"Concerned? If you're so damn concerned, why the hell didn't you do a better job of keeping her? Or making her well again? Last time I visited, she couldn't stop drooling. The time before, she couldn't sit still. What with all the shit you've been feeding her, it's no wonder she's taken off."

Raymond bit his lip. No one could've predicted how she'd respond to antipsychotics, but letting Nancy slide deeper into schizophrenia meant institutionalization if not suicide. He'd explained that, the limitations of both behavioral and medical treatments for schizophrenia, and the risks and possible benefits of every drug they'd ordered. Neither he nor Taylor were at fault for Nancy's allergic reactions, her extreme sensitivity; they'd used low doses, tried antidotes, discontinued the offending drugs. Every drug had its side effects, every treatment its problems. But that wasn't why Nancy ran away. "I don't think that Nancy ran because – "

"No! You don't think. That's the trouble with you young guys, today. All you're in it for is the bucks. Where the hell is your boss? Did he tell you to call the police?"

"Doctor Taylor is in Washington. I wasn't able to reach him." Should he say he checked it out with White? Screw it! That wasn't the Senator's business. With Taylor away, the decisions and responsibility were his.

"No wonder things got fucked up," said the Senator. "What an ass! To leave you in charge. I can't believe it – you called the police. As if she's a criminal or something."

Raymond squeezed the phone. "I called them to try to find and protect her."

"Protect her? Her mother always protected her – and look what happened. For Christ's sake, the girl's turned fifteen. I ran away when I was fourteen, and it didn't hurt me a bit."

"She's not you. She's sick. She's very dangerous to herself."

"Then find her, God damn it. Find her and do something to make her well."

The door opened. Out on the ward, a food cart rattled by and a woman said something. Raymond looked up. Fremmer came in and shut the door behind him. Raymond raised his eyebrows as a question.

Fremmer's cigarette was in pout position. His head wagged from side to side.

"Did you call my wife?" asked Senator Brill.

"I tried. She wasn't home," said Raymond.

Fremmer stepped toward the table.

"I'll tell her," said the Senator. "I'll get my aide to find her and to cancel my appointments. We'll be down to the hospital by six. You make sure you find Nancy by then. I can't have the newspapers making this the story of my campaign."

"I'll do my best," said Raymond, eyeing the silver cigarette case and lighter Fremmer drew from his pockets.

"Your best? No! Do better than that!" The Senator banged down his phone.

Raymond dropped the receiver on its cradle. "Bastard," he muttered.

Fremmer tapped the end of his one cigarette on the lighter. "World's full of 'em." He sat down on the edge of the table and lit his cigarette.

"Any sign of her?" asked Raymond. He saw Fremmer wasn't about to be rushed – not by anything other than nicotine. Raymond eased himself into the nearest chair. Nothing to do now but wait. No one else to call. And the big security man was sitting on his ass. On the table, no less.

Fremmer shrugged. "Maybe – maybe not. There's a large storage room in the basement. Either she was there or we have another weirdo loose." He reached across the table for a plastic ashtray. "A big carton was emptied and pushed on its side. The packing material was all over the floor."

"Couldn't anyone have knocked it over?"

"Sure. But it was right side up two hours ago. At least a janitor swears it was. He's not all that reliable; I think he's got a bottle stashed here and there." Fremmer took a drag on his cigarette. His body appeared to shrink as he exhaled. "Anyway, the carton was pulled back out of sight from the doorway, and a stool had been moved close by. I figure the kid used the stool to climb in, then couldn't reach it and had to tumble the carton over to crawl out." His facial expression soured. "One other thing."

Raymond leaned forward. "What?"

"There was a brown mark – like a scorch mark – in the box. Does the kid smoke? Have a cigarette lighter?"

"Not that I know of."

"Well, there weren't any matches in the box. Maybe it was

something that happened to the box before. Where will she go now, Doc?"

"I honestly don't know. You think the basement was right, then?"

"Who knows? I only know I don't like a nutty kid running loose. Did you call the police?"

Raymond nodded. "That was the father giving me a hard time about it on the phone."

"Don't let it bother you. The wolves feel freer to try to bring you down when you're not top dog in the pack. You and I, Doc, we're not top dogs; we're plain old hounds following a scent through a pond of piss." Fremmer took another long drag. He blew the smoke out slowly. "So where will she go?"

"Look, stop asking me that. I don't have the faintest idea."

"That right?" Fremmer looked sadly at his cigarette. "Then I guess we've done all we can. I shouldn't be smoking, anyway." He ground the half-finished cigarette into the ashtray. "Shit." He rose from his perch on the table. "Kids are like germs, Doc. Can't let them run loose."

Static coming from Fremmer's walkie-talkie startled them. "Mr. Fremmer! Mr. Fremmer! It's Erik. I've got her."

Fremmer grabbed the walkie-talkie from his belt. "This is Fremmer. What's happening?"

"The girl's with me. We're walking back toward the Emergency Room. Be there in three or four minutes. She was just wandering on Madison. Everything's okay, but she wouldn't get in my car."

"You sure it's the right girl?" asked Fremmer.

"Yup. She said her name's Nancy. Wouldn't tell me her last name. She's dressed like you described, only no sweater. She said the Devil took it."

"That's Nancy," said Raymond. Thank God they found her. Raymond smiled at Fremmer. The man wasn't all that bad.

Fremmer lowered the walkie-talkie to his side. "That shithead!" He saw Raymond's surprise. "He should have called as soon as he spotted her. He had no back-up. He has no brains. We're lucky she didn't run. Out there, he has no legal right to touch her." He spoke into the walkie-talkie. "Okay. You all heard the good news. Everyone except Erik can return to their regular assignments. I'll be making rounds in ten minutes, you hear? Make sure you're where you're supposed to be. Erik?"

"Yes, Mr. Fremmer."

"Doctor Daniels and I are coming down to meet you in the Emergency Room. Stay with Nancy until we get there."

"Sure. Ask the doctor if Nancy's allowed to smoke."

Fremmer raised an eyebrow at Raymond but didn't wait for a response. "Did she ask you for a cigarette?" he said into the walkie-talkie.

"Yeah. No. Sort of," said Erik. "She asked if I had a match."

26

Telephone Calls

"She wanted to stay up to see you, but it got too late," Lisa whispered.

Raymond nodded. With a sad smile, he bent over the bed and kissed the head of their three year-old daughter. Her red hair was silky and smelled freshly washed. Her eyelids fluttered but she didn't awaken. Another day in Julie's life without him, he thought. What could he do to make it up to her?

"Come," said Lisa. "I've saved your dinner."

"Thanks." Raymond followed her out of the tiny bedroom, through the living room and into the kitchen. They'd made the previous tenant's picket fence and sunflower wallpaper more tolerable by placing a frosted globe on the overhead light, but there was no easy replacement for decade-old appliances on a resident's salary. Still, the warmth of the kitchen meant that Lisa had gotten another day's work out of the temperamental stove, and the odors of oregano and sautéed onions made him realize how hungry he was. Lisa went to the stove and wrapped an apron over her blue maternity dress while he headed for the small table at the far end of the room. There was only one place setting and a glass of water on the white laminate tabletop. "Sorry I'm late." He chose to sit in the chair with the cracked and taped plastic seat, leaving the good one for her. "Is there anything I can do?" he asked.

"You'll clean up your dishes." Lisa transferred a baking dish from the top of the stove into the oven. "The casserole has to reheat. You can start with the salad." She cocked her head at him. "Why so late?"

Raymond sighed. "I should've called. I'm sorry. That psychotic 15 year-old girl that I've been helping Doctor Taylor with ran off from the hospital. Taylor was in Washington and unavailable, so I had to deal with it." He backhanded the air in front of him. "I created a shit-storm by calling the police."

"Did they find her?"

"Yes, thank God." His hands came to rest on the tabletop. "One of our security people found her out on the street."

"You still should have called me." Lisa opened the refrigerator, took out a small bowl of salad and placed it in front of him. She grunted as she sank onto the other chair. "Wasn't calling the police the right thing to do?"

His lips turned down in an ironic smile. "I thought so — but I caught hell from her father for doing it. He's a politician, up for re-election, and he wants to keep any unfavorable news from getting out. Anyway, there were no beds for her on the adolescent unit, so I had to admit her to Adult Psych, but I had a hell of a time getting her father to approve the transfer. That started another problem — the only open bed was in a room with the suicidal co-ed I have there. And she made a fuss about having a kid for a roommate, so I had to get them both settled, and then I had to write the whole runaway incident up." Raymond picked up his knife and fork. "Doctor Taylor's going to have a fit when he hears about it. His secretary said he usually calls in for a briefing at the end of the day, so he might even call me tonight… Anyway, how was your day?" With fork and knife, he dug into his salad. The blue cheese dressing made his mouth water.

"Oh, not that exciting," said Lisa. "I spent my afternoon picking little pieces of Pooh Bear out of the living room rug, with Julie hysterical and Helen's three year old bear-killer bouncing around like a Mexican jumping bean. In the midst of it, my mother called. I didn't know which baby to take care of first." Lisa shook her head. "Then Helen came back from the doctor and fell apart in my arms. The doctor told her that the lump in her breast needed a biopsy, but not to worry too much about it being cancer; if it was, a mastectomy could easily take away the problem. What kind of idiot says something like that?"

"A surgeon," said Raymond. "I'm sorry about Helen… Well, at her age it's probably a cyst. And I'm sorry you had a lousy day, too."

"Your being late didn't help. So why didn't you just call?"

Raymond grimaced. "To tell the truth, I was so caught up in this mess, I didn't think of calling until I was on my way out of the hospital. I was worried about what this big-wig politico was going to lay on Doctor Taylor, and whether I'll still have a job tomorrow, much less whether Taylor will give me a fellowship for next year."

"You mean we may to have to move before I have this baby?" Anxiety pushed Lisa's voice higher. "Won't it mean anything that I'm seven months along?"

He speared a piece of tomato. "To the Army? Not with this bloody war going on." Separation would be terrible for her, he thought. If he were fired, the Army would grab him as soon as they found out. Even if Taylor let him finish this year, the Chairman would certainly veto a fourth year fellowship.

"I heard on the radio that President Nixon ordered the withdrawal of 35,000 troops from Vietnam," said Lisa.

"Good for them, but it doesn't change our situation. And it doesn't change Ethan's death." He grit his teeth and swallowed hard. Lisa reached over the table and covered his free hand with her own.

"Thanks," he murmured. "It's not easy." He put down his fork. "Despite what Nixon ordered, we still have hundreds of thousands of Americans fighting there. *Life* magazine just had this article saying that they're dying at the rate of forty-two per week. Not that it's likely the Army would put me in a field hospital, but I'd still have to go somewhere for basic training and then God knows where. Maybe you could go to your mother's until after the baby is born."

Lisa withdrew her hand. "No. Maybe I can get my sister to come from Philadelphia for a week in December. And Helen would help — if she's alright. I told her to call me after she talks to Joe. She was in such an anxious state."

"When she calls, try to make it short. If Doctor Taylor is trying to get in touch with me, I don't want him to have another reason to be pissed off."

"You shouldn't have taken this job with him. Not after the awful things he said to you last spring."

"I can't undo what's done." He expelled a sigh of frustration. Would he ever stop grieving the deaths of his parents and Ethan, or the manic depressive illness that had institutionalized his father's mother and brother? "There are worse things than getting fired," he said.

"I know. I'm sorry. I'm not making anything better by carping."

"It's okay. You're not carping." He offered a small smile. "So what's in the casserole?"

Her smile was broader. "You mean besides Silly Putty? It's hamburger and macaroni and this wonderful cheese — "

The ring of the telephone startled them.

"It's probably Helen," said Lisa. "I'll get it."

"No." He put his hand on hers to stop her. "I'll get it; it may be Taylor. Anyway, it's easier for me to get up."

He pushed back his chair and was out to the living room before she could rise.

"Hello," said Raymond.

"Doctor Daniels?" a male voice inquired

"Yes."

"I received a letter from Maggie Saxe."

"Who are you?" asked Raymond.

"She said she was going to kill herself before her birthday — that's September twenty-third, two days from today. I'm sure she means it."

"What's your name? How do you know Maggie? "

"Not important. What's important is that Maggie doesn't lie. Protect her!"

The click of the receiver rang loud in Raymond's ear.

27

The Stone

The night's being stolen, thought Maggie. Robbed of purpose, stripped of its value. She might as well toss it on the junk heap of her past. Fucking Daniels, putting a lunatic in her room tonight. Without any warning, and with the nurses and attendants popping in and out, there was no opportunity to get the stone. So what if the only vacant bed was in her room – he could have waited another day to fill it. If only she'd risked another search, kept the stone in a drawer or under her mattress – dear Jesus, was she to be denied forever? What choice now but to lie in the dark, feign sleep – and listen to Nancy Brill rock back and forth in her bed. Minute by minute, hour after hour, the crazy girl was stealing the night.

Footsteps. Bedcheck again? That's nine since shift change. From the door, a channel of light, a shadow climbing the wall. Don't just stand there and wheeze Gareaux! Give crazy Nancy a sleeping pill; otherwise, disappear.

"Still having trouble sleeping, Nancy?" the aide asked.

You're really too much, Gareaux, thought Maggie. Too fat to breathe, too dumb to whisper. How is it *you* have the keys?

Nancy stopped rocking. "Trouble sleeping? No, I can't sleep. Did the Devil send you?"

"Heaven forbid. Don't talk like that. You lie still so you can go to sleep."

The shadow backed down as Gareaux retreated. Darkness filled the channel as she closed the door. Nancy rocked back and forth.

One more hour, give it one more hour, thought Maggie. There'd still be five hours to bleed out. But what if Nancy was still awake — who could predict what a crazy kid might do? No choice. Tonight was the last full night before her birthday. Let F. Dexter go out and celebrate her deathday. He could finally stop writing those checks. Wanda would play the inconsolable mother. How would she explain it to Father Boyle? An accident? Leukemia? But John would know, and her parents' friends would guess. Like in Luke, Chapter Twelve: *For there is nothing covered that shall not be revealed; nor hidden, that shall not be known.*

You were right, Wanda, the Bible should be studied every night; too bad you never studied your family that well. Didn't want to know? Didn't care enough? It makes no difference now.

The rocking stopped. Maggie listened intently. Had Nancy finally surrendered to sleep? A few minutes more and it might be safe to get the stone. A scratch of fingernails against a sheet – the rustle of bedclothes, a creak from Nancy's bed. Going to the john? Hard to hear bare feet on the carpet; she's such a puny thing, anyway. Smells like lilacs –

Maggie sprang to a sitting position, hands protecting her head. "What the fuck do you want?"

The black shape standing over her gasped, lurched backwards and jumped into Nancy's bed. "Don't scare me like that!" said Nancy.

194

Maggie lowered her arms, adjusted her nightgown. "Scare you? Are you cra – I mean, what the fuck were you doing?"

"Don't use dirty words. The Devil will punish you."

"Tough shit. He already has." Maggie peered through the darkness. At the head of Nancy's bed, the girl had merged with her pillow into one dark and bulbous form. "What were you doing here at my bed?"

"I just wanted to see if you were asleep."

"And what if I was? What would you have done?"

"Let you sleep. Really." Her tone was childlike, convincing.

Maggie extracted her legs from under the bedclothes and swung them over the side of her bed. It felt good to move, to play possum no more. "And if I was awake? What then?"

"I – do you know Melissa Tolliver?"

"No," said Maggie. "Do you know Gloria Steinem?"

"No. Do you know Valerie Murphy?"

"No. Do you know Mary Margaret Saxe?"

"Aren't you – "

"No. I'm Maggie. Mary Margaret was a different kid. She didn't use dirty words."

"But you did. Did the Devil send you?"

Maggie rolled her eyes. "He tried. I ate him."

Nancy dropped her pillow, sat up straight. "You ate the Devil? That's impossible."

"My mother always said I was full of the Devil." Maggie smiled. "You calling my mother a liar?"

"Oh, no. What did the Devil taste like?"

"First tell me what you were going to do if you found me awake."

"Promise you won't laugh?"

Maggie nodded. "Cross my heart and hope to die."

"I was going to ask — because it's very dark and I couldn't sleep — sometimes, at night I mean, sometimes my mother holds me."

"Oh." This kid belongs in a nursery, thought Maggie. Still, she couldn't help but feel sad for her. "I'm sure being held feels great, but I'm not the mothering type. I'm sorry."

"That's okay. I shouldn't have asked. Daddy says I have to grow up. What did the Devil taste like? You promised you would tell."

A puff of air escaped Maggie's lips before they twisted into a smile. "Salty. Some people gag, others spit a lot. I just swallow the little devils."

"But there's only one Devil."

"No. Do you remember in the Bible, where Jesus met a man crying and cutting himself with stones? Luke told us that Jesus asked the man his name, and the man said, *Legion; because many devils were entered into him.* You're not going to disagree with the Bible, are you?"

"Well how many Devils are there, then? I just hear one."

Maggie shrugged her shoulders. "God only knows. I'm only one person, but I must have taken – I don't know – maybe six or seven devils inside me. I was thinking tonight might be a good night to let them out. Want to help?"

Nancy hid behind her pillow. "No. They'll hurt us. They'll truth us with fire."

"No they won't. I promise it won't hurt you one bit. But first we have to lie down and pretend to be fast asleep. That fat bit – big nurse will be back. If she sees us up, she'll keep us from having fun with the Devil."

"No," said Nancy. "The Devil isn't fun."

"Maybe for you he's not. But lie down and pretend you're sleeping, okay? Until the nurse goes out and I say we can talk again. Then I can tell you a secret."

"And you'll hold me?"

"No, but I'll help you grow up a little. Now get under your covers and make believe you're asleep." Maggie watched until Nancy complied, then lay down and covered herself. Nancy was so immature, so pathetic. Because she was hungry to be held? What about Mr. Hyde's nightmare visits? Weren't any arms desirable then? Yes, but being held by a man was different than clinging to a surrogate mother, wasn't it? Shit, what difference did it make – holding Nancy Brill was a stupid idea. Gareaux would walk in – Fatso Gareaux, with her floppy-mop hair and Lestoil brain. One look at the two of them in a single bed and Gareaux would run off screaming, "the Lesies are coming, the Lesies are coming." All the loonies on the ward would rise to the occasion. No, the kid would have to do the best she could on her own.

Nancy didn't stir during the next bed-check. After Gareaux lumbered out, Maggie counted to one hundred, then got out of bed. "Okay, Nancy. Just keep your voice down."

Nancy flipped over and kicked back her bedclothes. "Down where?"

"I mean quiet – like a whisper."

The armchair was in the corner, a few feet beyond Nancy's bed. Maggie dragged the chair across the carpet. Marks in the carpet wouldn't be visible in the dark; tomorrow, those marks wouldn't matter.

"What are you doing?" whispered Nancy.

"Come help me lift this up."

"Lift what? Where?" Nancy came forward to help.

"The chair, silly. Onto my bed. Grab the frame at the bottom and lift when I say three. Easy now. One – two – three. No! Swing it over this way – down more to me."

"Are you going to let the Devils out?"

"Shh! Whisper, remember? Now hold on to the chair. I have to get the stone."

"What stone?"

"You'll see. Just balance the chair." Maggie climbed onto the bed, grabbed the chair's wooden arms and stepped up onto the seat. Cautiously, she straightened and raised her hands to the acoustic tiles. She pushed gently on one ceiling tile, then another, until she found the one that was loose. Raising the tile with one hand, she reached into the ceiling and pulled out a white envelope. She put the envelope between her teeth, then reached in again for the stone. Her fingers found natural indentations in the stone's rough convex surface. She brought it down and let the ceiling tile drop softly into place. Nancy helped her take down the chair.

"Show me," said Nancy.

Maggie insisted they first put the chair back in the corner. Then she showed Nancy the stone.

"I can't see it good," said Nancy. "Can I put on a light?"

"No. Just feel it. Here, give me your hand." Maggie took the thin fingers in her own and helped them trace over the surface of the geode. "Feel how rough the outside is – this stone was formed from volcanic ash, millions of years ago – even before God created people. Now let me turn it over so you can feel the cut surface... Here, give me your hand again."

"Oh, that's smooth — like glass."

"Yes, I ground and polished most of it. Put your finger in here – into the heart of the stone. Tomorrow you can hold it up to the light and watch the amethyst crystals glitter like hundreds of tiny windows, each one sealed perfectly by God. We can look back through those windows, but we can't go back with our bodies. Only our spirits can return with Jesus to God."

"Ouch!" Nancy pulled her hand away. "Something's sharp."

"I'm sorry. It's just a spur I haven't smoothed."

Nancy gripped her finger. "It hurts," she whined.

"Let me see," said Maggie.

"No. You hurt me."

"Suit yourself. Everything will be okay by morning." Maggie walked over to her bed and stuffed the stone and white envelope addressed to Daniels under her pillow.

"I'm bleeding," wailed Nancy.

"Nonsense."

"My finger's wet. It's blood. I hate blood." Her voice became shrill. "Blood gets the seeds red, like fire. The seeds are bleeding! They're rotted."

"Shh! Lower your voice." She walked toward Nancy. "I'll fix your finger. It'll be okay."

Nancy retreated to the far side of her bed. "No. Go back!" she shouted. "Your devils cut my finger. Help!"

Maggie stopped. The bed lay between them. "Be quiet! You'll ruin it, you little nut." She picked up Nancy's pillow. "Come into the bathroom, I'll put on the light."

"No, I don't want to see blood. The Devil is red like blood."

Maggie sensed the girl's arms waving her off.

"Go way, Devil! Don't punish me! I won't do it anymore."

"Be quiet, Nancy. The Devil wants me, not you."

"It's dripping," wailed Nancy. "Mommy! Help!"

Maggie rolled onto the bed and over it before Nancy could yell again. She pushed Nancy against the wall, tried to cover her head with the pillow to muffle her shouts. Nancy dove for the floor and

Maggie dropped on her, pillow extended to capture Nancy's head. Then the door slammed open against the wall, there was blinding light and Gareaux shouting, "Mr. Mills! Mr. Mills!" Maggie was startled. She relaxed her grip. Nancy squirmed out from under the pillow.

"She's cutting me open!" Nancy yelled. "I'm bleeding. My finger is dying."

Gareaux reached down to pull Maggie off.

Everything ruined, thought Maggie. Nothing matters anymore. "Get your hands off me," she yelled. "Leave me alone." She came up swinging and felt her fist sink into a fat stomach. Gareaux grunted and pivoted away; her elbow thudded into Maggie's eye. Maggie's head exploded with red pain and white stars, then strong black forearms grasped her from behind. Crying, cursing, she twisted and kicked. Gareaux grabbed Maggie's hair and yanked down. "Stop it right now," she yelled, "or I'll pull it out by the roots."

As they dragged her out toward a seclusion room, Maggie heard the frenzied voice of Nancy Brill: "She has devils inside her! They told her to cut me! Her name – her name is Legion!"

28

Seclusion

He felt a poke in the back, heard Lisa mumble, "Ray – the telephone." Then he heard it ring. And again. He rolled on his side, reached out to the night table and knocked the clock-radio to the floor. "Shit," he muttered, picking up the phone.

"Doctor Daniels?" A female voice, hospital tone.

"Uh-huh." He couldn't hold back a yawn.

"This is Donna Richards, from Palmer 3. Sorry to wake you. We've had to put Maggie Saxe in seclusion for assaulting another patient. She had her down on the floor and was trying to smother her with a pillow."

"What's that? Why?" He sat up and jammed his pillow between his back and the wall.

"Maggie won't tell us why. She's having a nutty – cursing and crying and pounding the seclusion room door. She refuses to take any meds — not even ice for her eye. She's really upset everyone on the ward."

"Her eye?"

"It was an accident. Mrs. Gareaux heard yelling, went in and tried to pull Maggie off Nancy, but Maggie punched her and Mr. Mills had to help restrain her. In the midst of it, Maggie got elbowed in the eye by Mrs. Gareaux. Her right eye's swollen, but there's no sign of bleeding in or around it. It really was an accident — Mr. Mills confirmed it."

Raymond tried to shake the fog from his head. "Maggie attacked Nancy Brill?" No, tell me no, he thought.

"Yes. Nancy's still raving about Maggie trying to cut her apart. She does have a small cut on a finger. We searched Maggie before we put her into seclusion – the only sharp thing on her was her temper. And there was nothing on the floor where they were fighting. Nancy probably got cut grabbing the metal frame of her bed."

"Do you know what started the fight?" He rubbed the back of his neck to awaken more brain cells.

"No. I haven't been able to get two coherent sentences from either of them."

Raymond felt his gut squeeze tight. He'd have to go in, calm everyone down, get the facts himself. He swung his legs over the bed to the carpet. With one hand, he started unbuttoning his pajama top.

Taylor was going to have another shit-fit, he thought. Even long distance from Washington, the Chairman had singed his ears: notifying the police was judged short-sighted; transferring Nancy to an adult unit without Taylor's personal approval was insubordinate. Never mind that there was no bed open on the adolescent unit and that Doctor White had agreed to the transfer. Taylor was in charge of the Brill case, hadn't he made that perfectly clear? There was no excuse for disobedience. Now Taylor would learn that Nancy was attacked on the adult unit. He'd be out to burn balls, not ears.

"Doctor Daniels? You still there?" asked the nurse.

"Yes. Did you give Nancy her PRN medication?" Raymond

tugged his pajama bottoms off, letting them fall to the floor. His eyes began to adjust to the dark. He found the clock-radio and set it back on the night table.

"The diazepam? I gave it to her twenty minutes ago – it hasn't done anything yet. Doctor Berents is the resident on call. He's in with her now."

Berents. A first year resident, less than three months into the program. Raymond headed to the closet for a pair of pants. "Tell Doctor Berents not to order any anti-psychotic meds. Her white blood cells nose-dived on the last one, and Doctor Taylor doesn't want her to have any other antipsychotics until her white count comes back up. Did Berents authorize seclusion for Saxe?"

"When we first called him. He hasn't seen her yet. He's seeing Nancy first."

"Tell him not to start up with Saxe. I'll drive in right away."

At the emergency entrance, two attendants were unloading a patient from an ambulance. The old man was clutching his chest, moaning through an oxygen mask. Raymond raced through the automatic doors, bypassed the bleary-eyed woman at the reception desk and headed for the elevator bank. He clenched and unclenched his hands as the elevator hummed its way up to the third floor. The corridor was dimly lit and seemed endless. The sound of his footsteps ricocheted off tall plaster walls and raced ahead of him, meeting no one. He passed an abandoned gurney; beyond it, the open door to a surgical ward from which came the beeps of cardiac monitors and a lung-wrenching spasm of coughs. The loneliness and pain of illness was much more palpable at night. What pains twisted Mary Margaret Saxe? What had provoked her to go off? He had no answers, only questions, frustration. He was like a blind man reaching out to someone who refuses to see.

As he unlocked the outer door to Palmer 3, he heard the pounding of hands against metal. Maggie Saxe was beating on the seclusion room door. Richards came to greet him with a roll of her eyes. "It's been like a zoo," she said.

Down the hall, Mr. Mills was filling an open doorway. "Knock it off, Arnold. Go to sleep!" His voice resonated up the hall.

"Where's Berents?" asked Raymond.

The nurse brushed strands of dirty blonde hair back from her forehead. The armpit of her blouse was a darker green than the rest. "He went back to bed. Nancy quieted down and I told him you would see Maggie. He wrote a note on Nancy's chart. He said you could call if you needed him."

"Has Saxe been banging like that since she was put in seclusion?"

"She alternates that with screaming curses at the top of her lungs. I was just down there to look in. She called me a few things I'd rather not repeat."

He offered the nurse a small smile. "I've been there, too. Don't take it personally. Can I borrow Mrs. Gareaux or another female while I'm down there with her?"

"Mrs. Gareaux is still in the E.R. She has pains in her abdomen and back from trying to pull Maggie off Nancy. She said Maggie punched her in the stomach. I doubt she'll come back to work tonight. If she files an injury claim, she may be out longer."

"It gets worse and worse. Any better idea since I spoke with you about what set Maggie off?"

"No. But I'll come down with you to find out."

"Thanks," said Raymond. He followed Richards down the hall to the seclusion suite, where she unlocked the door to the anteroom and stood aside to let him enter. Two gray doors were to his right, a folding chair stood propped against the wall to his left, and a curtained alcove with toilet and sink was straight ahead. The pounding on the gray door farthest from him reverberated throughout. "Maggie," he called. "It's Doctor Daniels."

Richards hung back out of sight, but Raymond peeped through the plexiglass window. Strands of long black hair streamed over Saxe's swollen, bruised eye and down her flushed and tear-stained face. Her body looked lost in a white paper johnny. Behind her, a plastic mattress lay on the floor; a coarse grey blanket was bunched up beside it.

Saxe stopped pounding but kicked the door with the sole of a bare foot. "What the fuck took you so long?"

"I was asleep," he said. "I got here as fast as I could."

"Okay. Let me out." She turned away but edged closer to the door.

Were her shoulders shaking from exertion, fatigue? Or was she trying to hide her tears? "We have to talk first."

"Go fuck a porcupine." Hair and paper rustled against the metal as she sank out of sight, to the floor.

"How's your eye?"

"I can't see it and I don't want you to."

He took a step back and turned toward Richards. "May take a while," he whispered. "I'll come get you if I need her unlocked. Just don't lock the outer door."

"Good luck," mouthed Richards. She closed the outer door carefully.

"You still there?" Maggie called.

He moved the chair close to her door and sat down. "Yup. What do you think about that?" He leaned forward and opened the slot in the door through which food was passed. He only saw black hair on white paper.

"At least you're not a fucking deserter. Got a cigarette?"

Still hurting about that boyfriend. Had a parent left her, too? "You know I don't smoke. Couldn't give you one in there, anyway. What happened tonight?"

"It was all your fault. You put crazy Nancy in my room. But I wasn't trying to hurt her – trust me on that."

How could he trust someone who held so much back? Even now, she offered no explanation. "Believe me, I want to – but isn't there something in the way?"

She coughed, then cleared her throat. "I suppose you mean the stone."

What stone? he thought. Don't show surprise! "Yes. And the pillow." Two birds for the price of one.

"I just wanted her quiet. She flipped out about the blood. I wasn't trying to smother her."

"And the stone?" Was it a gem? A rock?

"It was an accident. I was showing it to her. A sharp spur nicked her finger."

He shook his head. "So why didn't you tell the nurse? Or get her a Band-Aid?"

"I think your brain needs a tune-up. I didn't want them to take the stone."

"Oh." His tone was knowing, but what did he know? She'd hidden a rock or a gem with a spur on it in her room. Maggie tried to silence Nancy, who freaked out after an accidental cut? Even if it was all true, Taylor would blame him for putting Nancy in danger.

"Do you like it?" she asked tentatively.

"What? The stone?"

"What else do you think we're talking about?"

"To tell you the truth, I haven't seen it yet."

Silence.

"Did they tell you what was with the stone?" she asked.

He heard her suspicion loud and clear. Best to play it straight; she'd soon find out, anyway. "No, because we haven't found anything. Either you've hidden it very well, or someone has taken it."

"Crazy Nancy didn't tell how she got cut?"

"No. She kept your secret, if that's any comfort."

"Then I went and — " Her head banged against the metal door. "Shit! Raymond, you do lead a girl on."

He straightened in his chair. Raymond? She'd never called him by his first name before. Lead a girl on to what? No, she wouldn't tell. "We'll search the room, we'll find the stone."

Maggie uttered a curt laugh. "Look, you jerk, the stone is for you – payment for services rendered. Don't thank me. I figured you needed another rock for the collection in your head. Let me out of this tomb and I'll lead you right to it. You shouldn't have to hunt for your own present."

"I'm impressed by your generosity, but how do I know you're on the level? Tell me where it is – I'll bring it back here, along with whatever else is with it."

"No trust, Daniels. You have no fucking trust. The whatever is a note to you. Now that you mention it, I'd like it back still sealed. The circumstances have changed, what with me being – indisposed. I'd be very embarrassed if you read it now. Mushy girl stuff, if you know what I mean."

Raymond laughed. "Maggie, you may be many things, but mushy just doesn't fit."

"You'd be surprised," she said.

"I probably would. Tell you what – I'll bring the note back here sealed and we'll talk it over before I decide whether to read it. If I have to do a big search for it, you can be sure I'll read it."

"You're a bastard, you know that? I'll bet you're gloating that I'm in here, freezing my ass on the floor. Just like my mo – oh, go to Hell!"

"Your mother used to gloat? She locked you up?"

"You're a nosey s.o.b. What happened to you? Did the fairies jerk it every time you lied?"

He shook his head. "Come off it, Maggie. Why do you hide behind this sexual garbage?"

"Is that what I do?"

"Of course. Don't you recognize it?"

"You're not telling me anything I don't know. I doubt you ever will."

"You're so damn good at putting people down. It makes me wonder what they did to you." Locked up, raped – what else was she hiding?

"Wonder away. Go take your big nose and put it under my pillow – that's where you'll find the stone. If you read the note I left, you're fired as my shrink. I won't ever talk to you again. If you don't, you can come back and let me out – this is one coffin I don't want to be in."

"You sure act like you're running the show. I think I have more than the two alternatives you've allowed."

"You're lucky I gave you two."

"Doesn't feel that way to me." He stood up, folded the chair and put it back where she couldn't reach it. "You want that slot left open?"

"Yes. It's a breath of stale air."

"Can you keep from pounding on the door? Other patients do need to sleep."

"Go apologize to them. It's your fault. I never asked to be in here."

"Well, have patience. I'm just going to look under your pillow."
He did. Nothing was there.

29

One At A Time

This time he knew why he couldn't sleep, why his body couldn't relax in bed. He was under again on his tolls. Five dollars and thirty-five cents. Had to have been more than one mistake. Mistaking a five for a ten would have been stupid enough, but even that wouldn't account for the shortage. No, something freaky was going on. Mike had said the transaction tapes couldn't be wrong, but people could screw up anything if they wanted to. Was someone targeting him?

George pulled more of the blanket away from Denise. She murmured something and rolled closer without waking. He envied how soundly she slept. She just burrowed into her groove, folded up her limbs and went out like a light. Every night. No matter what happened. Did other women sleep through a fuck? Hardly better than fucking a corpse. So he had to lie awake thinking about where he might have been shorted five dollars and thirty-five cents. Short change people accidentally, they bitch and holler; give them too much, they don't say a word. So what if they were coming at him heavy today. He'd handled the busiest lane lots of times. It was probably the red Firebird that had thrown him off. For a minute there, when he noticed it back in the line, he saw Garbage Mouth coming again. One-handed Vinnie, head bashed in, reaching out to redeem his toll. More spells like that, he'd go mental. Or lose his job.

"Your third shortage in the last month," Mike had said. "That's not like you at all. What's happenin' out in the booth?" As if supervisors didn't listen through the intercom. As if they'd ever catch him saying something wrong.

"One transaction at a time," he told Mike. What could the supervisor make of that? Those were the little man's favorite words, his formula for living. One transaction at a time, one day at a time, one step at a time – Mike had even made one mistake at a time.

"Any problems at home, George?" Mistake number one. Things at home were none of Mike's business. Perhaps Mike thought the smile and soft-spoken "No" meant a happy home, a good marriage. If so, that was mistake number two. If not, his next question was.

"You wouldn't be comin' in hung over, or usin' anything, would ya?"

Who would say yes? If he came to work drunk or stoned, even if they found booze in his car, he could be fired on the spot. "I don't drink or use drugs," he'd told Mike. "I don't even smoke." First time his mother caught him, she'd whaled his ass with her brush. Second time, she'd burned his hands.

"No wonder you grew so big. You're a man without vices. Maybe it's the strain of holdin' down two jobs – throwin' you off in the booth, I mean."

Too many questions, Mike. Curiosity killed the crow – Cat! Curiosity killed the cat. Damn crows kept pecking at his brain... Maybe a cat would chase the crows from the yard. If he brought a cat home as a present for Denise, she'd probably like it. Hadn't she asked for a puppy a few months ago? Like it or not, she'd keep it if he told her to. Denise didn't have a mind of her own. Her mother owned it until he came along and planted that line of trees eight years ago. What good shape he was in that summer, working at the nursery every day – not picking up flab in a barrier booth or running meat through a saw. He'd been foolish enough to think that his hands could make things grow. Weed-pullers, hole-diggers, choppers, that's what they were. Even perennials died in his hands. That line of trees was the only exception. Hardy as Denise's old lady. She stood on the porch and watched him sweat – wanted to see he did it right, she said. Bull! She liked his bulging muscles, the bronze color of his skin, even the sweat dripping down his bare chest. Not like that wimp of a husband, with his little manicured hands. Owning two shoe stores did nothing for his muscles. Down on his knees before the ladies a lot. Got plenty of practice at home. Denise's mother ruled the roost: one wimp and a dumb little chick she'd hatched when she was only sixteen. The old bird thought he was a dumb one, too – easily led, quiet, an ox to be yoked and ridden. He gave her a few rides she'd never forget. He had the tapes to remind her. Made her willing to give him Denise and anything else he wanted.

Could the tapes at work be wrong? Played with, like the way he'd played with Denise's mother? Five thirty-five was such an odd number; maybe the number had some other meaning. What was the number on Garbage Mouth's license plate? No, Vinnie was dead and buried. If anyone was coming at him, it wasn't from the grave like in a monster flick; it had to do with work, that's all. Maybe Mike was trying to get him transferred back to a ticket booth. Maybe there were suck-ups who wanted to bid on a barrier booth job to collect the tolls. Well, they'd regret trying to take his job away from him. He'd thought that they'd learned not to mess with him. Until Mike had brought him up short.

"You gotta do it without messin' up again, George. I might have to move you, next time. Just be more careful — take one transaction at a time."

That's when he went red hot and slammed Mike's glasses right into his eyes. Mike screamed and fell backward, his face a bloody mess. He reached down and dragged Mike up by his neck, squeezed hard with both hands and watched him gasp and squirm like a fish. He only let go of the little man when there was no life left in him.

And then he saw Mike walking away.

He'd tell Daniels about that spell – toned down, of course, like he'd told him last week about the other two. "Fantasies," Daniels called them. Not a bad word. Except they were more vivid than life. How could he feel alive in a fantasy, so dead at other times? How could he see, hear and touch what never happened? Would he snap back and find that it had? Maybe there was another world where these murders really took place. Perhaps the future was giving a sign. Should he ask Daniels whether such things were possible? No it was best to crow slow. Go! Not crow. Damn them. He had to go slow.

30

What I Have

"There wasn't anything under your pillow, Maggie." The legs of the chair scraped against the vinyl tiles as Raymond dragged it back to her seclusion room door. Through the slot, he saw only coarse grey wool. She'd wrapped herself in the blanket. He stood on his toes to look down through the Plexiglas window. She'd moved the mattress in front of the door. One hell of an observation room, he thought. Sitting against the door, she wasn't visible. And her silence – surprise? satisfaction? "No stone, no note, not even a hair," he said.

"Are you telling me the truth?"

"Yes. Will you do the same for me?"

"I told you the truth." Her tone was impatient. "They were under my pillow when I was dragged out of there. Crazy Nancy must have ripped them off."

Had she? He sat down, noticed the finger marks on the green door. It really needed a scrubbing. "I thought you'd say that, so I woke Nancy up and asked her."

"What did she say?"

Gibberish, he thought. Seven devils cutting off her finger. "Nothing about a stone or a note."

"That little nut." She sounded relieved, not angry.

Was she pleased that Nancy had taken the stone? No, not the stone – the note. That's what had bothered her. Not mushy romantic, but even more revealing – probably a suicide note that said too much. That's why she'd threatened him, why she now felt relieved. "If Nancy took them, she hid them cleverly," he said. "We did a quick search of the room."

"Let me out. I'll get them back and give you the stone."

Without violence if Nancy refused to give them up? "You know where she's hidden them. Tell me, and I'll get them."

"No! You have to let me out first. Otherwise you have nothing."

Incredible, he thought. The less she had, the more omnipotent she sounded. She'd been that way from their very first meeting. "Uh-uh, sorry. As a young woman I knew once said to me, 'I don't *have* to do anything'."

She hit the metal door. He jumped in his chair. "Fuck you, Doctor Jekyll. Do you have a tape recorder up your ass? Or do you just remember every word I say?"

"Neither. I wouldn't tape our talks without your permission. And the profanity doesn't impress – it just makes you sound cheap."

"I don't give a flying fuck."

"And I don't think that you are." No, not cheap, he thought. She's angry, tantalizing, infuriating – and hurting so much. "Even if I'm wrong, why advertise a sleazy you?"

"Wake up, shrink-brain, the world loves sleaze. Who's sleeping with whom gets around faster than the sperm. Even priests get hard-ons in the confessional. And don't tell me you shrinks don't lick your chops as you say 'tell me more about that'."

He rubbed his fingers across his face, felt reassured that his lips were dry. "I don't salivate at other people's pain. Not even at their sexual intimacies. If they had it so great, they wouldn't be talking to me in the first place. Can it be that you're worried I might get too close? Maybe you test me – test most men you meet – test by playing the sleaze."

Silence.

"What do you think?" he finally asked.

"I think I'm tired of all this horseshit. Let me out and you can go home."

He exhaled loud enough for her to hear. "Okay, no horseshit. I'd be a fool to let you out now. I believe you weren't trying to kill Nancy – or even hurt her. God knows why, but I do. But if she has taken the stone and the note, how do I know what you'll do to get them back? She may have stashed them in a different place than the one you used."

"I won't hurt her."

Probably not, but the risk's too great, he thought. "It's the middle of the night. Let's all get some sleep and talk about it again in the morning."

"You have to get me out of this cell – I'll go crazy in here." Fear had displaced her demanding tone.

"No you won't. It's just four walls and a locked door. Lots of security so no one gets hurt."

"I can't stand being locked up." She sounded sincere. "I get the horrors, you know what I mean? That's how I started reading the Bible – to hold a few decent thoughts in my mind, to keep the crazy ones from taking over."

His head inched upward, his sleepiness vanished. "You mean when your mother locked you up?"

"Yes, in the – no – oh, hell, what difference does it make? In the cellar. I had four walls there, too. Stone walls and one forty watt bulb. She took out the others. Said she was conserving electricity. And there were rats, so she put rat poison in the corners. Believe me, I was tempted; except I thought she wanted me to, so I wouldn't. Thank God she couldn't refuse me the Bible; that would've made her feel guilty. But it was okay to go to Bingo, or to leave me with – you ever feel terribly guilty, Raymond?"

"Yes." He put his hand over his mouth, remembering the argument with his father, his refusal to go work with him in the pharmacy because of a chess tournament; and coming home to find the police there, Sarah and Ethan in tears, his father dead in his store. That was the last time he'd played chess. What had Maggie said about Bingo? "Your mother left you with…?"

"With the horrors. I'll go crazy in here."

He shook his head. "It's not the craziness that haunts you – it's memories and painful feelings coming back; they're getting to you now because your escape routes are blocked. You need to deal with them, remember things and make some peace with them." So do I, he thought. "Otherwise there's no lasting escape, no real freedom at all. You're a prisoner, shackled to the past, condemned to relive it."

"It's damned easy to be glib when you're outside the cell, you know that? Keep your chin up as you suffer, my dear; it's good for your soul – your psyche – your backbone, your character. I'm fed up with you spineless mouths, you armchair assholes." She smacked the door. "Go away and let me die."

He stood up, put one foot on the chair, used a handkerchief to wipe his brow. "You're right and you're wrong. Right that I'm too glib about other people's suffering – wrong because we all have our own. You think you're the only one in a cell? Every one of us is in some

God-damned cell, wanting to touch each other without reaching out, fearfully guarding that little slot in the door."

"Do me a favor, Daniels. Shove the sentimentality up your slot. You have the keys, I don't."

"Don't you?"

"Oh, go to Hell. You know what I mean."

He pocketed his handkerchief. "Yes. You feel powerless, the helpless and abandoned little girl, victimized, right? All too ready to die. It doesn't have to be that way. Not anymore. You do have the keys to that."

"Don't tell me what I have!" she shouted. "I know what I have." The blanket lifted from the slot, brushed the door as she rose. "I have no hope and not enough faith. I have a Church-going family that excels in sin. I have a heart full of hatred, a belly full of guilt – and nightmares that drive me insane."

Raymond looked through the Plexiglas. Framed by a tangle of black hair, she stared back at him. Her right eye was swollen and tears slid down her cheeks, bypassing a reddened nose.

"Yes, go ahead and look at your guinea pig, your freak in a cage." Her tone was bitter and defiant. "I have nowhere to hide — no one to love except one tired old Greek that cares. And here I have you – you stupid, maudlin son-of-a-bitch – keeping me locked in this room. Well, you're making a big mistake if you leave me in here. Don't leave me, Daniels. Don't leave me alone."

31

Don't Tell Me You Understand

Maggie's chest was heaving, she couldn't catch her breath. She sank down on the mattress and sobbed. Mother of God, it hurt so much, so deep in her throat, her chest. Why wouldn't he free her? She would go crazy in here.

"Damn it! Did you hear what I said?" Daniels' voice reached through the slot, but it was impossible to answer, barely possible to breathe. "I said I'd stay with you until it's light. Then I'll get someone else to stay."

Pity. That's what it was – pity for the quivering freak. Stop these whimpers and tears, these animal noises – right now! If only she could control her voice, she'd tell him what to do with his pity.

"Will you let one of the surgical residents look at your eye?" he asked.

She slipped her hand through the slot and raised her middle finger. Fuck what he thought about her.

"How about some ice? Will you accept an icepack for your eye?"

She could barely see out of that eye. It felt like a knife was stabbing it again and again. But even ice could have strings attached. Did he want her grateful, subservient, his plaything in bed?

She used a corner of the blanket to wipe her nose. Uggh, she needed tissues. Oh hell, there probably wasn't much harm in accepting an icepack.

"Okay, an icepack. Some tissues, too." How meek she sounded. Dear God, lend me the strength not to give in.

"I'll be right back," said Daniels.

She heard him walk to the outer door, heard the lock snap home. Alone, always alone. Ever since her sister ran off with Emilio. That fucker killed Tricia when he first put a needle in her vein. So what if he wasn't around for the final speedball? That was no suicide, that was murder. Oh, Tricia – no more tears, now. No more anything — what's the use? Where the hell was Daniels?

Maggie got up, readjusted the blanket around her shoulders, stepped back onto the mattress and sat. "No worry so much," she said, imitating Petro. Daniels had said he'd be right back, that he'd stay until dawn. He hadn't lied to her yet. Probably didn't know her well enough. Intimacy and deceit went to bed together; sure, and she always got fucked by both. Daniels would stay because he wanted the stone and her note. Stupid to have included her parents' address. No, she was stupid for failing to kill herself. Wanda and F. Dexter deserved proof that they fucked up both daughters; they deserved to feel some of the pain.

Where was he with those tissues? She tore a swatch from the bottom of her paper gown and blew her nose. Would Daniels let her out tomorrow? Petro was coming on Sunday. Couldn't let him see her like this. Explaining her eye would be bad enough. Damn it! She never asked to be Petro's substitute daughter. What was she, a lightning rod for pain? She was the one who should have died; Tricia was much kinder, more loving. More of a mother than Wanda ever was, that was for sure. Damn it, Tricia, you didn't mean to do it – did you?

Even Sister Gemma couldn't convince her it was accidental, couldn't explain why God chose Tricia instead. "We're not always capable of understanding God's will," Gemma had said. "That's what faith is about." Drowning in a sea of grief, she'd clung to Gemma's frail body and strong faith. Had Gemma lived a few more years, there might have been a different Mary Saxe emerging from the whirlpool of adolescence.

Maggie heard the key turn the lock, then whispers in the anteroom. Who the hell did Daniels bring? To see her in tears, in a toilet paper gown? "I'm not up for company, Doctor Frankenstein. Send the creature back to the lab."

"It's only Miss Richards," said Daniels. "I'd like to come in and take a look at your eye."

Richards! That bitch had ordered her stripped and thrown in this cell. "My, Miss Richards, your voice has changed. Did Doctor Frankenstein screw you up?"

"Maggie, that's very inappropriate," Richards said.

"Throwing me in here was very inappropriate. I wasn't trying to hurt Nancy."

"I'm coming in," said Daniels as he unlocked the door.

"Wait! First pass me those tissues." Yes, that sounded stronger, better. Let them wait for her.

"I brought you a washcloth, too – although it's probably not very warm by now." He offered the washcloth through the slot.

"Thank you." Sitting on the mattress, she took the warm cloth, then the tissues, and cleaned her face. Thoughtful of him to bring a washcloth – but he was after something. Everyone wanted something. The warmth of the cloth evaporated much too fast.

"Coming in." Daniels opened the door outward and stood on the threshold, his forward progress blocked by the mattress upon which she still sat. He knelt on the mattress and offered her an icepack. His eyes were bloodshot; he hadn't shaved.

She saw concern, fatigue, perhaps sadness in his face. Not a trace of pity. She took the icepack and started to raise it to her eye, but he touched her wrist softly to stop her.

"Let me examine your eye," he said. "I'll be as gentle as I can."

"You do that." Damn. Her sarcasm sounded like acquiescence. She felt his fingertips on her cheek, her nose, the rim of bone above her eye. His touch was softer than John's.

"I want to try to feel your cheekbone. It will hurt when I press."

"Then don't press."

"An x-ray would be better. It wouldn't hurt."

"Tell that to my unborn child."

His hand pulled back. "Are you pregnant? Didn't they test you?"

"Does that make me untouchable?"

"No, of course not." His hand hovered over her cheek. "But are you? Pregnant, I mean."

She had him waiting, wondering, that felt good. And that bitch was standing outside, lapping up every word. "Better press carefully, Raymond."

Pain flashed to her ear, into her eye. She grit her teeth and pulled back. Endure it! Show him you can, you're strong.

"I'm sorry," he said. "One more time. Try not to clamp your teeth. It tightens your facial muscles." He offered her his other hand. "When it hurts, squeeze my fingers, hard as you can."

His offer felt like an itch she dared not scratch. "I might hurt you. I'll squeeze the icepack."

"Do it now," he said, resuming his examination. She winced but managed not to grit her teeth or pull back. The icepack burned her hand.

"Okay, you can relax. There's no obvious fracture, but we'll still need an X-ray to be sure." He reached into his pocket, produced an ophthalmoscope and turned on the tiny light. "I'm going to lift your eyelid so I can see your pupil. Look straight ahead at the wall behind me."

One part of her stayed with him and followed commands to look this way and that. Another Mary was years away, staring at her bedroom wall. "I love you, Mary, remember that." Big lips, a scratchy cheek, the ritual kiss good-night. As if what went before could be put to rest, as if love could extirpate pain. Then her father was getting out of her bed, padding off to his own, leaving her to study the wall.

Suddenly he had his cheek next to hers, only the black head of his instrument between them. "Get a – " she uttered, choking off the rest as she spun away. Daniels, not Fucking Dexter. Now, not then. For God's sake, don't scream.

"What's the matter? Did I hurt you?"

All she could do was cry. She shielded her face with her hands.

"Talk to me, Maggie. Sharing's better than suffering alone."

"Go away!" This wasn't how it was supposed to be. His nearness was driving her insane.

"Alright." She heard him click the instrument off, rise to his feet. "You won't forget the icepack, will you? I only got a quick look inside. Okay if I ask an ophthalmologist to examine it later?"

She nodded. He was leaving. She feared to ask.

"I'll be right outside the door."

Jesus, Mary and Joseph, could he read her thoughts? The tissues, where were the tissues?

She heard Richards leave, heard Daniels reclaim his folding chair. After that, she didn't hear anything. She picked up the icepack and put it to her eye. The paper gown rustled as she moved. Was he falling asleep? Why didn't he say something? Anything.

"I'm not pregnant," she said.

"Is that good or bad?"

"Bad for me, good for the baby."

"Bad for you? You mean you haven't used any contraceptives?"

"No, I've been a fucking nun. Idiot. I've used the pill."

"I heard about that 'nun' comment. I understand that the women in the group were very upset."

"I don't care what you heard, that's not what I said." She brushed a cold drop of water from her cheek. "They were acting like a bunch of prissies, talking about how they loved their jobs and their husbands and weren't their kids such angels. You'd think they were in a beauty salon, not the nut house. And I didn't say anything until they jumped on my case for closing my eyes." She heightened her voice to mock their squawking. "'Withdrawing from the group, withdrawing from the group!' Parrots – that's what they were. Six parrots performing for a monkey with a Ph.D. Too bad I didn't think of that, then. Anyway, I didn't get nasty. All I said was, 'I feel like a whore in a room full of nuns'."

"Is that all?"

"Well, after I said that, they all had to prove how bad they were, how their problems were worse than mine. This one beats her kid, that one is a dominatrix with her husband, even old Myrna was fucking her janitor. It was real group puke – no one was clean. So as we were all getting up to leave, I felt I had to admit I'd been wrong, so I told them 'I'm sorry. I was very wrong. I'm a nun in a room full of whores'."

"That must have gone over real big."

"If looks could kill, my problems would have been over." Her smile ended with a wince.

"Either way, nun or whore, you're the one who stands out from the group – is that it?"

She waved off the idea. "No, that's not it. They're a bunch of hypocrites. They deserved to be dragged out of the closet. Anyway, it served them right for getting on my case."

"I'm on your case."

"That's your problem – at least I think so. How did you happen to get my case?" Did John arrange it? she wondered.

"Why is that important?"

Because John cared? Because he wanted to shut her up? "Just believe that it is."

"I was assigned your case by the Chairman of the Department."

She kicked the mattress. "Why?"

"I thought it was because I met you at City Hospital. Do you have another idea?"

Her lips tightened. Daniels didn't know. He was just being used. "Are you sorry you got me?" She heard the scrape of his chair.

"Only on those few occasions you do something particularly – outlandish."

She laughed.

"And you?" he asked. "How do you feel about having drawn me?"

Better, now, she thought. "I'm just sorry you'll feel bad when I die. You shouldn't. It's not your fault."

She heard him laugh. What was so damn funny? "No, I'm very serious," she said.

"I know. That's — I appreciate your concern. But why are you so intent on killing yourself? You'd have a lot of years in which you could change things, enjoy some of the good things life offers."

"I'm very fucked up, Raymond. There's no way to unfuck me. Maybe that's gross, but it's the truth."

"Fucked up by whom?"

"Mostly myself. Which is why I have to die."

"You told me you don't *have* to do anything. And you said 'mostly.' Who else?"

"People. Everyone."

"Including your parents?"

What should she say? He'd tell her it was a fantasy. Evil thoughts and lies. The same as Wanda and Sister Alfreda. No, Daniels would believe her — he'd know it was true. But then he'd use it, throw it back in her face like a prick demanding more, until she had to spit out the truth or gag on lies. Mother of God, get me out of this room!

"Including your parents?" he asked again.

He knew. He was playing with her. Waiting for her to crack wide open, to give him what he wanted, like any other man. Was there another way out of here?

"Especially my parents."

She heard him twist in his chair. "It was incest that hurt you; that's what it was, wasn't it?"

She managed a laugh, then used her most patronizing tone. "No, dear Raymond. Incest didn't hurt me. Incest is just a word. To be accurate, my father hurt me. To be precise, he stuck his great big prick up my cunt. That's what hurt me." Enough! She'd said enough. "Maybe it hurt because I was only eight the first time he did it. Before that, finger-fucking did fine." She turned away. "Of course, there were times he stuffed his cock in my mouth so I could give him head.

228

He said that proved I loved him. F. Dexter needed frequent proof." Her body shook, her eye throbbed, her mouth kept going — she couldn't stop any of it. "He said he was teaching me what I'd need to know as a woman. And when I was older and wouldn't give in so easily, he'd knock me down and stuff a coke bottle or even a lightbulb into me so I'd stop struggling and beg him not to break it, to take it out." She punched her thigh. "For which there was a price, always a price. Good women were those who served their men in and out of bed. Honoring your father meant doing whatever he asked, without question. And I believed it – for a while, I believed all his lies."

"I understand," Raymond said.

"Understand?" She struggled up and turned to the door. "What the fuck do you understand? You're not in my skin. You weren't there. You never went through it. Did you?"

"No."

She smacked the door. The metal resounded. "Then don't tell me you understand! Go suck your father's cock – maybe then you'll understand something. Go get raped once a week for seven years." She spun away and kicked wildly at the mattress. "Live with the fucker every day of the week and try to believe he loves you. Understand?" she shouted. "Don't tell me you understand. Go tell your mother and have her smack you across the face for lying, have her lock you in the basement until you confess you lied. Then wait every night for your father to climb into your bed, wondering what he'll do because you told that dirty secret that she fucking knew anyway." The room was whirling about her. "Feel that you're a body spawned by his scum, a receptacle for his waste, an abomination punished by God – then you straight-laced son-of-a-bitch, then you'll really understand."

Done! Finished! She collapsed onto the mattress. Her eye throbbed, the bitter taste lingered. Why was he silent? What was he thinking? Mother of God, did that matter so much?

32

One Must Choose

"What did you say to her?" Bergstrom asked. He took another sip from his cup of tea. Rain pit-patted against the office window behind him.

Raymond leaned back in the rocker and rubbed his tired eyes. It had been a long and painful day. "I told her that I didn't know what to say. I mean, what can you say when someone shares such torment – how awful? I'm sorry? You have every right to hate your father?" Damn, he sounded so defensive. Fatigue – it was fatigue. Up all last night, then Taylor landing on him today. Surely Bergstrom knew – he had to.

"Sometimes there isn't anything that feels right to say." Bergstrom replaced the cup and saucer on his desk blotter, next to the geode. His swivel chair squeaked as he turned back. "In those cases, silence is often best."

"I think Maggie would have taken silence as a rejection."

"Even though you stayed with her until dawn?"

"She was locked in that room. I thought she needed to hear my voice. Especially with the door between us."

"She needed that door between you," said Bergstrom. "Perhaps it offered safety for you as well."

Raymond's lips turned down at the suggestion. "Sure, I wanted to comfort her, but that's not the main reason I stayed. She insisted that words without action were empty; what she needed from me was to let her out of that room. I understood that her 'let me out' referred to the past as well as the present, to her psyche as well as her body. But letting her out would have smacked of a trade — or pity, I suppose. Yet nothing had been resolved." He gestured at the rock on Bergstrom's desk. Half of a large orange in size and shape, its rough, gray surface hid a concavity of dazzling purple, violet and blue crystals. "We didn't have the stone, then; Nancy was still at risk. Even as a symbolic act, letting Maggie out didn't make sense. I can't open some magic door to free her of her agony — she has to work her way out."

"True," said Bergstrom. "Yet — "

"No! If I walked away from that cell, she'd have viewed me as a bastard who didn't care. I would've been just like her father, her mother — maybe the worst of both. She felt trapped in that cell, but she turned it around — turned the passive role into the active one, so I ended up feeling trapped, too."

"An unenviable position. I see why you stayed." Bergstrom reached for his tea.

"More enviable than the one I'm in with Doctor Taylor." Raymond rocked forward in his chair. "Did he tell you he removed me from Nancy Brill's case this morning?"

"Yes." Bergstrom took a sip of tea, then put down his cup. "I'm sorry I wasn't available when you called."

"Would you have advised me not to call the police?" he challenged.

"If I understand the situation correctly, you were aware of the political ramifications of calling the police, yet you had reason to believe that Nancy might've left the building?"

"Yes." Raymond's finger drew a small circle on the arm of his chair. Someone had scratched a groove there.

"Then I probably would have told you that one must choose between the practice of medicine and the practice of politics – and accept the consequences, of course." Bergstrom opened his desk drawer and extracted a paper clip.

"That's all you would have said?"

"No. I would have asked you to consider who bore the greatest responsibility for that child at that time?"

"Who did or who should have? Senator Brill wouldn't have let me call the police. That was clear when he yelled – when I spoke with him afterwards."

The professor stopped straightening the paper clip and looked up. "How could he have stopped you? Don't question only the validity of what you did; question the way you did it."

Was Bergstrom right? "But if I'd called Senator Brill first and then didn't do what he said, you probably would've had to scrape me off Doctor Taylor's shoe. He would have fired me from the residency program."

"Perhaps." Bergstrom started uncurling the clip again. "It's probably impossible to be both a good doctor and a good politician."

"You ever share that observation with Doctor Taylor?"

Bergstrom's smile was fleeting. "On a number of occasions. Please don't interpret my remarks as a lack of support. Neither our laws nor common sense allow parents the right to physically harm their children. But what is the price of allowing deviousness into any helping relationship?"

He met Bergstrom's gaze squarely. "I would have paid a higher price for doing it the other way. Nancy might have paid a higher price, too."

"No! Deviousness protects the deceiver. All the rest is rationalization." Bergstrom pointed the straightened paper clip at him. "Don't ever forget that, Raymond." The professor dropped the piece of wire into the ashtray on his desk. "And I think you're misreading Doctor Taylor's — irascibility. He's been under a lot of pressure in the past few years. Money for research and training has been drying up because of the war, and everything we do costs more. But I don't believe Doctor Taylor would have dismissed you from the program for trying to protect Nancy Brill. From the case, yes – that was politically expedient. Not from the program."

"Well, I can't say I like being a political casualty – or that Doctor Taylor did anything to separate the politics from the reality."

Bergstrom picked up the geode. "Politics is a large chunk of his reality. Harrison's been building and protecting this department for more than twenty years. Bergstrom pointed hand and rock toward the door. "Where do you think it all comes from? I've had the joy of doing my work because Harrison's fought the political battles. I don't think recognizing that has made me blind or docile. I would have fought to keep you in the program."

Raymond felt a lump in his throat. "Thank you," he said. How different Bergstrom was from his uncle, always the apologist for others, never drawing a line he'd defend. And his real father – dying in order to defend what? The drugs in his pharmacy? There had to be a middle ground, there had to be.

"Who found this?" asked Bergstrom, holding the geode up for inspection. The central cavity looked like a laughing mouth – teeth and gums of sparkling amethyst crystals, surrounded by gray and white lined lips.

"Gail Eggers. One of the aides remarked on the dirt under Nancy Brill's fingernails, and Gail thought about the flower pots – the window boxes – in the dayroom. Gail washed the dirt off."

"I see. And the note that Ms. Saxe mentioned?"

"It wasn't there. Nancy must have hidden that elsewhere."

"Have you told Ms. Saxe you have this?"

"A couple of hours ago. She didn't seem surprised. I suppose she expected us to find it sooner or later. All she said was, 'Now that you have it, you can keep it and use it. It was a present for you, anyway.'"

"Use it? How?"

"Paperweight, I guess. I didn't ask her. She'd have said something profane."

Bergstrom offered a small smile. "You should've asked – tried to get some idea of what expectations and fantasies accompanied the gift. No gift comes free and clear."

"I think she intended to cut herself with it. There's a sharp spur on it. I don't know why she chose the stone rather than something else that might be more effective. I'll ask her about that and her expectations. Meanwhile, I let her out of the seclusion room and put her on room confinement and suicide precautions with five minute checks – until we've gotten her through her birthday."

"It's her birthday?"

"Tomorrow, September twenty-third. She'll be twenty-one. They're even giving her a little party on the ward."

"On room confinement?"

"The plan is for her to come out for candles and cake after lunch. We have enough staff on that shift to supervise her closely."

"Are you concerned she might cause trouble?"

"Only about how she and Nancy Brill will interact. I know

Nancy's not my patient anymore, but still I vetoed Maggie's choice of birthday cake."

Bergstrom's brows converged. "Because?"

"It might set Nancy off. Maggie asked for devil's food."

33

He's Your Saint, Too

Maggie had waited for the right opportunity for two days. It came when a new patient went berserk as a nurse and an aide tried to search him. Every staff member on the unit ran to help, leaving Maggie and Nancy in the doorways of their respective rooms.

Maggie ran down to Nancy's room and took her by the arm. Although a head taller and much stronger than Nancy, she was careful that her grip not cause pain. "I need to talk to you," she whispered. "Come."

Nancy's eyes bulged, her jaw quivered. "I don't want to," she said, but she offered only token resistance as Maggie pulled and jostled her into the ladies' room.

"Don't hurt me. Let go!" She pawed at Maggie's hand.

Maggie released her grip but leaned back against the door. "I won't if you give me the note you stole. Letters are private, don't you know that?"

"I didn't mean to." Looking down at the white tile floor, Nancy massaged the sleeve of her blouse. "The Devil made me do it."

"Bullshit. I asked the Devil and he said it was your idea."

"He's lying. The Devil always lies."

"He's not the only one." Maggie leaned forward. "Look at me! I said look at me!" She waited until Nancy complied. "I want my note. It's bad enough they found the stone."

"I'm sorry. I didn't mean to. I hid it for you, too, true."

"I'll bet you did. Where's the note?"

"I tore it up and flushed-gushed it down there." Nancy pointed to a stall.

Better than staff finding it, thought Maggie. "You had no right to destroy it. That was *my* note."

Nancy examined her finger. "You made the stone cut me. You put the pillow on my face."

"I didn't mean for you to get cut. I'm really sorry, but it was an accident. The pillow was to keep them from hearing you scream. I wasn't going to hurt you."

"Yes you were. You're bad. Your name is Legion."

And yours is Nutcase, thought Maggie. She sighed. It wasn't Nancy's fault that she was sick. Why make it any harder for her. "I swear I wasn't trying to hurt you. I may be bad, but I don't hurt young girls." That was F. Dexter's specialty. "I was one, once. I know what it's like to be hurt. I wouldn't do that to you."

"You swear?"

"Cross my heart – " She made the gesture. " – and hope to die."

"I hope to die, too."

Mother of God. "Why?" she murmured.

Nancy's jaw trembled. Her eyes welled with tears. "Because I'm sick and I'll never get better."

Maggie tried to swallow the lump in her throat. "Lots of people are sick worse than you, and they don't try to kill themselves. And what makes you think you can't get better?"

"The Devil told me, scolded me."

"But the Devil lies. You told me yourself."

Nancy looked puzzled. "But what if he's telling the truth with proof?"

"Then I wouldn't trust that he's really the Devil. I think you have to wait and see. Maybe the doctors can help you get better. And you can help yourself. Maybe you ought to pray to Jesus instead of listening to the Devil."

"Will Jesus make me better?"

Maggie shrugged. "I don't really know. I can only tell you that he's helped me."

"Then why do *you* hope to die?"

A torrent of reasons flooded her mind. "Because I've – because I'll be better off with Jesus than I would be anywhere else."

"Will you be with Jesus after you die and cry?"

"If God forgives me." The muscles of her face tightened; her voice dropped to a whisper. "I've sinned very badly."

Nancy peered wide-eyed into Maggie's face. "Did the Devil make you? My mother says the Devil always makes you do bad things."

"I don't think it matters who makes you."

"It does! My father says he doesn't believe in the Devil. He's Senator Joe Brill and he makes laws that make people do things." Nancy scrunched up her face. "But I think he lies, too. I've heard him say the Devil is in the details."

"Your father's a Senator?"

Nancy nodded. "Mommy said he couldn't keep a regular job."

The commotion outside had stilled. Maggie glanced at the door. "We better get out there before they think we've taken off."

"Taken off what?"

"Run away."

"Oh. Will you talk to me again? I don't like the old lady they put me with."

"Sure. And I'll pray for you."

"To Jesus?"

"To God, to Jesus, the Holy Virgin, and Saint Jude."

"Who's Saint Jude? Does he know Valerie Murphy?"

"He's the Saint who cares for people with – serious sickness."

"Then he's my Saint, too?"

"Yes, he's your Saint, too. Let's go out now."

Nancy smiled. "I never had a Saint before. Wait until I tell Mommy…"

34

Birding A Window

Listening for sounds other than the chirping of crickets, George stood behind the privacy hedge that bordered the driveway of his supervisor's home. How long after the lights went out would it take Mike and his family to settle into sleep? he wondered. No need for them to die tonight. But even a crow could have a horrible death. George smiled in the dark. Oh, how that grubsucker had flapped. Back and forth along the fence, no longer knowing which way was up. No birdbrain instinct to survive could overcome his poison. This last batch had hit the jackpot. His mother's Harpies would soon be dead meat. He'd taken that first dead crow out to her and dropped it right on her. She couldn't ignore that. Would she call them off before he had to kill more?

"Horrible," Denise had said. Well, hadn't Denise insisted on watching that crow die? Like those monster movies she freaked out on. Except this time it didn't disappear. Even after it'd fallen, that black mother had fought in the grass. "Horrible," he'd agreed. Even hugged her. Well, he'd felt — really felt — great. Because of that crow. Spasm after spasm. Maybe there was a God, after all — collecting tolls. Mike might have to pay at both of their booths.

Leaves rustled. A breeze tickled the back of George's neck. He tugged his cap down and looked behind him. One and two family homes, a few with porch lights on, no people — cars parked in driveways, a few on the tree-lined street. No, no crows. Too bad Mike had parked in his garage...Doesn't matter. George patted the bulge behind the zipper of his leather jacket. One bagged bird to collect another.

He brought his wristwatch close to his eyes. Twelve-twenty. Almost forty minutes since the upstairs light went out. Did Mike and his wife sleep on the second floor? If only he'd had a day or two more to look around. But Mike wouldn't give him more time. Mike was going to stick him in a ticket booth, where he was supposed to smile at the grubsuckers and hand out tickets all day. Not touch anyone, anymore. No way Mike was going to punish him like that. So when his objections went nowhere, he'd said "okay" as if he accepted Mike's decision and asked him about a dog.

"By the way, I'm thinking of getting my little girl a puppy for her birthday, Mike. You know how to housebreak a pup?" No, bowel-bound Mike, the big expert on all the political shit and paperwork of the Turnpike Authority, hadn't known diddly about dogs. The question that couldn't be asked was whether Mike had his house and garage wired for an alarm.

George touched the wire cutter in the back pocket of his jeans, then the penlight clipped to his belt. His fingers followed the belt around to where he'd taped the icepick and glasscutter. Gloves in one pocket, suction cup in another — yes, everything ready to go. He put on his gloves.

His sneakers made no sound on the driveway blacktop. The garage was about twenty feet from the back corner of the house. An overhead door, a window on each side. Four, five running steps from the garage to the back porch — no, Mike wouldn't come out in the dark. Not alone. He'd put on the porch light, but it wouldn't reach around the far side of the garage, so that was the window to go in.

Locked! No problem. He licked the suction cup and affixed it to the windowpane, an inch above the lock. Taking the glasscutter from his belt, he etched a circle around the rubber, then retraced the groove with more pressure. He jerked the cup toward him and the glass circle came away. No alarm yet, but the real test would come in opening the window. He pocketed his tools and lay the circle of glass down on the ground, ready to run at the first shriek of an alarm. With one finger, he reached through the hole and pushed back the lock. The sash rose easily. He brushed splinters of glass from the sill, reached inside with the penlight and clicked it on, aimed at the floor. Cement. Two bags of fertilizer. Mike's Chevy. Easy! Just avoid the spreader against the wall. He clicked off the light and hoisted himself inside. His nose scrunched up at the odor of turpentine.

He removed the plastic bag from his jacket and extracted the dead jay. Too bad — Mike deserved a crow. Well, more crows would die if Ma kept sending them. Leaving the jay on a bag of fertilizer, his jacket on the fender of the car, George lay down on his back and squirmed underneath the chassis. He could barely see the lower control arm extending from the ball joint. He clicked the penlight on. Upper control arm, caliper — yes, the brake hose. With the icepick, he gouged a small hole in the rubber. Perfect! Normal air pressure would hold most of the fluid in — until Mike stepped on the brake. Each time he braked, he'd force fluid out. Would he make it as far as the Turnpike? One way or another, Mike had to be out for a while. Maybe forever.

George put the jaws of the wire cutter around the emergency brake cable. Easy now — not all the way — better to have the Chevy's momentum snap it. He applied pressure gradually, then checked the depth of his cut with the light. After three repetitions, he was satisfied.

He put on his jacket, returned to the window and listened. Crickets chirping, no other sound. George closed and locked the window from the inside, then used the wire cutter to shape the hole irregularly. Now for the bird! He stuck a few fragments of glass into its head and neck, then poked the head through the hole and impaled the body. Would they believe the jay got trapped in the garage, was desperate to get out? No matter. He had all his tools, left no fingerprints, no clues. And Mike would have his accident.

He went out the other window, leaving it closed but unlocked. Who'd believe someone birded one window to get in when the other was unlocked? To think that, they'd have to be crazy.

PART IV

December 1969

35

The Dream

Maggie tucked her feet up on the sofa and rearranged the blue blanket from toes to shoulders. There, maybe she'd be warmer now. Knee socks and jeans weren't enough, that was for sure. How could Raymond sit there in short sleeves while she shivered in her sweatshirt? Didn't he feel the visiting room's chill? She leaned back against the brown sofa pillow propped up on the armrest and closed her eyes as sunlight flooded her face. Yes, that was better.

"Aren't you cold?" she said.

"Are you concerned about me or just changing the subject again?" he asked.

Let him wonder. Oh, yes, that sun felt good. She heard him shift his position in the wing chair.

"How many times have you mentioned that dream, only to run away to another subject?" he asked.

"I haven't counted."

"Is this another tease?"

Sweet Jesus! Was he going to harp on that again? "No. Just forget about it."

"Why did you mention it, then?"

"I don't know. Forget it!"

"That seems to be your solution to most of life's problems." He sounded annoyed.

"So?" What was bugging him, lately?

"So it hasn't worked very well, has it?"

"That's not my fault. I didn't ask for those problems." She burrowed deeper beneath the blanket. "Hell, I didn't even ask to be born. You think I chose any of it? That I want to have that nightmare again and again? Forgetting it is the best I can do."

"No, it's not."

Easy for him to say; he didn't have to live with her pain. "Maybe forgetting is all I want to do."

"Sure, you want to forget. The deeper the wound, the more you want to look the other way — except deep wounds don't heal without proper attention. They bleed — or they fester inside."

On his high horse again! "Come off it! I don't want to hear it."

She heard him rubbing bare skin and half sleeves. Well, the cold wasn't her fault. He should've known about the broken radiator. Served him right for dressing that way in December.

"I guess…" His voice sounded hoarse. He cleared his throat and began again. "I guess that's the Second Law of Maggie's Universe: if you can't forget it, avoid it."

No, don't get up! Don't look at him; don't answer. That's what he wanted, to get a rise out of her.

"I take your silence as a way of avoiding. Am I wrong?"

She opened her eyes and glared at him. "No, Doctor Daniels, you're a peckerhead. You think I'm going to bare my soul to you? You're just a lightweight cheerleader for the U. of Freud."

His lips turned down. "I see. Back to the insults again. Third Law of Maggie's Universe: if you can't avoid it, piss on it! Sexualize it! Crap it up any way you can." He stood up. "For God's sake, haven't we come further than that?"

What was he doing? Walking out? "Our time isn't up!"

"I'm not leaving." He turned. Flapping his arms, he came back. "I just have to move around a little. It's freezing in here."

"Serves you right for wearing a short-sleeved shirt."

He stood over her, looking down. "Sure. My misfortune is always deserved; yours never is, right?"

"Oh, don't be so — so self-righteous. I know better than that." Yes, she liked his little mocking smile, and his puppy eyes, too, God help her. Too bad he was always so serious. How could she get him to just be a person? "Mice ate your sleeves, right?"

He laughed. "You're really something."

She felt warmth rising within her. She withdrew her feet from the far side of the sofa. "Do you want to share my blanket?" Jesus! What a dumb thing to say! "I didn't mean it the way you're thinking."

Grinning, he raised his brows. "What was I thinking?"

"See!" She sat up. "You're the tease!" She sprang from the sofa, bunched up the blanket and tossed it at him. "Wear this!" She headed for the door. "I'll be right back. I have a fu — a dream to tell you. And next time, you'd better wear the right shirt."

She glared the two middle-aged men in the hall into silence. Jesus, Fat Ernie had covetous eyes. Why didn't Daniels understand her? She wasn't a tease. Sure, sometimes she liked to flirt and have fun, aggravate a little — no more than anyone else. One dumb remark didn't prove his case.

The door to her room was closed. She slammed it back against the doorstop. Shit! Her room was a mess. Not that her new roommate, Mrs. — what's her name, Bannack? Bunnock? — was any help.

Where was she? Poor woman was getting senile before her time. Oh, well…

She began stripping the remaining blue blanket from her own bed. Sure, they thought they were smart, giving her much older roommates. Don't infect the young people, Maggie. Were they still blaming her for Nancy Brill? It wasn't her fault that they packed the poor kid off to the state hospital. If Raymond had still been Nancy's doctor, he wouldn't have done it. Why had he given her up when she needed him so much?

Maggie draped the blanket around her shoulders and started back. Did Raymond have to choose between her and Nancy? Poor Nancy never had a chance. Well, it wasn't her fault. Nancy wouldn't have offered to share her junk collection if she'd held any grudge. Who would've dreamed she had some L.P.N.'s nametag? A good swap — worth the perfume. Hope Nancy never finds out it's "My Sin."

"Thanks for the blanket," Daniels said, greeting her from the wing chair.

Well, at least he was using it, hadn't refused her offering. "You're welcome." She draped the second blanket around her, sat down on the sofa and afforded him a satisfied nod.

Had the blanket she gave him taken on her scent? Don't be stupid. He's not going to stick his nose in it. Mark used to love her fragrance, John was oblivious. Would Raymond — Forget it! He's a shrink, he's married…Wasn't John? "No sense you freezing to death," she said. "Your wife might miss you." Watch your mouth! "You'd think they'd get this radiator fixed."

"My wife?"

"Yes. Remember her? The little woman at home."

"I know. I'm just curious about why you mentioned her."

No way! "Beats me. You ready for my dream?"

"There you go — changing the subject again."

"Just shut up and listen. I'm praying in a room — it's not a church, but there's an altar and three small figurines on the wall. One's the Holy Mother, the other's Jesus on the Cross, the third looks — it's stupid, it makes no sense…"

"Tell me anyway." He readjusted his blanket. "In a dream, your mind disguises important clues; it makes them seem trivial or ridiculous so you'll discard them."

"Well, don't laugh at this, okay? It may not even be right because the light's not too good and I have trouble making it out — the third one looks like Elvis."

She spotted the slight elevation of his eyebrows.

"See! I told you it's stupid. Anyway, there's a tiny table and chair — just enough for me, that's all, because it's my hiding place, my secret room. Suddenly, this monster or creature — I call him Mr. Hyde — he bursts through the door and comes after me." She shuddered. "He's sickening, revolting. I hate to think about him."

"I believe it. Try to describe him to me, anyway."

Why was he putting her through this? She closed her eyes and took a deep breath. "He's burned all over. Both of his eyes are – they're burned down to the bone. And what's left of his mouth is bloody. He wants to grab me — to cut me open and burn me. I try to scream, but nothing comes out; I try to get away but my legs can't move. He reaches out to get me — it's awful, his hand is on fire, black and burning. I feel the heat. Just as he's about to touch me, I wake up." She opened her eyes, relieved to see daylight, hopeful that he might do something to help. "Lots of times, I wake up screaming — although that hasn't happened as much in the hospital. There!" She sucked in a deep breath, blew it out, then eased herself back against the pillow.

His silence troubled her. She turned her head to look at his face. A few lines in his forehead, sad eyes, but no sadder than usual, tight lips and jaw — Why didn't he say something? What more did he expect her to say? No, he couldn't feel her horror, much less relieve it. She could talk until her voice gave out, feel 'til she writhed in pain. Peace would always be beyond her grasp. Yes, that was the tease.

"What else do you see in that dream?" His tone was kind.

She looked down at the carpet; her fingers pressured her forehead. "I told you."

"Look again. Picture it with your mind's eye. What else do you see?"

"No! It's awful. I don't want to go through it again." Did he think she was a petulant child?

His hand emerged from the blanket to roam through his hair. "What thoughts do you have about it, then?"

"You're not hearing me. Let's drop it."

"You might be less frightened if you understand what it means."

Damn him! "I know what it means. You think I'm stupid? That I don't know Mr. Hyde is my father; that he's burned in Hell like I want him to be, but he's come for me?" Her hand shot from her blanket. "Is that knowledge supposed to be reassuring? Maybe you should tell me a nuclear missile is on its way over and will explode on top of me. You think the more I know, the better I'll sleep?"

"When did you realize Mr. Hyde is your father?"

"Why do you keep pushing me, keep trying to pin me down? What are you, some kind of sadist?"

"Like Mr. Hyde? And your father?"

"I didn't say that."

"That I'm pushing you into something you'd rather avoid, trying to pin you down and make you suffer — isn't that the way you see me?"

"No! Yes!…I don't know." She searched his face, looking for deviousness. "Alright, maybe you're not a sadistic monster. Does that mean I can't get bur — " She was pinned to that beach again, being crucified in the sand, feverish faces above her cheering each fucking shaft, inventing new ways to torment her. The burning stick was their idea of a joke, although Cal was crazy enough —

"Get burned?" asked Daniels.

— and angry enough after she spit in his ugly face. But what else could she have done to resist? Judas Dave had his portion before he surrendered her to them. Hadn't John done the same?

"Hey! Where are you?" asked Daniels.

"What?… Oh, at the beach." Virginia Beach, she recalled. She suddenly felt cold.

"Running away again?"

"As a matter of fact, I was."

"Will you share what you were thinking?"

"No." She saw his face harden. Sure, he'd accuse her of teasing again. She sighed. "Oh, alright… When I was fifteen, I ran away from home — it wasn't the first time — but that time I got all the way to Virginia Beach. I met a guy there. His name was Dave. He dealt pot and pills to keep from working, but I didn't know that right away and he was cute and seemed decent."

Daniels was staring. She had to move. Grappling with the blanket, she got up and started to walk. "Now I'm cold, okay? Dave let me stay in his apartment, bought me some clothes — he didn't even push me to sleep with him." Forget Daniels — walk and talk!

"Maybe that should have made me suspicious, considering what I'd been through with my father. But it was so good to have someone care without demanding anything. I felt free. I felt very grateful. He made me — no, he didn't make me — I wanted — to be loved in a different way. I was so stupid, then. I told Dave what'd happened to me. It was the last time — the last time I ever told anyone."

She came up behind his wing chair. What was he thinking? Why didn't he say anything? Jesus! Was Raymond any different?

"Why did you stop?" His voice was gentle. "Are you worried about telling me?"

"Yes." She gripped the top of his chair, looked at the curly hair on the back of his head. If only she could see inside his mind. Well, he couldn't see hers, either. "You want to know the truth?"

"Sure."

"I'm wondering how you're going to fuck me."

His head turned but an inch. "How? Not even an 'if'?"

"Why should you be any different?"

"For God's sake!" He got up and faced her. "What makes you think I'm the same? Look, if I told you that I believe incest is a vile betrayal of trust and that fucking a patient is just as bad, would you believe me? One word that I said?"

She looked away. "No, not really."

"I didn't think you would. Actions, right? Well, what've I done to earn your distrust?" He unwrapped himself from the blanket, held it out to her. "Was taking this a mistake?"

"No. I wanted you to have it."

"But worried when I took it?"

"No."

He dropped the blanket on the chair that stood between them. "Well, what misdeed have I done, then?"

"Nothing. I never said — "

He didn't let her finish. "Can't you see that you're transferring old attitudes and feelings onto me? That I'm not Dave or Mr. Hyde?"

"Yes, yes, but that doesn't matter — because it's not you, it's not Dave — " She squeezed her blanket as if it were Dave's neck. "Don't you understand?"

"Not really."

No, don't you dare cry in front of him again! She turned away. Her jaw worked against resistance. "It's me. I do that to men."

"Do what?"

"I make them want me — that way — until they really get to know me; then they can't stand me any more."

"I see. You believe it's your fault for being so attractive, for inspiring lust and betrayal. Where did you get that idea?"

"Don't mock me! It's true!" She headed for the door.

"I'm not mocking you." He was close behind. "Truth is learned, isn't it? How did you arrive at that particular truth?"

"It's what happened all my life." She grabbed for the doorknob.

He put his hand against the door. "Well, it's not happening now. Must you keep running away? Do you want to stay a screwed-up adolescent?"

"Damn you!" Her fist hit the door. "Don't look down your nose at me. Understand?"

"I wasn't — "

"Just don't!" He's infuriating! Patronizing! Like F. Dexter, when he lectured her about her adolescent behavior.

"How about if we sit down again?" He withdrew his hand from the door.

She looked back at the sofa. Hadn't F. Dexter taught her the limits of confession and absolution? God forgive her, hadn't F. Dexter's catechism come first? She bit her lip, looked at Raymond, then the door, hearing her father's voice in her head. *Who do you love best, Mary Margaret? Tell me the truth. You want your father in jail? Want your mother to die of shame? You know what God does to children who destroy their parents?*

"Jesus.." she groaned. *Tell me the truth, Mary Margaret, you really like it, don't you?* "No! I don't. I can't! I don't want to go back there!" She pushed at him wildly. "Get away from me, Raymond." She yanked the door open. "Do us both a favor; leave me alone!"

She slammed the door shut behind her. One way or another — an oath before You, Holy Mother — one way or another, I'm getting out of here.

36

Balancing Out

"I guess I'm late," said George, easing himself between the puny chrome arms of the chair closest to the door.

"Guess?" Daniels smiled and sat down in the swivel chair, his back to the littered desk.

George folded his arms across his chest. His fingers stroked the coarse brown wool of his sweater. Was Daniels trying to be cute? To mock him? Just like that woodcut above the desk, that line of faceless children holding hands — touching. Why didn't Daniels come right out with it and put up a picture of crows? First Fish-Eyes, then Daniels — they were laughing up their sleeves at him. Working together?

"I bumped into a friend of my mother's downstairs," said George. "I haven't seen her since the funeral." Until she'd stepped off the elevator coming down from the Outpatient Clinics. With her long purple coat and multicolored scarf, the bony hag'd looked like a tropical fish, not a crow. A disguise? What was she hiding in that black handbag?

Daniels adjusted his striped tie, placing the fat end atop the thin end. "What was it like for you to see her again?"

"No big deal."

"You'd rather not share your impressions?"

He shook his head. "It doesn't matter. She said she waitressed with my mother a long time ago. That's all." All Daniels needed to know. The shrink would make a big deal of the nothing conversation he'd had with that fish-eyed hag.

"Why didn't you have any visiting hours for your mother at the funeral home?" Fish-Eyes had scolded. "That wasn't right."

"I didn't know she had any friends," he'd replied. What else could he have said? The less attention the body they buried got, the better?

Daniels crossed his legs. "Didn't the woman say anything more than that she worked with your mother?"

"No." Keep the past in the past; don't give this guy an opening.

Daniels just stared at him. Fish-Eyes had, too. He lowered his eyes.

"She did have friends," Fish-Eyes had told him. "Only she got hard to take when she was drinking."

"When wasn't she?"

Fish-Eyes had scowled. "You shouldn't look down your nose at your mother, Mister. She didn't have a real mother. Only foster mothers."

"So what?"

"Well, she did a lot more for you than your father ever did, that's for sure."

He'd wanted to slit her open, see if she was a crow. "My mother tell you to say that?"

"Don't be stupid. She never told me to tell you anything."

"Did the woman say anything that made you worry more about your spells or about crows?" asked Daniels.

Startled, he looked up. "What crows?"

"The ones that bother you. Look, I don't want to repeat my big speech about psychotherapy, but I can't do anything to help you if you stay so unwilling to share." Daniels raised a hand from his lap. "Even your getting here has become problematic again."

George looked over his shoulder. No, the crows were outside. This office didn't even have windows. Maybe Daniels was right; he had to know some things to be able to help. "The acting supervisor at our toll booths doesn't know his ass from his elbow. It's been hard to get out on time." Mike had been much more efficient. How long for a fractured pelvis to heal?

"And once you get here, why has it been hard to talk?" Daniels asked.

"I don't know — I guess I'm not much of a talker."

"I've seen you talk fine when you've wanted to — about your motorcycle, for instance. But, most of the time, I think you conceal far more than you say."

He tried to look surprised. "Why should I do that?"

"I don't know. You tell me."

"Maybe there's less to regret that way."

"You're worried about me getting to know you better?"

"I don't worry."

"Except about your spells, and the crows."

He gripped the arms of his chair. "I'm not crazy."

"I'm not implying that. But those worries come from feelings you're keeping locked away."

"What feelings?"

Daniels passed his hand through his hair. "Aren't you in touch with any?"

"In touch? I don't — Maybe I'm missing something. Some of these feelings you say I have."

"Or can't recognize them. Do you ever get angry?"

"I get even."

"Well what do you think it is that makes you want to get even?"

"I don't know." He folded his arms across his chest. "I never thought about it. A grubsucker messes with me, he pays for it. It's that simple."

"No feeling about his messing with you in the first place?"

"I don't like it. No more than you like to pay a toll. You don't get angry about that, do you?"

Daniels shook his head. "That's different. A toll isn't a personal injury."

Sure, big college degree, but he doesn't know diddly about tolls. He lowered his forearms to the chrome armrests. "When you got to pay a lot, you either take it personally — that the State is out to rip you off — or you get used to it. That's the way it is. I'm used to it. Sometimes I pay, sometimes I collect. No feelings either way."

"Did you have to pay a lot of tolls growing up?"

"My mother didn't have a car."

"I meant about your life in general. Did grubsuckers mess around with you back then?"

"No queers, if that's what you mean. Sometimes my mother's boyfriends got drunk-ugly."

"Beat up on you?"

"Her, mostly."

Daniels leaned forward. "And what did you feel when that happened?"

"I guess I got used to it. I'd take off. She did what she wanted to."

"And who paid the toll?"

"Sometimes her, sometimes both of us." He waved it off. "That's just the way it is. You can sneak by without paying once in a while, but there's always another collector down the pike."

"But it sounds like you paid younger than most."

He shrugged. "So now I'm not paying, I'm collecting. It balances out."

"Does it?" Daniels extended a palm. "Can anyone give you back what you paid?"

"That's not the way it works. Maybe my mother's paying — paid — for me, and I paid for her. Shoot! I'm paying your toll to come here, right? So you're my collector for now. Maybe you're paying my toll by listening to this crowshit, so then I'm your collector. There's always a collector." He looked down at his hands. "That's how it balances out. Everybody pays — for the road."

37

They've Got It All

"Why?" From her chair, Gail Eggers pointed to the world outside her office door. Her willowy form stiffened beneath her maroon skirt and tweed jacket. "Because I can't hack it out there, anymore — that's why." Her eyes watered, her lips curled in an apologetic smile. "Too much, too long," she said.

Raymond rubbed his forehead. Surely she was wrong. She was making a mistake. "Palmer 3?" he asked.

"Not just Palmer 3 — University Hospital. Nursing. You understand?"

Raymond's hand started toward her, paused, then retreated to the arm of his chair. "I understand you're feeling down, but you're a fine nurse Gail, and this place needs you. Are you letting these go-rounds with Maggie get to you?"

Eggers sniffed. "Don't be ridiculous. I hold my own with her. All I need is roller skates to catch her and soap to wash out her mouth."

"Then what is it?" he asked.

"You think this place needs me? What, the bricks and mortar? Who, Raymond? The patients? To most of them, nurses are vending machines." Her finger jabbed forward. "Push the button, get a goody; if it doesn't come instantly, kick the withholding bitch, right?" Eggers' hand swatted aside any objection. "Your friend Maggie's a good example. Who goes around kicking doctors, Raymond?"

"Lawyers?"

"Don't be a wise-acre; you know what I mean. The docs and the patients won't miss me."

He grimaced. "I will."

"I know. That's why I wanted to tell you personally." She looked down at her lap. "You really are a very…well, you're a nine on a scale averaging three. To some of those other wheeler-healers out there, I'm — I'm a handmaid or something." Her tone was bitter. "A brainless doer who should follow orders. Especially if it means taking the rap so a doc doesn't get screwed — or taking the pill so he can."

"Oh, c'mon Gail."

She looked up. Her gray eyes bored into him. "You don't think so? Well let me tell you something." She raised a forefinger. "The first month after I told a couple of people here I was getting divorced, I was propositioned by two residents and an attending psychiatrist, all of whom said they cared about my feelings." She touched her chest. "Imagine if I were pretty, Raymond — if I had the face and figure of your friend out there. I'd never have to spend a lonely night then, would I?"

Raymond rubbed his palms on his lap. Why couldn't Gail be satisfied being herself? Which of his colleagues were such nitwits?

"Psychiatry residents?" he asked.

"You think they're special? That they're immune to jock itch?" Eggers sniffed. "Really, Raymond, except for you and Doctor White and a couple of good friends on the nursing staff, who'll care a crumb that I'm gone? I'm not a Bobbi Stowell, you know."

He shook his head. "I don't know. I don't care how good a head nurse Bobbi Stowell was. I never knew her and I'm not comparing you to her, to Maggie Saxe or to anyone else. You're the one who keeps comparing. Don't you see how it hurts you?"

"I can't live in a vacuum. Look — " She touched her tweed jacket. " — I don't have the money to buy in Bloomingdale's, but I can't pass the window without looking in, can't go in without trying on a designer dress or two, thinking all the time how marvelous it would be if I could really buy one and still pay the rent. Am I so unusual? Haven't you ever wished to have more than you do — be more than you are?"

Being choked from behind, pulled into the alley, the smell of old garbage, then puke — memories before him like the nose on his face. "Sure," he said. "I was a short, skinny kid. I got picked on a lot. I would have given anything to have been bigger, to have had less fear." Less pain, less hatred. How much confidence had he lost because he'd been cheated of his parents?

Eggers scratched her neck. "Then you know what it's like to be dissatisfied with yourself."

"Who doesn't? I had some junior high hoods grab me into an alley and beat the shit out of me." He touched his nose. "Broke my nose, knocked out a tooth. My father called their parents and they laughed at him. The police wouldn't do anything." He shrugged. "What could I do? I had to settle for what I was; I had to accept I'd probably never be able to get back at them. We are what we are, Gail. We're dealt a certain hand; all we can do is play it the best we can."

She raised her eyebrows. "You think I haven't been doing that?"

"No, no." He reached toward her. "I'm not criticizing you. You've helped a lot of people — staff as well as patients. I'm sure many appreciate it. Really!" His hand dropped to his lap. "If you stay, you'd help a lot more."

She shook her head. "But I don't want to help a lot more. I've had it with helping; don't you understand that? On the radio this morning, some deejay said there were twelve shopping days to Christmas, and I thought 'shit! I've been giving forever'." She pointed at her office door. "You know this big Christmas party we're having on the twenty-third? Every patient is doing something special, from making decorations to telling a Christmas story or playing the violin. We're engaging the healthy parts of these people, and every staff member is helping and excited about it." Her finger poked at her chest. "Except me. I'm acting. I'm spent." Her hand darted upward. "Thirty-four, and I feel old and spent. If I don't try to find something different now, before I know it my whole life will be spent — and what will I have to show for it?"

"Look, I understand. It's just that I like and respect you a hell of a lot and I'm really upset you've resigned."

"Thanks, I know you mean that."

They sat in silence. What more could he say? Yes, he was angry at her; sure, he'd miss her. "So what will you do?" he finally asked.

"Doctor Taylor asked me to stay until they found a replacement. I told him I would stay to the end of January, not longer." She smiled. "Then I'm going to Phoenix. It's warm. It's far enough away. And I have a cousin there with whom I can stay for a while."

He rubbed his jaw. "It's the divorce — isn't it?"

"What?"

"That you're running from. It's not — it's not only the job."

She leaned forward. "I'm not running. I'm trying to make a fresh start. There's quite a difference."

"Is there?"

She pointed at him. "Don't play therapist with me, Raymond Daniels. I knew you when you were an ignorant intern."

He pretended to cower behind raised palms. "Okay. Relax. No more feeble attempts at insight." His hands dropped to his lap. "As an ignorant friend, I wish you the best of luck."

"You're angry that I'm leaving." Sadness and regret were in her tone.

"I won't insult you by denying it."

"Thanks." She leaned back in her chair. "I'm sure they'll find someone good to take over Palmer 3."

"Are they cloning Bobbi Stowell?"

Eggers smiled. "I'll bet Doctor Taylor would if he could. He recruited her from City Hospital when he was a consultant there. He really thought she was terrific — a real go-getter, just like he is."

Raymond stifled a yawn. "So why did Taylor let her get away?"

"He didn't. Not really. I mean she left Palmer 3 after she got married, but she stayed in the family. She married Doctor Taylor's youngest son. She's Mrs. Roberta Taylor, now. It was a beautiful wedding. I was a bridesmaid. It was really grand."

Raymond spread his arms wide. "And the lovely couple lived happily ever after?"

"Yes." Eggers sniffed. "Why not? With her looks and his money, they've got it all. They have a big house and two adorable children — they've got it all, Raymond. They've got it all."

38

The Fast

Raymond looked at his wristwatch. Twelve minutes to make a cheeseburger, he thought. Stupid to have ordered it; he wasn't even hungry. No matter what Leroy White had said, it was too early for lunch. Following him down the cafeteria line had been a mistake. Leroy's appetite was contagious, his plate had no rim. He'd teased and sampled his way down the serving line, addressing each server by name. The same woman — had Leroy called her Hedy or Betty? — who had cackled gleefully as she'd hustled Doctor White's specially prepared salad from the kitchen, had suddenly developed Parkinson's Disease when she'd turned to serve Doctor Daniels. Yup, some people had it made, while others couldn't even order it. Not that he couldn't be satisfied with a cheeseburger, but Mrs. Parkinson had overcooked the burger, and she'd melted more time than cheese.

"Cheeseburger, a fountain drink, thirty cents," said the bleached blonde cashier.

He gave her three dimes and she rang up the sale. Carrying his tray, he headed toward the doctors' section, trying to tune out the cafeteria clatter, the laughter and general babble.

"Daniels!"

He looked over his shoulder. Jack Kenman was approaching with a bag of chips in one hand, a bottle of Coke in the other. Raymond forced a polite smile and stopped so that the lanky Neurology resident could catch up. "Hello, Jack. No lunch, today?"

Kenman's scowl sucked up his lips and narrowed the space between his blond eyebrows. "I have a fucking attending who's got me making rounds with him at lunchtime… By the way, I appreciate your follow-up on that woman with M.S. She's been cooperating much better since she began talking to you. Seems less depressed."

"She is. The family meeting was important. Her husband couldn't accept — "

"Can't talk, I gotta run. You'll keep seeing her?"

"Sure. I'll call you." Not that Kenman would be interested in the family's dynamics, thought Raymond. Kenman wanted to treat the disease, not the patient.

Raymond found Leroy White at a table by a window. Rain was splattering the glass and blurring the view of the hospital wing across the courtyard. Leroy's white coat was unbuttoned and his midsection bulged under his black shirt and vermilion tie. Set out before him were his salad, a platter of haddock and vegetables, two corn muffins, pecan pie and coffee. An empty soup bowl had been moved aside.

"I hope you don't mind that I started without you." White poured dressing on his salad from a small Tupperware container. "It looked like you were going to be a while."

"That's okay." Raymond transferred his burger and root beer from tray to table. "I don't mind. I'm just glad you had time to see me today." He placed his tray on an extra chair and sat down opposite White. "I'm sorry it had to be at lunch."

White used his knife to scrape the last of the salad dressing from the container. "I made this dressing myself – it's chutney." He frowned at Raymond's cheeseburger. "Is that all you're having?"

"I'm not very hungry."

"You look like worry is eating you for lunch. Worry is always hungry. Is it that Saxe case again?"

"Yes and no. I'm still pissed off that they sent Nancy Brill to the state hospital. I worry about the treatment she'll get there. Had Doctor Taylor kept me on the case, I would have argued to keep her here."

White picked up his fork and tablespoon and began tossing his salad. Red stones in his pinky ring sparkled. "From what I hear, nothing we tried was helping her that much. And once her Papa lost his election — well, you know our Chairman's ways and means…But that's not why you wanted to see me, is it?"

"No. It is Maggie Saxe. I can't figure out what's going on with her. I thought she and I were building a relationship, making some progress – then boom." He tapped the tabletop. "She won't talk, won't eat, and sits like a statue in our sessions. I haven't felt so out of my depth since my first test in medical school when I studied for a solid week and got a D, I thought what the hell more could I do? Maybe I didn't have what it took to become a doctor."

"But you persevered," said White. "Graduated third in your class, I was told." He put a forkful of salad into his mouth.

"Doesn't matter now. This is about life and death for Maggie. She's done a lot of things that are willful and self-destructive, but this one is planned, not impulsive. She hasn't eaten for five days. Juice, water, coffee — that's been it." His lips and gums pulled inward with a sucking sound. "I don't know what more to do. And I only have a few days left."

White's head bobbed as he swallowed his food. "Left? Did Doctor Taylor — "

"No, he hasn't fired me. Not yet. But don't think I haven't been sweating it. I can't afford another Nancy Brill fiasco." Damn, why was he being so self-centered? Leroy and Nancy had been hurt worse than he had. "Have you heard anything about your tenure?"

White snorted. "Tenure's a white man's umbrella. I don't see anyone raising it for me, okay? What did you mean by only a few days left?" White's mouth opened wide for another forklift of salad.

Was Leroy right? Sure, prejudice and politics — hand in glove. Raymond ripped the corner off a foil package of ketchup. "Lisa's due next week, on the twenty-fourth." He squeezed the ketchup onto his cheeseburger. "I'm going to take off from work to be with her as soon as she goes into labor and then I'll have to take care of Julie — my daughter — she's three. I'll be a full-time daddy 'til after New Year's."

"Congratulations! I didn't know it was so close…Big Daddy Daniels! I'll expect a see-gar from you, Big Daddy." White's grin seemed as warm as it was wide.

"It'll be my pleasure. But that's why I feel so pressed for time. I don't want to leave Maggie like this. It's not fair to her or to Al Spiva, who'll be covering for me."

"You know better than that, Raymond. You can't control whatever crazy shit people might be into anytime you go away. You can't even control other people's behavior while you're here, okay? Spiva's an excellent resident; he'll manage just fine. Chances are, the girl's acting out because you're taking time off. Did she stop eating after you told her?"

"No. I told her three weeks ago. She didn't seem put out. Maybe a week later, she asked me whether I was taking vacation because my wife was going to have a new baby." Raymond wiggled the top of the bun around on the burger. "She said she was told that by another patient, who heard about it from someone else. One of the ward staff probably said something out of turn." He took a napkin from the metal dispenser and spread it on his lap. "Anyway, Maggie seemed to handle the news appropriately. She congratulated me, asked if I wanted a boy or a girl — I said I just wanted a healthy baby — and she wished my wife an easy time of it. I tried to get at whatever fantasies she might have had about Lisa's pregnancy, but she got off onto something else — I don't remember what it was."

"Mmm," grunted White, his mouth full again.

"Boy, it's frustrating not to remember — I know we got into something else..." Raymond took a bite out of his cheeseburger. What had Maggie said? About Lisa's pregnancy; his taking time off? God! Like eating wet cardboard. "Could you pass the salt, please?" He shouldn't have ordered anything. "Thanks." He sprinkled salt on his burger, set the shaker back on the table.

"Anyway, I'm almost positive whatever she said didn't have to do with my taking time off. She didn't start missing meals until last Friday, so there was at least a week between the conversation about Lisa's pregnancy and the start of her fast. And when Gail Eggers asked her why she wasn't eating, Maggie said that Jesus fasted for forty days and she was going to fast longer. That's the last thing she said to anyone."

"Really?" White glanced up from his salad bowl.

Raymond nodded. "If she wants something now, she writes notes. With me, she just sits in silence. I've suggested a couple of times that maybe she's angry with me for leaving her, but she didn't react at all."

"Well, you can't see what's cooking when the lid is on, okay? Could be she's simmering about your leaving; she doesn't have to boil right up and over." He stuck his fork into a slice of lemon and squeezed juice onto his fish. "Sometimes, people get so angry they don't feel like talking or eating." He grinned. "Some of us do the opposite... Maybe she's so angry that she wants to 'chew you up and spit you out,' or 'bite your head off' — angry words often reflect oral sadistic impulses? But if she sinks her teeth into you too hard, she's gonna frighten you off, maybe lose you, okay? So what's her defense against those impulses? She grits her teeth and says nothing, eats nothing. She swallows her anger, and nothing else... Excuse me, I'd better tend to this fish."

"Sure." Raymond picked up his cup. Sure, Maggie acted out oral sadistic impulses. Weren't her put-downs part of that? And her wrist-cutting and attention-seeking? She was so terribly needy beneath her outer shell.

He took a sip of root beer; his throat closed and he coughed. He covered his mouth with the napkin and set down the cup.

"You okay?" asked White.

"Fine. How's the haddock?"

"Fair to middlin'. I prefer it baked with onions and heavy cream... She say anything else about Jesus?"

"No."

"Hmmm." White speared some greens from his salad bowl. "What do you make of her desire to fast longer than Jesus did?"

"Well, until you just showed me that her fast might be a defense against her aggressive impulses, I was thinking it represented a penance — either for real sins or some she's imagined." He shrugged. "Who knows? It might be self-purification; not so she'll live better, but as a prelude to suicide."

White chewed his food slowly. He swallowed and nodded. "I should've used more dill in the dressing. What else?"

"What ?"

"Well, let's look at it again," said White. "Feeling so bad about herself for so long, is she likely to think she can purify herself by fasting?"

"Probably not."

"Is she cleansing herself in any other remarkable way?"

"No."

"And why would she fast for penance when up to now she's been cutting and overdosing and bent on suicide? Isn't suicide the greater punishment?"

"Yes."

White's fork captured a cherry tomato. "So what else could she be up to in trying to out-fast Jesus?" He popped the tomato in his mouth with obvious pleasure.

C'mon, Leroy! thought Raymond. Leroy looked like a little boy who'd just swallowed the only red jellybean. What was tickling him so?

"You think Maggie's putting on a show for us?" Raymond asked. "To convince us of her holiness — her zeal or something?"

"Could be. But what if it wasn't Jesus? What if she said, 'I'm going to fast longer than – Joe Nobody'?"

"Trying to outdo him, I guess. Some sort of competition."

White split a corn muffin and began to butter it. "And what kinds of competition are there?"

Raymond reached for his root beer. What was the purpose of all this? If Leroy had figured something out, why didn't he just say it? Types of competition? "Well, there's sibling ri — Wait!" He put down the paper cup. "Are you saying she views Jesus as a sibling to be outdone?"

"My guess is she doesn't think that at all." White took a large bite of muffin and reached for his coffee.

"Then I don't understand." What a lousy place for supervision, thought Raymond. The supervisee sits and gags on his ignorance while the supervisor stuffs his mouth full of muffin. Sorry, my boy, coffee comes before clarification.

"This is only guesswork," White finally said. "We've got an interesting serving of behavior here, and we're guessing at the ingredients that got put into this dish, okay? The ingredients may be half-forgotten, half-jumbled in her head." His hand wiggled in the air. "Know what I mean?"

"Sort of. " Leroy approached neurosis as if it were some sort of goulash.

"You and I, we can guess about ingredients — the causes and influences that determined this behavior — but chances are we'll be wrong, or at best only partly right. The ingredients have to come from her. And even then, there are always more ingredients than we'll ever know — even more than she'll ever know. So never think that's all there is, okay?"

"Sure." Raymond crumpled his napkin into a ball.

"Then let me tell you about my oldest sister, Nessie, okay? Her name is really Vanessa, but I always used to call her Nessie because she hated it." White grinned. "I won't tell you the things she called me." He took another swallow of coffee. "I don't even know why I'm — well, it's how I learned it, and how you learn something can be more powerful than the knowledge itself. Maybe it'll help you and Miss Saxe." He set down his cup. "As a kid, I had asthma and was the baby and the only boy of four sibs, so looking back on it, it's easy to understand Nessie's resentment. She got the brunt of everything, what with my mother away so much, cooking for some rich folks." He pointed at his pie. "See that, Raymond? That's not real pecan pie. My mother made real pecan pie. Every now and then, she'd bring a piece or two home from work and we kids would have ourselves a little piece of Heaven."

White sighed. "Well, anyway, I had asthma and I couldn't be out running with other boys. I stayed in our apartment a lot, hiding out in the bedroom with secondhand copies of *Plastic Man* or *The Crypt of Terror* because old Nessie was coiled around the TV in the living room. And way after my other sisters came in and Nessie fixed dinner for us, Mama would come home all tired out and criticize Nessie for not doing the kitchen floor just so, or for losing socks at the Laundromat, or for giving us peanut butter and jelly for the third night in a row... Anyway, those times Mama would produce some treat left over from the rich folks' dinner, I'd usually get the biggest piece — not by much, but the biggest — because I was `sickly' or `sproutin' or `doing all of us proud in school'." White pushed his haddock plate aside. He shook his head sadly. "It's not surprising that Nessie picked on me, is it? Or that sometimes she'd lay into Mama, shouting `You treat that little lard-ass nigger like he's Jesus Himself.' Then Mama would give her what for, and Nessie would take it out on us the next day."

Raymond rubbed the back of his neck. What did this have to do with Maggie Saxe?

"Gradually, Nessie listened less and stayed out more. When she stopped going to church with us, Mama told her she was truly evil." A puff of air shot from White's lips. "Well, it wasn't long before Nessie went to live elsewhere."

Mothering! thought Raymond. Wanting children, fearing to have them. Fearing she'd be a bad mother — that was the issue Maggie had raised in response to Lisa's pregnancy.

White reached for his coffee cup. "Which may be a long way round, Raymond, but that's how I first learned it — learned it the hard way from my sister, who learned almost everything the hard way herself." White sipped from his cup.

Learned what? Raymond ran a hand through his hair. Had he missed the point by thinking of Maggie? "I'm sorry. I think you lost me."

White grinned. "Not yet. I'm just coming around the corner slowly." His hand rose in explanation. "Consciously, Mary Saxe probably venerates Jesus as the Son of God, much as Nessie did then and I still do. But unconsciously — " He tapped his head. " — who does Jesus symbolize for her? Even now, Vanessa feels terrible at Christmas, for all of us Christians are celebrating and worshiping the Holy Infant and showering our mortal children with gifts Vanessa never had."

White put his fists on the table. "Transference, Raymond — transference. We even deliver our family feelings and attitudes unto God. For Vanessa, God was another absentee father, and His Son became – well — let's just say a pain." White grimaced and reached for his pie.

39

The Lunatic Child

Maggie scratched and picked at the loose threads surrounding the hole in her jeans. From beyond the scrape of her fingernail on denim yet nearer than the radiator's hiss and splutter, she heard Raymond shift his position in the other wing chair. Well, as long as she stayed bent over the hole on her knee, he couldn't see her face and she wouldn't see his, and the ravenous ache in her stomach was more bearable. Why did he sit there pretending the patience of a saint? Saint Raymund Nonnatus, lips pierced by a red hot iron and padlocked. Yes, Sister Wilhelmina's saintly gore for children. Maggie grit her teeth. Forget it! This Raymond was as ignorant of saints as she was of chastity... Giving up food and speech was much harder than giving up sex. She'd become a sluggish, hollow-eyed scarecrow. If only she could turn off her thoughts...

Out of the corner of her eye, she saw a black shoe and navy blue trouser bottom rise as Raymond crossed his legs. "I don't understand what you gain by silence," he said.

So what? He could never understand her pain or her religious faith. Even that first time they'd met, when he burst in and found her praying, hadn't he run from her in confusion? Yet he hadn't run from the foul-mouthed slut. Men wanted sex, not prayer and penitence. She dug her fingernail beneath a stubborn thread. Hadn't F. Dexter chosen her over her mother? Her finger jerked; the thread snapped. Got it! And the boys in the neighborhood were no different, corrupting her name to Mary Margaret Sex, calling it out as she walked home from St. Theresa's. What fourth grader could look sexual in baggy blue serge, that demure pleated skirt and white collar? No, it wasn't her appearance and it wasn't because they knew her secrets. She was just marked and sold by her devils. They tempted her, pressed her to give in, to give what men wanted, be what they wanted, draining her dry, leaving her dirty, empty. That's all she'd ever be — foul and empty. Pull apart the threads, Raymond, and all you'll find is a hole. An empty stomach and an empty soul.

"When you pick at your clothes that way, you're often angry," he said. "Are you angry now?"

Moron. When wasn't she angry? Did life exist without helplessness and rage? Maybe for the nuns. Some, anyway. For a while, their faith had sustained her. Sister Gemma's love had nourished her — even Sister Wilhelmina's punishments hadn't bothered her. That look on Wilhelmina's face? Priceless! "Go ahead and hit me, Sister. I deserve it. You can put me in the Spanking Machine." Maggie smiled. Oh, that mythical Spanking Machine.

"Something amuses you?" asked Raymond.

Tell him nothing! She yanked a thread; it unraveled others. There! Maybe she'd have been better off if there had been a Spanking Machine. Or a giant washing machine for dirty secrets. No, she wouldn't have told Wilhelmina, anyway. Wilhelmina was too hard, Sister Gemma too important; Sister Alfreda had seemed the best choice. Well, who'd ever taught choice at St. Theresa's? Maybe life was the Spanking Machine.

She heard the friction between fabrics as he shifted about. Good, let him be uneasy, too. He'd go home soon enough. His wife was probably some cutesy little thing that cooed and curtsied. He would go home. She never could. Well, since when did loonies need a home? Stuck in the Nuthouse: My True Life Story. Always been stuck… except for Sister Gemma and school, Mrs. Hilliard in eleventh grade…and the Holy Virgin and Jesus. Most of all, Jesus. Who knew suffering and redemption better?

"My guess is that you're very angry with me for leaving you, but you're afraid of verbalizing it," said Raymond.

Idiot. Was he still stuck on that track? Did he think she was blind to his needs? Of course he needed time off, to be with his wife, his new baby. His wife was probably so small she'd need a Caesarian. Or want one, anyway. Saint Raymund was born by Caesarian. Now if she had Raymond's baby — of course she couldn't, but if she could — forget it! This hole's really getting bigger, now. She inspected her fingernails. If she could muster the energy, she'd file and repolish them later. It would be the high of the day.

"Why hold in your anger?" he asked. "What do you gain?"

She opened and closed her hands, then rubbed them together. Too bad she wasn't a brain surgeon; he could be her first case. That would put an end to his intrusiveness, his attempts to seduce her with false hope, false promises. Like John — the bastard never wrote, never called. No, no man could cure her sinfulness, her emptiness. If she had any chance of Salvation, she had to chastise her own mind and body. Mary Magdalen had redeemed herself, hadn't she?

She straightened up in her chair, felt a moment of dizziness and put one hand to her head. How much more time? Should have worn her watch. She glanced at Raymond. Long-sleeved shirt and sweater. Sure, now that the radiator was going full blast. Stop worrying about him! Can't be his or any man's vanity bag. John was the last. Sorry, Raymond — psychic penetration hurts a lot more than fucking. And there won't even be a baby to show for it. So go back to your wife — she's the one that needs your earnestness and pity. She'll bear the baby, I'm stuck with the pain. Even the patron saint of midwives can't deliver me. "She having the baby here?" Had she said that aloud? Imbecile! Couldn't she be resolute for more than five seconds?

"You mean my wife?" asked Raymond.

Idiot. Whom did he think she meant? The Blessed Virgin?

"Why do you ask that?" he questioned.

She smacked her forehead. It sounded worse than it felt. Small penance for opening her mouth. She bent over her knee again, began picking at her jeans.

"Yes. Here," he said.

She plucked another thread, gave no sign she heard. What mattered now was getting a knee patch. Too late for a mouth patch.

"Jesus, Maggie — don't shut me out. We will both survive your anger."

She stopped picking, looked up. He had leaned far forward. His cheeks were flushed. "You're the one who's angry," she told him.

A burst of air from his nose, a guttural chuckle — he seemed to deflate back into his chair. "You're right. I am. And you are." He nodded. "We are."

"You conjugate beautifully." Jesus! She wanted to die. At least cut out her tongue.

She saw him fighting back the grin, trying to minimize her embarrassment, but his body was shaking with mirth.

"Don't shut it in." She mimicked his tone, his words. "We will both survive your laughter." Let him feel embarrassed!

He raised his hands, surrendering to laughter. Yes, and to her. She couldn't suppress a smile.

"Will you share more of your thoughts about my wife delivering a baby?" .

"I have to patch my jeans."

"Now that you've torn them. At least tell me why you're fasting."

Her hands spread wide. "What is this, *Let's Make a Deal?*"

"No, it's not a show; it's not a game." He leaned forward. "It's truth, between us, because we're important, and truth is — it's our gift to each other."

Gift? She looked down at her lap. One of her hands massaged the other. "*Every one that is of the truth, heareth my voice,*" she quoted.

"New Testament," said Raymond.

She looked up. "You're learning."

"And the fast?"

She bit her lip, studied his face. Reproachful eyes. Oh, shit... "I asked help from Jesus. I don't want to be here forever, you know. The words were in Saint Matthew and Saint Paul."

"Tell me."

"I'll give you The Book. It's good reading."

"I'll read it. But tell me."

"You sure you'll read it?"

His hands shot up. "Maggie, I know you're serious and I don't want to sound unappreciative — " His hands descended slowly. " — but the way you drag things out has the effect of a tease. The same is true of your days of silence. People have to quit or keep coming after you. Either way, the result is frustration."

She closed her eyes; her lips tightened. Was he right? Maybe. But he was missing the point. Her eyes opened for another try. "Are you sure you'll read the New Testament?"

"Yes, I said so. But you're still teasing."

"No, I'm not. Well, maybe I am. But I also want to show you the best part of me. Maybe then I can show you the worst." Slowly, she got up, blinked away her dizziness, and shuffled toward the window. "The story in Chapter 17 of Saint Matthew is about a lunatic child." She looked out at the buildings, the traffic below. Getting dark already. "A boy, but that doesn't matter." Yes, winter's coming. Can't spend winter locked up here. "I always wished I was a boy, anyway. F. Dexter took Mory fishing and to ballgames. You know where he took me." Her face hardened. "Ballgames," she growled.

"Mory?" asked Raymond.

She moved back to her chair. "Little brother. Maurice Hermann. Named after the Saxon bastard who founded our line of bastards. I mean literally. Count Maurice Hermann Saxe." She sat down, slipped off her shoes and drew her legs up beneath her. "Good old Hermann was the illegitimate son of a Polish king, or so F. Dexter said. F. Dexter was an expert on bastardry. Impulsive bastard."

"F. Dexter?"

"Him, too. I meant old Hermann. Did you ever hear of Adrienne Lecouvreur?"

"No."

"His mistress. Great French actress." Maggie smoothed back her hair. "Did you know that I'm also related to George Sand? Old Hermann was her grandfather. As a family, we're very classy bastards." She cocked her head. "I think F. Dexter let us down."

"You're doing it again," Raymond said.

"What?"

"You were going to tell me about the lunatic child."

"You're right." She smiled sadly. "But all of us are lunatic children... So anyway, this lunatic boy's father asked the disciples to cure him, to drive out the devil that made him loony. And they couldn't do it, but Jesus did." Her hand rose to make the point. "See, the disciples and the doctors failed! And when the disciples asked Jesus how come they failed, Jesus said they didn't have enough faith in God, and they hadn't used prayer and fasting. Get it?"

"Got it. And Saint Paul?"

She shifted position, put her feet to the floor. "I have mixed feelings about Saint Paul's first letter to the Corinthians. He wasn't big on incest. `...deliver such a one to Satan for the destruction of the flesh...' I quaked when I read that as a kid. Maybe that's what made me feel I — " No, Raymond would think her ludicrous. "Of course I missed the whole point of saving the spirit. All I saw was my corruption, and that I should be excommunicated and ripped to shreds by Satan." She shook her head. "It's crazy, I know, but I was always drawn to that passage — a moth to the flame, sort of. Well, I couldn't exactly ask anyone for clarification, either."

"And the fasting?"

"Saint Paul was big on chastity. Of the spirit as well as the body. Fasting was a way of self-discipline."

"Anything else?"

"Read The Book." She leaned back and stretched.

He ran his hand through his hair. "Miss Eggers said that you told her you were going to fast longer than Jesus."

Lying bitch! Maggie bent forward; her hands gripped the chair. "I can't ever do anything better than Jesus. That's absurd. Old Egg-Face didn't understand — or maybe you didn't get the whole picture."

Raymond nodded. "One person never has the whole picture. You're not competing?"

"Competing?" She grabbed her head; her words tumbled out. "Eggers asked me how long I was going to fast and I said 'I don't know,' because I didn't and that's my business, not hers; and she said 'fasting can be dangerous,' so I told her 'Jesus Christ did it without advice from a twiggy nurse, and I can, too'." Maggie slapped the chair. She took a quick breath. "Then old Egg-Face was stupid enough to tell me that Jesus was the Son of God and didn't require professional help, while I was merely a hospital nut-cake — well, she didn't exactly say the last part, but something like that. She kept asking me how long I intended fasting, so to bug her I said 'Forty days and nights. No, definitely more'!" Maggie shook her head. "Communications around this place — "

"Are definitely improving," said Raymond.

She frowned at him. "Maybe." Had she said too much? Resolute for all of five seconds. Competing with Jesus? Absurd. Mory, yes; never Jesus. Is that how they viewed it? Imbeciles!

Raymond looked at his watch. "Uh-oh, we've run over. Look, I don't question your faith and I know it's entirely up to you, but I hope you'll at least consider some solid food."

Maggie turned away from him. No, no matter what she said, they'd doubt her words, count the days of her fast and lay bets on whether she could beat Jesus.

"How about it?" he asked.

Eat? For them? She stood up, felt light-headed and grabbed on to the back of her chair.

He started to rise, but she waved him back down. "Don't push me, Raymond. Don't push me. You know me better than that. I hate being used... Bring me a Big Mac and a strawberry shake."

40

The Baby

"Bear down, Lisa!" The obstetrician's command and encouraging tone came through his surgical mask crisp and clear.

At the opposite end of the delivery table, Raymond felt Lisa's sweaty hand crush his fingers as her back arched, her abdomen went tight, and her grunt turned into a scream that sent a shock wave through his own body. "Push Lisie! You can do it!" he urged, hoping his words might get through her pain and be helpful. After eight hours of labor, she was exhausted, and he felt weak in the knees. The second time might be easier for some women, but it hadn't been for her because their baby had come down "sunny side up" instead of face down. Thank God Doctor Vostenza had been able to turn it without forceps. Still, Lisa had endured extra hours of agony while every worst case scenario he'd learned in medical school and internship had to be pushed out of his mind. No doubt who was stronger; he could never have endured so much pain for so long.

She fell back against the table with a small cry of disappointment. "Hang in there, you're doing fine. Do the panting," said Raymond. Her pressure on his fingers eased, but he left them in her fist. With his other hand, he used a gauze pad to wipe the sweat from her forehead, the strands of red hair away from her eyes, and then his own sweat from under the collar of his shirt.

"It won't be long, now," said the obstetrician.

"It's all worth it; I have three," said the masked and gloved nurse by his side.

"Two may be enough for me," Lisa mumbled. Her body tensed as another contraction began.

"Let's just get through this one," said Raymond, wishing he could do more to help her. He'd had the same wish with patients, but it was so intense now that his body ached with inaction. Seeing her go through this again was just as hard as it was three years ago.

The mound of Lisa's belly quivered and went into spasm. Her face contorted, her feet dug into the stirrups, her hand crushed his fingers. A ragged scream ripped from her throat.

"Baby's coming! Push!" Doctor Vostenza commanded.

Raymond leaned forward, trying to see their baby, the new life they created emerging between Lisa's legs and the doctor's gloved hands. Beneath the slime, was a well-formed head and reddish hair, a tiny shoulder and arm.

"Come on out, don't be shy," Vostenza crooned. "Time?"

"Twelve-oh-two," said the nurse. "December twenty-second by two minutes."

The baby let out a cry. "A boy!" announced Vostenza. "Damn if he isn't pissing already. Mrs. Harris, give me a towel! Trying the new equipment, are you, junior?"

"A boy!" said Raymond. Awe and gratitude brought tears to his eyes. "You okay, Lisie?"

"Yes." Her voice was hoarse and weighed down by fatigue. "From nothing, a little person. A miracle." She put her head back against a pillow. Her smile was broad and loving.

Raymond bent over and kissed her damp forehead.

"Oh," Vostenza muttered. He placed the baby on Lisa's abdomen and snapped a clamp on the cord.

"Oh." Mrs. Harris raised her shaped eyebrows.

Raymond stiffened. Words died in his throat. A bright red fleshy growth sat above the baby's eye. The strawberry mass extended onto the eyelid, weighing it down. *Hemangioma*. The word came to mind on a wave of sadness and fear. It's not malignant, he told himself. What else did he remember from Pediatrics, from Dermatology?

"Please," said Vostenza.

"Sorry," said Mrs. Harris. She smacked another clamp into Vostenza's palm.

"What's the matter?" asked Lisa.

"Your little genius pissed on me, that's all." Vostenza snapped the second clamp in place, cut the umbilical cord, then exchanged his scissors for a test tube. "I'm just taking some blood from the cord. It's very routine." Raising his eyebrows, he glanced at Raymond.

He wants *me* to tell her. Raymond cleared his throat. "Lisie, our baby's all pink and fine, but he has a little strawberry growth above his right eye."

Her head and shoulders lurched upward. "Let me see! Let me see him!"

"Mrs. Harris, give Mom a look and then clean the baby up." Vostenza rattled on as the nurse carefully wrapped the baby in a blanket. "It's almost certainly a benign growth. It's called a hemangioma, a tumor of tiny blood vessels. Often they go away without treatment."

Mrs. Harris brought the baby close. Lisa sucked in a breath. "Oh, my God. How can he see?"

Yes, thought Raymond, without enough light, would their baby's retinal cells die? Would their son be forever blind in that eye? He put his hand on Lisa's shoulder. "Don't worry. The pediatrician will ask for an ophthalmologist to examine him. Between the two of them, they'll know what to do."

"Let me hold him," said Lisa.

The nurse looked at Vostenza. "For a minute or two," he said. "We have to get the placenta out and the baby cleaned up. We have to make sure that's the only one on his skin."

"There could be more?" Lisa's voice quavered, her hands trembled as she reached for the baby.

"I didn't see any, but they could be just little reddish patches," said Vostenza.

"I didn't see any, either." Raymond shut his mouth with his fist. Even if he'd had a good look, the danger wasn't on the skin. Hemangiomas could be inside the baby's organs. A slim chance – still, this wasn't the time to tell Lisa. He grit his teeth. How was he going to show optimism he didn't feel without lying?

As if she didn't trust the outstretched hands, Mrs. Harris lay the baby on Lisa's chest. "Here, Mrs. Daniels. Say hello to your son."

41

A Christmas Party

Well fuck them, fuck their Lilliputian applause! thought Maggie.
What did those idiots know about poetry, anyway? Spotlit in front
of an eight-foot, plastic Christmas tree decorated with popcorn and
cookies, she bobbed her head to the audience. How light her head felt
without the braids. Was her poetry that empty? No, the real airheads
were seated in the rows of folding chairs facing her.

She stuffed the folded papers into the pocket of her velvet skirt.
This Christmas talent show was a stupid idea. Even in party clothes,
they were a gathering of loony-tunes. Gathered from the locked and
unlocked wards — nuts, plain and candy-covered. Not that she was
any better — just packaged more attractively. With a harder shell.

She paraded toward her chair in the rear of the gym. She nodded
at Juanita, silently thanking her again for the loan of the satin blouse.
It had positively shimmered in the makeshift spotlight. As she came
toward Louise, Maggie smiled and touched her short hairdo in salute.
Even now, the others were watching her pass as if she were a movie
star. Was she crazy for wanting to pass as a poet? Well, lust into dust,
let's crave to the grave. None of us will ever get what we want.

"Thanks, Mag," said Arnold, reclaiming the spotlight. "You read those poems real good... And doesn't she look great, all dressed up, without the hairball?"

Maggie stopped. Arnold was the teen-age hairball. No, don't turn back — don't ruin it! They were applauding her more enthusiastically. Stupid wolf whistles. Wasted breath all around. She smiled and blew a kiss to the audience. Idiots! Poetry was beyond them. She walked on. Hadn't she told the committee her poems were morbid, that they weren't Christmas party entertainment? Christmas was a big enough downer without any contribution from her. Two days to Christmas, two hours to freedom. But first things first — the pizza man had to deliver.

"Your poems are so sad, so beautiful," said Stacy Wilner. Maggie sat down in the chair next to her. Stacy's eyes, hazelnuts protruding from her anorexic face, were moist with tears.

"Thank you," said Maggie. Stacy was just trying to be nice. Part of her sickness, most likely.

"And now," proclaimed Arnold, "Russell Meachum is gonna play a Mozart thing in G Major on the violin, and Andrea Broule is gonna play with him on the piano. Let's bring 'em up here with a nice hand."

Idiot! Arnold couldn't M.C. a slug's sleep-over. The idea that everybody had to contribute was as crazy as the guest list. Reluctantly, she joined in the applause. Hadn't she warned them? Wasn't Arnold living proof? A pretentious nothing. Just like her poetry.

She was startled by the hot breath on her neck, a jowl hovering above her shoulder. Mr. Carlson, leaning forward from the seat behind her. "I really liked your poems. Especially `Betrayals.' You should get them published."

"Sure." The man was undoubtedly brain-damaged. Probably drinking his Aqua Velva.

"I mean it," he insisted. "My sister-in-law's nephew got published."

"Shhh." She leaned forward to escape him.

Stacy came to her rescue. "Doesn't Russell look handsome in a suit?"

Maggie looked at the pale, thin young man tucking the violin under his chin. "Yes." Like a frail David Bowie. Except Russell was wilting in the spotlight. The pianist looked cute in her pixie cut. Louise was truly an artist when it came to hair. Yes, Louise deserved to be in a chic beauty salon, not the nuthouse. She'd been right about this Italian cut, too. Came out so nicely. Definitely was time for the braids to go. Especially with the pizza man delivering her to freedom. Best leave the braids of her adolescence behind. She'd miss Louise and Juanita more than the others. Poor Russell, he's going to sink into the floor up there.

"He dropped out of the Conservatory," said Mr. Carlson.

"Shhh." Oh, Russell, don't back down, thought Maggie. We're all scared to perform.

The violin lurched from Russell's chin. Sweat was visible on his forehead.

"You can do it, Russell." In the first row, his roommate, Danny.

"We all want to hear Mozart, Russell." Was that Gwynn, the PCP freak?

Bow in hand, Russell used his sleeve to mop his forehead. "Concerto...Concerto in G Major. Wolfgang Amadeus Mozart." The violin remained at his side.

"Go ahead, Russell," Maggie shouted. "Otherwise the bastards will make me read more of my poems."

The patients laughed.

"Anything but that!" yelled Arnold. "I'm already crazy."

Even the staff was laughing.

Russell smiled. He took in a deep breath, then slowly exhaled. Andrea sounded an A on the piano. Russell took another breath, brought the violin to his chin. An A from the piano. The violin responded. Andrea smiled, Russell nodded. And they played.

What elegant music. Fantastic! Maggie brushed away a few tears. Sweet Jesus, wasn't she the biggest nut of all? Sitting here, crying for this kid she barely knew, when she couldn't even stand her own brother. If only F. Dexter hadn't given Mory the lead in the family melodrama. F. Dexter the fanciful. F. Dexter the inadequate. Feeding off his children — and his ancestors. Hermann Maurice of Saxe, the macho Grand Marshall of France; king's bastard, military genius and hero, lover of the greatest French actress of his day. Why didn't they make men like that nowadays? The Grand Marshall was everything F. Dexter wanted to be and was not. So it all got shoved down the throats of his children. Or up the other end. Forget him! Listen to the music.

No, it wasn't all F. Dexter's fault. Mory was always a brat. Why not? To Wanda, he was the Second Coming. All he had to do was pop out to eclipse his older sisters. Because he was male? Because he followed two miscarriages? That didn't mean Wanda had to treat him like Baby Jesus, did it? Shit! Even a whore could have produced a better-looking baby. Wanda over-reacted to everything except incest. No, that she wouldn't believe. Sex only existed for procreation. Once she had her Baby Jesus, Wanda acted like the Last Catholic Virgin — and wanted to be treated like the First.

That's the way, Russell! Lift us out of this place. Jesus, Mary and Joseph! How does such talent end up in the nuthouse? Why did Tricia end up junkie dead? No wimp tears, now, sister. Be strong.

"You okay?" whispered Stacy, offering a tissue.

Maggie took it, nodded, and wiped her eyes.

"Why are you crying?" Stacy asked.

"For Russell." And Tricia. For all of them. For what might have been. For being born a girl, too attractive, too sexy. For loving F. Dexter — and hating him. For not being able to write like Sylvia Plath or Anne Sexton, to create beautiful music, to cut hair like Louise, to have a baby like Mrs. Daniels. Yes, and for not having enough faith in God's reasons. Forgive me Father, for I have sinned and don't know how to stop. Except by dying.

42

Escape

Maggie sat on the edge of her bed, waiting. Up the back staircase, from two floors below in the gym, came faint reverberations of Mr. Carlson's saxophone.

Jesus! At least she'd been spared that penance. After Mr. Carlson, they'd have the staff skit and a few carols. That was it for entertainment. If only the pizza man would come! Maybe, they'd even enjoy the pizza. Probably not, seeing as how she'd coaxed them into it. Well, that was their problem. Did they think she'd volunteered for the refreshment committee because she loved to bake Christmas cookies? With Sister Claire, she had. With Sister Claire and Kathy O'Reilly. Fifth grade? Another life. Well, before they had their cookies and ice cream tonight, the patients were going to have pizza. And she was going to have her freedom.

Had she forgotten anything important? Flats instead of heels, the ten dollar bill and her poems in her skirt pocket, a white turtle neck and beige cardigan instead of Juanita's satin blouse — and a reasonable explanation to Nurse Richards. "I have to change out of this blouse before I carry the pizza down, Miss Richards. Juanita will kill me if

I stain it serving." What else? Anything important? The nametag! How could she have forgotten the nametag. It was her passport, her insurance.

She got up, went to the small dresser and rummaged through the middle drawer until she found the balled up brown socks. From inside a sock she extracted the nametag. Nancy Brill's gift of atonement. God knows where she'd found it. R. Boone, L.P.N., didn't work on Palmer 3. Poor Nancy. Please Jesus, comfort and cure her.

The saxophone's wail intensified momentarily as the door to the back staircase opened and slammed shut. She pocketed the nametag and threw her socks in the drawer. Footsteps came down the hall toward her. Leaning against the dresser, she slipped off a shoe and made a show of putting it back on.

The knock was a formality. Her door was open. "How ya doin', Maggie?" The baritone was scratchy, the tone good-natured.

Jim Mills! Shit! She looked up and smiled at the huge attendant. The party had prompted alterations in his self-selected uniform: his khaki pants were neatly pressed; his enormous chest and muscular arms were jammed into a red sport shirt instead of a sleeveless jersey.

"Fine now, Jim. My high heels were killing me. Why aren't you down enjoying the show?"

"Mrs. Eggers asked me to come up and help you carry the pizza downstairs."

Eggers! That tight-lipped sourpussy wouldn't trust a saint. Maggie stood tall, smiled reassuringly. "Miss Richards is in the nursing station. She and I can handle it."

"That's okay." Jim smiled back but shook his head. "The way that man is playing the sax, I'd just as soon be up here... How come you put on a sweater?"

He knows! She feigned puzzlement. "Oh!" She smiled as if she'd decided he wasn't being impertinent, merely ignorant. "I was wearing Juanita's blouse. She'd kill me if I stained it eating pizza. I guess I must have gotten overheated downstairs, because I really felt chilled when I took it off... How do you stay so warm?"

"I take a cold shower every morning. It keeps me temperate."

Was he teasing? No matter; get rid of him! He'd ruin it all.

The door buzzer sounded. "That must be the pizza," said Jim.

Fuck! No time to do anything. "Well, let's go get it. I'm starving." She brushed by him and strode up the hall.

Keys in one hand, a wallet in the other, Richards came out of the nurses' station. She and Maggie reached the outer door simultaneously. Jim Mills was two steps behind. Richards fumbled for the right key.

Jesus, Mary and Joseph, let this go right. No way she could bolt with Jim Mills right behind her. He'd outrun her in the corridor, grab her and carry her back like a sack of potatoes. Like F. Dexter did, when she was little. She heard the lock click. Oh Jesus! Why couldn't You have sent Eggers, Gareaux or any of the others? Was Jim a sign to stay here?

The door swung open. Two men, one grizzled, the other young and greasy, both carrying stacked boxes of pizza. She didn't hesitate. "Here, I'll help you," she said to the older one, taking all but two of his boxes, turning, handing them to Jim. "Here Jim, I'll get the others."

"Let them come in, Maggie. I have to pay them," said Richards.

Maggie reached toward the younger man's boxes, then darted out between the delivery men. "I hate pizza," she yelled.

She heard shouts but kept running down the corridor. She imagined Jim Mills reaching for her shoulder. Faster! She came to the Exit sign, slammed down the handle, franticly pushed the door open. He'll take three steps to my one, she thought, catch me going down. So go up! She'd rounded the bend in the staircase when she heard the door below burst open. She stopped, heard Jim clattering downwards, then resumed her climb to the fourth floor door and let herself in as silently as she could. Except for a couple of parked wheelchairs, the corridor was deserted. Panting, she leaned against the wall and looked about. A fire hose behind glass, a door marked SINK, signs with arrows offering choices: Blood Bank to the left or Elevators and 4 South to the right. Blood Bank meant technicians, even at this hour. She pinned the nametag on her cardigan and turned right.

Roxanne? No, Rosalie, that was plainer. Rosalie Boone, L.P.N., on an important errand. What? Well, she needed to find a restroom soon. Fruit punch didn't mix well with frenzy. It wouldn't take Jim long to figure out what she'd done. Maybe he'd think her lead was bigger, that she'd made it out the second floor door before he'd blown by to the first. Richards would have called for help. They'd watch the exits. Uh-oh. Who's that? Doctor? Technician? They all looked the same in green scrub suits. She smiled primly as he approached. "Hi," he said absently. Good! His mind was obviously elsewhere. Elevator? No, too easily trapped. She needed another staircase. There! The red EXIT sign.

The signs on the fifth floor indicated that Outpatient Medical Clinics were to the right. Proctology, BRIDGE, and Maternity were to the left. What was BRIDGE? she wondered. Well, at least she had some possibilities. The medical clinics would be deserted; she could hide until morning. Sleep here? No, they had to have a night watchman or someone. Her very presence in an empty wing would guarantee more questions than she could answer. Proctology? No thanks. But Maternity might have people in and out all night long… Would Daniels' baby be in the window with the newborns? Wouldn't that be a lark — to see his baby? Little puppy-eyes. Risk it? She smiled and headed left.

Halfway down the corridor, she stopped before a wooden door. Female Staff Only. Well, wasn't Rosalie Boone female staff? Better go now than pay later. That's what Sister Wilhelmina used to say when she'd lined up the first graders in front of the bathroom. Yes, grim Wilhelmina and her threats of The Spanking Machine had scared the pee out of most of them. Okay, Sister, this one's for you.

The restroom was dark. She groped along the wall for the switch. Yes! Two small rooms. The outer with lockers, two wooden stools, an open hamper of dirty scrub suits — no, scrub dresses — and a shelf with clean ones. In there? Stalls, sinks and mirrors. Terrific!

She emerged in a green scrub dress, nametag in place, a smile on her lips. She passed by doctors' offices and examining rooms, following the orange arrows, even offering a cheery "Good evening" to a nurse hurrying in the opposite direction. The bridge was a passageway to another building. A blue-uniformed security guard loitered at the entrance. Her eyes darted about for an alternate route.

"Excuse me, Miss. Where are you coming from?"

Too late! "Coming from?" she echoed. He looked like he'd come from bed or a bar. Receding grey hair, hollow cheeks, bags under his eyes. "The ladies' room," she said. "Before that I was at the Blood Bank. I — delivered a sample. I'm going back to Maternity." She saw the two-way radio clipped to his belt. His nametag said E. Snead, Security.

"Did you see anyone around who doesn't belong?" asked Snead.

"Belong to whom?" Why was she trying to bait him?

His hand flapped impatiently. "To the hospital. To the staff."

"I don't think so. Do you have a description of him?"

"It's a girl. Beige skirt and sweater. White turtleneck shirt."

"What did she do?"

He touched his temple. "She's a mental case. Escaped from the psycho ward."

Did he think she was some lower form of life? "Is she dangerous?"

He shrugged. "Who knows with crazies, right?"

"Right." She forced a smile. "Fruitcakes are unpredictable, right?"

Snead nodded. "If you ask me, they should ship the whole bunch of them out to the state hospital and throw away the keys. The streets would be much safer."

"And cleaner. Wasted humans are human waste, right?" She glanced at the entrance to the bridge. "Listen, do you think it's safe for me to go on alone?"

"Oh, yeah." He smiled protectively. "She won't get by here. She's probably back on the street by now."

"I hope she's not an axe-murderer. I passed an axe in a case next to a fire hose."

"No, they're just for fire. I can walk you over to Maternity if you'd feel safer, Miss – " He squinted at her nametag. "What does that say — Boone?" His gaze remained fixed on her breasts.

"Yes. Boone. Mrs. Rosalie Boone. My husband is a state trooper. Thanks for offering, but you'd better stay here. I know how nasty supervisors can be." She tried to step around him.

He turned to prolong contact. "Yeah. We have one like that. My boss, Fremmer."

"You'd better stay here." She waved him off. "Bye-bye."

"Nice talking to you. Stop back again."

She felt his eyes on her ass. Stupid! Stupid! Flaunting her superiority, daring him to catch on, to catch her. Did she have to demonstrate how much smarter she was? So bogus! She hadn't even recognized what the BRIDGE sign meant. False pride and profound shame were a lousy combination to live with. She looked down at the cars passing five stories below. A running dive would do it. Not yet. She wanted to see Daniels' baby. Yes, her freedom was newborn, too. What a high — to look at their children simultaneously.

She followed the signs to the newborn nursery. Good! No one in front of the glass panels. Well who would be at this hour? What reason could she give? Why were the babies in plastic boxes? Weren't they uncomfortable like that? The enclosed ones must be incubators. Such sad, tiny babies. A masked and gowned woman was giving one a bottle. A white-capped nurse was writing on a chart. Why were all the lights on at night? No wonder most adults were insomniacs. And which one was Baby Daniels? The baby boxes were on wheeled carts that were turned in every direction. Hoffer, O'Malley, Johnson — no way she could see all the names. Damn! What if she asked? As one hospital employee to another. She tapped on the glass. The woman inside looked up. Maggie smiled and signaled. The nurse pointed around the corner, met her outside the door of the nursery. She was overweight. A pretty face except for the mole on her cheek. She had bangs and lovely dark lashes. Natural.

"Excuse me — " Maggie read her nametag. " — Mrs. Cortland. I'm Rosalie Boone. I'm an L.P.N. over in Palmer Pavilion. I heard that Mrs. Daniels delivered, yesterday. I work with her husband, Doctor Raymond Daniels, and I thought maybe I could just peek at the baby before my shift ends."

"I'm sorry — "

Maggie interrupted. "I don't want you to do anything against the rules. I just thought maybe you could point out which baby was his and I could look at it through the glass, that's all. I'm just so excited for Doctor Daniels. Do you know him?"

Cortland shook her head. "Not really." Her tone was apologetic. "I saw him when he visited his wife earlier this evening."

"Don't they make an adorable couple?"

"Yes, she's very pretty. It's too bad about the baby."

Mother of God! "You mean it died?"

"Oh, no. He's fine except for his eye. An hemangioma."

Hemangioma? Don't ask! Rosalie would know. "May I just have a quick peek at him?"

Cortland looked down the corridor. Her lips tightened. She shook her head regretfully. "I'm sorry. He's getting a feeding from his mother now."

"She's breast feeding him, I bet."

"Yes. Do you know Mrs. Daniels?"

Know her? Maggie smiled. "Doctor Daniels introduced me to her. Would it be okay to pop in for a minute to congratulate her?"

"I don't think — "

"Because I'm sure she could use support and she must be awake if the baby's with her. I'll just be a minute, no more. Promise."

Cortland glanced at her shoes, then looked up with a small smile. "Well, alright." She raised her finger. "But make sure you keep your composure when you see the baby. The tumor looks like little red worms on his eyelid. I don't want Mrs. Daniels feeling worse than she does already."

"Don't worry. I don't shock easily."

"Good. She's in 514." Cortland pointed down the corridor. "It's a single at the end, on the right. If Mrs. Hoover stops you at the desk, tell her Miss Cortland said it was okay."

The door to 514 was open halfway. Maggie knocked.

"Come in." The voice was gently appealing.

She entered. "Excuse me, Mrs. Daniels — " Holy Virgin! That red hair against the white nightgown! Not petite at all! She was propped up in bed, cradling the sleeping baby in a blue blanket.

"Oh, I'm glad you came. I think he's had his fill for now — " She stroked him with her fingertips. "He's a very contented little fellow. I'm sorry, I don't think I've met you. I'm Lisa Daniels. Have you just come on?"

"Yes." Country-pretty face, but pale, nothing fantastic. But she cared about that baby! "I'm — Rosalie Boone. I'm an L.P.N. Miss Cortland said it was okay to check and see how you were doing."

"Thank you." Mrs. Daniels smiled. Appreciative, yet sweetly sad. "I think I'm doing better." Her face said she was trying.

"I'm glad," said Maggie. Why? Because of Raymond? More. "I'm sure, no matter what the problems are, you'll be a wonderful mother."

"Thank you." Her eyes filled with tears. "That's very kind of you to say."

Maggie shrugged. "I say what I feel. I have confidence in you and Doctor Daniels. May I take a peek at the baby?"

"Oh, of course. Come over here where you can see him. Confidence about what?"

Maggie approached the bed. "To — to raise happy children. Nothing's more important." She bent over. "Hi, baby Daniels." The tumor was a purplish-pink mound on the baby's eyelid. Even without it, he wouldn't have been a Gerber baby. Well, Daniels wasn't any Robert Redford. She smiled. "He looks like his daddy."

"Do you know my husband?"

Maggie straightened up quickly. "Yes. We used to work together. Speaking of which, I have to get back to my other assignments."

Mrs. Daniels cocked her head. "I was watching your face when you looked at the baby. It didn't bother you at all — did it?"

Should it? Did it mean she was hard, unfeeling? "What?"

"The tumor. It didn't upset you. You didn't feel any pity."

"Is it cancer?" asked Maggie.

"No. But he may lose his sight in that eye."

"Mays usually become Junes." Maggie shook her head. "I'm sorry. I'm being facetious and I shouldn't. I have enough trouble dealing with realities. Possibilities are — well, they're like creatures from outer space. I'll worry when I meet one face-to-face."

Mrs. Daniels reached out and took her hand. "Please don't misunderstand. I'm relieved that it doesn't bother you. Everyone else is smothering us with concern, with pity. My own mother said she can't bear to look at the baby. I'm sure they put me in a single room so I wouldn't see another baby and another mother wouldn't see mine."

"Maybe no one else could bear listening to your mother."

Mrs. Daniels laughed. "If you only knew..."

Yes, a nice gift, to leave her laughing. Both for her and for Raymond. Maggie gave her hand a quick squeeze, then disengaged. She looked around in a conspiratorial manner. "I'll probably get fired for telling you this," she murmured, "but this hospital is desperate to win the National Hospital Association's competition for Hospital Fuck-Up of the Year." Mrs. Daniels giggled, Maggie continued. "We've been National Champion four times. Our motto is, 'We Fuck-Up Harder'."

They were laughing together like irreverent schoolgirls. Who would have expected? But she'd overstayed her time. "I really have to run."

"Wait. Won't you take Joshua back to the nursery?"

Carry the baby? "Joshua?" Raymond's baby.

"My grandfather's name. He didn't live long enough to see the Promised Land. Not even in this country. I pray Joshua will see it all for him."

Maggie nodded. "I'll pray for that, too."

"Here, hold him! He molds himself right into your body."

What was she doing? She took the baby, smelled the powder. This was crazy! Carrying Raymond's baby. "You're right. He snuggles in."

"Isn't he special?" asked Mrs. Daniels.

"Yes. He is. He's a dream."

43

Christmas Tidings

The television was on. The anchorman was interviewing American soldiers in Vietnam at their Christmas Eve service, but Raymond had turned off the sound. The telephone call interrupted the imaginary tea party he, his daughter and her Chatty Kathy doll were enjoying on the living room rug.

"I'll be right back, Julie," said Raymond. "Daddy has to answer the phone." He put down his tiny tea cup and scrambled up from the rug.

"Mommy? From the hospital?" Julie's face lit up.

"I don't know," he said.

"Raymond, the telephone is ringing," his mother-in-law yelled from the bathroom. "Where does she keep her Babo?"

"The what?" he shouted on the way to the kitchen phone.

"The cleanser. She has stains in the tub."

"Maybe on the floor of the broom closet... Hello?"

"Doctor Daniels?"

"Anita?" Why was he no longer Raymond to Anita DeSimone?

"Yes. Doctor Taylor asks that you come in for an important meeting at eleven o'clock today."

"Today?" They knew that Lisa'd delivered, had approved his time off. Anita had even called Lisa to congratulate her.

"Yes. Doctor Taylor is aware that it may be a great inconvenience and apologizes for the short notice, but he — "

"C'mon Anita. You sound like the recorded message you get from the electric company after the power goes out. What's going on?"

"I'm sorry, Raymond. I'm not at liberty to say. But it is very important."

"Am I being fired?"

"Don't be ridiculous. Why on earth would Doctor Taylor do that?"

"Tomorrow's Christmas."

"Don't be — just be here at eleven, okay?"

"Okay. Thanks." His lips tightened; he hung up the phone. Not fired, he thought. What other big trouble could he be in?

*   *   *

He got to the hospital a few minutes before eleven but chose to dawdle on his way to Taylor's office so as not to have to stew in a chair longer than necessary.

As he entered the outer office, Anita looked up, frowned, then tilted her head toward Taylor's door. "They're waiting," she said.

"They who?"

"Go right in."

"Tell me, does `not at liberty' imply bondage?"

"Don't be bitchy, Raymond. I know you're under stress about the baby, but we all have our problems."

"The baby has nothing to do with this." Stressed and bitchy, was he? "I see you finally got your new air conditioner. Just in time for Christmas. Congratulations." He saw her frown. Well, from burned

312

bridges, one has to move forward. He knocked on the Chairman's door and opened it.

"Ah, Raymond," said Taylor, rising from behind his desk. He realigned his wire-rimmed glasses. "I believe you know Mr. Fremmer, Assistant Director of Hospital Security?"

Fremmer turned his head but made no effort to extract himself from one of the twin leather chairs facing the desk.

"Yes," said Raymond, wanting to add "we played hounds in a puddle of piss."

"How do, Doc," said Fremmer. It wasn't a question.

Raymond acted as if it was. "Could be better." Well, at least he wasn't in huge trouble. Taylor had addressed him as Raymond. "Yourself?" he asked Fremmer.

Fremmer winked. "Could be worse."

"Please sit down. We have a lot to discuss." Taylor's tone was businesslike.

As Raymond sank into the chair parallel to Fremmer's, Taylor stretched taller before his wall of diplomas. "Thank you for coming in on your vacation time, Raymond. First, I want to congratulate you on the birth of your son. I know that you and your wife must be worried about him. Please convey Mrs. Taylor's and my best wishes to Lisa. If there's anything we can do to help, don't hesitate to let Anita know." He pulled out his chair and sat down.

"Thank you, sir." Was Taylor sincere? Gracious as a pompous ass can be? Or were he and Fremmer the pawns in another game?

Taylor folded his hands in front of him. "I'm afraid we had a great deal of difficulty last night." He pursed his lips, then drew out each word. "Mary Margaret Saxe escaped."

"She did?" Raymond straightened up in his chair. "Why wasn't I called?"

"You were on vacation," said Taylor. "Doctor Spiva was notified. But there were other ramifications."

"A suicide attempt?" Raymond clutched his thighs. Dead? Oh God.

"Yes," said Taylor. "Unsuccessful, fortunately. But she suffered a broken collar bone and three cracked ribs."

"What? How?" Raymond ran a hand through his hair.

"There's more," said Taylor.

"More?"

Taylor raised a reassuring hand. "Please try to stay calm. Miss Saxe is being well taken care of." He pointed his hand at Raymond. "Most important, you must understand your wife and baby are fine and you can see them right after our discussion."

"I don't understand." Lisa and the baby? he thought. What do they have to do with Maggie Saxe?

Taylor folded his hands on the desk and leaned forward. "After she escaped, Miss Saxe put on a nurse's scrub dress and a hospital nametag. She visited your wife, tricked her into giving up the baby and started off with it."

"Lisa gave Joshua to Maggie?" Raymond sagged against the leather backrest and stared at the Chairman. "Maggie took our baby?"

It was as if Taylor read his confusion and disbelief. "Your wife and baby are perfectly fine," he repeated. "And it wasn't your wife's fault. Mary Saxe tricked her. You're perfectly within your rights to involve the police and bring charges of kidnapping against her. Fortunately — " He nodded at Fremmer. " — our friend here was on his toes and apprehended her before she got off the floor."

Involve the police? Raymond glanced at Fremmer. The man's face was stony, but a hint of pride was in his eyes. Yes, a professional soldier receiving a commendation.

"Mr. Fremmer relieved her of the baby, who was not injured in any way and he and one of his men — "

"Edward Snead," interjected Fremmer.

" — Edward Snead," echoed Taylor, "were walking Mary Saxe back to Palmer 3 when she attempted to escape."

Raymond felt warmth on the back of his fingers. He glanced down, became aware he was rubbing them and stopped. "What happened?" he asked Fremmer.

"She was a lamb until we got to the fifth floor bridge, then she broke and ran for a header out the windows."

"She — she fell five stories?"

Fremmer shook his head. "She never made it. This black boy over on Palmer 3 — Jim Mills — well, he was out hunting her, too. Felt responsible for her escape, I gather. Well, when one of my people told him we'd located her on Maternity, this Jim came running. He came onto the bridge and made the best damn flying tackle I've ever seen outside a stadium." Fremmer's hand whipped forward. "Both in mid-air – bang! Like a 747 hitting a Learjet taking off. But he saved her damn fool life. The boy's an honest-to-God hero. Saved us all a mess." Fremmer looked at Taylor. "Did you know he was cut by the Colts?"

"No," replied Taylor.

Fremmer shrugged. "The Dolphins I could understand. The Colts should have kept him."

They were bizarre! Inane! Raymond pounded his fist on the arm of his chair. "Why the fuck wasn't I called?"

Taylor's arms spread apart to indicate what he saw in front of him. "Because you might have acted just like this. We had a crisis on our hands." His own hands dropped softly to the desktop. "Don't you think we knew the strain you and your wife were under with your baby? Why subject either one of you to this in the middle of the night?"

"You mean Lisa doesn't know? No one told her?" Involving the police and attorneys would complicate everything even more, thought Raymond. Thank God, Lisa and Joshua weren't hurt.

"I stopped by as an old acquaintance of yours, making my normal hospital rounds," said Fremmer. "No need at that point to worry the little lady. Hell, she'd had a fine old time with Rosalie Boone."

"Who?"

"That was the name Miss Saxe was using," explained Taylor.

"Remember the last crazy kid you had that ran off?" asked Fremmer. "Well, R. Boone was the nametag we never found. Always did bother me."

Raymond ran a hand through his hair. "So Lisa doesn't know any of this?"

"No," replied Taylor. "I thought you'd want to tell her yourself, that it would be less traumatic."

"She sent the baby back to the nursery, and that's where the baby ended up," said Fremmer. "Happy ending."

Dare he believe it? "You're sure that Lisa and Joshua are fine."

"Certain," said Fremmer.

"And Maggie?"

Taylor's fingertips struck the desktop. "Medically, she's in no danger, but — "

"She just won't be taking any deep breaths for a while," said Fremmer.

"But," Taylor said, "she remains dangerous to herself and others, despite months of your dedicated efforts. That's clear, isn't it?"

Raymond felt cold. "You sent her out," he murmured.

"This morning, to the state hospital — after she received proper medical attention here."

"Without letting me talk with her." All the pawns pushed. All the moves made.

Taylor waved away his objection. "She endangered your family; she compromised her treatment here."

"That's my decision," Raymond snapped. "I'm her physician."

"No longer," said Taylor. "Remember, Doctor Daniels, you are a trainee, not a full-fledged psychiatrist. You're not autonomous, yet. Is that clear?" He glared across the desk.

The threat? How could he miss it? One more wrong move, checkmate! Raymond looked down at his lap. Game's over. Pick up your pieces and go home. No, there had to be a way to fight him! Raymond looked up. "You told me you weren't going to be involved in this case — that I could handle it."

Taylor leaned forward. "I had no idea she'd do what she did. Understand me, Raymond. I must do what's best not only for you and your family and that miserable woman, I must do what's best for the department and for this hospital."

Lord Protector of his fief, was he? Raymond rubbed his forehead. Miserable woman? Miserable? That much trouble? "Did you meet with Maggie Saxe to tell her why she was going or that she was going — or anything?"

Taylor leaned back in his chair. "Of course not. Doctor Spiva took care of that."

"Did you ever meet or speak to her?"

Taylor offered a small smile. "What a strange question. No, I never have. What prompted you to ask?"

"You called her a 'miserable woman'."

"Did I?" Taylor looked to Fremmer. The security man nodded.

Taylor shrugged. "I meant poor and unfortunate. I suppose it was a poor and unfortunate choice of a word. Honestly, Raymond, I have tried and continue to try to do the best for all concerned. I don't expect everyone to agree with or like all my decisions. I do expect my faculty and trainees to abide by them. Is that clear?"

Raymond felt his throat constrict.

"Is that clear?" Taylor demanded.

Raymond nodded.

"Good." Taylor looked at his watch. "Do you have any further questions? I have a luncheon downtown, but you'll be able to get any remaining details from Mr. Fremmer."

Raymond rubbed his face. His cheeks were hot. Questions? So much, so fast. Taylor had used time to his advantage. The master moving his pawns. And where were the knights that protected this pawn? "Was Professor Bergstrom informed about what happened last night?"

"Of course. I called him this morning. No need to disturb him in the middle of the night when he's expecting such bad news, already."

Bad news? Bergstrom? What the hell, why not? "Right. Then he still hasn't heard?" asked Raymond.

"No. The boy is still comatose." The Chairman shook his head sadly. "Our children can be our biggest tragedies." He pointed his hand at Raymond. "Let me tell you, no one can better appreciate what you and your wife are going through with a child with a birth defect than Erik Bergstrom. He invested so much time and effort in that retarded son of his." Taylor's hand sliced the air. "And then some drunken fool destroys it all. Senseless, absolutely senseless."

"Yes," Raymond agreed. At least Taylor had some empathy in his craw. Retarded? Comatose? Joshua's tumor seemed even smaller, now.

Taylor looked at his watch and stood up. "I'm going to have to be on my way."

As he and Fremmer rose, Raymond asked, "Did Professor Bergstrom agree with this decision?"

Taylor walked to the paneling beyond the closed door to his office. "In its substance, yes. He thought you should get a final interview with her. We disagreed only on that point." Taylor pressed on the paneling. The door to a concealed closet sprang open. "I mean how can you be objective with someone who tries to kidnap your baby?" He extracted a blue topcoat and gray fedora. "I really believe that it would be best for you and your wife to put all this behind you as quickly as possible."

Fremmer stepped forward to help the Chairman don his coat. Taylor kept talking. "I'm sure you have enough to worry about without Miss Saxe. It would probably be best for you if you never saw her again." Taylor closed the closet. "She'd just bring more trouble your way."

"I'll think about it."

Taylor smiled. "Do!" He opened the office door and walked out.

"C.Y.A., Doc." Fremmer shook his head. "Didn't I tell you?"

"Look, will you get the fuck off your smug — " Raymond stopped as Taylor reappeared in the doorway.

"I'm sorry," said the Chairman. "I almost forgot. Merry Christmas!"

PART V

February 1970

44

The Attic

Denise would regret it, thought George. Yes, he'd see to that after he found the old pictures. "In some box in the attic," she'd said. Another lie, most likely. Two lies with one bowl of stew.

Enough boxes up here to build a bonfire. Ought to build it right under her ass. Hadn't he told her to get rid of all his mother's junk? Denise saved more shit than a farmer. Maybe in this one...why didn't she ever label anything? The old shower curtain? Why was she storing that? What would she do when she ran out of attic; take over his basement room? No, she wasn't going to mess with his guns the way she messed with his mind. She'd regret lying — he'd make her eat her words. Maybe he'd flavor her dessert with the poison he'd bought for the crows. Trying to poison his brain with that lie! No wonder he'd freaked out, that he'd choked her until her hands stopped clawing his, until her fat face was blue and her eyes popped out and the stench of her bowels letting go became too strong.

Finishing dinner hadn't been easy afterwards, what with the baby crying and Carol spilling her milk and Denise yakkety-yakking about how he'd looked so strange for a minute and maybe he should see a real doctor instead of that shrink and those neuro people, or at least take vitamins fortified with iron.

Could a corpse talk? No — but he'd seen her do it, hadn't he? So she wasn't dead. Or wasn't human. Or maybe certain corpses could talk. The grubsuckers were trying to confuse him. Brown cushions? Crap! He'd taken that sofa to the dump two years ago. Was Denise waiting for it to come back? She was just a giant squirrel, that's what she was, hoarding upstairs, chomping away downstairs, with just a peanut for a brain. No, she had to be smarter than that — the way she'd slipped in that lie so casual, mixed in with her jabber like a tiny piece of bone hidden in his bowl of stew, a sharp little fragment to stick in his throat.

"Rita said that Carol had your eyes and dimples, George, but I told her no, she was wrong — Carol! Use the spoon, not your fingers. — because you have gray eyes and Carol's are more green. Carol has your mother's eyes and mouth. I swear she favors your mother more than she does me. Rita said the boys will swarm to her like bees around honey — "

He'd shut her up, hadn't he? Choked her and killed her. Too late to stop the lie. But maybe it wasn't a lie. What seemed real, sometimes wasn't. He was real — when he cut himself shaving, he bled. Yet he could strangle Denise like he had at dinner, feeling it with every sense, and there she'd be afterwards, yakking away, barely stopping to swallow her food. So either his spells weren't real or Denise and the kids weren't real. Could he only tell which was true afterward? Like that cop who gave him a ticket, and Deg at the meat-packing plant, and all the others he'd butchered who were still walking around. But what if they were crows, pretending to be the people he killed?

Dolls! This box couldn't be his mother's, it had to be Denise's. She must have kept every scraggly one of her dolls. No, some of the grubsuckers he'd killed were definitely alive. Bowel-bound Mike had his ass in a sling but most of the others looked and acted no different than before. Maybe he'd never killed anyone. Maybe Garbage-Mouth Vinnie was still out there on the street, clutching the wheel with both "LOVE" and "HATE." Had the newspaper stories about that killing been lies? Denise lied. His mother had lied. Were the newspapers any better?

Carol couldn't have his mother's eyes and mouth. His mother was dead, her face rotting with her. That had to be real. Hadn't he buried her? Maybe she'd been right after all. Maybe he should have cremated every ounce of her flesh. Then there'd be no doubt, no need for old pictures. No way for her to come back. Where the hell was that album?

"Did you find it?" Denise was huffing up the folding stairs.

"No." He shoved aside two broken chairs to get to the boxes piled behind them. "Try to remember which box you put it in."

Denise looked down the steps. "You want to come, too, Carol? I'm not going away, sugar. Wait a minute, George, I'm going to bring Carol up. The baby's in for a nap." Denise started down.

"No. It's not safe up here." He stripped packing tape from a cardboard box.

"It's okay; I'll watch her," Denise called up to him.

"Too many nails sticking out," he shouted. Damn her fat head! He opened the long box. Shoot! Her wedding gown.

Carol's head poked up through the opening in the floor. Her ponytail bobbed up and down as she looked into the attic, then down at the ladder.

"That's right, keep going," Denise encouraged from below. "Climb over the top and let Mommy up."

"It's high," said Carol.

"Take another step, sugar." Denise's dark brown hair appeared above the trap. "That's right."

"Will you use your brain instead of your mouth for a minute? Which box did you put the album in?"

Denise took another step up. Her plump face registered an apology. "I told you I don't know. I packed away so much."

"I can see that." He pulled over another box.

"There you go, Sugar; stay away from this big hole, now." Denise climbed into the attic and took Carol by the hand. "I'll help you find it, George. I'm really glad you want to look at the pictures. I know you felt terrible about her death and all, but it wasn't right not to have one picture of your mother in the house."

"What the hell is this? Rags? You packed away rags?"

"Can I see the pictures?" asked Carol.

"Remnants. You can see the pictures after Daddy. Why don't you try that Del Monte box." She pointed to a pile of boxes in the corner.

He dropped the box of remnants; it hit the floor with a thud. "I thought you didn't know which one it was." He headed for the corner.

"I don't. I'm only guessing. Carol! Look in this one, look at the dolls! You know, these were once Mommy's dolls."

He ripped open the Del Monte box.

"I want that one," said Carol.

"That's Raggedy Ann. I loved Raggedy Ann, too. Here, you hold her."

The album! Found you, you sucker. Never mind Carol's squeals and Denise's chatter, here's the proof that Denise was lying. At the very least, that she didn't know what she was talking about. If he couldn't remember his mother's face — a mask of make-up, yes, but no face underneath — how in hell could Denise?

No, not surprising that the album felt lighter than it had when he used to study it, examining each photo for a male face that looked like his, asking her directly, then slyly, then not at all, but imagining each man as his father. She never said. Wouldn't even say why. Well, let her rot. He hated to look at her face again. There was no person inside.

Pages getting brown, crumbling at the edges. Black corner tabs falling — dead flies? Childhood pictures of her? No, this was better — a close-up. Shoot! Right there, in black and white. Ma was alive in his kid! The album fell from his hands. "Carol!"

"George, look at this — my wedding gown!"

"I saw it. Carol!" Alive in that little body. "Carol, come here!" Stupid! Stupid! Why hadn't he seen the resemblance before?

"George! Look!"

Denise in her bridal veil, holding the dress in front of her. Carol coming with that stupid doll. His mother's face laughing, the doll grinning, Denise's face dissolving under that veil. No one real. Crows, just crows. Clawing and shredding his brain.

He felt Carol stiffen when he grabbed her and hoisted her up to the rafter, heard her scream as she flew, then the snap of her small body against the stairs, the tumble and thud below. He saw Denise drop the wedding gown, shrieking "Carol! Carol!"

His fist hurt as it smashed through her veil to teeth and bone. He watched Denise fall backwards over the cartons, spilling them every which way as pots and pans clattered down behind her. He felt himself moving, reaching, pulling her up by the hair, backhanding the bloody lace from her head. She wasn't Denise, but a faceless, gurgling doll spewing blood onto his hands. How easily his fingers did the rest.

Yes, she bled, Denise bled; she must have been real... Or would she start yakking again?

45

The Letter

Lisa folded the dishtowel and hung it on the rack. "That woman sent another letter," she announced.

Maggie? Raymond looked up from sweeping supper crumbs from under the kitchen table. "Did you open it?"

"This one's addressed to you only." Lisa turned on the faucet and wet the sponge. "Why didn't she mail it to the hospital?"

"I don't know."

She throttled the sponge, turned off the tap. "I don't like her letters coming to the house."

"I know." Was he going to get another earful about Maggie? "Where's the letter?"

"On the dresser in the bedroom." She began to sponge the counter around the sink. "I wanted it to wait until the children were asleep."

"I'll get it." He leaned the broom against the table.

She looked annoyed. "Aren't you going to finish the floor?"

"Sure." He frowned at the broom, grabbed it and resumed sweeping. When had the first letter come? Mid-January? A denial that she'd tried to kidnap Joshua, an apology for the worries she'd caused. What made him believe her? Lisa sure hadn't. She'd really flown off the handle. How dare he defend someone who'd deceived her, who had duped her into surrendering her baby.

"Where's the dustpan?" he asked.

"Where it is every night."

"Oh, right." Sure, later they'd recognized that their worries about Joshua's tumor had heightened their anxieties. But she'd labeled him an ostrich and he'd accused her of hysteria and she'd flared up like a rocket, accusing him of hiding behind psychiatric mumbo-jumbo and a superior attitude that —

"I'm beat," said Lisa, on her way out. "I'm going to bed. Will you put the chairs back?"

"Sure. I'll be in soon." She really did look exhausted. It wasn't only the pre-dawn feedings and lack of sleep, it was running back and forth to the hospital with the baby, the worries about blindness, the talk of surgery. Hadn't he cried when alone in the car? How could he blame Lisa for being less than understanding about Maggie Saxe? There was too damn much to worry about without her.

He finished his chores, turned out the kitchen light and headed for the bedroom. He heard Lisa brushing her teeth. The envelope lay face down on the dresser. A mixture of excitement and foreboding coursed through him as he picked it up, opened it, and extracted a single sheet of notebook paper. Maggie's handwriting was embellished with curlicues.

Dear Raymond,

I don't like to ask for your help, but I'm not asking for myself alone. Nancy Brill is here on this ward. Did you know that? Remember what happened to me as a child? It's happening here, but mostly to Nancy. We need to see you as soon as possible. Please don't let us down. Maggie.

Shit! Sexual abuse there, too? He sighed heavily. Don't let us down. He'd have to go.

"What did she say?" asked Lisa. She was in her nightgown. She hadn't bothered to brush her hair.

He handed her the note, unbuttoned his shirt as she read.

"What happened to her as a child?" she asked.

"Sexual abuse."

She tossed the note on the dresser. "That's happening at the state hospital?"

"With an attendant, a doctor — I don't know." He dropped his shirt on the floor, started to unbuckle his belt.

"She wants to see you. You going?"

He looked at her warily. "Yes."

"Good."

"You. — you don't mind?" He pulled his belt free.

"Of course I do." She quickly raised her hand. "I don't want you to ever see that woman again."

"But you said `good'," protested Raymond. He tossed his belt on the chair.

She nodded. "I feel that, too."

"But that's opposite — "

"I have both feelings, what can I do?" She retreated to her side of the bed. "Help me with the bedspread, okay?"

"Yeah, sure."

"No one should face something like that alone," she told him as they folded back the bedspread. "The police won't believe a mental patient. I wouldn't believe that woman either, except it's happening to someone else too, isn't it?"

"That's what she wrote."

"You'll make sure it's true, won't you?"

"Yes."

"Good. Give me your end."

He relinquished his part of the bedspread, sat down on the end of the bed and took off his shoes. Lisa draped the folded spread over the back of the chair.

"Just one visit," she said, coming to stand over him. "Then I don't want you to see that woman again."

Raymond smiled. "I know." He stood up and kissed her.

46

Wretchville

Maggie forced herself to walk with composure. She wanted to fly up the corridor and kiss him. He'd come! He'd really come!

"Hello," said Raymond, advancing to meet her. "It's good to see you." The attendant who'd unlocked the door walked back past them as they halted awkwardly in the windowless hallway. Above the first four feet of pale green tiles, the plaster walls were cracked, the yellow paint was peeling.

She felt like a glowworm on the scuffed linoleum. "Welcome to Wretchville," she said. "Glad you could pop by." She planted her hands in the pockets of her jeans. Yes, safe there.

"Wretchville?" he asked.

"I changed the name. Capital `W' or capital `R' — they both fit. I like `W' because Doctor White once told me a capital `W' made names easier to remember. I suppose he's forgotten mine, already. Well, nuts in, nuts out — that's the way it goes." One hand sprang loose. "Would you like the penny tour? The whole fucking place isn't worth two cents."

He smiled. "Calm down. You sound like you're speeding. You cut your braids?"

"Sorry. My cup and mouth runneth over. I'm glad you came. Yes, I cut my hair before — " She put a hand to her hair. "Does it look awful?"

"I think it looks better." Raymond's eyes focused over her shoulder. "We have company."

Maggie turned to face a gray-haired, tall but withered black woman. She'd emerged from the side-bedroom in a safety-pinned sweater, faded housecoat, slippers, and high socks. "Oh, Lady Agnes! Let me introduce you to my — visitor, Doctor Raymond Daniels. Doctor Daniels, this is Lady Agnes, one of my five roommates."

"Hello," said Raymond.

Lady Agnes' mouth puckered and twitched. Her eyes seemed dull with despair.

"Would you like to shake his hand, Lady Agnes?" asked Maggie. "They say Lady Agnes hasn't talked for more than thirty years, but she has an outstanding handshake."

Lady Agnes raised her hand slowly. Her fingers twitched in an arrhythmic dance.

"Thank you, Lady Agnes," said Raymond as she clasped his hand.

"Lady Agnes represents the Wretchville State Department," said Maggie. "She greets all the visiting dignitaries. We get one coming through every ten years or so, don't we Agnes?"

Lady Agnes smiled slightly and kept pumping Raymond's hand.

"You have a very strong handshake," said Raymond.

Lady Agnes grinned. She was toothless.

"I'm sure her great-great grandfather was a Zulu nobleman," said Maggie. "I've asked her and she's never denied it. Please let go now, Lady Agnes. He's a special friend. If anybody's going to wear him out, it's going to be me." Mother of God! "Ignore that!" she told Raymond. "I didn't even think it." She put her good arm around the older woman's shoulders. "Lady Agnes and I share three things — royal blood, a cold room and a hot sense of humor; don't we Agnes? Her idea of a joke is to hold visitors' hands until they turn blue." Tugging gently on Agnes' forearm, she helped Raymond disengage. "It's a good joke, Agnes. Another thirty days here, I'll be doing the very same thing. Good. Will you please excuse us now? We have to go talk."

Lady Agnes frowned.

"Don't pout. I'll come shake your hand later," said Maggie, motioning Raymond to follow her.

She led him down the corridor, passing another six-bed unit, the dining room and the large bathroom that contained the showers.

"I don't want to take you into the dayroom," said Maggie. "Who knows what the Duchess is doing in place of croquet." Maggie stopped at the nurses' station. Mrs. Larabee was standing on tip-toe, head back, chubby arm extended, placing a large medication bottle onto the highest shelf of a crowded cabinet. Beneath her straggly gray hair, the nurse's face was pink; her blouse was ready to pop its buttons.

"Excuse me, Mrs. Larabee," said Maggie.

"Huh?" Larabee's body came back to earth before she took her eyes from the bottle. "Maggie, have you seen the stepstool?" Larabee saw Raymond. "Oh!" She put a hand to her chest.

"No, I haven't seen it today," said Maggie. "This is Doctor Daniels, my psychiatrist from University Hospital."

Larabee's smile was marred by stained teeth. "Hello, Doctor. Maggie told me you might be coming." The smile became sheepish. "Someone keeps hiding the stepstool."

Squire Tommy, thought Maggie. "Could you be so kind as to open the conference room for us?" she asked. "I feel a pressing need for Doctor Daniels to cure my lunacy once and for all. How much time do you have?" she asked him.

"About an hour."

Maggie nodded. "With luck, we can do it."

Larabee grinned. "I hope so. I'll unlock it. Use it as long as you need. Just let me know when you're done." She winked at Maggie. "I've always wanted to see a miracle."

There were enough plastic chairs, armchairs and sofas around the perimeter of the room to seat two dozen people. Maggie chose a padded armchair that caught sunlight from a high window. Raymond moved a white plastic chair from against the wall so that they faced each other.

"How's the baby?" asked Maggie.

Raymond sat down. "Okay. Except the tumor's not shrinking, yet." His lips tightened. There was an unspoken question in his eyes.

She leaned forward. "I didn't try to kidnap him. I swear I didn't."

"What happened?" His tone had a hard edge.

"I was walking back toward the nursery when I saw a nurse waving S.O.S. to that Neanderthal security guard. I got spooked and turned back toward your wife's room. I should have just stopped immediately and given the baby over. That's what I did do, but not until I saw there was no other way out without running." She put her hand out toward him. "I wouldn't hurt any baby, much less yours." Her breath caught in her throat until he nodded.

"I believe you… How's your collarbone?"

"Okay. It hurts without the sling, but I need my hands free in here. There are a couple of guys sent here by the Court who are a little too free with theirs." She inhaled deeply, leaned back against the chair, then exhaled. "At least I can breathe without my ribs making it feel like hot knives were sticking me... Do you know Joe Mills has come up to see me a couple of times?"

"Really?"

"He feels awful about it. He's really a good guy, but I made him feel worse." She pretended to be a wilting flower. "I acted like Camille, except I didn't dare cough."

His lips hinted of a smile. "Why did you give him a hard time?"

She straightened up. "Why should I let someone who's hurt me off the hook?"

"The way I heard it, Joe Mills saved your life."

She shrugged. "We all make mistakes."

"What about the John who dumped you at the hospital? Why protect him? Who is he?"

Damn her big mouth! He'd not forgotten her slip of the tongue in that awful seclusion room. "I can't, Raymond. I promised. Stupid of me, but I was terribly upset. Anyway, I'm sure he's hurting, too."

"What makes you think so?"

She pressed the back of one hand to her forehead, lifted the other hand skyward, showing him Greta Garbo. "Vhat mahn who hahd me vould not suffer vidout me?" Her hands descended, her voice returned to normal. "The problem is that anyone I like seems to suffer worse with me." She tried not to look grim. "It's hopeless. Forget it."

"And where are your suicidal feelings at?" he asked.

Why was he so fucking serious? Was it a Freudian sin to enjoy their time together? Closing her eyes, she poked a forefinger in her mouth for a count of three, then held her finger in front of her and examined it as if it were a thermometer. "Ninety-six point seven, doctor. Getting close to rigor mortis."

Raymond put both feet to the floor and leaned forward. "Maggie, would you stop trying so hard to entertain me. I know you're glad I came. But I'm here on serious business, right?"

She looked down at the floor, wanted to sink out of sight. "Sorry — all my life I've been playacting. It's hard to change." She bowed her head and shielded her face with her hand. "Today I don't feel like killing myself, because you came to see me. If you care, maybe I'm not so terrible. Especially because you know me pretty well. Joe comes. Petro was here. That helps, because none of you are out to use me. And being here, I see people living lives that are a lot worse than mine. But — " She tried to rub away the pain in her forehead. "But there are many days — days when I'm deep down in Slut-City and feel I can't make it out." She bowed her head. "No, that's not true anymore. It's that it's not worth the effort. It's too painful to change. And even if I do, I'll still be — damaged, still be alone."

"Wake up!" His sharp tone jarred her. "Everybody's damaged. It's how you put the pieces back together that makes you strong — and beautiful. The A.A. people have a very good saying: `Live one day at a time'."

Beautiful? She looked up. "I'm trying. But I can't last long in here." Did he really think she was beautiful? "I would have taken off already if it weren't for Nancy."

"What's going on?"

She snorted. "The psychiatrist running this ward is a pervert. He likes exposing himself to yuffies. If we don't scream or pass out, he asks for a blow job."

"A real son-of-a-bitch, is he?"

"Not when you first meet him. He acts like butter wouldn't melt in his mouth."

"We'll need to convince the superintendent that the doc isn't what he appears to be." Raymond looked puzzled. "What are yuffies?"

"Young, unbalanced females." Her hand moved as if petting a snake. "The man is sickeningly smooth. He gets your case history before he decides whether to unzip."

"He did it to you?"

She nodded. "He started by talking to me about my sexual experiences, asking what turns me on. I told him I was aroused by nude pictures of eunuchs. When you're crazy, you can say anything, right?"

He shrugged. "So what happened?"

"So he said that men must have hurt me very badly in sex — how he was different, could cure me of my castration complex. From live pigs, you only get pigshit."

"And he exposed himself?"

She rolled her eyes. "Well, I wasn't about to scream or faint. I have seen — never mind. The only real pervert I ever knew was my father." She shook her head. "No, that's not true — there was a guy named Cal that raped me." Her hand brushed aside all feeling. "Well anyway, I was curious to see if there was a resemblance where it counted. I was even toying with the idea of biting it off. Let him explain that!"

Raymond shifted in his chair. "Did you — do anything?"

She pointed at his face. "Seems to me I once asked you the same question, but you never answered it. You said I should have been a surgeon."

"You don't have to answer."

Her hands flew up. "Why not? I've got nothing to hide from you anymore — well, practically nothing." She brought her hands down to her lap and clasped them demurely. "No, I didn't lower myself. I simply waited until he had it out and said, `Is that all, doctor? Now you've lost my respect in every dimension.' Was that gracious and ladylike, or what?"

Raymond nodded. "Much more gracious than biting it off."

"Please. I'd rather make do with a Tootsie Roll." She looked down at his shoes. "The truth is I've never fought back. Only with my mouth."

"Why didn't you tell the Superintendent?"

She met his gaze squarely. "I can tell you, because I trust you'll believe me. Even then, I hide a lot behind my jokes and zingers." She gripped the arms of her chair. "I can't tell a stranger. Besides, the bastard said that if I told, he'd call me mentally unbalanced and say I was having a vivid sexual fantasy as part of the fucking transference. Who's going to believe me? What man will say I'm not 'provocative'?" Her hands swept the air in opposite directions. "It doesn't matter. I can take care of myself. But the bastard is doing it to Nancy." She thumped her chair. "I want him dead!"

He nodded. "And I want him out of the profession."

"Dead would accomplish that."

"Will Nancy talk about it?"

"In her crazy way. `Sucking the Devil's Pipe' she calls it. You know she smokes now? Another new trick she learned here." She saw his displeasure. "Don't look at me like that — I didn't teach her."

"That's not what I was thinking," he said.

"Good. I think the bastard deliberately fit his prick into her Devil delusions. Maybe he just buys her with cigarettes." She shrugged. "I don't think her parents give her any. Why is she hospitalized so far from home?"

Raymond passed his hand through his hair. "Her father was a — is a V.I.P. He didn't want her where people who knew him might gossip. Do you know of any other women who've been abused here?"

"One girl who left a week ago. But she wasn't about to go public with it. She said her father would beat the shit out of her and throw her out of the house. I told her we should have switched fathers at birth... " She shook her head. "Men are so bizarre when it comes to sex."

Raymond cleared his throat. "You know you'll have to testify in order to get him fired and his license pulled. Also, if you decide to go ahead with legal action."

Her eyes sought his. "Will you be there to testify for me?"

"All the way." His eyes reassured her. "But at some point Superintendent Kroft or an ethics committee of doctors will demand to talk to you alone. You probably will be able to have a lawyer with you."

"I wouldn't know who to go to."

"I'll help you find someone. A woman."

"I just can't be alone in it, Raymond. I mean I'll try. I really will. I can do it for Nancy more than myself. God knows she can't defend herself, either." She crossed her arms on her chest, massaged the flesh beneath her sleeves. "All my life I've been trying to do it alone. So don't leave me more than you have to."

"I'll do my best. What's the psychiatrist's name?"

She told him. They went to get Nancy.

47

The Court

"Don't inhale," said Maggie, leading him through a communal bedroom, "the disinfectant will burn your lungs."

Raymond paused for a sniff. "It's not that bad."

Easy for him to say — he didn't have to live in it. Maggie glanced back. Well, give him a few minutes to let the bleakness sink in. A dozen beds, the piss pine odors and brain rot — like vacuous Lord Charlie over there, and poor Czarina Walker, body flopping every which way with Huntington's Disease. Fucking place's full of made beds and unmade people. Too easy to lose hope and compassion, too easy to become less than human.

"Come on." She started down the center aisle. "The dayroom's through here." Yes, beyond young Charlie, eyes and mouth agape, bean bag body propped up by two pillows and belted into his geriatric chair with sheets. "Good afternoon, Sir Charles." No, not even a flicker.

"Mahhg…" called Czarina Walker from the next aisle over.

"Hi, Czarina," said Maggie. Sweet Jesus! Why did they leave her back there? She glanced over her shoulder at Raymond. "I'll just be a second." She strode to the Czarina's gerry chair. The thin, gray-haired woman jerked against the sheet and safety bar which restrained her. "Easy, Czarina." Maggie placed her hands on the woman's shoulders and gently pressed down. "I want you to meet my visitor. You up for a formal introduction?"

"Shhh — ure!" She managed a spastic smile.

"Then sit back, okay?" Maggie tugged Czarina Walker's gown into place, then got behind the chair and released the brake. "Doctor Raymond Daniels," she announced as she wheeled the Czarina toward him, "I have the great honor to present you to Her Most Imperial Highness, Agnes Muriel Abernathy, Czarina of all the Russias and Rumanias." Oh shit, he wasn't smiling.

Raymond nodded. "I'm pleased to meet you, Czarina."

Was that all? No feeling? Maggie stomped on the brake. "You needn't bother to bow and scrape, sir," she said. "All the Czarina requires is a kiss."

"A kiss?" His voice shot higher than his eyebrows.

"K..Keh…iss." The Czarina's arms flopped open, her fingers writhed in anticipation.

Why were men so awkward? Maggie stepped around the chair. "On the hand, sir. Nobility demands respect from all of us." She reached out and secured the Czarina's right hand.

"I see," said Raymond.

He's so damn impassive! She offered him the Czarina's hand.

He took it gently between his. "May I offer my respect, Czarina?"

"Shhh – ure!"

He kissed Czarina Abernathy's hand. She nodded at Maggie. "Thaa — aank you." Her right eye twitched.

"My pleasure," said Maggie, returning the wink.

"You think there's nobility in suffering?" Raymond muttered as he followed her into the hallway.

She glared at him. "What am I supposed to do with it? Fall apart? I have to watch these people struggling and suffering with their illnesses day after day. If I shut my eyes to their humanity, I lose some of my own. The better I treat them, the better I feel about myself." She heard loud voices competing with the television set in the dayroom. Where was the staff?

"I understand. I'm sorry," said Raymond.

"What's wrong with making a loony bin into a palace?" she asked, stepping into the dayroom. The volume had been turned up, but the TV soap opera was losing to a Marxist harangue from old Squire Tommy and the cross-eyed Duchess shouting at God. Maggie stopped short. Raymond's shoulder brushed hers.

"Sorry," he said.

For touching her? Jesus, Mary and Joseph! Raymond would fit right in. "That's Squire Tommy — " Maggie pointed with small movements of head and chin. " — and that's the Duchess. The one in the purple robe is the Empress."

Raymond shook his head. "And I suppose the woman sitting over there drooling on her sleeve is the Princess?"

"No. That's the Infanta. See those two playing backgammon? The one with the mustache is the Mogul; the little guy's the Barrio Duke. The Court sent them for evaluation."

"A Court of Law, I presume," said Raymond.

"I doubt it." She indicated the half-dozen nobles walking aimlessly about. "See how they dance? It's called the Thorazine shuffle. Court ordered. Do you call that law?"

"I call it poor doctoring," said Raymond.

"There's Nancy." Maggie pointed toward a corner of the large room. Wearing a white blouse, a pleated pink skirt and slippers, Nancy was rocking in a motionless chair. "Come on." Maggie started toward her, Raymond close behind. Poor kid, thought Maggie. Maybe he could get them both out of here.

"Let's go, Princess. Our champion's here. We need to talk."

Nancy stopped rocking. "Someone's here?" Her white blouse was dotted with a red sauce; the pleats in her skirt were crushed almost flat.

"Hello, Nancy. Do you remember me?" asked Raymond.

"Remember me?" Nancy echoed.

"Yes, I remember you. I'm Doctor Daniels. I helped take care of you at University Hospital."

Squire Tommy looked over and broke off his attack on the robber barons of Wall Street. The Duchess stopped talking to God.

"Let's go, Princess," Maggie urged.

Squire Tommy stepped toward Raymond. "Are you any relation to Patty O'Daniel, the union organizer?"

"Will you be my doctor?" asked the Duchess in a booming voice. "The one I have now is a fart."

"No. I'm sorry, I'm not allowed. I can't," apologized Raymond.

"Then you're a fart, too," the Duchess scolded.

"Capitalist scum!" screamed Squire Tommy. "They beat Patty to death!"

"Shut the fuck up!" yelled a brawny knight.

"Let's get out of here." Maggie grasped Nancy's hands. "Let's go." She pulled Nancy from her chair.

"Is the castle crumbling?" Raymond asked.

"You're a bean-blowing fart!" the Duchess shouted.

"See — " Maggie glanced at Raymond. "– and I had you pegged as the asshole." She tugged Nancy toward the door.

"An asshole is a hole in an ass," said Nancy.

"Only sometimes," said Maggie.

Raymond appeared at her side. "What are you angry about now?" he demanded.

"Angry? I'm not angry. You'll know when I'm angry. But whose fault is it we're stuck in the dark ages, doctor?"

"I wish I knew," he said. "I'd like to blame someone, too."

In the conference room, Raymond pulled a third chair over for Nancy.

"Sit down, Princess," said Maggie. She bobbed her head defiantly at Raymond. His hands asked for a truce. She nodded, then guided Nancy into her seat and sat down in the chair next to her. Nancy's lips were moving in silent conversation.

"How have you been, Nancy?" asked Raymond.

Nancy looked at him. Her face showed no sign of recognition. "A bin is a box for vegetables."

Or people, thought Maggie.

"Do you remember me talking to you at University Hospital?" Raymond asked.

"Yes, I was bad. I tried, but the Devil blew it out."

"What did he blow out?"

Hope, thought Maggie.

"The match." Nancy rubbed a fingernail against her skirt. "Scratch, scratch. I found a match." She looked at the floor.

"I know," said Raymond. "But he blew the match out. No one, not even the Devil, wanted you to start a fire."

"The Devil truth-proofs with fire."

"Nancy! Look at me." He waited until she did. "Fire's not needed for truth... Maggie says the doctor here does more than talk to you. That he does other things."

Nancy grabbed her head and began rocking. "Things. Rings are things. Swings are things."

Maggie gently pulled Nancy's hands down and held them. "Tell Doctor Daniels what Doctor L did."

"Tell?" Nancy glanced at the ceiling. "Don't yell." She looked at Raymond. "The Devil is angry. Did the Devil send you?"

"No."

Nancy frowned. "Then I don't know — the other one said the Devil sent him."

"Doctor L ?" asked Raymond.

Nancy nodded.

"What else did he tell you?"

"I have to go to the bathroom."

"In a little while," said Raymond. "What else did Doctor L tell you?"

Nancy squirmed in her seat. She pulled her hands away from Maggie.

Damn! She leaned toward Nancy. "Say it, Nancy."

"Nice — nice Nancy, sweet little Nancy. Oh yes! Oh yes! Oh yes!"

Raymond looked grim. His voice was gentle. "Nancy, what were you doing when he said that?"

Nancy looked at her, not at Raymond. "May I go now?" she pleaded.

No, don't. She stopped short of touching Nancy's hands again. "Not yet. Tell us what you were doing when Doctor L said, `Oh yes! Oh yes! Oh yes'!"

Nancy's face contorted as if she held a hot coal in her mouth but dared not spit it out. She flapped her hands in distress.

"Please, Princess. Doctor Daniels is here to help us. I'm counting on you to tell him the truth...Our honor depends on truth. Jesus lived and died for the truth." She placed her hand on Nancy's knee. "What were you doing when Doctor L said, `Oh yes! Oh yes!'?"

Nancy shuddered. "Suh — sucking the Devil's pipe."

"I'm sorry, Nancy, but I'm not sure what the Devil's pipe is," said Raymond.

"You do too know!" Nancy rocked faster. "Don't lie, cry, die. Jesus died for the truth."

Raymond leaned forward. "Is the Devil's pipe a penis?"

"The Devil's going to wash your mouth out with fire!" Nancy yelled.

"But is that what you were doing?" asked Maggie. "Did Doctor L make you suck on his — what Doctor Daniels just said?"

"He made me, paid me with fire, cigarettes to burn the sperm germ," she blurted out. "I didn't want to!" She braced herself back against the chair, ready to spring. "I have to go to the bathroom."

"Nancy, I know the doctor made you do it," said Raymond. "It's not your fault. But you and Maggie and I must see that it doesn't happen again. After you go to the bathroom, will you come with us to talk with the Superintendent?"

Nancy jumped up. "No. Told you and her. No Stupidintendent."

Raymond's hands and voice tried to placate her. "Okay, Nancy. Okay. But Superintendent Kroft isn't stupid. I've met him. He's a nice man. But you don't have to see him today. Maggie and I will go instead. You did fine in telling us about it."

Maggie came out of her chair. "Fine? Wonderful!" She put her hands on Nancy's shoulders and kissed her cheek. "Princess Nancy, I love you."

Nancy looked away. "The Devil loves me, too. He said not to tell."

"He doesn't love you as much as I do, does he Ray — Doctor Daniels?"

"I'm certain of that," Raymond said.

"He truths me in fire. He blew out the match. I sucked on the Devil's pipe." She looked down at the floor. "I was bad."

Maggie put an arm around Nancy's shoulders. "It's not your fault. It's the Devil's fault."

"And the doctor's," added Raymond.

Nancy peered into Maggie's face. "How come you have seven Devils and I only see one?"

Raymond's chair squeaked as he shifted his weight.

Damn! thought Maggie. The kid remembers what I told her before they threw me into that seclusion room. "I don't know." She released Nancy with a gentle push. "Why don't you go to the bathroom, and then back to the dayroom. I'll talk to you later."

"The Devil says you won't."

"Fu — Forget the Devil! I'll be there."

"I can't forget Him." Nancy glanced at the ceiling. "He talks with me. He truths me in fire."

"What does that mean, Nancy?" Raymond got up.

Nancy edged away. "I have to go to the bathroom, zoom, groom, tomb. Come soon, okay?" she said to Maggie.

"Okay, Princess… "

Nancy left. Raymond sighed and stretched. "We're going to get the creep."

"Good."

He took a step toward her. "What did Nancy mean about you having seven devils?"

"This is hardly the time to go into my — whatever."

"I don't know about that. Our appointment with Kroft isn't until three-thirty. If that clock on the wall is right, we still have some time."

Her eyes went wide. "You set up an appointment with him before you came?"

"He knows why I'm here. I told you — he's a good man. I met him several times when I worked out here."

Her thumb jerked toward the door. "You worked here?"

"I did a two month rotation — not in this ward — in another building."

"You chose it?" She shook her head. "You're crazier than I am. But, then you believed my note — you didn't even wait to speak with me!" Suddenly her hands were on his shoulders and she kissed him. Fleetingly tender, but he stiffened. "I'm sorry!" she said. Spicy aftershave. She backed away. "I didn't mean... "

"I know." He grinned. "You didn't even think it. Still, it was very nice. Thank you."

He liked it! "You mean it?"

"Will you tell me about those seven devils?"

She spun away. "We don't have time for that. If we're going to meet the Superintendent, I have to get into something presentable." She started for the door.

"Wait a minute." He strode after her. "This isn't a formal hearing or anything. All he wants to do is — "

"Fire!" A hoarse voice from the hall. "Fire!"

They were out in the hall in two seconds. Lady Agnes raced from her room with a khaki blanket and ran into the bathroom. Nurse Larabee was running toward them.

"Nancy!" screamed Maggie. She ran to the bathroom. The smoke bit her eyes. Nancy was on the floor, screaming, flames rising from her clothes. Lady Agnes beat at them with the blanket. A fire alarm shrieked.

"Agnes! Give it!" Maggie pulled the blanket away, opened it in front of her and flopped on Nancy's thrashing body, using hands, arms and legs to gather the material in, to keep it tight against Nancy. Heat singed Maggie's hands; the smell of burned flesh revolted her. "Ouch! Owww!" Crying, she hung on for dear life. Nancy was screaming and screaming.

"Let her up!" shouted Raymond. His hands were pulling her off Nancy.

"She's burning!"

"It's out! The shower! Help me get her into the shower. Agnes! Go put that shower on. Cold! Only cold water!"

They scooped up Nancy in the blanket, bundled her toward the nearest shower stall, where Agnes was inspecting the handles. Nancy shrieked at their touch, lashed out at the blanket and at them. Water spouted from the shower head.

"I called in a Code 99," yelled Larabee from behind. "The rescue squad is on its way."

Maggie glanced back at her. On its way? Jesus, the smell —

Raymond stepped into the shower stall, yanked Nancy in with him. As the water hit them, Nancy screamed in agony.

"What are you doing? You're hurting her!" cried Maggie. Water splattered out onto her jeans.

"Cold water — for the burn!" He was struggling to hold her up, fumbling with the blanket. "I gotta get this off! She won't even stand! Help me! Get in here and help me undress her!"

"Oh God, what have we done?" Reaching out to help, Maggie stepped into the shower."Why did we — " The cold water made her shut her mouth; it didn't keep her from crying.

48

Kroft

Raymond shifted his weight. His wet underpants had plastered the flimsy bathrobe against the plastic seat. He reached under his buttocks and peeled the robe away from the plastic, then away from his skin. Conscious of how this might look, he glanced at the women sitting beside him. Nurse Larabee was making her report to Superintendent Kroft, Maggie was looking at her bandaged hands, and Lady Agnes was staring into space. Crazy to worry about embarrassment after trying to save a life. Still, it was a relief that all the other patients had been escorted back to their rooms, and that Superintendent Kroft had told the staff to stay out of the dayroom during his inquiry.

"– but I had to sound the fire alarm and call for help first," he heard Larabee say.

"You bet. That was good." Kroft swept a shock of dark hair away from his eyes. His voice was throaty, his nose and eyes were sharp. Once Nancy had been taken away by ambulance and the firemen had departed, he'd shed his jacket and tie and popped chewing gum in his mouth. Now, in his dress shirt and gray, pin-striped trousers, he sat on the threadbare sofa in front of which the four of them were sitting in a line like errant school children. Moist sounds came from Kroft's mouth as he chewed; meanwhile, his fingers played a silent tune on an arm of the sofa and his feet took turns tapping the floor. The man's perpetual motion and gum-chewing made him seem younger than his forty-some years.

"What happened next?" asked Kroft.

Why did he have to hear it three times over? thought Raymond. Hadn't Maggie's account verified his own? He'd already cancelled all his afternoon patients; could he get back to the city in time for the evening ones? He tuned out Larabee's voice as she detailed Nancy's suicide attempt. How would Nancy's parents deal with yet another tragedy? Like the biblical story of Job, were some individuals or families targeted by God to suffer more than others? No, not just a philosophical question, not with his mother's premature death, his father gunned down in his pharmacy, his brother's death in VietNam, now Joshua's hemangioma. Still, lots of people had it worse than he did. Weren't tragic losses a part of life? Was a person's life and death determined by the roll of the genetic dice and then chance from womb to tomb? Of what use were his skills and best intentions when both Nancy and Maggie ended up here, suicidal and burned?

He looked over at Maggie. She tilted her head toward Larabee and rolled her eyes. He noticed they were bloodshot, the skin around them puffy. At least she'd allowed them to bandage her hands and to help her into a sweatsuit. But she was hurting and Nancy was in agony because of his stupidity. *Scratch, scratch, I found a match.* Why had he assumed it was back at University Hospital? *The Devil is angry — truth-proofs in fire.* That awful smell of burnt hair. Would she be permanently scarred? No doubt Maggie was also blaming herself for letting Nancy go the bathroom alone – and getting her to talk in the first place. What would Maggie do to herself if Nancy died?

"– and Maggie had her down on the floor with the blanket on top of her — " Larabee was saying.

"Agnes got the blanket," said Maggie. "I wouldn't have thought of it."

Except for the sucking, twitching motions of her mouth, Agnes was expressionless. Her arms were folded across her chest, her gaze seemed fixed on a wall.

"Well, you might've," said Larabee.

"No," said Maggie.

"What about you, Agnes?" said Kroft. "Want to tell me your side of what happened?"

Agnes looked down at her housecoat.

"We know you can talk," said Kroft. "Maggie says you're the one who yelled `fire'. Doing that and getting the blanket saved that girl's life. You did yell `fire', didn't you?"

Agnes didn't respond.

"It's safe to talk now," urged Kroft. Without taking his gaze from Agnes, he took a scrap of paper from his shirt pocket, the gum from his mouth. Pocketing the wrapped gum, he leaned forward. "Agnes, I want to thank you for what you did. You're a real hero, and you should feel proud of yourself." His hands lifted and spread to include all four of them. "You all should feel proud of yourselves. I thank each of you for taking such prompt and effective action." He scanned their faces. "Stop looking so glum! You saved Nancy's life. Don't get hung up on side issues." He offered a rueful smile. "That's what the State pays me for." His smile disappeared. "Don't worry. Doctor Urzaki thinks she'll be okay."

"Urzaki's an asshole," said Maggie.

Kroft's fingers fluttered on his knees. "You had a bad experience with him?"

"Not the kind you're thinking," said Maggie. "I've just seen how he treats sick people here."

"Well, he won't be treating Nancy Brill, if that's some comfort to you," said Kroft. "We sent her to the burn unit at Baptist." He rose from the sofa. "I'll keep you all informed. And I'll certainly commend you all in my report to the Commissioner. Who knows, maybe we can get him to give Agnes a citation next time he's down here." Kroft stepped toward Agnes. "Then he'll have to shake hands with you, okay?" He flashed a boyish smile.

Agnes got up and extended her hand.

Kroft patted her shoulder as if she were a friend. "No, not now, Agnes. I have to talk to Doctor Daniels alone. Please excuse us, ladies." He nodded at Mrs. Larabee. The nurse rose, took Agnes by the arm and guided her to the door.

Maggie raised her eyebrows.

Raymond shrugged. "I'll see you in a few minutes," he said. Did Kroft want to chew him out? He certainly deserved it. How could he have missed Nancy's intent?

Maggie got up. "Don't disappear on me." She followed the other women out. Mrs. Larabee reached back in and pulled the door closed.

Rising to his feet, Raymond tugged on the back of his bathrobe. Yes, his stupidity went far beyond refusing to surrender his wet underwear for drying. Even thinking about that now was asinine.

"Okay, Raymond." Kroft's tone was sharp. "I know what Nancy Brill did and what everybody else did after. Now tell me why the hell she did it."

"I pushed her to talk about being abused here." Resting his hands on the back of a chair, he told Kroft the important details of Nancy's history and treatment, including the reactions of Senator Brill and

Chairman Taylor, ending with an account of Maggie's note and the meeting that preceded Nancy's suicide attempt.

As Raymond spoke, Kroft hovered nearby, walking this way and that in small circles and spirals, with hands in pockets, then out again, fingering keys, rubbing his neck or brushing back hair from his forehead. When Raymond finally stopped talking, Kroft perched on the arm of the sofa and unwrapped a new stick of gum.

"Real nice of you to drop by with these small problems. If I got it right, the only American-trained psychiatrist on my staff's a sexual deviant, I've got a burned girl to worry about and explain to my ass-licking Commissioner, and an ex-Senator with lots of clout is probably going to sue me, crucify you, and jam our remains through the Governor's nostrils." With a shake of his head, he put the gum in his mouth and began chewing.

Raymond nodded. "I think you've got it right."

Bowing his head, Kroft pinched the bridge of his nose and chewed on more than his gum. Finally, he took a deep breath and lifted his head. "You know, I thought all I had to worry about today was scrounging five grand that's not in my budget to fix an elevator for the handicapped, and finding a way around the hiring freeze to adequately staff eight wards. I didn't look forward to hearing grievances from the union reps but I did want to steal some time to figure out how we're going to close a crumbling building built in the 1880s. Oh, and my wife asked me to pick up tomatoes and cucumbers on my way home." Kroft smiled. "Shit! I thought it was going to be an easy day." He looked at his wristwatch.

"What are you going to do?" asked Raymond.

"Ask my wife to do the shopping. It's going to be another late one." He jumped to his feet. "Where the hell are they with your pants and shirt?"

"That's what I'd like to know," said Raymond. "Can you fire him?"

Kroft looked puzzled. "It's a woman in the laundry."

"I mean the psychiatrist."

"Fire him? Without due process?" Kroft's arms spread wide with exasperation. "I can't even suspend the fucker!" His arms descended. "Not that I would hesitate if this turns out to be true — even ten-percent true. But meanwhile, who's going to medicate the two wards full of patients that he's in charge of? I've got a Ph.D. in psychology — I can't write prescriptions." He bent over a waste basket, spit out his gum and turned back to Raymond. "You want to come here and do it? No, you have a full-time job, right? I doubt if I can get a replacement until July."

Raymond tried to suppress his indignation. It's not Kroft's fault, he told himself. "So you'll leave this turd here because you need him to push pills?"

"No! Because of due process. I'm just saying we need the medical coverage and the pills desperately." Kroft reached out toward him. "Listen Ray, out here we always have to do more with less. You think Senator Brill ever cared about this place before his daughter went bonkers? You think anybody but the relatives ever give a fuck about these people?"

"I think you care — and most of your staff does. But not that bastard who's a disgrace to the profession. You said two wards. What if he's abusing women on the other one?"

"I'd be damn surprised. It's geriatrics. Don't get me wrong." Kroft brandished a fist. "I'm going to call him in and notify him of these allegations and their seriousness. Believe me, I'm going to grill his ass and notify Central Office to get an independent investigation going."

"But meanwhile he's allowed to see patients?"

"That's his job, Ray. While the investigation is in progress, I'll make sure that he doesn't see another female without female staff present — although where I'll find the staff for that — oh well, that's a problem for tomorrow." Kroft raised a finger in warning. "It all may boil down to his word against theirs — isn't it wonderful? Your witnesses are a suicidal hysteric and a schizophrenic arsonist — God knows what will happen when the shit hits the fan. Who the fuck knows what's true these days, anyway."

"I'll vouch for their credibility."

"And I'll vouch for yours. Your two months here, you treated these patients like people. I'll tell you, though — by the time this alleged pervert's lawyers get through with you, you'll need God to vouch for you. Don't be surprised, Ray. They're going to say some nasty things – whatever dirt they can find, and even more they'll dream up."

"I can't do anything about that. Meanwhile, will you look into the possibility that this doctor abused young women who've already been discharged? Maggie can give you one name."

Kroft's palms came up empty. "Can't promise. Our patients move a lot because they can't pay the rent, can't get along with their families — don't expect us to go search for people or push them to talk. Central Office has all it can do to handle the problems making headlines; it's not going to go looking for a scandal."

"It doesn't need to." Raymond jerked his thumb toward the ward. "It's right out there. You'll follow up on any name Maggie gives you?"

"I'll try. Anything else?"

"My clothes?"

Kroft turned toward the door. "They should have been back. We better go see. Let's hope some patient isn't wearing them."

49

Crowpox

Slipping two fingers between the buttons of his shirt, George leaned back in the office chair, scratched his belly and scanned the hanging woodcut of faceless children, the framed posters of flower show and circus. Where would they hide a microphone? He glanced up at the acoustic tile ceiling and fluorescent fixture, then down at Daniels. A wire under his jacket, his tie? No, it would be wireless. Lousy itch! So hot in here! Sure, even in this windowless little cage the shrink called an office, there were plenty of places to hide electronic bugs.

Daniels shifted position, one elbow retreating over the back of a swivel chair to touch the desk behind him. "Why did you stop?" he asked. "What are you looking for?"

"Nothing," said George. For starters, they'd have bugged the phone. Would they need another bug to pick up room conversation? A backup, anyway. "I was thinking that there aren't any windows." He withdrew his fingers from his shirt, took hold of the chrome arm supports of his chair. Hard, cool — hollow?

"Does that bother you?" Daniels asked.

Under the mess of papers on the desk? Maybe in that hollow rock the shrink used as a paperweight. "What?"

"The lack of windows. Does that bother you?"

"It's hot in here."

Daniels glanced at the door. "I'm sorry. There's only one thermostat for this whole row of offices."

"Forget it," said George. "It's not important. The crows can't hear us — can they?"

Daniels' eyebrows rose a fraction of an inch. His eyes were brown, not black; wide and bloodshot, not beady. Could contacts change them that much?

"You still worried what you say won't be kept confidential?"

"No. I can handle all you — all the grubsuckers."

"You think I'm a grubsucker, too?"

He scrutinized Daniels again. Brown contacts? A nose job? Artificial skin? Those lizard guys on that T.V. show, what was the name of that? No, the shrink's hands were too soft, his gizzard was too weak. "You may be different," he said.

"All I ask is for you to tell me directly if you think I'm — " Daniels rubbed the back of his neck. "– that I'm acting like a grubsucker. Because sooner or later you seem to think that about everyone. And that you give us a chance to talk about it. Fair enough?"

Fair? Crowshit! George shrugged. "If you want it that way."

"I do. You want to finish telling me what happened in the attic?"

George touched his forehead. Sweat!

"What's the matter?" asked Daniels.

Had they poisoned the air? "Maybe I'm coming down with something." He sniffed twice. Musty, maybe something else. "My sinuses are clogged up. You smell anything?"

Daniels sniffed the air half-heartedly. "No. What did you expect I'd smell?"

Crows. Or cyanide. George wiped his hand on his jeans. "I'm not sure."

"I don't know if you realize it," said Daniels, "but you became distracted as soon as you started telling me what happened in the attic."

"It's not that." George scratched his chest. What difference did it make, anyway? The grubsuckers lurking under the eaves of his house knew what happened. No doubt they'd flown off to tell his mother — maybe all the living dead — yes, the crows were their eyes and ears. If Daniels were a crow, wouldn't he know about the attic? Or was the shrink just sucking him in? Either way, there was nothing to lose by saying it.

"I — I threw Carol down the attic steps, then I did Denise with my hands. I choked her; I beat her face in." He rubbed his knuckles, showing them to Daniels. "It hurt here — and she was bleeding, so I knew it was real. At least I thought I knew." Daniels looked uptight. Mistake to tell him? "Then Carol was jerking at my jeans, showing me that stupid doll. Shoot! I don't know what's real anymore."

Daniels leaned forward. "Then they're okay?"

"Carol's broke out in some red spots she's been scratching. She's got a fever. Denise thinks it's chicken pox."

"But you didn't hurt them? It was one of your spells?"

"I... " He shrugged. "Who knows? Maybe I'm in two worlds, and it comes out different ways. All I know is they're still walking around in this world and if I'd touched them, they'd be dead." He pointed at Daniels. "You better do something about these spells. One of these days, I'll come in and it will've been for real."

Daniels frowned. "The pills aren't helping?"

"Those pills aren't worth crowshit. What did the blood test show?"

"There's plenty of it in your blood."

"Yeah? Well, it's no different with it than without it. Why isn't it working?"

"I don't know. Maybe the spells aren't partial seizures. I think we should try a different kind of medicine."

We? Who was Daniels trying to kid? Damn itch! George scratched his belly. No bloody way he'd be a guinea pig. "So what now?"

"A phenothiazine. A major tranquilizer."

His back stiffened. "A zine? You mean like Thorazine? Like they give to crazy people?"

"That wasn't the one I was thinking of, but it's in that chemical family. They're anti-psychotic agents, but they have other uses, too."

Like poisoning? His throat went tight, his cheeks hot. "I don't want to be drugged up."

"I would give you one that's not too sedating."

"Follow my lips, Doc." He put a finger below his bottom lip and hardened his tone. "No more pills. I'm not crazy."

"But you're having trouble knowing what's real, trouble controlling your impulses."

Brainwashed! He was being brainwashed. Daniels was injecting poison by mind-control.

Daniels extended a hand. "How about coming into the hospital for a few weeks so we can try to figure out what's going on? I don't want anybody getting hurt, and I doubt that you do, either."

"No frigging way!" He shoved himself up from his chair.

"Look, you say you want me to do something, but then you turn down my advice. What do you expect me to do?"

He towered over Daniels in a show of strength, then bent over to look the shrink in the eye. "Tell me what to do to stop these spells!"

Daniels' eyes widened, his face became taut. "Why don't you sit down? Please." Daniels' hand indicated the chair.

And have them listening, laughing? Maybe Daniels himself was their bug. Well, bugs could be stepped on. "Answer me! You think I'm crazy?"

Daniels' Adam's apple bobbed. "What do you mean by crazy?"

"You're the shrink. You tell me."

"Can you handle whatever I'll say without losing control?"

"I can handle it." There was sweat on Daniels' forehead. Did artificial skin sweat?

Daniels licked his lips. His face was pale. "How about backing up a step or two so I don't have to strain my neck looking up?"

Trick? No, scared. The shrink was scared. George smiled. "No problem." He backed up a step.

Daniels took in a breath, then exhaled slowly. His hands moved to his thighs. "You tell me you have trouble knowing what's real. That you have these spells – violent impulses and not much control over them, isn't that right?"

"Sometimes."

Daniels nodded. "And you don't trust people. You even conceal a lot of things from me. And you have this obsession with crows. What do you think it adds up to?"

He clenched his fists. "You saying I'm crazy?"

"I don't know what you mean by crazy. I'm not calling you crazy. I do think you have a mental illness."

Mental? No! He felt throbbing in his head, blood warming his cheeks. Brainwashing! They'd gotten to Daniels, bribed him, feathered his nest. Damn itch! Scratch and it gets worse. His voice came out a whisper. "You think I'll lose my mind?"

"That's one possibility. Really hurting someone's another. That's why it's so important you come into the hospital."

For the crows? Him in the cage and them out with Ma? Dizzy! He reached for the back of his chair with one hand, scratched his chest with the other.

"What's the matter?"

"I'm not gonna be caged up!" Better to take a few grubsuckers with him. Or just ride off. The pigs weren't that smart. And the shrink? "If I did — really hurt someone, say if I killed them, would you testify I was insane?"

Daniels grimaced. "Why speculate about something that hasn't happened? If we work together on this, we can probably prevent any harm."

"You'd have to, wouldn't you?"

"Testify?" Daniels rubbed his chin. "You planning to hurt someone?"

"No." He tried to smile reassuringly, forced himself to sit down again. "Shoot, Doc. You know I don't plan these spells. You agreed I don't have any control over them, remember?"

"I feel like you're setting me up," said Daniels.

"I wouldn't do that. I don't even need to. You have a suspicious mind, Doc. You don't trust people, either."

Daniels frowned. "I weigh what they do heavier than what they say. How about doing what's best and coming in to the hospital?"

"No way. You can't commit me, can you?"

"Only for several days of observation. Commitment is a legal process. There'd be a hearing in front of a judge; you'd have a lawyer."

Another grubsucker? His eyes narrowed, his mouth went dry. He forced himself to smile. "You planning to commit me?"

Daniels smiled back. "Now who's suspicious? No, I'd rather that you bring in your wife to meet with us next time."

"Denise? Why?"

"Because she cares about you, and she and the children share some of the risk."

George scratched his belly. "And what if I don't bring her?"

"Why wouldn't you?"

The itch had jumped to his back. Leave it! Daniels wanted to tell Denise her Georgie was nuts. No doubt about it — the crows were closing in, forcing his hand. This shrink might have to take early retirement. He looked down at his hands. No. Better to have Daniels as insurance in case something did happen. Or if anyone ever found out about Garbage Mouth Vinnie. Wasn't insanity what got people off?

George rubbed his back against the chair. So what if the shrink talked to Denise? She wouldn't go against her Georgie. "Did I say I wouldn't? I'll bring her next week." He'd tell her about this crazy grubsucker and his weird ideas. It wouldn't take much to sour her on this whole psychiatry bit.

"Good." said Daniels. "Will you try a new medicine, meanwhile?"

"You deaf or are you dumb?"

"Neither," said Daniels. "Same time next week, then?"

"You got it." George stood up slowly. The three of them were barely going to fit in this office without playing kneesies. Daniels didn't get up.

George opened the door and walked down the long corridor toward the elevator, passing offices on either side. Denise wouldn't like it here any more than he did. She'd come with wax in her ears and scoot home with nothing more in her head. Even with her mother babysitting, she'd have ants in her pants to get home to her poor sick Carol. Damn cr–chicken pox. Crow pox? Maybe that's why he'd been so hot and itchy. Shoot! Ma's black grubsuckers would do anything to get at him, wouldn't they? Infect the kid, she'll give pox to the parents. Oh yes, they'd use anyone to destroy him. Ma wouldn't rest until he was buried, too. He should have burned the cancerous bitch. Then there would have been no eyes to give to Carol, no malignant brain to direct the crows.

"Good-bye, Mr. Cruber," said the receptionist.

"What?" He stopped short of the elevators. What did she want?

"Have a good week."

"Sure. Why not?" He strode to the elevators, jabbed the down button and looked up to see what floor they were on. Two. One. Both elevators down there? Shoot! He clawed at his chest. Crowpox! Her grandmother's eyes, the grubsuckers' pox — what else did Carol have in store for him? Was Ma really alive in Carol's body? Then who had he buried? And the hands?

Air! He needed air! He bolted toward the stairway, depressed the handle, shoved open the door. Crowpox. He rushed down the stairs. Crowpox. Reverberations in the stairwell, thunder in his brain. Crowpox! If Carol had given him crowpox, he'd kill the little bitch. Crowpox! It was a long way down.

50

Nausea

Superintendent Kroft's voice pulsated from the telephone receiver. "Ray, I have bad news, worse news and terrible news. You decide which is which, I don't have the time. You sitting down?"

"Yes." Gripping the phone with one hand, he placed the other on the edge of his desk.

"Nancy Brill has some third degree burns," said Kroft. "Most are first and second, but her belly got it worse. She'll need plastic surgery and her father is suing me, you, the ward physician, the Commissioner, and the Department for negligence and malpractice. Five million dollars."

"What?" Raymond's gut began to ache.

"For five million. And that's without him knowing about the sexual allegations. I expect you'll be hearing from his attorney. What else? Oh, yeah, your other girl, Saxe, took off yesterday morning. As the poet said, we're in deep shit. You ever been sued before?"

Maggie gone? Five million dollars? There was a lump in his throat. "No," he managed.

"Well, you'll get used to it. They don't let you stay a virgin, these days. You have malpractice insurance?"

"Yes."

"Good. Because the State's attorneys won't defend you, being that you're not our employee. Don't feel bad, sometimes they won't even defend our own people. I don't want you to worry yourself sick about it, the way I did the first time. You weren't Nancy's doctor when she torched herself. You were a visiting hero. You feel like a hero?"

"I feel sick to my stomach." How could he get through three more patients this afternoon?

"I'm not surprised," said Kroft. "Did you know that nausea and headaches are the most common diseases of state employees? Listen, if the girl makes contact with you, let me know. She's not living at that Howard Street address, anymore. I had a social worker check."

"How did Maggie get off the locked ward?"

"You won't believe this. I'm even embarrassed to say it. She tickled her way out."

"Tickled?" He felt like throwing the phone.

"Somehow she knew that one of the male attendants was ticklish." Kroft coughed. "Excuse me." He cleared his throat. "The asshole still won't level with me about how she knew that. She got him as he was opening the door for old Agnes to go out with a student nurse, and your girl tickles him to the floor. Honest to God! No wonder they call this a funny farm."

Jesus Christ! Raymond shook his head. "Why didn't the nurse grab her?"

"Agnes had the nurse by the hand. It was a set-up, Ray. Your girl set it up."

"She's not my girl, God damn it! She's not even my patient. She's yours!"

"Only on paper," said Kroft. "If she's not back within forty-eight hours, we'll discharge her. Another bureaucratic cure for the state." Raymond heard a beep on Kroft's line. "Hold on," said the Superintendent. "Be right back."

The phone clicked in his ear. Shit! Didn't Maggie realize how important it was to stay and testify? And now with a lawsuit…

Another click. "Sorry," said Kroft. "Anyway, we've notified the police. Not that they'll go out of their way. You have any idea where she'll go?"

Here? He rubbed his forehead. She'd know he'd urge her to go back. Maybe back to her lover John, whoever he is. Or to Petro? Yes, Petro. Was that wishful thinking?

"You there?" asked Kroft.

"Yes. Look, there's an old Greek guy who visited her here. She used to work in his restaurant. But he wouldn't talk to us at all; I'm sure he'll play dumb with the police."

"Then that's that," said Kroft. "But without her, I'm not going to be able to do anything about the allegations she made. You understand that, don't you?"

Raymond rubbed his forehead. Oh Maggie, how the hell do you get me into these things? "I'll find her."

"You? It's really not your problem."

"Whose is it? I won't like myself if I sit on my ass, knowing damn well that other women will be abused by that bastard who's calling himself a psychiatrist."

"Then bravo and good hunting," said Kroft. "Keep me informed." His voice became gentle. "Ray, are you sure you're not acting out some rescue fantasy about this woman?"

"I'll keep you informed," he said. He hung up the phone. When had he ever been sure?

51

The Pub

Greek music, red and white checkered tablecloths, a rush of warmth and oregano. Cheery little place, thought Raymond. He closed the door and looked around as he slipped off his gloves. The bar and the booths opposite it were occupied by an assortment of middle-aged couples, young professionals and students. Cheap prints of the Parthenon and the Greek Islands clung to the walls. A waitress was off-loading moussaka and stuffed grape leaves from her tray; another was clearing dishes from an empty booth. Shouted Greek and loud laughter came from the back. Two tables of men back there. Regulars, most likely. The other tables were crowded as well. But no Maggie. Was she in the kitchen?

Raymond hung his coat on the rack and made his way to a stool at the short end of the L-shaped bar. He sat down between the wall and a squat, balding man in a plaid shirt and gray trousers.

"No I'm not kidding," said a muscular youth in a University polo shirt to a slim, goateed guy on the long side of the bar. "He looked at the engine and said `it's fucked, man, it's fucked'."

"Then it must be fucked," said the slim guy.

"Is Petro here?" Raymond asked the elderly, bespectacled bartender.

"Mmm." The bartender whisked away the used glass and napkin. His chapped, large-veined hands did a quick mop-up with a towel and placed a new napkin on the bar in front of him. "What you drink?"

Better give if he hoped to get. "Do you carry Michelob?" asked Raymond.

"No, but Greek beer is better," said the bartender. "You try FIX Hellas?"

"Fix what?"

The bartender opened a refrigerator and took out a brown bottle which he plunked onto the bar. "FIX Hellas, best beer. You try?"

Raymond nodded. "Where's Petro?"

The bartender popped the cap. "Kitchen."

"Can I see him?"

The old man shrugged. "Do you have eyes?" He tilted a glass and poured the lager down the side.

"Stavros, *fere mas ena boukali Ouzo*," a man called from a back table.

"*Perimene!*" the bartender called back. He set the glass and bottle in front of Raymond. "Why you want Petro?"

"He's a good friend of someone who was my — friend. I would like him to give a message to that person."

"You want Petro to be postman?"

"I want to speak with him about our friend. Petro will decide what he wants or doesn't want to do."

"*Endaxi.* I tell him. But you must wait. We busy." He turned and made his way to the other end of the bar, stopping to inquire about refills and collect cash.

Raymond picked up the glass. Your health, Maggie Saxe, wherever you are. To your health and long life. The beer was heavy and cold. He swallowed hard.

The bartender rang up a bill on the register, which looked as old as he did. Raymond took in another mouthful of beer. He remembered his father taking Ethan and him to the Prospect Park Zoo and then a luncheonette counter for egg cream sodas. Both the drink and his life were sweeter then.

The squat man next to him burped. "Excuse me," he said. "It's the damn olives."

"I know," said Raymond. "They can really get to you." How could he convince Petro to let him see Maggie? He certainly hadn't convinced Lisa.

"Especially Greek olives," said the man. "I used to import them." Skin pouched beneath his eyes and wrinkled into folds on his forehead, yet his scalp was tight and shiny. "Their dogs piss on the trees."

"Uh-huh." No, there wasn't any logical reason for Lisa's anger. He wasn't chasing after Maggie; that'd been absurd. Jealousy, irrational jealousy. Still, he shouldn't have snapped back at her. Lisa needed reassurance, not more anger.

"Stavros, *pou sto thiavolo ine to ouzo*," said a pouting young stud, advancing on the bar from a back table. His hair was slicked back, the deep vee neckline of his silk shirt showed off a gold chain, his black pants emphasized the bulge in his crotch.

"I have only two hands," said the bartender, giving the stud two bottles of ouzo.

How could he have brought Lisa here? Had to say no. With his luck, Maggie Saxe would've turned up as their waitress. If she's still alive. Well, worrying was the price of caring, wasn't it? Maybe arguing with Lisa was, too.

The bartender pushed through the swinging door of the kitchen.

What if Maggie were back there, if she came out to speak to him? No privacy. They'd have to go for a walk.

"You know about Israeli olives?" asked the man.

Raymond emptied the rest of his beer into his glass.

"Do you know what makes them special?"

Raymond thumped the beer bottle down on the counter. "Look, I'm not interested. I'm in a rotten mood, okay?"

The man looked at him and sighed. "I told you. Greek olives."

"Yeah, right," Raymond muttered. Could he convince Maggie to return to the State Hospital? No chance. University Hospital? Not with Doctor Taylor in charge. As an outpatient? What if she turned him down; could he just get up and walk out of her life? Shit! Lisa was partly right — his interest in Maggie went beyond a professional relationship. Raymond put down his glass. Was he holding on too long again? Raymond the Rescuer? The Rescuee?

Stavros emerged from the kitchen, returned to the bar. No one followed. Where the hell was Petro?

"It's because they piss on the trees," he heard the olive man telling another barfly.

Raymond finished his beer. He watched Stavros as he dispensed drinks for other customers, then chatted in Greek with a swarthy man in a black shirt. What had happened out in the kitchen? Raymond lifted the empty bottle. "Excuse me — ," he said, but Stavros either didn't hear or chose not to respond. Was he being ignored deliberately? Raymond put a five dollar bill on the bar in front of him. "Excuse me — ," he repeated, louder.

"*Perimene!* Wait!" said Stavros, dismissing Raymond with two words and a wave of his hand.

How he hated when people brushed him off, dismissed him as if he didn't exist. Like Uncle Jack did, after he took the three of them in. More interested in their father's estate than the grief or day-to-day problems of his little niece and teen nephews. If it weren't for Aunt Rachel, their lives would've truly been miserable. Easier to talk about that in analysis than it would be to talk about his feelings for Maggie. No, not looking forward to that.

Finally! Petro was wearing a white apron over a tee shirt and black trousers. His brow showed perspiration, his features impatience. "*Pios ise?*" he said, coming close for a good look. "Who are you?"

Had Petro forgotten? Raymond got up and offered his hand. "I'm Raymond Daniels. I was Maggie Saxe's psychiatrist at University Hospital. She introduced us once on the ward."

Petro kept his hands at his sides. "So? What you do here?"

Raymond's hand descended. "I don't know where she is. I'm worried about her. I thought you might see her and give her a message."

Petro shook his head. "I don't see her."

Lying? "If you should happen to see her, if she calls you, would you tell her that I came here looking for her? That it's important that she call me."

"I don't see her." Petro's lips tightened.

"I'm worried that she may try to hurt herself again."

"No more. She not crazy."

"I know. But she tried before."

Petro shook his head. "*O Kathigitis! O Bastardos* is no more with her."

Raymond's eyebrows shot upward. "Kathigitis? Was that her boyfriend's name?"

"No. *Kathigitis* means professor. She think him her boyfriend, that goat's asshole."

"You mean John?" Go for the name! "John Hancock?"

"No. John Taylor."

"Taylor? Son of a bitch!" Raymond banged his fist against the barstool. Used! He'd been used!

"May a sick horse piss on his mother," said Petro.

"I never saw that in Greece," said the olive man.

"And shit on his father." Raymond headed for the coat rack. "You tell Maggie I said that. And tell her to call!" He was out the door before Petro could refuse.

52

Cards on the table

"I want to see Doctor Taylor," Raymond demanded.

Anita DeSimone looked up from her typewriter. "I'm sorry, Raymond. Doctor Taylor's all booked up today."

Raymond shut the outer door behind him. "Is he with anyone right now?"

Anita took one look at him and stopped typing. "What's the matter? Is it the baby?"

"No, it's Taylor." He advanced toward her desk. "Who's in there with him?"

"Doctor Walton, from Medicine, and Doctor Sklar, from Neurology. They'll be in for another forty-five minutes," said Anita.

His hand flicked forward. "Get them out!"

"I can't do that, Raymond."

"You can and you will." He planted his hands on her desk and leaned over them. "Otherwise, I'll go in there and announce that Doctor Taylor's son has been fucking one of our patients."

Anita's cheeks turned pink. Raymond withdrew his hands to his sides. Damn! He shouldn't dump on her. She wasn't responsible for her boss.

"You don't have to be coarse. Which son? Harry or Edgar?"

Were there only two? "John."

"Impossible. He's happily married."

"And happily screwing my patient on the side."

Anita shook her head. "I don't believe it."

"She was his student." He pointed in the direction of the main campus. "John teaches philosophy and fucks his students. Does that sound like a happy marriage?"

"I don't believe it." Her face looked grim. "I know Bobbi. I talk to her on the phone every few weeks. She wouldn't stand — "

He cut her off. "Who's Bobbi?"

"Bobbi Taylor. John's wife. She used to work here."

Raymond's gut squeezed, his hand rushed to his belly. He sat down on the edge of Anita's desk. "Bobbi Stowell?"

"Yes," said Anita. "What's wrong?"

"God! It all makes sense! It all makes sense."

"What does?" Anita squinted in puzzlement.

"Why John ran off at City Hospital — " Raymond's hands dragged stiff, unwilling fingers back over his scalp and down his neck. Yes, the Chairman had recruited her from City.

"John ran off? When?"

"And why John never came to visit her here, and why Maggie's clothing showed up on the ward before — Shit!" He stood up. "It was a set-up! The whole fucking thing!"

"What was?" Anita shook her head. "You've lost me, Raymond. What was a setup?"

"Maggie's admission here." Sure, Doctor Taylor would have had her admitted to Palmer 3, anyway. If Doctor White had said no,

Taylor would have overruled him. No wonder Maggie hadn't revealed John's name. And whom had they chosen as their stupid pawn? Well, it was time to fight back, to speak truth to power like Ethan would have had he survived Vietnam. Raymond leaned over and slapped his hands down on Anita's desktop. "Get them out of there, Anita!"

"Control yourself, Raymond." But she had the telephone to her ear. "Doctor Taylor? Something urgent has come up in regard to — your son John. Doctor Daniels is out here and insists on speaking with you right away... He won't. He's prepared to make a scene."

Scene? You bet! Raymond glanced over his shoulder at the door to the inner office. Yes, this pawn was going after the king.

"Yes, sir." Anita hung up the telephone.

"What did he say?"

"He'll be out in two minutes."

Raymond glanced at his wristwatch. This time, the tempo would be his. The move would be his. And if he was right, checkmate! Pawn wins. Ethan would be proud of him.

The inner door opened within a minute. Raymond watched them emerge. Yes, Thomas K. Walton, the pin-striped aristocrat himself; behind him, in a white coat, the plump and bald Sklar. Where the fuck was Taylor?

Raymond nodded. "I'm sorry, gentlemen."

They eyed him curiously as they passed in front of him.

Ignored again! Well, he'd never be able to work at University Hospital again, anyway. "I'm carrying plague," he said.

Sklar smiled.

"That can be fatal," said Walton, heading for the outer door.

"Don't worry. I know whom to bite."

The Chairman was standing behind his desk, before his wall of awards and diplomas. Raymond shut the door to Taylor's office and strode toward his desk.

"Sit down, Raymond."

"I'd rather stand." He pointed an accusing finger. "You set me up to treat your son's mistress. You wanted me to fail. You wanted her in a state hospital and me in disgrace."

Taylor blinked; his face remained impassive. "Only the first of your accusations is true, Raymond. I think I'll sit, if you don't mind." He pushed back his swivel chair and sank into it with a sigh. "I can understand your anger, but I did what I did for good reasons."

Raymond's eyes appealed to the ceiling. "Where have I heard that before?"

"Your sarcasm is wasted. Don't you think I've examined my motives over and over?" Taylor raised his forefinger as if testing the wind. "My son wanted and needed to return to his marriage." Taylor raised his middle finger next to the other. "That young woman was suicidal and needed help." His ring finger made it a threesome. "A scandal would have cost him his marriage and his job — yes, and hurt my reputation as well, I'll own up to that. But what would you do after years of — alienation, if your son came to you and asked for your help?"

"I wouldn't manipulate other people. You chose me for this job because I'd seen Maggie Saxe at City Hospital, not for any of the other reasons you gave me. You wanted whatever she might have told me about your son to remain limited to our therapeutic relationship, with you in control of whether I have a fourth year here."

Taylor's hand sloughed away all opposition. "Your future is a separate issue. Miss Saxe wanted to be here. Don't you understand?" Taylor reached out. "The fact that she never told you about John makes that perfectly clear. She knew who I was. She traded her silence about John for free care."

Raymond shook his head. "No, it's you who doesn't understand. Maggie made a promise, and kept it because she has integrity. Maybe she did know it was her ticket for professional help. So what? Underneath it all, your son victimized Maggie, just like her father did." He walked up to Taylor's desk and looked down at his boss. "And you and I — her supposed helpers — manipulated her into the same Goddamned pattern: you shut up about who's fucking you, Maggie, and we'll take care of you, maybe even love you; but tell the dirty secret and you're gone — you might as well be dead, kid. You won't have anyone left." He slammed his hand on the desk. "You made me a party to that!"

Taylor removed his glasses, put them down on the desk. He rubbed his forehead and eyes. "Raymond, I didn't know — " He looked up. "I swear it. I didn't know she was an incest victim until Dr. Bergstrom told me. If John knew, he never said a word to me about it."

Bergstrom? Another betrayal? Raymond backed away. "Dr. Bergstrom told you? Didn't you assure me you didn't want to know the details of her treatment? That you'd stay out of it?"

"I did what I said I'd do. Until Ms. Saxe escaped, took your baby and tried to kill herself. That presented behavioral and legal issues that this department cannot tolerate. Dr. Bergstrom was trying to change my mind about sending her to the state hospital, so he told me some of her history. My son was not involved in any way. I promised John I'd stay out of her treatment. He promised to do the same."

Was it true that John didn't know? Maybe Maggie had only disclosed the incest because of her seclusion room agony. Raymond bumped against a chair; his hand reached back and touched leather.

Taylor shook his head. "Remember, Ms. Saxe was free to leave at any time. I wanted no part of the misery she brought to my family."

"Except I was telling her if she tried to leave, I'd go for commitment. Oh God!" Raymond sank into the chair. Secrets! They hurt everyone. "Why did you ever permit her to be admitted?"

"She overdosed with barbiturates. She was unconscious. John called the police and she was admitted directly to the I.C.U." Taylor's hands reached out for a fair judgment. "Even if I could have, do you really think I'd have blocked her admission to the I.C.U?"

"No. But I meant the transfer to Palmer. Why did you decide to keep her?"

Taylor smiled ruefully. "Even though my son doesn't like me, he happens to think I run the best psychiatric program in the state. Sometimes, I wonder if one is the price of the other." He sighed. "Anyhow, John insisted she be given the best of care; I insisted he stay out of her life." He put his glasses on carefully. "A bad bargain, Raymond, a bad bargain. Unfortunately, it was the best we could come to."

The best? For whom? "Bring her back," said Raymond.

"What?"

"Let's bring Maggie back here and do it right."

"I can't re-admit her! She tried to kidnap your baby."

"You sure?"

"Yes. We have incident reports from everyone involved."

"Maggie told me she was going to take the baby back to the nursery, but she panicked when she saw Security."

Taylor's skepticism was plain on his face. "Raymond, she's a bright, very troubled woman. Do you think she'd confess to kidnapping?"

"Frankly, I think she has more integrity than you do. If she'll agree to be admitted, I want her back in Palmer."

"You only have four months left in the program," said Taylor. "It makes no sense."

"Maybe." Raymond rubbed his chin. "Why did you pick me in the first place?"

Taylor shrugged. "She met you at City Hospital. John thought she liked you. I told you all the reasons at the time."

"I think there are more."

"Oh, do you? Why?"

A puff of air escaped his lips. "There are always more."

The Chairman glared at him. Raymond stared back.

"Remember, after she was admitted," said Raymond, "I approached you about transferring her to a female therapist?"

"Yes. I suppose I was reluctant to give her care to a faculty member who might be around for a number of years. Frankly, I was hoping you would finish your third year and go, and take Mary Margaret Saxe with you."

Raymond nodded. "We were to disappear silently."

"Why air dirty linen?"

"To make it smell better. Well, I have a bargain for you, too."

Taylor raised his eyebrows. "Oh, and what's that?"

"You let Maggie Saxe back in for the next four months — "

"And you'll be discreet?"

"I will. But she'll be free to say what she chooses to whomever she chooses — and she doesn't get bounced out until June thirtieth, when I do."

"I see." Taylor flashed a cold smile. "Anything else?"

"I need a decent letter of recommendation for my next job, wherever that takes me."

"I'd have no trouble writing such a letter. And it will be

professionally sincere." Taylor's chair squeaked as he shifted his weight. "I'll just leave out that you've been a personal pain in the ass."

"My pleasure," said Raymond. "And one more thing — "

"There's always one more thing. What?" The word crackled with Taylor's anger.

"Leroy White's tenure. You're to approve it within thirty days."

Taylor's eyes narrowed, his lips tightened. He scratched the back of his hand. "Raymond, my boy. You're stepping into the big leagues now. Hardball, is it? Well, I'm going to disappoint you."

"Then we have no bargain."

The Chairman grimaced. He straightened in his chair. "Do you think I'd agree to such blackmail? You underestimate me, boy. I endorsed Doctor White before the Tenure Committee last week and I'm sure they'll vote favorably. We need more black faculty. More than just Doctor White." Taylor folded his hands on the desk. "Now, are you certain there's nothing more you want?"

"That's all I wanted."

"Good. Now I'll tell you what I want." Taylor pointed a finger at Raymond. "I want that woman out of my son's life." His voice got louder. "I want her out of mine. She's not to come anywhere near this department or its employees again."

Raymond stiffened. "But you said — "

"I don't repeat my mistakes. I won't make another bad bargain."

"You're risking disclosure," Raymond warned.

"And you're risking your job, possibly more." Taylor rose to his feet in front of his wall of diplomas and citations. "Disclosure to whom, Raymond? Do you have her permission to tell my faculty? You can't exactly go public about my son without revealing intimate matters about your ex-patient, can you? Where is your sense of professional ethics?"

Taylor accusing him? That was the pot calling the kettle black. Raymond found it hard to swallow. "Suppose she gives me permission to tell the faculty?" Stupid. Taylor knew he wasn't a blabbermouth —or did he? Had Taylor appointed him Maggie's therapist to silence him about what she might have confided at City Hospital?

The Chairman leaned over his desk. "Her permission is irrelevant. If you disclose anything, I'll call you unprofessional and fire you. Then I'll file a complaint with the Ethics Committee of the Medical Society. That's clear, isn't it?" Taylor straightened. "I would hope you'd rather finish your residency quietly. Then I'll give you that letter." Taylor's lips fought and lost to a smirk. "Which way makes the most sense for everyone, Raymond?"

There must be some way to beat the bastard. "I'll think about it."

"Do that." Taylor pointed to the door. "Now please excuse me. You interrupted my work."

"As you did mine." Raymond rose to his feet.

"Never at a loss for an answer, are you," said Taylor.

Raymond felt sadness drowning him from within. "Only when it's important," he said.

PART VI

April 1970

53

Denise

"You ready for us?"

The whisper startled him. Raymond's head jerked up and around, body and swivel chair following after. George Cruber filled the doorway of Raymond's small office. The toll collector's mackinaw was half-unzipped, his hair glistened with melted snow. Cruber's lips were pursed in amused appraisal.

"You ready for us?" This time, Cruber added voice to the question.

Ready? How late were they? Raymond resisted the urge to look at his watch. "Sure." He tossed his pen onto the report he'd been writing at his desk. "The receptionist didn't — "

"She wasn't out there." Cruber stepped into the office. "I know we're late — I'll get the slip later. This is Denise." Cruber's head gave short shrift to the woman in boots and quilted coat who followed him in. Her long dark hair was windblown and wet; her eyes darted about, avoiding contact.

Raymond pushed himself up from his chair. "Hello, Mrs. Cruber. I'm Doctor Daniels."

"H'lo," she muttered. Her cheeks were pink, her features delicate; a clear droplet leaked from her upturned nose.

Raymond gestured toward the chairs. "Please make yourself comfortable. Would you like to take off your coat?"

"I'm still cold," said Denise in a thin, high-pitched voice. With a trembling hand, she took a crumpled tissue from her coat pocket and wiped her nose.

"We can't stay long," said Cruber. "Denise's mother is watching the kids."

"Well, please, sit down. I'm glad you came. It's really important. Otherwise, I wouldn't have called you."

Cruber looked around cautiously. "We — uh — we would have come, anyway." He nodded to Denise, then eased his bulk into a chair. Denise moved forward and sat down tentatively in the one next to him.

Raymond walked around them to shut the door. Yes, a faint medicinal odor — Vicks? Ben-Gay?

"I had to cancel last week because my schedule got messed up," said Cruber.

Denise looked at him. "No, George, because of Carol." Her tone indicated a desire to help, not criticize.

"My schedule," asserted Cruber. "I took time off for Carol, but then my new supervisor switched my days. The grubsucker put me in a barrier booth, giving out tickets. That's why I couldn't come here."

"How come you didn't call to cancel?" asked Raymond as he sat down again.

Cruber looked surprised. "I did. Didn't you get my message?"

Another lie? "I didn't." Raymond's lips tightened. No, there were bigger issues. Was Mrs. Cruber reachable? "Carol getting over the chicken pox?" he asked.

"Real good," said Cruber.

Denise nodded. "It's the concussion we were worried about."

Raymond's eyes widened. "The what?"

"The concussion. In her head." Denise bit her lip.

"A little accident," said Cruber. "She's okay now."

"She could have been killed." Denise dabbed her eyes with the tissue, then looked at Raymond. Beneath her left eye, a muscle twitched. "She fell down the basement steps. You should see her black-and-blues."

Beaten? Pushed? What the hell had happened? Raymond straightened in his chair. "I'm sorry she got hurt. How did it happen?"

"She tripped," said Cruber.

"How?"

"Over her shoelaces, probably." Cruber's hands separated; his lips hinted at a smile. "You know how careless kids are."

"Were you both home when it happened?"

"Yes," said Denise. "I was in the shower. The baby was sleeping and Carol was watching TV, so I thought it was okay. I told George to keep his ears open." She offered the reproof sorrowfully.

"I did!" said Cruber. "I left the basement door open so I could hear." He shook his head sadly at his wife. "See, you try to do something right and it backfires. I shouldn't have told Carol I was down the basement. I don't know — maybe you shouldn't have showered then." He turned toward Raymond. "Go figure it. The kid's gone up and down those steps a thousand times." Cruber's mouth twisted to one side as his hand flicked upward. "That's life. You never know."

Denise put a hand on his arm. "We can't keep blaming ourselves, George. The important thing is that she's better."

For how long? Raymond rubbed his chin. "Was she ever able to tell you what happened?"

"She doesn't remember," said Denise.

He turned to George. "Did you have one of your spells?"

Cruber's eyes narrowed. "Is that what you think? No. I never touched her until after she fell and I carried her upstairs."

"What's he saying, George?" Denise withdrew her hand to her lap.

Raymond leaned forward. "Mrs. Cruber, did your husband ever tell you about his spells?"

"Yes, after his last appointment here. Maybe he did before — I don't remember." Her eyes darted toward Cruber, then back to Raymond. "He was upset because you wanted to put him away."

Raymond shook his head. "No. That's a — a misunderstanding. I want him to come into this hospital. Here. Not away. And not for very long." His hand reached toward her. "A few weeks, that's all. Just enough time to figure out what's causing the spells. Meanwhile, everyone will be safe."

Cruber chuckled. "Safe? Isn't he something else? See, Denise? He thinks I'm crazy."

"George isn't crazy," said Denise.

Raymond's hand smoothed the air. "I didn't say he was crazy."

Denise looked puzzled. "Then why do you want him in the hospital?"

"Because he has times where he loses touch with reality and becomes very dangerous."

Cruber shook his head. "This guy's too much." He looked at Denise, commanding her with hand and voice. "Tell him! Did I ever hurt anybody?"

"George never hurt anybody on purpose, except a kid in high school." The muscle beneath her eye twitched again and again. She pressed a finger beneath her eye in an attempt to stop it.

"What kid?" asked Raymond..

"Ohh — " Cruber's hand flicked impatiently. "– just some bozo. That was years ago." His forehead wrinkled as he looked at Denise. "Did I tell you about that?"

"No, your mother did."

Cruber stiffened. "My mother? When?" It was almost a whisper.

Denise looked down at the carpet. "A few years ago. She – uh — she said that the kid was picking on you. She said you got kicked off the football team, but you didn't deserve it. They had it in for you."

Cruber bowed his head and began to rub his temples, creating a rustle of hair.

"Will you share what happened?" asked Raymond.

The big man's fingers stopped moving. His head stayed down as if pinned in place. "I didn't need to play football, anyway. The coach got after me to play. I was in his class and he kept talking to me about it because I was so big." Cruber looked up. His fingers retreated into fists on his lap. "What difference does it make? It was years ago."

"Is it hard to talk about?" asked Raymond.

Cruber scowled. "No! It was nothing! I replaced some senior grubsucker on the line, that's all. He kept hassling me. Him and his friends." Cruber pointed at Raymond. "I warned him — but he didn't stop. So I whipped his ass."

Raymond sucked in his lower lip. No, it was a threat all right. Better to face it squarely. "You saying I should stop?" His heart picked up speed.

"I didn't say that — but it wouldn't hurt if you did."

No, he couldn't back off. Cruber would know he was afraid. "Why did you get thrown off the team?"

Cruber frowned, glanced at Denise, then at Raymond. "I – uh — well, let's just say they had to scrape his face off a locker." Cruber shrugged. "It was his own fault; he was asking for it. He said some things about my mother. I told him not to, but — some people don't listen." His icy glare told Raymond not to be one of those people.

"And then?" Raymond's gut tightened.

"Then he made another mistake." A smile flickered and died on Cruber's lips. "He didn't see me coming."

"Well, he shouldn't have talked that way," said Denise. "You warned him."

Cruber nodded. "I warned him. Right, Doc? If it was you, you'd try to see me coming, wouldn't you?"

"Sure." A chill shot up Raymond's back. His shoulders inched up, his arms moved close to his torso. Did Denise live with such fear? Her choice; but the kids… "Mrs. Cruber, your husband has been worried about his spells getting out of control, about hurting or killing you and your children, or people outside your family." Raymond glanced at Cruber. "It's a credit to him that he's worried about it, but he needs to get help before he's done something violent. I need your help to convince him that he needs to go into a hospital."

Denise looked at George, then at Raymond, then at the door. "I can't — I don't believe it." She glared at Raymond. "George isn't crazy! He's a good husband. He doesn't smoke, he doesn't drink, he goes to church when I ask him. And he's never hit me or the children. Even when he shot Carol, the police and the social worker from Protective Services agreed it was an accident." Her mouth twitched. "So I think this whole thing is stupid."

Shot Carol? Raymond's muscles tensed, his heart sped up, but he kept his body still, his face impassive. Ask the wrong question, and they're out the door, he thought. But criminal — no, negligent, not to ask. "You accidentally shot your daughter?"

Cruber turned his glare from his wife to Raymond. "In the leg. I was cleaning one of my guns. I didn't know it was loaded. It fell out of my hand."

A well-practiced recitation, thought Raymond. Facts without remorse, without any feeling at all. "How did you feel after it happened?"

"Like any father would feel. I mean how would you feel if your child got shot?" Cruber's cold smile was unnerving.

"We're different people. We might not feel the same. What were your feelings?"

"I don't remember. That was more than a year ago."

"Why haven't you mentioned it to me before this?"

"Because it's not important." Cruber dismissed the subject with a flick of his wrist. "It had nothing to do with why I came here."

Didn't it? Was there any chance that Mrs. Cruber could recognize the danger to her children? Was she already too afraid? Or so loyal?

Raymond cleared his throat. "What if — and I'm not saying it's true — but what if Carol didn't trip? What if she did something to annoy her father and, before he realized what was happening, he hit her and knocked her down those steps?"

Cruber's eyes narrowed, his jaw thrust forward. "You don't give up — do you? That's a mistake."

"George, that didn't happen, did it?" Denise pleaded.

"Of course not." Cruber's gaze remained fixed on Raymond. "The doc's playing head games. Next he'll say that you probably beat the kids, that you're a no good mother and our kids should be taken away."

Raymond gripped the arms of his chair. "You're the one playing head games. He's trying to scare you, Mrs. Cruber. I never questioned your abilities as a mother. That has nothing to do with this."

Denise stood up. "George, take me home. I can't stand this."

"Please, Mrs. Cruber. We need to discuss this. Please sit down."

Cruber was on his feet. "I'll take you home."

Raymond stood. "Mrs. Cruber, you're putting your children at risk; it's not only you."

"Now who's trying to scare her," said Cruber.

"Look, I'm not trying to scare anyone. But it's my ethical and legal obligation, my duty, to warn you." Raymond ran a hand through his hair. "And if you can't or won't hear me, for the sake of the children, I'll have to involve Protective Services. They'll send a social worker out to the house to talk with you."

"See!" Cruber brandished a fist. "He won't be satisfied until we lose our kids. Wait for me outside, Denise."

"It's not to take them away; it's to protect them," said Raymond.

"Let's go, George." She tugged at his arm.

Cruber shook her off. "I said wait for me outside. I want to talk with him."

"We need to face the truth here," said Raymond.

"Come with me, George." Denise sounded desperate.

"Go! I'll be right out."

"Don't be mad, George. He's just making a mistake."

"Yes, he is." Cruber's tone was icy. "But don't worry, we'll straighten everything out. You go wait by the elevators."

Raymond watched Denise leave. He felt helpless.

"What's the matter with you?" Cruber asked. "You must have a wife and kids. Do you know what you'd be starting with an investigation?" He took a step forward.

Raymond's hands opened in front of his chest. "I'm sorry. I'm not doing this to hurt anyone. I'm trying to protect the kids, and her, and you — although you probably find that hard to believe."

"Maybe you should think about protecting you, not us."

Raymond's hands dropped to his sides. He struggled to keep fear from his face, cracks from his voice. "I don't like your threats."

"What threats? I don't think you listen good. I'm just saying you don't have to worry about my family so much. If you need to worry, you can worry about yours." Cruber raised his forefinger. "Now if you tell someone that's a threat, I'll say you're a liar. I don't need to make threats."

"Look, we need some time to think this through, to discuss this. How about making another appointment?"

The toll collector chuckled. "I think you're the one that's crazy."

Cruber wouldn't be coming back. Good riddance! No, he'd lost him. And what would happen to Denise, to the kids? "You did push Carol — didn't you?"

"I didn't push her."

"You did it some other way?"

Cruber shook his head. "It's none of your business, now. You really think I'd tell you anything?"

"I think you just did." Stupid! Shut up and let him go.

"You have a good imagination, Doc. That will make it even better."

Raymond's mouth went dry. "Make what better?"

Cruber winked. "You're in the telephone book, you know."

"You stay away from my home. If you want to see me, you come here."

"See how your imagination gets working? It's nasty." Cruber took another step forward. "So drop this Protective Services crowshit, okay? Hey, we both have families, right? Let's keep it that way."

"Get out of here!"

Cruber smiled. "Okay, okay." He walked to the door. "But

remember, grubsucker, you call Protective Services, you won't see me coming – back — either."

54

On the Line

"Ray! It's for you," said Lisa.

The frost in her voice nipped between his ears and severed his thoughts from the article on schizophrenia he was reading. He glanced up.

With fiery hair igniting her cheeks and streaming onto the shoulders of her terrycloth robe, Lisa thrust the telephone receiver toward him as if it could reach across the living room and poke him from his easy chair.

Cruber? Shit! Raymond dropped *The American Journal of Psychiatry* onto the carpet next to his slippers. "Who is it?" he asked, getting up.

Lisa covered the receiver with her hand, her face with a scowl. "I think it's that woman."

Maggie? He felt his heart jump. "Really?" Good old Petro!

"Really." Her tone was sarcastic.

God, she's pissed. Tightening the cord of his bathrobe, he started toward her. "I'm sorry." Apologizing? For what? It wasn't a crime for Maggie to call. "I'll take it in the bedroom."

"Why is she calling?" Lisa demanded. "You're not her therapist any more, are you?"

Raymond's hands rose, palms up and empty. "I don't know."

Her eyes lit up. "What do you mean you don't know? After what Doctor Taylor said to you? And what about your promise you'd only see her once?"

"Let me take the call. Then we'll talk." He stepped around her.

"You bet we will," she said to his back. "Tell her I don't want her calling here. If she has to call you, let her do it at the hospital."

"Okay, okay." No, he couldn't tell Lisa the story of Maggie's life or describe their work together; Lisa would forever view Maggie as the devious mental patient who took her baby. It was all he and the hospital's attorney could do to get her not to press criminal charges.

Raymond switched on the light, shut the bedroom door, and picked up the telephone on his night table. "Hello?" He heard a loud click as Lisa hung up the other receiver.

"Do you hate me?" asked Maggie.

From frying pan to fire. "What makes you think that?"

"I've let you down. I'm sorry. I told you when we first met that I drag people down with me."

Had she heard Lisa? "How do you mean?" He sat down on the bed, the soft green comforter beneath him.

"You know — like with Nancy. That was the worst. I can't even get rid of that smell."

"That wasn't your fault. I should've picked up the clues."

"We both failed." Her tone conveyed her remorse. "And after that, whenever that pervert doctor showed his face on the ward, I thought about killing him. Burning him up like Mr. – even worse than Nancy. Then I'd feel suicidal for the rest of the day. I had to leave."

To Petro? To John? "Why didn't you tell me?"

"You weren't there."

"I mean about John Taylor."

"Oh…that." The words were barely audible.

He looked at the clock on the night table. Ten-twenty. Why didn't she answer? Where was she tonight? "Yes, that," he prompted.

"I promised John I wouldn't."

"But still, you could have. It would've made things so much clearer."

"I couldn't! Don't you understand? My word is the only decent thing I can give, that I have left to give. If I break it, I'm not — I have nothing worth anything."

"And you're afraid there's no one that will believe, that will understand."

"That, too." She cleared her throat. "At first, I didn't know whether you were in on it or not." Her tone was apologetic. "For all I knew, you were Doctor Taylor's spy, and he could have been telling John things about my treatment or pressuring both of you — it was a mess. I was a mess. I needed the hospital. I hated it but I needed it." He heard her snort. "I even needed Doctor Taylor to keep me there after my thirty shitty days of Blue Cross ran out. That's my karma, Raymond — I need everything I hate and I end up hating everything I need."

He massaged the back of his neck. "Me, too?"

"Not yet. Are we ending up?"

"No. And I wasn't Doctor Taylor's spy. I was his pawn."

"Hey! Welcome to the club." Her tone was ironic.

"I think the dues are too high. We've got to stop being used, Maggie."

"How?"

"Well…" He paused to think. "For openers, there can't be any more secrets if we work together."

She chuckled. "I'm fresh out of secrets. You want to tell me some?"

"No. I mean I don't have secrets." Liar, he thought. Everybody has secrets. "At least not about your treatment. You do know that Doctor Taylor doesn't want you at University Hospital, don't you?"

"When did he? He only let me stay to guarantee that John would go back to his wife. At least my father had the balls to fuck me personally."

He shook his head. "That's a warped yardstick to measure people by."

"Maybe, but it's all I have."

"No! All you had."

"Don't get technical; you know what I mean. How's Nancy?"

"Not good. She had some second and third degree burns. She'll need plastic surgery — but she's alive. So hope's alive."

Maggie was silent.

He rubbed his thigh. "What are you thinking?"

"Four-letter words. I never should have asked her to speak up. The wrong people always get hurt."

"No. Nancy hurt herself because of her illness, not because you spoke up. Her illness hurt her, and that piss-poor excuse for a doctor hurt her — not you! You have to stop measuring everything with that incest yardstick."

"Oh sure. That's easy for you to say. You find a more realistic yardstick, you let me know."

"I'm part of that better yardstick, Maggie. Petro is part of it. And there are other people out there, too."

"People use and hurt each other, Raymond. The only difference is that the nice ones apologize before they do it again."

He stood up. "Have I hurt you, used you?"

"I'm waiting. Everyone wants his pound of flesh wrapped in a different package. I'll know it when I see it."

He looked at the bedroom door. Yes, Lisa was waiting, too. He looked at the clock. "You tell me when you think you see it. Don't just run off, okay?"

"I'm not making another promise. I'll try. You deserve that much."

"So do you...Where are you living?"

"With Petro. Will I see you?"

"You mean professionally?"

"Is there another way?" Her voice smiled.

"I don't — I mean no." Too attached to her? No wonder Lisa —

"Then I mean professionally," she said.

He ran a hand through his hair. "Sure, but it really might make more sense for you to see another psychiatrist."

"You don't want to see me?" She enunciated each word carefully.

"It's not that. It would be better for you to have a fresh start — to have a therapeutic relationship without — " Me, he thought. " — all this old baggage."

"I'm a pain. Is that it?" Hurt drove her tone.

"No. That's not true." He sat down on the bed.

"Then Taylor's gotten to you." Now her tone was bitter. "Why couldn't you come right out and say it?"

"Damn it!" He punched the bed. "You're listening to your own suspicions, you're not hearing me."

"Well, what the fuck are you saying? Listen, Raymond. I won't go to another shrink. I didn't even want to talk to you, remember? It tore my guts out to tell you about — about me. I won't do it again."

"Okay. I hear you! Now you hear me out, okay? I care about you, and I want to keep working with you. I really do." He clutched the comforter. Risk losing Lisa's trust by treating Maggie? Or kill Maggie's trust by walking away. "Look, in less than three months, I end my residency program. Taylor won't let me stay on at University Hospital. Within a month or two after that, the Army will grab me. I don't know where I'll be after June thirtieth."

"Did you hear me asking for a lifetime contract?"

"No, but you — "

"Three months is better than nothing, isn't it?"

"It depends on your goals." Hypocrite. And he expected truth from her?

"And who says I won't die before you move?" she asked. "Or move before you die? I can't worry about tomorrow — I have to get a grip on today. Are you going to help me or not?"

He bit his lip. How could he turn her down? Or deny his desire to help her? "Yes. I will." He was trapped! Like Maggie, like Lisa, trapped somewhere between love and loss. With both of them? Schmuck! "But you'll have to come to the office at night. After everyone else leaves. Doctor Taylor isn't to know you're coming. Which means John isn't to know."

"John won't tell him."

"I can't take that chance."

"Now who's playing secrets?"

His throat ached. "I'm sorry, Maggie. Truly sorry."

"Don't. It's my fault."

"It's not. It's me. I — my career is on the line. I'm willing to risk it — I am — but don't ask me to bet it all on the word of someone who cheats on his wife to sleep with his students."

"You don't think much of him, do you."

"I don't want to be anyone's judge. I have enough trouble with me."

"Me, too."

"Look, I'll see you this coming Thursday night. In the Adult Outpatient Clinic, seventh floor."

"Okay. It'll be our secret," she teased.

He glanced at the door. "No. I'm going to have to tell my wife why I'm working that late."

"Won't she mind?"

Yes, he thought. "Why do you ask that?"

"She will. Won't she?"

His eyes roamed the wall to his wedding picture. "You didn't answer my question."

"But you answered mine. Tell her not to worry. I'm not out to wreck anyone's home, especially yours."

He lowered his gaze. "I know that."

"What happens, happens — right? It's usually bad, but there's not much anyone can do about it."

"Most times, there is — certainly, about this. Look, unless it's an emergency, try not to call me at home, okay?"

"Oh, she's on your case about me. Once you live together, you have to pay dues, right?"

"If you call me at the hospital, say you're — Mrs. Lieberman. I wouldn't put it past Doctor Taylor to have the receptionist monitor my calls."

"Oh shit, I'm Jewish and my doctor's paranoid. Is that double jeopardy?"

"It's no joke."

"Sorry. You just seem — I hope your wife won't be too hard on you. Tell her not to worry. I didn't want to steal her baby, and I certainly don't want to steal her husband. He's too good and boring for the likes of me."

She hung up before he could think of something to say.

55

Flowers

George looked through the window of the small flower shop to make sure the young salesgirl was alone. A chime rang as he stepped over the threshold and the heavy scent of well-nourished plants and flowers washed over him.

"Good afternoon. Can I help you?" asked the salesgirl.

Frosted hair, bogus smile, thought George. "Six white daisies," he said. Yes, phony as those silk flower arrangements. Probably stuffed her bra, too.

The salesgirl tucked her pen into the pocket of her green apron. "Only six?"

"Six," he repeated.

"Okay." She turned and headed toward the walk-in cooler.

Was everything in here carefully arranged but false as the silk flowers? "Real daisies," he said, following her. The cooler's hum taunted him. She slid its door open. He stepped back as a chill breath pushed the sweet stink of cut flowers up his nose. He glanced over his shoulder. In front of the window, the hanging plants seemed to stir. Whispering? Warning him? The clock on the wall was supposed to look like a sunflower. Yes, everything here was designed to deceive. He checked his wristwatch. Three-thirty. The clock was wrong!

"Do you need a vase or anything for these?" asked the salesgirl.

His head jerked. "What?" He saw her holding the daisies. "No, I've got what I need."

She slid the glass door shut. He followed her to the counter. These daisies plus the stuff in his car should do it. He had the vase from the flea market; the first six daisies and some ferns from the other florist; gold foil and the Thermos from his house; and a dead crow from his yard. It would just take some arranging. If the grubsuckers tried to backtrack him, they'd come up empty-handed. For fifty bucks each, Deg and Tony would swear he was at the plant, butchering meat. Meanwhile, he'd close in for the kill. He dropped a five dollar bill on the counter.

"Remember to cut the stems diagonally and put them in warm water," said the girl as she wrapped the daisies in green paper. "You can help yourself to a card, if you'd like."

Were they the same "Happy Birthday" and "Get Well" crap he'd seen in the other store? He walked over to the rack and scanned the rows of small cards. He smiled when he saw "Thinking of You." George glanced at the salesgirl; she was busy at the cash register. He folded another card and used it to pick up "Thinking of You." He selected an envelope the same way. No fingerprints, no writing, no clues.

Outside the store, he walked quickly, eyes darting from face to face, to rooftops and sky and back to faces. The public telephone booth reeked of urine. He wrinkled his nose, hesitated, then closed the door behind him. Cradling the daisies in one arm, he used the other to make his call.

"Good afternoon. Psychiatry Clinic," said the receptionist.

"Doctor Daniels?" he asked.

"I'm sorry. He's with a client. Would you like to leave a message?"

"When will he be free?"

"He has patients scheduled until six. If you'd like to leave your name and number, he may be able to call you between appointments."

"It's not that important. I'll call him tomorrow."

As George stepped out of the booth, his eyes scanned faces, street and sky. Scheduled until six, she'd said. Plenty of time. Only two blocks back to the car.

He drove through the park until he found an isolated strip of grass bordered by tall trees. He parked his Plymouth, put on his gloves, took out the dead crow, his knife and his purchases. Using the car to shield him from the road, he sat down on the grass to work.

Much better to do this with his own hands. A professional arrangement would lead back to a particular florist, and a florist might remember, might talk. And this way he could touch the daisies as much as he wanted. Too bad he wouldn't be there to see her face when she went to smell her daisies and saw the crow's eyes staring up at her.

George stretched the crow's neck and cut off its head. Would flowers ever look the same to her? Not that it made up for the way Denise looked at him ever since Daniels planted doubts and fears in her mind. George wiped his knife against the grass. Well, now that Protective Services had given him a clean bill of health, maybe Denise would relax. And he'd collect a few tolls. His new supervisor would have to pay for moving him to a barrier booth job. But Daniels was first in line.

He placed the knife on the grass next to him, unscrewed the top of his Thermos and poured a small amount of water into the vase. Once the Thermos was secure again, he began wrapping the vase in gold foil. Oh yes, the daisies would make it a pretty package. First she'd smile — then she'd scream. Hadn't he warned Daniels to forget about Protective Services? Now the grubsucker would see who needed protection. Pretending to be so innocent, so eager to help, when all along he'd been in cahoots with the crows...

Good enough! George unwrapped the daisies. Last time he'd touched daisies was at Ma's funeral. He removed his gloves to feel the white petals. Why hadn't she ever let him touch the ones that she wore? Stubborn bitch! Wouldn't even die like everyone else. Was that why she'd sent the crows? To tease him, like with the daisies? He touched each flower gently before placing it in the vase. Had she sent the crows to test him or to torture him? Because she'd been buried? Well, after Daniels, Ma, after Daniels, I'll come for you.

George drove carefully, the vase braced by his thighs, the daisies and ferns leaning against his sweatshirt. A block away from the apartment house, he found an unmetered parking spot big enough for his Fury. After setting the vase carefully on the floor, he tucked the screwdrivers and small hammer in his belt and transferred more water from Thermos to vase.

The vestibule of the apartment house smelled of cooked cabbage. Six rows of black buttons and nameplates protruded from the yellow wall next to the intercom. He tried the glass-paneled door that led to the lobby. Locked! He returned to the nameplates and found Daniels' name. 4C. For Crow? He pushed the button. Come on! Be home! He pushed the button again. Next time he came, there'd be broken locks on a basement window or two. And the door to the roof, if that had a lock.

"Hello," a woman's voice said through the intercom.

George smiled. "Crow Brothers' Florists, ma'am. I have a delivery."

"Flowers? For me?"

"Mrs. Raymond Daniels?"

"Yes. I'll buzz you in."

The buzzer tripped the lock. George pushed open the door. Yes, what woman didn't like flowers? Well, this bitch was going to pay big for her daisies.

56

What Do I Do?

"So what do I do about him?" asked Raymond. "He's a psychopath."

Bergstrom studied the paper clip he held between thumb and forefinger. The furrows in his brow deepened. "There aren't many options." He looked up over his bifocals. His eyes seemed deeply recessed, his face wrinkled with concern. "If you send Cruber to the state hospital on a detention order, he'll play Mr. Innocent and the psychiatrist who evaluates him won't consider him dangerous and will let him go. Even if they admit Cruber, he'd be out within a few days."

Raymond gripped the arms of the Kennedy rocker. "With another grudge against me."

"Apparently he only needs one." Bergstrom looked down at the paper clip. His hand closed around it and descended to his lap. "You could only play the detention card twice. Even after the first time, some lawyer might call and threaten to sue you for harassment or inflicting emotional injury or some-such..." He looked up again. "Won't the police do anything more?"

Raymond shook his head. "A dead crow in a flower arrangement isn't high on their list of priorities. As far as the police are concerned, there is no crime, no witness and a suspect who doesn't even have a traffic ticket. It's just a sick joke, they say." His throat felt tight. He loosened his tie, undid his collar button. "I don't think this guy will stop." He remembered being beaten, his nose broken, by four bigger kids who didn't like Jews living in their neighborhood. "Either we beat the shit out of you, or we do it to your little brother right here in front of you," Domenic had said. "You run or hit back, we'll take it out on him." Now Cruber was taking his malevolent toll from Lisa, knowing that there was little he could do to stop him short of offering himself up as a sacrifice.

"What do you think he'll do?" asked Bergstrom.

"I don't know." Raymond tasted bile. "I feel sick every time I think about it. Cruber doesn't want to get Lisa, he wants to get me. This was his way of making me sweat… The police sergeant's attitude was like `hey, if he's crazy, you should handle him — we put these guys away, and you shrinks let them out'."

Bergstrom threw the straightened paper clip into his waste paper basket. "And the detective?"

"He said he'd go out to Cruber's house to talk with him. It took him two days to get out there and another day to find a telephone to call me." Raymond shook his head. "Of course, Cruber denied everything. He even had the balls to say that I was angry because he told me that I wasn't helping him and that he was going to switch to another doctor. He told the detective that he could prove he was at the meat packing plant when the flowers were delivered, that they could check his time card. The clever bastard probably paid someone to punch in for him. As it is, the detective did all he could. He checked that Cruber had valid licenses for his guns, and he warned him to stay away from me, my family and my apartment." Raymond looked up. "You and I both know that's like spitting in the ocean. Even if I went to Court and could get a restraining order, it wouldn't mean diddly to Cruber."

"No. Not to any man that sick or that vengeful." Bergstrom took off his bifocals and rubbed his eyes. "What about calling him? You might acknowledge his — cleverness — no, call it brilliance. Trade flattery and another opportunity at outpatient treatment, not with you, but here at the Adult Outpatient Clinic, in exchange for a truce."

"I don't think it'll work."

"Work in what way?" Bergstrom put his glasses on again. "I agree that it's not going to stop him. The man is obsessed with these crows and what they represent. To him, you're just another — what does he call them?"

"Grubsuckers."

"Yes. Just another grubsucker to be exterminated."

Raymond's eyes rolled upward. "Terrific."

"Hardly. The purpose of the call is to buy you a few days. I doubt that he'll acknowledge anything to you over the telephone; he'll believe it's tapped."

"I could offer to meet with him. At the clinic, I mean — or somewhere very, very public."

Bergstrom shook his head. "He'd admit nothing. He'd think you or the room were wired. No, it seems to me that the best you can do is to buy a few days. You might be able to do that with a temporary commitment order, but if he got word of it before the police picked him up, he might come right after you... Even if they did apprehend him and take him to the state hospital, he could act normal and be out very quickly."

"Or he could escape like Maggie did." Raymond massaged the back of his neck. The tightness in his muscles didn't ease.

"That's why calling him may work better. At least it won't provoke him. Especially if you pretend to believe his statements that he never did you any harm, that he would never stoop to such behavior. Meanwhile, you can get your family to a safe place and wrap up your affairs here by the end of April."

Raymond gripped the rocker's arms. He felt queasy. His life was falling away. Bergstrom wouldn't help, couldn't help — just like Korline, hiding his ass up his damn analytic posture. "You're telling me I should run away?"

"Not telling you — suggesting."

"And what's a safe place? What if he comes after me?"

"The chances are less."

"But what if?" His hand tried to brush such thoughts away. "Anyway, I doubt that Doctor Taylor would give me credit for completing the entire year. I'd have to repeat it somewhere else. And I doubt the Army would let me; they're so hungry for docs. And what then? Do Lisa and I have to stay out of the telephone book of every major city for the next ten years? Do I stay off the lists of the medical societies, resign from the A.P.A.?"

Bergstrom shrugged his shoulders. "What's your alternative? Do you fight him in the trenches? Do you buy handguns for you and your wife?" He pointed the paper clip at Raymond. "'You'll never see me coming.' Isn't that what Cruber said?"

Raymond nodded. Shit! He had to do something. He got up from the chair and walked around Bergstrom to the window. Gray! Where was the fucking sun? He shook his head at the tall brick buildings that comprised the medical center. "I never knew psychiatry was going to be like this."

Bergstrom sighed. "Sometimes you do the right thing and it has tragic consequences — I'm referring to your report to Protective

Services, not to your decision to become a psychiatrist. I don't want another tragic consequence here..."

"Another?" Raymond glanced over his shoulder. Bergstrom looked pained.

"I'm sorry," said the professor. "That's personal. I didn't mean for it to intrude."

Raymond turned to face him. "I'm very sorry about your son."

"It was a blessing. He was wasting away on that respirator." He threw another straightened clip into the wastebasket. "These are no damn good, any more. He — you probably don't know that he was retarded. That's why I can truly appreciate the anxiety you have about your son. Is he continuing to do well?"

Raymond shrugged. "The radiation treatments seem to have helped. The tumor's smaller; he can open his eye wider – but who knows the long term effects? Forgive me if I'm speaking out of turn, but does any of what we're talking about have anything to do with those paper clips?"

"Remember what I taught you? Follow a person's thought associations long enough and it will lead you to the heart of the problem, and of the person. Even the teacher... " Bergstrom's smile seemed terribly sad. "Once, when my son was young, he got into my desk at home and unbent a couple dozen paper clips. When I reprimanded him, he got so remorseful that — well, I was too hard on him, I was reprimanding him for his condition as well as for his mischief. So I had to find something we could do with those useless paper clips. We made a miniature wire swing. It's amazing what people can do with something others consider useless..." Bergstrom reached to his pocket for a handkerchief. "Excuse me." He swiveled around in his chair and blew his nose.

Raymond bit his lip. What could he say? "I'm sorry." He walked back to the rocker and sat down.

"Thanks." Bergstrom stuffed the handkerchief back in his pocket. "In any case, my son was so enraptured by that swing, and I suppose the closeness that we shared in making it, that he wanted to make swing after swing." Bergstrom managed a brighter smile. "In self-defense, I had to find other little sculptures we could make with paper clips. Eventually, he became very good at it... I'm sorry. I didn't mean to get so far away from your dilemma."

"You're not far away; I feel you're very close. And I feel good that this can be more than a one way street, sometimes."

"It always has been. I've enjoyed working with you. I want you and your family to be safe."

Raymond's hands rose from his lap, then silently fell back. "I asked Lisa to take the kids and go to her mother's for a while. She won't do it. If I don't call her every couple of hours, she calls to check up on me. This crow thing really threw her, but she's hanging tough. She calls Cruber 'that abominable crowman'."

"She's suffering from over-exposure to your sense of humor, Raymond." He reached for another paper clip. "If you were George Cruber, out to get Raymond Daniels, how would you do it?"

Raymond heaved a sigh. "I'd get him when he's alone. At night. On his way home from work, maybe. Just as he's driving away from a toll booth and thinks that he's finished paying for the night."

"You work nights?"

"Only one. There's only one patient I see after dark."

"Who?"

"I'd rather not say."

Bergstrom cocked his head. "Oh?"

"It's someone who — has ties to the Department. We agreed to anonymity."

"I see." Bergstrom's tone suggested he didn't. "Well, perhaps that patient could come on Saturday or Sunday morning instead of after dark."

"I'll ask. And I'll get a security man to walk us to our cars."

"Cruber could show up at your house again."

"I know. I'll be careful. We've gotten a deadbolt put on our door. We're on the fourth floor, so he can't come through the windows. I don't know what else I can do."

"You can move somewhere else for a while." Bergstrom's hands rose, offering. "My wife and I could make room for you and your family."

Raymond swallowed hard. "Thank you. I sincerely appreciate that. But I can't do that. All he'd have to do is follow me there one day, and then your house would have to become a fortress — if we found out in time."

Bergstrom sighed. "As much as I don't like to, I keep coming back to the option of you leaving town for a while."

"I'll talk it over with Lisa. She'd go in a minute if I would." Raymond shrugged. "Maybe it's not rational to think that Cruber would follow me, that I'd be lulled into a false sense of security somewhere else. I don't know… One of my problems is that sometimes I'm too persistent. I just hate to be pushed around again. I had too much of it when I was a kid. My younger brother never tolerated it; whatever the odds, he always fought back."

"This isn't the same, Raymond. You're not fighting kids on the street. You've done all anyone could have reasonably expected. You can walk away without any shame."

"I wish I could." He sighed. "I don't know — maybe I can. Meanwhile, I'll try to buy a few days."

57

Self-service

George reached the row of trees bordering the self-service gas station just after dusk. Cars sped by on the divided highway, their headlights falling short of his observation post. He set the tire iron and black helmet down on the ground, pulled off his goggles and leather gloves and looked the station over. Three cars. Five — no, six — people, counting the bald guy collecting money in the hut. The girl filling the VW Beetle wouldn't be a problem. Neither would the nerd with his wife and little boy in the Chevy Bel Air. The two jocks alongside the Mustang might be likely to horn in. Well, they'd be gone in a few minutes, anyway. The nice thing about self-service was the rapid turnover.

George unzipped his leather jacket and took the Baretta from his shoulder holster. He released the safety, then tucked the pistol away again, zipping up his jacket to conceal it.

A brown Javelin pulled in and stopped at pump 8. The nerd's Bel Air coughed as it started; its headlights flicked on. A roly-poly guy in a suit got out of the Javelin and headed for the booth. The Bel Air pulled out. One of the jocks approached the girl, who was using a squeegee on the Beetle's windshield.

Shoot! Why couldn't the grubsucker go to a bar if he wanted a pick-up? Joe College thinks he's so cool. The stupid crow-turd comes to a self-service station and expects to get laid. Well, best to settle down and watch the show — a good bike might be a long time in coming. Meanwhile, his Fury would do fine on that residential street. If he couldn't get a bike, he'd walk back to the Fury, drive home and call to cancel the ride to work in the morning. Good, the girl was getting into the Beetle. Joe College couldn't do shit.

Come on, you lucky bike. Wouldn't need much power to catch Daniels' old Valiant. Still, if the cro — cops showed up, he'd need a bike that handled when he let loose the horses. Something no cruiser could catch that he could ditch later. His old Harley was too slow and it could be traced back to him. Yes, he was too smart for the police, and too smart for Daniels. The grubsucker'd said it himself, called and begged to be left alone. Had Daniels thought him dumb enough to admit anything? How many crows were on the wires, listening? "Gee, doc, I don't know what you're talking about. Your imagination must be working overtime." Nothing he said could be used against him.

He watched arrivals and departures for more than thirty minutes before a red and white Suzuki Cobra rumbled up to pump 8. The biker wore a red helmet, black goggles and a red knapsack. Even his jacket had red stripes down the sleeves. Showy grubsucker, thought George. Red might stand out too much, but the Cobra had a 5-speed transmission and could get over a hundred mph. That's my ride! He slipped on his gloves.

Two teen-age girls fluttered around the gas tank of a Camaro; two more were in the back seat. No problem. Neither was the gray-haired gent filling the red Mercury. The black guy paying for the Thunderbird's appetite needed watching; with his woman in the car, would he play hero?

The biker cut the engine, engaged the side-stand and walked to the hut. When the black guy walked away from the window, the biker stepped up to pay.

George put on his goggles, picked up his helmet and strapped it to his head. With the tire iron concealed vertically under his arm, he sauntered out into the light. The biker was pumping gas. He glanced up as George approached.

"My Jughead broke down," said George, indicating the highway with a thumb. "My wife's coming with the pick-up. Can you give me a lift back to the bike?"

The biker eyed him warily. "Sorry. I don't give rides to — anyone." His bug-spattered helmet jerked toward the cars. "Ask one of the gropers."

"C'mon man, I don't want to ride in one of those piss-pots." George stepped behind the pump. "Tell you what, I'll pay for this tank."

The biker withdrew the nozzle from the Suzuki"s gas tank, snapped the lock cap closed. "No, I don't think so." He reached out to hang up the hose.

"Too bad." George smashed the tire iron down on the biker's exposed wrist. Bones splintered; the biker screamed and dropped the hose. His knees buckled. "Rape my little sister, will ya!" George yelled. He whipped the tire iron up, then down against the biker's shoulder. The biker shrieked as he fell; his helmet butted the pump. His arms were useless. "Get her pregnant with your bastard, will ya!" George turned and glared at the man next to the Thunderbird. "This grubsucker raped my little sister! You want to mix in?"

"No way, man. He ain't nothin' to me."

"Damn right!" Tucking the tire iron under his arm, George looked at the girls next to the Camaro. They were bug-eyed with fear. He bent down for the hose. "Here, let me hang it up for you," he said, aiming his words and the nozzle at the whimpering biker. George heard one of the girls scream as he drenched the biker with gasoline.

"You crazy bastard!" cried the biker.

The black guy jumped into his car. The hose went dry. Baldie in the hut was sucking up a telephone. No time to waste, thought George. "Anybody want more gas?" he yelled, throwing down the hose. He pulled a cigarette lighter from his pocket and held it aloft. "Get out of here! I'm going to blow it all up!"

Baldie dropped the phone and ran out of the hut, leaving the door wide open. The others scrambled into their cars, gunned the engines, fought for position to get onto the highway. George started to smile, then frowned as he saw the biker struggling to his feet. Stupid grubsucker! He chopped the biker down like a side of beef; his red helmet smacked hard against the blacktop.

Good! The grubsuckers that sped by weren't stopping, no matter what they saw. Did any of them have C.B. radios?

George slid the tire iron into his jacket and down through his belt, then grabbed paper towels from a dispenser and stuffed them into his pocket. He ran to the Cobra, kicked the stand back and rolled the bike away from the gas pumps. The key was in the ignition. He mounted the bike, crumpled the paper towels into a tight ball and set it on fire. He tossed the flaming ball at the prostrate biker. The gasoline ignited with a whoosh and a rush of flame. The biker screamed in agony.

Key, clutch, starter button — the Suzuki's engine rumbled into life. His toe shifted the bike into first, his hand snapped back the throttle. The engine screamed like a jet, the rear wheel spun, the front wheel jumped off the ground. He threw his weight forward, released the throttle and kicked into second gear. The tires smoked and screamed against the blacktop as the Cobra hurtled out onto the highway and careened into the left lane. Behind him, a gasoline storage tank exploded.

A quarter mile down the highway, George downshifted and slowed the bike for a wide left turn. Standing up on the pegs, he cut squarely across the grassy median and headed back slowly in the opposite direction. A car passed him, then a moving van attempted it. He increased his speed to keep the truck on his left until they passed the inferno that had been a gas station. Up ahead, on the other side of the highway, flashing blue, white and yellow lights were approaching rapidly.

Too late, thought George. The crows were too predictable, too stupid. He'd left no fingerprints, no clues; the biker was dead, his body and identity in ashes; the witnesses were scattered. Meanwhile, he had a great bike and a night's entertainment. No doubt about it — self-service was wonderful.

58

What's Hurting

Maggie's fingers clung to the silver crucifix; the back of her neck stiffened against the braided chain. "It's not getting better. I feel worse than when I left the hospital."

"In what way?" asked Raymond.

How much pressure would snap the chain? Don't! Petro would be heartbroken. She relaxed her grip and looked over at Raymond. Only two feet away, with no furniture or argument between them, yet he was gone. His eyelids drooped; his body sagged in his chair; his tie and brown jacket looked permanently wrinkled. Had he tired of her? "In every way," she said.

"How about some specifics? What's getting you down?"

"Everything – everyone. I don't know…"

"You look like you're in mourning."

"You don't look so good, either." She took her hand from the crucifix so he could see her black blouse. "This is pure silk. I saw it in the mall, yesterday. I just knew it would be right."

"For your mood?"

"For this skirt." She touched the soft black leather skirt, then spread her arms wide. "You like the outfit?"

He tilted his head. "It's a — attractive."

Her hands fell to her lap. Sure, his idea of style was a button down collar and striped tie.

"What's hurting, Maggie?"

"I don't — well, maybe I do. I'm rattling around Petro's house like his daughter's ghost. Now he wants me to learn to cook all those Greek dishes. You see me stuffing grape leaves?" She rolled her eyes. "And he wants me to go to his church with him, celebrate the Greek Easter. I can't even handle mine, much less another one. I'm not Maritza, I'm just not."

"Have you talked with him about it?"

"I tried. He couldn't really handle it. He felt badly, so he went out and bought me this." Her fingers framed the crucifix. She pressed her lips together until the ache in her throat subsided. "I can't hurt him. He's been there for me when I needed someone."

"You think Petro will abandon you if you don't satisfy all his needs?"

"Don't make it sound dirty. There's nothing dirty about it."

Raymond shook his head. "I wasn't implying anything sexual between you and Petro. You heard it that way?"

"No, you said it that way. Just drop it!" Drop it yourself, she thought. You don't want to fight with him — he's not John. "I finally found out who that bastard is fucking."

"You mean John?"

"Yes, John the philosofucker. Humping an eighteen year old freshman. Eighteen — can you believe that? I told him that if he didn't have the guts to tell me, I'd go ask in every class." She snorted. "I hope her little box is crawling with crabs."

"Even though you know he's a bastard, you're feeling rejected?"

"I don't give a — yes, I do. And I'm angry. And I'm feeling — " She had to push the words past a lump in her throat. Her voice came out low and ragged. "– all alone. I'm feeling all alone. Next Sunday is Easter. As much as I love Petro, I can't substitute Greek Easter for mine. But who do I have?" She looked down at her lap. "My pervert father's quite happy to send me a once-a-year check to keep my big mouth out of Baltimore. And my mother — " Her head and hands jerked upward. "My mother's Christmas and Easter cards include little exhortations to pray for my sins. *My* sins." Her hands came back to her lap. "You know, Hallmark's missing a trick — they need repent cards. She'd buy 'em by the truckload. God knows she doesn't send me birthday cards… So where the fuck do I belong? I haven't even been able to force myself into a church. See, I can live as Petro's daughter or John's mistress or your patient. Hell, I can be any man's — whatever. But I have no life of my own, Raymond. None! Zero. And I never will."

"Bullshit." His tone was calm. "First of all, you can go to church. God understands everything — don't you believe that?"

"Yes. At least I hope so. I did think about going to Easter Mass." Her hands spread wide. "I thought I'd wear a sign saying `Give me resurrection or give me death.' You think the priest'll understand?"

He smiled. "Is his understanding the issue?"

"Well, it would be good to have someone around here understand… The thing is, I don't know if I can connect. All these years, I've used religion to keep me going. What happens if it's not like I remember it? Like I need it to be?" She picked up her pocketbook and pulled back the black leather flap. Her hand found the half empty package of cigarettes.

"Nothing is how you remember it after ten, twelve years. If you work at it, you'll connect. Give yourself time."

"It used to be so good, so pure. Now I feel so dirty. So sinful." She took a cigarette from the pack. "I feel that I have devils inside me that even you haven't seen."

"What kind of devils?"

She tucked the pack into her pocketbook and extracted a metal lighter. "I don't know... You've seen my vulgarity, my profanity — that's just the beginning. I'm very ugly when you get to know me." She set the pocketbook on the floor, flipped open the Zippo's cap and thumbed the spark wheel to get a flame.

"Tell me about the devils and the ugliness," he said.

She dragged on the cigarette and held the smoke in her lungs as long as she could before exhaling. If she told him, he'd laugh. Or leave her, like John. 'Devils united, devils delighted.' Which nun had said that? "You know what John called me? 'Self-centered, perverse and vindictive.' As if he isn't... Still, he's right about me. But not from what I said today; I was just giving him a hard time."

"You spoke to him?"

"I called him. Got an ashtray?" She took another drag and put the lighter back in her purse.

"I think so." He turned to the desk, lifted a few papers and journals, finally found a glass ashtray under a pile of pink message slips. He tucked the messages under the geode she'd given him. "Only one cigarette, okay?" He handed her the ashtray.

"I remember," she said. Why didn't they have better ventilation in a room without windows? "The call wasn't a big deal. I wanted to congratulate him on his new lover. I told him I was going to post signs around campus. 'Beware of John Taylor. He fucks students in more ways than one'." She tapped her cigarette against the glass ashtray, saw the ashes crumble away. "You know, people should come with warning labels stamped on their foreheads. Everyone's dangerous, but you don't know how until it's too late."

"You didn't know what you were getting into with John?"

"Maybe I didn't care. But he shouldn't throw stones. He's more self-centered and promiscuous than I am."

"Is that comforting?"

"Don't get nasty." She pointed at the geode. "You want to throw a stone, use the one on your desk. Or be like John — fuck me, screw me and then throw it."

He frowned. "Why are you inviting something you don't want — inviting me to be someone you don't want me to be?"

"How should I know? You're the psychiatrist."

"But it's your life, your mind, isn't it? Work at it." He picked up the geode and showed it to her. "Why did you give me this?"

She stared at the rock's laughing mouth, at the sparkling teeth of amethyst crystal. "I didn't give it to you; Eggers found it."

"You said I could keep it, that you would have given it to me anyway, right? What did you want me to do with it?"

She glanced up at him. "In my generous moments or my rotten ones?"

"Come on, Maggie." He sounded annoyed.

What did he want from her? She took a quick puff and blew smoke toward the bookcase. "I guess I hoped you'd keep the stone as a souvenir. Something to remember me by, after I was dead."

He placed the geode on his desk. "Did you give a stone to John?"

"A Petoskey stone. It was a birthday — " To Mark, to James. Mother of God! She closed her eyes, smacked her forehead with her palm.

"Tell me — "

She looked down at the ashtray. "I always give them. To my boyfriends, to you, to Petro." She ground her cigarette against the glass. "I'm asking for it — aren't I?"

"Asking for what?"

"To be hurt, to be stoned." She blinked back her tears. "Why? Why do I keep doing it?"

"You tell me."

"You're no help, you know that?" She thrust the ashtray toward him. "Here! Take it and shove it."

His fingers closed on the glass. "Who am I right now? Who needs to take it and shove it?"

She saw F. Dexter's face, felt his thick fingers pinching her, squeezing pain from her nipples, the pain, oh the pain as he put his fingers inside her and pulled and tore and the blood — "You bastards! Sadistic bastards!"

"Who?" asked Raymond.

"You know."

"Say it, Who are the sadistic bastards?"

"Fuck you!"

"Fuck all of us, right? And why do you give us stones?"

She clutched her head. *O my God,* she recited silently, *I am heartily sorry for having offended Thee. I detest all my sins because I dread the loss of —*

"Why do you give us stones?" demanded Raymond.

She glared at him. "To hurt me, all right?"

"No, it's not all right." He set the ashtray on his desk. "Why?"

Hands on her head, she looked up toward the ceiling. Jesus, Mary and Joseph, make him leave me alone.

"Why, Maggie?"

Her head jerked downward, her fists shook with rage. "You think they're fucking souvenirs?" she shouted. "Hey guy, you want this to remember our fuck?' Stone for a bone?" She thrust her fists into her lap.

"You need us to remember your gift?"

Away, she needed to get away — .a joint, yes, a joint. "All I need is to get — " Stoned. She needed to get stoned.

"Get what?" asked Raymond.

"Fucked!" she screamed. "Screwed! Stoned!" She gulped for breath. "In that order." Her head ached and her throat burned as hurt spouted upward, overflowing muscles, reason, will, a flood reclaiming old territory. Then she was sobbing aloud, body balled up in her chair, knowing she was crazy as well as sinful. Nothing mattered anymore.

"Maggie…" He sounded far away.

How long had he been sitting there watching her cry? Her throat felt raw. Had he handed her these tissues? She wiped her eyes, then blew her nose noisily. He always saw her like this. Oh, God. She dabbed at her blouse. She'd have to get it dry-cleaned.

She glanced up. "I'm sorry."

"It's okay." His face was comforting.

"No, it's not. How do you put up with me?"

"I'm not `putting up' with you. We're on the same side of the struggle."

"To live?" she asked.

"To live in peace, to trust, to love — you name it."

"I — "

"What?" he prompted.

"I almost trust you."

He smiled. "Thank you. I almost trust me, too."

"You're really not like them, are you. It's hard to believe."

"Like whom?"

437

"Like John and Dave and Mark and James — "

"Mark and James?"

"Boyfriends. Old boyfriends. I told you about them."

"No you didn't. They're all Biblical names."

"So? Lots of people have Biblical names."

"Is it possible — "

She covered her ears. "I don't want to hear it." It wasn't true. Even if he said it, that didn't make it true, did it?

"I don't understand. I think that — "

"I don't give a shit what you think!" She sprang from her chair. "It's a coincidence." Her fist thumped the wall. "Just a coincidence. David wasn't a disciple. Carlos wasn't even in the Bible. I fucked them, too." She buried her face in her hands. Did the exceptions prove the rule? Had she been testing all of them? Corrupting all of them?

"Hey, wait a minute. I'm not accusing you. I'm not blaming you. I just want you to consider — "

"Stop it!" she screamed. Her arm lashed out, sweeping books and papers from the top shelf of the bookcase. "You're wrong! You're wrong!" She had to destroy his papers, his records. She charged toward the desk, but he was getting up, arms stretched wide to block her. She felt her head hit his nose, heard his grunt of pain as he recoiled, his arms locking around her shoulders as he tripped against his chair, dragging her with him over the back of the chair, onto the floor. He let out a gasp as she fell on him.

"Fu–ugh," she grunted. His body felt warm and forgiving. Crying, she clung to him.

He held her gently. "Are you hurt?"

"No — no — I'm sorry." She was shaking, sobbing, her face pressed to his neck. "I'm sorry, I'm sorry." She felt him hugging her protectively.

"It's not your fault. I tripped. It's not your fault about the other stuff, either." For an instant, his arms tightened, then they withdrew completely.

She raised her head, brushed away tears with one hand. "Your nose is bleeding," she told him. "I'm sorry. I'm really sorry."

"I know." Raymond touched his nose. "There are tissues on the desk."

"I'll get them." She disengaged her leg from the chair, her body from his. Her left knee hurt as she got up. "With a nosebleed, you're better off lying down."

"Good advice," he said as he sat up, "but I feel a trifle awkward lying at my patient's feet."

Giggling through her tears, she handed him a bunch of tissues. "And how did you feel lying next to me?"

He pressed tissues to his nose. His voice became nasal. "There are no words to describe it."

"Bullshit."

"No, that word doesn't do it, either. Let's consider it a very special, once-in-a-lifetime experience, okay?" He struggled to his feet.

She grinned. "That's entirely up to you." She righted the chair, then began picking up papers and books from the floor.

"Why don't you leave that?" he said. "I'll get it later."

"I did it. I'll fix it."

"You have more important things to fix. How about sitting down again?"

"Don't tell me what to do." She stuffed a bunch of papers into the nearest manila folder.

"I'm not. I was telling you what I think. And you didn't like it. Can you handle it now?" He looked at his wad of tissues, then threw them in the wastebasket.

"You don't know when to give up, do you?" She put the manila folder on the bookcase.

"It's a failing I have."

"One of many." She squatted to retrieve a few books from the carpet. "Well, say what you have to say. Maybe you'll feel better for it."

"Maybe we both will." He touched his nostrils lightly, looked for blood on his fingers. "How about sitting down?"

She put the books on top of the manila folder. "I'll stand, thank you. Get it over with."

"Okay. I think part of your hell is participating again and again in the corruption of the man you love — not that you're responsible for that, except by picking losers — but you witness it over and over, always hoping for a happier ending than you've come to expect." He ran his hand through his hair. "I don't know, maybe your hell is to be betrayed again and again, and your penance is unending guilt."

Was he right? Well, a little. About the guilt...and the betrayals. Not the names. She returned to her chair and sat down. "I picked you. Are you a loser?"

"I thought Doctor Taylor picked me."

"Well, he assigned you. But I spoke to you, didn't I?"

"Sure..." He rearranged his tie to cover its tail. "Did you think I was a loser?"

"I never think the men I — care for are losers."

"Not to begin with, anyway." He reached to his desk for a tissue. "But then you give each one a stone. You expect to be fucked, screwed and stoned. In that order, right?" He dabbed at his nose gently.

Why was he pushing her? Did he have to bare all her secrets

before he screwed her? No, no! Those were fucked-up thoughts. Old patterns. "I — "

"What?" he prompted.

"There's something else. From long ago." She took a deep breath. "I never put all these things together before. I don't even remember when I first thought I was like her. I just knew she was bad, but she believed in Jesus and Jesus saved her."

"Mary Magdalene?"

"*He that is without sin among you, let him first cast a stone at her.*" She laughed at the irony. "You know who wrote that?"

"Jesus said it. I don't know who wrote it."

"It was Saint John. Well, what's in a name anyway, right?"

"Did Mary Magdalene's name provide some – uh –a bridge for Mary Saxe to become Maggie?"

She shrugged. "I don't know. The more I knew about Mary Magdalene, the more I saw myself in her. In how she was before Jesus cast out her devils. But Margaret was also my grandmother's name. F. Dexter hated her. After she died, I asked all my friends to call me Maggie." She gave him her best wicked grin. "In my family, we went out of our way to screw each other."

"You're smiling, but that's terribly sad."

She felt her smile cave in. She swallowed hard and looked away.

"Our time's almost up for tonight," he said. "There's something I have to bring up. I need to change our appointment time. I can't meet in the evening, anymore."

"Your wife?"

"It has nothing to do with my wife. There's another reason that I can't tell you about right now."

She feigned a heavy sigh. "For a guy that doesn't believe in secrets, you sure own a bundle. I thought we couldn't meet during the day because Doctor Taylor might find out."

"That's right. I was thinking about Sunday mornings."

"Sunday?"

He nodded. "Some of the faculty come in on Saturday to catch up on paperwork or finish their latest articles — it's too unpredictable. If they see me here, there'll be questions."

"Sunday at the shrink's?" She rolled her eyes up toward the ceiling. "Well, only for you. Oh, but not this Sunday — it's Easter."

"Church?" he asked.

She shrugged her shoulders.

"I hope so," he said. "Sunday after this?"

"I'm sorry. That's the Greek Easter. I'll have to be with Petro that day."

"Okay, we'll meet once more at night, next Tuesday, then we'll skip the week of the Greek Easter and pick up on the following Sunday."

"Is that okay for you?" she asked.

"I think so…" He rubbed his forehead. "I hope so."

Bike Attack

"Why is it red?" asked Julie from the passenger seat. She sat bundled in her brown toggle coat, secured by a seat belt.

"What?" said Lisa. She eyed a grungy young man who was approaching the driver in front of her with a fistful of individually wrapped roses. A white placard tied around his chest said, "Make Peace, Not War." She rolled up her window, checked the lock on her door.

"Why is it red?" repeated Julie, pointing at the traffic light.

"Oh. To make the cars stop so people can cross the street." Lisa glanced past Joshua sleeping in his car seat to check that the button on Julie's door was down. Oh, crumb! Frightened to take the kids, frightened to leave them.

"How does it know to make cars stop?" asked Julie.

"The drivers make them stop. They know a red light means — " Lisa's body jerked at the knock on her window. She shook her head vehemently at the flower seller.

"Flowers!" exclaimed Julie. "Can I have one?"

"No!" snapped Lisa. Flowers were the last thing she wanted after seeing that dismembered bird in the daisies. Her body relaxed as the man moved away to the next car. "We don't buy or take anything from strangers. You remember that. We buy what we need in stores." Was there a store that sold security?

"Can we get flowers in the store?"

"No, not today. We're not going to any stores. We're picking up Daddy and going right home." She'd feel much safer with Raymond in the car. That crazy crow-man had made her so jumpy. She adjusted the rearview mirror. The flower seller was making a sale three cars back, with a station wagon and a motorcyclist in a black helmet and goggles remaining as potential customers. Nothing to worry about. She readjusted the mirror.

"It's green," said Julie. "Who changed it?"

"A switch," Lisa replied, shifting her foot to the accelerator. "Like on the TV, when we change channels." The Volkswagon in front of her hesitated, then lurched ahead. Lisa followed cautiously.

"But who changed it?" Julie repeated.

"It changed itself. There's a timer in it."

"What's a timer?"

"A little clock. When it gets to a certain time it makes a switch do something. Like the buzzer on Daddy's alarm clock." A bad time, it was just a bad time. Too many changes. Joshua's tumor, Raymond having to leave his job, planning a move —

"Does the timer tell the switch what noise to make?" asked Julie.

"Yes. Now don't ask any more questions. I have to think about driving." She stopped at the YIELD sign before turning onto the parkway. Damn! Heavy traffic. Wait for a clear opening. The people behind her would just have to be patient. She looked in the mirror. Only a station wagon and that motorcyclist.

Julie squirmed upward. "Why are we stopped? I don't see a red light."

"Stay in your seat belt! We'll go in a minute." No, she wouldn't go. Raymond could talk himself blue in the face. She'd never leave him in danger. How could she ever forgive herself if something awful happened?

The motorcycle rumbled up beside her. Impatient man! She glanced over. Goodness, he's huge. Why do bikers love black? The biker pointed for her to move onto the parkway.

"Don't be ridiculous," Lisa muttered, gesturing for him to go ahead. He could kill himself if he wanted to.

"I'm not ridiculous," said Julie.

Lisa looked over and smiled. "No, I didn't mea -"

The motorcycle roared. Lisa's body jumped, her head spun to her window. Black helmet! What was that? "No!" she screamed as she stomped on the accelerator. The tire iron shattered the window behind her, stinging her neck with glass. She heard Julie scream "Mommy!" and the screech of brakes as an oncoming car swerved to avoid her but failed, it's front bumper bashing the Valiant's tail light. The impact jarred Lisa, made her clutch the wheel tighter as the Valiant skidded into the breakdown lane. She twisted the wheel desperately, saw trees and then cars again. Horns blared as drivers tried to avoid her. She regained control of the wheel, felt herself trembling, sweating. Should she stop? Joshua whimpered. Lisa glanced over. "Julie, are you okay?"

"I'm scared, Mommy."

"Don't worry, honey. We're all okay." The wind whipped through the broken window. That crazy man! She glanced at the mirror. Motorcycle coming! My God! She floored the accelerator, pressed her hand to the horn. Oh, God, wouldn't anybody help?

"Why are you ringing the horn?" asked Julie.

"So these bastards will get out of my way!" She steered into the left lane, put on the headlights, kicked the floor switch to get the bright beams. Emergency lights! She pressed the switch; both blinkers came on. She looked in the mirror. Black Helmet moving up fast. She'd never outrun him.

"What are bastards?" asked Julie.

"Shut up. We're in trouble!"

Lisa weaved the speeding Valiant back and forth between lanes. Her blaring horn was answered by others, by curses and upraised fingers. The motorcycle roared closer, was behind her, coming up on her left. She swerved into the left lane, hugging the guard rail. Black Helmet fell back, tried to come up on her right. She twisted the wheel right, almost hit a Mercedes, saw the man's outrage as she passed him and moved close to a van. EXIT 2 MILES. Oh God, they'd never make it. Coming on the left! She turned the wheel sharply, heard the screech of metal against metal as the Valiant grazed the guard rail and bounced back. My God! I'll kill us all! She glanced in the mirror, weaved right and then left. That sign, NO U-TURN. A break in the guard rail? Oh, my God! The only way!

She braked hard, harder. The motorcycle veered right to avoid a collision, roared up beside the Valiant, next to the back window, then Julie's window. Black Helmet's hand drew the tire iron from his jacket. He raised the iron rod above his head, looked into the front seat and paused. Lisa dug her foot into the brake pedal and twisted the wheel. Brakes locked, wheels sending up a shower of dirt and gravel, the Valiant skidded into a U-turn. The car seat pitched against Julie, pushing her to the door. Joshua yelped, Julie cried "Ouch," Lisa flung up a hand and grabbed for the baby. As oncoming drivers flinched and gave ground to avoid a collision, the Valiant careened across the road, then across the breakdown lane, onto the grass. Black Helmet looked over his shoulder, but the motorcycle's momentum and the traffic carried him onward toward the exit.

Lisa struggled to take a breath. No, mustn't cry, mustn't cry! "You okay?" she asked hoarsely. Her hands were trembling.

"I don't like the way you drive," said Julie.

"I'm sorry. I won't do that again." Hope not, anyway. A mile and a half to the exit — a three mile lead. How fast can a motorcycle go? She pulled the car seat next to her. "Quiet, Joshua, I need quiet." She dried her hands on her skirt, turned off the emergency blinkers and took a firm grip on the wheel. Who was chasing them? The Crowman? Some other crazy? No time to think about that now.

She maneuvered the Valiant back to the breakdown lane, waited for an opening and floored the accelerator. The baby was crying. "Shhhh, Joshua." At least we're alive. Tears ran down Lisa's cheeks. She wiped her eyes with the back of her hand, then dabbed the moisture from her neck. Blood? Oh, shit. Alive, we're alive! Joshua cried louder.

Julie yelled "Shut up, Joshua. We're in trouble."

"No, not now," said Lisa. "And don't talk to your brother like that."

60

Starch

"Your wife's got some starch in her," said Fremmer, pin-striped and stiff behind his well-disciplined desk. "She didn't panic." His gray crew-cut dipped in a nod of approval.

Didn't Fremmer understand? Raymond leaned forward in the straight-backed chair that faced the security man. "My wife and children could be dead now, Mr. Fremmer. The police don't give a shit; they let Cruber go. He's going to try again. I know he will — he's crazy."

"I don't understand what you get out of working with crazies. Every time I see you, they're giving you trouble... Why'd they let that old boy loose?"

Raymond's hands rose in frustration. "Cruber had an alibi. He was at work. His card was punched in at the meat packing plant."

"Could have punched in and left," said Fremmer. "Or had somebody punch in for him. Couldn't they figure that out?"

"His foreman claimed he was there." Raymond's tone was bitter, his fists empty. He wiped his hands on his trousers.

Fremmer shrugged. "Then maybe he was there."

"No, it had to be Cruber. He must have bribed the foreman. Maybe he's blackmailing him. He's capable of doing almost anything." Raymond shook his head. "I can't believe that someone else would just ride down the highway and attack a woman and two babies for no reason."

Fremmer reached into the breast pocket of his suit, pulled out a silver cigarette case. "It happens. Read your newspaper."

"I'm telling you, it's Cruber. He rides a motorcycle."

"So do lots of people." Fremmer snapped open the cigarette case. It was half full. "Could your wife identify the bike?" He extracted a cigarette and closed the case.

"Not really. She described it to the police the best she could, but she couldn't pinpoint a specific make or model. Not that it matters."

"Why not?" Fremmer tapped the cigarette on the silver case.

"Cruber showed the police that his bike was in the shop for repairs. A paranoid thinks of every angle." Raymond grimaced. "If you ever need a lawyer, hire a paranoid."

"So the foreman says this guy's at work, and his bike is out of commission. And you still think he's the one?"

"I don't think it. I know it. I threatened his family — his cover, really — by initiating that Protective Services evaluation, so he punished me by threatening my family."

"Seems like he wanted to kill your family."

"No. I've thought about that, believe me." Raymond massaged the back of his neck. "He could have reversed direction at that exit and made up the three miles lickety-split. Hell, he could have caught them. Or he could have used a gun if he wanted them dead. No," Raymond jabbed a finger forward, "killing them wasn't his goal. Lisa said he even hesitated before he struck at Julie's window. Not that he would have cared if they died. He doesn't feel guilt or compassion.

His aim was to hurt me, to terrify me about what he could do, what he's out there planning to do. And he wanted my wife out of the way."

"Why?" asked Fremmer, producing a lighter from his pocket.

Raymond's hands separated, palms up. "It's like in chess. You attack the queen so that she'll withdraw and leave the king vulnerable. The object of the game is to checkmate the king."

"Does Cruber play chess?"

"No, I did. But that's only a game. I need your help, Mr. Fremmer. You've seen combat. You've worked in security. Together, maybe we can nail this guy."

Fremmer raised his eyebrows, lowered them, lit his cigarette. He took a long drag and let the smoke out slowly. "Together?" he finally said.

"I can't do it myself." Raymond shook his head. "I don't know how to use a gun. Physically, I'm no match for him. I have my family to worry about. All we could do is run away."

Fremmer coughed. Covering his mouth with the back of his hand, he coughed again, then cleared his throat. "If this Cruber's as crazy as you say, running away may not be a bad idea."

"I'm tired of running away. I did that as a kid; I can't do it as a man. I have to do something else."

"Well, that's up to you, Doc. But why drag me into it? I don't only preach C.Y.A., I practice it. My responsibility is to the patients and staff of this medical center while they're on our property. Once they step off our grounds, they're on they're own."

"He could come after me here. Then whatever happens is your problem, too." Raymond extended his palms toward Fremmer. "Look, I'm not asking you to do anything illegal or beyond your abilities. I'm willing to pay you or pay anyone you recommend as being very capable of protecting my family. The truth is, I don't know anybody else, and I'd rather go with someone I trust."

"What exactly do you want done?" Fremmer tapped the ash from his cigarette into an ashtray.

"Like I said, Cruber's going to come after me. I want Lisa and the kids snuck out of town so they won't get hurt." Raymond rubbed his neck. "They can stay with Lisa's sister. Then, when Cruber makes his move against me, he has to be caught, disarmed, and turned over to the police." He pointed a finger at Fremmer. "Before he hurts me. If I can't have him dead, I want him locked away for a very long time."

"You should get the police to protect you. I haven't seen any action since Korea."

"Get someone good to help you, Mr. Fremmer. The police think this is small potatoes. Cruber has no criminal record and he has an air-tight alibi for everything." Raymond scratched the back of his hand. "The police say I should call them if he shows up again. The problem is that Cruber told me I'd never see him coming. I'll never have time to make that call."

Fremmer coughed. He shook his head at the cigarette. "I don't know why I do this. It's not good for me at all." He stubbed out the cigarette. "How much will you pay?"

"Forty dollars a day."

Fremmer looked pained. "Ask the Girl Scouts to protect you."

"How much do you want?"

"Two hundred a day. That includes my man. I won't take this on alone."

"I don't have that kind of money."

Fremmer shrugged. "If you want something bad enough, you pay the price."

Bastard! he thought. Fourteen hundred a week? "But that's — uh — almost seventeen thousand dollars between now and June thirtieth."

"Look at it this way, Doc — you can borrow money, you can't borrow life."

Raymond started to rise. "Sorry, I'll have to try someone else."

Fremmer put up a pacifying hand. "Tell you what. For you, I'll come down to one-seventy-five. Remember, we may catch him the first week."

"And what if you don't?"

"I'll earn a little more toward retirement. I don't work for the fun of it, you know."

Raymond stood up. "Neither do I. Seventeen thousand is more than double what I make in a year."

"Tell you what, I'll give you a guarantee. If you or any member of your family get hurt by that crazy, I'll give you back every cent."

"Now who's crazy? You're treating our lives like they're on some bargain basement table."

"I learned from the government. You can apply cost-benefit ratios to anything. One-sixty. It's my final offer. If you don't take it, you're the crazy."

Raymond ran a hand through his hair. "I'm damned if I do and damned if I don't."

"That's the way it always is, Doc. There's no real security in anything."

61

Packing

Raymond set his coffee mug on the kitchen table. Beneath the table, his other hand gripped his thigh. "Thanks for making dinner," he said.

In the chair opposite his, Lisa stared at her mug of tea, but she nodded that she'd heard him. Above the scoop neck of her peasant blouse, a pink blotch the size of a quarter marred her fair skin. Half her portion of salmon and broccoli lay on the plate she'd pushed back, and she'd not had more than a few sips of tea. His only morsel of relief came from seeing her faded patchwork skirt and fuzzy slippers, which suggested she'd not ventured out of the apartment.

Aftershock or the calm before the storm? thought Raymond. Yesterday, once the children were safely lodged with her friend Helen, Lisa had been openly distraught about being attacked, but today she'd apparently gone through her chores in a robotic manner. He'd come home to a perfunctory kiss, the kids already in bed, her controlled manner and her reluctance to say much about anything. The upward tilt of her chin and the darkness in her eyes as she'd put dinner on the table told him that she was angry as well as afraid. Well, she certainly had good reason to feel both. He'd brought terror into their lives, and his apologies hadn't made her feel one drop better. How could they? Cruber was still out there. Yet silence just made things worse.

"You know, we have to talk," he said.

She looked up with a strained expression; she spoke in a weary tone. "What good is talking? You're stubborn as an ox about staying. Even with that madman on the loose."

"I'm not going to get hurt." He tried to sound confident. "Fremmer's going to be here — he's getting other men, too. There will always be two with me. I'll be very well protected."

"Well, if Mr. Fremmer can protect you, he can protect all of us. I'm not leaving without you."

Under the table, his fingernails bit into his palm. "Please, Lisa, don't make it harder. Two men can't protect a whole family around the clock. Not with me going to work, you needing to shop. You saw that yesterday."

"Don't put that 'making it harder' bull on me!" she snapped. "The easiest, smartest thing we could do is pack up and leave. But no, you have this thing about your job. Isn't your life more important than finishing this residency?"

Raymond frowned. "Of course. But I have patients who depend on me. What do you want me to do? Abandon them?"

"Transfer them! The department has other psychiatrists."

"C'mon, Lisa." His plea rode an undercurrent of anger. "I've worked hard with these people. I can't call them tonight and leave them tomorrow. They'd see it as a betrayal, an abandonment — and they'd be right."

She leveled a finger at him. "You're not their husband, Ray. You're not their father. Isn't leaving them better than abandoning us?"

"But I'm not abandoning you! I love you and the kids and want you safe. And you'll be safe in Maine with your sister."

"For how long? A week, a month? More than that if you don't come back?" Her tone was sharp, her neck and cheeks reddish pink. "You ask my sister to shelter us, my father for money – I don't like being my family's charity case."

"We'll pay your dad back. I promise. But to do that — " He reached out, palms up and open. "– for me to get anywhere in my profession, I have to finish this residency. Any clinical job in medicine has occupational hazards. A radiologist is more likely to get cancer, an infectious disease doc can die from a nasty virus, and a psychiatrist can get killed by a crazy person." He placed his hands on the table like a lawyer resting his case.

"Who's craziness are you dealing with? Cruber's? Or yours?"

"Thanks a lot." His tone was sarcastic. "I appreciate your support."

"Support?" She hit the tabletop. Tea sloshed from her mug. "Damn! For risking your life? For sending me away? What kind of support do you expect? What kind of support are you giving?" She grabbed a couple of paper napkins to wipe up the spilled tea. "Think about what you're doing to us because you're afraid to walk away."

"I'm not afraid to walk away. I'm not even afraid to run away. That's all too familiar..." A blood vessel throbbed in his temple. "I can't do that anymore. Don't you understand? I can't let everything I've worked for be destroyed by Taylor's vindictiveness or Cruber's craziness or my — cowardice, or your fears for me. I'm going to do my job."

"You're so blind!" She squeezed the wet napkins into a ball. "You have a job to do with our children. Isn't that more important? Isn't our life together more important than any job?"

"Sure. But we'll have many years together. I can't give my children a wimp father who runs away. You know that… And I can't really give much to you if I feel worthless and empty."

"What can you give me if you're dead?" Her voice cracked, her eyes welled with tears. She dropped the napkins and reached for his hand. Her fingers were cold. "I'm terrified, Ray. You lost your father. Wasn't he trying to be brave, too? Standing up to some drug addict? I don't want our children to lose their father. You should understand that better than anybody."

He pulled his hand away. "You think I don't? You think I want them to go through what I did?"

"Of course not."

"Then ease off. Fremmer is a combat vet who has years of experience in security. He and his men are more than ready for Cruber to try to get to me. They've laid out a protection plan I'll follow, but they say having you and the kids here poses too many variables, too much risk for everyone. And they're right. More important than anything, I want to make sure that you and the kids stay safe."

Her hands retreated to the table's edge. "I know that. But your safety is just as important to us. Putting your life on the line to prove yourself wouldn't make a whole lot of sense if you were single. But as a husband and father, it makes no sense at all." She looked him in the eye. "I hate to say it, but it's selfish."

He winced. "It's not only about me. Do you know how much time and effort it took to get Maggie Saxe to trust me? If I dumped her, she'd probably kill herself. Even if she didn't, she certainly wouldn't trust another therapist."

"Those are her choices, her problems." Lisa shook her head. "God knows I don't want anyone to commit suicide or live in misery, but I'm not responsible for that and neither are you. Is that woman worth dying for? Is she worth splitting up our family? Having our kids grow up without their father?"

"For God's sake, Lisa." He extended his hands. "I'm not going to die… And it's not only Maggie. I have a dozen people who are hurting and need me."

"Aren't the kids and I more important than a dozen strangers?"

"Yes, of course you are. But they're not strangers to me. They're people I care about. I know more about Mag — some of them — than I know about my brother and sister. I can't abandon them."

"Especially Maggie Saxe." Lisa pushed back her chair.

"Oh c'mon, Lisa. There's no need to — "

"You're sending us away so you can play doctor with her. Isn't that what it comes down to?"

"No, it's not!" he shouted. "I'm not doing it because of Maggie Saxe."

The baby cried out. Their heads turned toward the bedroom.

"Keep your voice down," whispered Lisa. Hearing no further outcry, she grabbed up her dinner plate and tea mug. "You may not be staying only for her, but you sure as hell aren't doing it for me and the children." She moved toward the sink.

"I'm just trying to keep us all safe."

"Are you?" She dumped her dishes into the sink's soapy water and turned back to look at him. "Then let's all go away together."

"I can't," he said quietly. "Please don't ask me again. I love you. I love the children. But I have to stay and you can't. We'd never forgive ourselves if he got to the children. You know that."

Tearfully, she went to him, reached out and pressed his head against her abdomen. "I love you," she said. "I'd never — never forgive myself if he got to you."

"He won't." He pushed back his chair and stood pressed against her, aching to comfort her. "Don't cry. Whatever happens, I don't want you feeling guilty. Like you said, these are my choices, my problems."

"I said that about that Saxe woman, not about you." She pulled her head back and brushed away her tears. "The relationship is hardly the same. We're supposed to share, remember?"

"Some things aren't sharable."

She pulled out of his grasp. "That's crazy! I'm your wife!"

"No! I'm telling you the truth. I have to do this. If that's selfish, so be it." At what price? he thought. His stomach knotted. No, we'll get through this.

Lisa's nostrils flared. "You know, for a psychiatrist, you're damned insensitive. And as a husband, you're a pig-headed jerk!" She headed for the door. "You clean up the dishes. I have packing to do."

62

The Roof

George climbed the last flight of steps to the roof door. He paused for his heart to slow down, and for his mind to think through the details one last time before opening the metal door. A 40-watt bulb caged his shadow against the opposite wall. His gloved fingers reached between the wires and unscrewed the bulb. If the crows were out there, would they shoot first and ask questions later? Probably not. If they were disguised as cops, they'd demand he lie down and then they'd search him. Private security crows would start out the same, but they'd probably go beyond threatening and beat him. Still, it was smarter to have come without a weapon, and smarter to test the enemy's defenses before launching an attack.

George sniffed the air, trying to strain out the odors of mildew and cooked onions and cabbage to sense what remained. No good. He put his ear to the door. The metal was cold. No, if they were on the roof, the metal door kept their scent and sounds from him. Could be that they were in Daniels' apartment, two floors below. Or both places. Had they let him get into the basement and up seven stories to bag him on the roof? Still, what could they prove? He was visiting his doctor to apologize, got cold feet, went to the roof for a breath of air — at worst, they might get him for breaking and entering. Without a weapon. And if he'd misjudged Daniels, if the shrink didn't have protection and was alone or with his wife in that apartment, why then Daniels would provide the weapon and a car to visit Ma — yes, and anything else he wanted.

He took a penlight from his shirt pocket and examined the lock. It hadn't been fixed. He bent over and aimed the beam at the base of the door. The broken toothpick was still propped against it, still pointed the right way. He clicked off the light. Did they notice the toothpick, have one grubsucker replace it after others had gone through to the roof? Would he open the door to find crows in black shoes and uniforms? Yes, disguised, like Ma peeping out of Carol's body, pretending to be so coy and innocent — like the way she tried to make up her face for every new man. Oh, they were clever. Except they underestimated him this time. The gorilla he'd hired would flush them from hiding, then the real gorilla would show Daniels and Ma and all her Harpies what for.

He opened the roof door a crack, peeked out at the blackness, felt a cool breeze on his face. Would the clouds be blown away? He heard hard rock throbbing from big speakers, raised voices from another apartment, a truck passing on the street below. He listened for a scratch of talons on the brick, a soft caw, a flap of wings. Nothing. The heavy door squeaked as he pushed it open. He crouched, listened, moved forward cautiously. Only shadows and pipes, a TV aerial. No, no grubsuckers here, but stay down — a night-scope could target him easy. Yes, they could be on that roof across the street — or that one — advising the crow-turds in Daniels' apartment. Only Ma could call off the crows, shut their infra-red eyes for good. And she wouldn't. He'd buried her. Well, he'd have to fix that or he'd never get rid of them.

In a crouch, he moved to the shelter of a brick parapet and looked at his watch. Too dark. Using the penlight might reveal his position. He settled down to wait. After a while, he began poking his head over different points along the parapet each time he heard a car stop on the street. What will the grubsuckers do when they see the gorilla? "Not ten fifty-nine, not eleven oh-one," he'd specified over the telephone. "Eleven o'clock. That's when my brother was born. It has to be exact, because my mother's going to be on the phone with him in Vietnam." All lies, but so what? Everyone lies and makes false promises to get what they want, but they're furious when others do it to them. No one could pin this little trick on him — cash through the transom, public telephone. But if that gorilla didn't come, he'd find him, chop off his hands and stuff his fingers into his balloons.

Another car coming. George poked his head up and saw the yellow van as it passed under a street-lamp. He couldn't see the letters on the side until the van double-parked in front of the entrance. Now all the crows would have their eyes on it, he thought. LOONY BALLOONS. He'd show them who would laugh last.

The driver got out, went to the rear of the van and opened it. He put on the head of the gorilla costume, extracted a bunch of large balloons, closed the van and headed toward the apartment house. Good! Now he'd flush out the crows — and ask Daniels to visit the late Mrs. Cruber.

His sneakers made no noise descending the steps. He paused before each landing to listen. Don't rush, plenty of time. It would take the gorilla a few minutes to gain entrance, take the elevator up four floors and find the right apartment. He'd be slowed by his gorilla suit and a dozen balloons.

Fourth floor. George stopped, held his breath and listened for breathing, for the click of a safety catch as a weapon was readied, for crow wings moving the air. Nothing. He took a quiet breath, opened the fire door a crack, and heard the whir of an elevator rising. They'd buzzed the gorilla in. Daniels would never've done that if he were alone. Yes, the grubsuckers were waiting for George Elton Cruber. What if Daniels was there with a gun? Wouldn't it be rich if Daniels shot the gorilla? He heard the elevator stop, the doors slide apart.

George opened the fire door wide enough to peek out. The gorilla pulled the balloons from the elevator and headed down the hall to Daniels' apartment. He rang the doorbell. The apartment door opened.

"Freeze, you fucker!" a hoarse voice yelled.

The gorilla screamed in fright.

"Move and we'll blow you away," another voice threatened.

George closed the fire door quietly and hurried down the steps. Neither voice was Daniels'. No doubt about it — Daniels worked for the crows. That grubsucker! Well, another day, another way. Let Daniels and that gorilla sweat. It was time to visit Ma.

63

Gorilla

The electric eye blinked at his gorilla suit; the sliding doors hissed back. Holding the red guide-ribbons of the balloons in one paw and a large gift-wrapped box with the other, George strode through the hospital lobby toward the elevators. A flock of evening visitors were on their way out, eager to get home now that their duty was done. The faces that turned his way showed surprise and then smiles.

Grubsuckers! Planning to trap him. A few were flitting this way and that to deceive him, but all of them were eager to stop him from incinerating their source of power. He was their prey, and they were his. Daniels was their bait, but he was also a witness and proof of their treachery.

"Look, Ma! Just like *Planet of the Apes*," said a pimply boy.

"I want a balloon," whined his little sister.

"Visiting your girlfriend?" a skeletal man asked at the elevator.

Grubsucker! George nodded. Under his costume, the canteen nagged at his hip.

A gumchewer in an **I Love Ringo** tee shirt touched his hairy sleeve. "You big ape," she said, giggling. Her girlfriend snorted and snickered. He glared at them through the mask.

The elevator door opened. Startled faces, a gasp, and an "Oh my God" from a lipsticked mouth all turned to smiles as bodies emerged from the elevator and passed close enough to leave the stench of crowshit in his nostrils. George jerked the balloons lower, stepped into the elevator and put his back to the rear wall. The balloons knocked about overhead. The skeletal man followed the two young women across the threshold and grinned at George.

"What floor, good lookin?" asked the gumchewer from the control panel. Her friend snorted. They looked at each other and giggled.

"Five," said George. The crows were testing him. A peck here, a scratch there – if he kept pretending to ignore it, they'd think him weak.

"Four, please," said the skeletal man.

The door closed. The elevator trembled, then rose with a whir.

"King Kong didn't need no elevator," said the snorter.

"I saw the old one on TV," said the chewer. "It looked so fake."

"It's still better than the one with Godzilla," said the snorter. She stepped toward George. "I'll bet King Kong's your hero." She snickered and reached out to touch him.

George let go of the balloons, dropped the package and drove his forearm into the snorter's face. Her neck snapped back, her head hit the wall. The chewer screamed. The skeletal man reached for his gun. George pivoted on one foot and kicked upward with the other. The man yelped and doubled over, exposing his neck. George chopped down with his cleaver, felt the impact, saw blood spurt everywhere. The chewer's eyes were enormous. "No, please!" she pleaded. He smashed the back of his cleaver into her forehead. Her body dropped to the floor.

"Isn't this your floor?" asked the chewer. "Five?"

"What? Yes," said George. Why were they giggling? Where was all that blood? Clutching the gift-wrapped box against the gorilla suit, he staggered from the elevator. The balloons danced on their ribbons as they followed him.

He found an empty stairwell. Leaning against the bannister, he descended a flight of steps to the landing between floors. His head ached, his vision was blurry. He put the box down, anchored the balloons to the banister, then pulled off his paw-mittens and gorilla head and placed them on the steps. It was hard to think clearly. What had seemed so real, didn't happen – or it had, and the crows had erased it from his mind. He felt exhausted and he hadn't even begun. What chance did he have of carrying it off tonight? No, the crows had sent that spell to stop him and they'd just send a worse one the next time. Even now, they might be massing outside the firedoors above and below, readying their attack. He unzipped the gorilla suit to get at the pills and his Baretta, popped a few of Denise's amphetamines into his mouth and swallowed them. Let the grubsuckers come. The high velocity hollow points would blow them away.

When they didn't come, he knew that they feared him. He was too strong, too smart. They'd expected him to sneak in a side exit to the clinic building, not walk right through the hospital lobby to get to the indoor bridge. He was beginning to feel better – the "speed" was kicking in.

He slipped the Baretta back in the shoulder holster, then poked holes in the gift wrapping so he could fire his silenced Walther with his hand still in the box. He put on the gorilla head, stuffed the right mitten into his costume and slipped on the left one to open the firedoor. It only took seconds to transfer the balloon ribbons to his mittened hand, and slip his bare hand around the gun in the box. The corridor was empty. He followed the signs toward the clinic building. At the bridge, a crow dressed in the body and uniform of a security guard rose from a chair. "That's quite a get-up. Where are you going?" The crow's mustache was too thick and brown to be real.

"Obstetrics clinic. My wife called to tell me the doctor said she was pregnant. After so many false alarms, I said I'd go ape if it was true."

"Congratulations," said the crow. "But that clinic closed at 5pm. She must have called from somewhere else."

"Oh, no." He turned in a circle as if unsure about what to do. The corridor was clear. "I took too long getting this costume. But, knowing her, she's probably still waiting there."

"After four hours? I doubt it, but I'll walk over there with you."

"Don't bother." The bullet that zipped from the Walther pierced the crow's heart, driving the body backward with one last flap of its wings before it fell. Shreds of cardboard and motes of dust settled more slowly. George set the Walther and what was left of the box down on the floor and slipped the balloon ribbons under the gun. He pocketed the crow's walkie-talkie, moved the chair away from the bridge and dragged the body over, seating it with the grubsucker's cap tilted down, as if he'd dozed off. Wouldn't fool them for long, not with a trail of blood on the floor, but maybe they wouldn't immediately assume the killer was on the other side of the bridge.

In the clinic building, he hurried down two flights of steps to put some distance between himself and any pursuers. There'd be more crows around Daniels, but the tattered remains of the gift box could no longer conceal the gun. Outnumbered, he'd need to surprise them.

The Cardiology Clinic waiting room was empty, the offices

behind it equally dark. George turned on the overhead light and looked about for anything he could use. Magazines! *TIME. LOOK. LIFE.* He secured the balloon ribbons around the arm of a chair, took off the gorilla head, then slid his right arm out of the costume. He quickly ripped the magazines apart, crumpled the pages and stuffed them into his empty sleeve, adding the remnants of the box for more bulk. Then he stuffed the mitten and forced it into the bottom of the sleeve. Push pins from the receptionist's desk served to fasten the fake arm diagonally across his costume.

On the elevator ride up to the Psychiatry Clinic, George positioned himself close to the door, his right hand on the gun inside his costume, his left holding the balloons low enough so they'd be readily seen. Seventh floor! The elevator trembled under his feet. The door opened slowly. Two crows were waiting, one tall and grizzled, one young and muscular. The young one had a hand in his jacket pocket. "You, again! I told you never – "

The Walther coughed, blowing the young one backward as the grizzled one dove for the receptionist's desk. The first slug missed him. The second exploded his back. The grizzled one jerked as if he'd been hit by a lightning bolt. He cawed once and lay still.

George let the balloons float up to the ceiling as he approached the crows. He kicked them hard to make sure they were dead. The older one groaned. George finished him off with a bullet to the back of his head. There was no outcry from the rest of the flock, no sound of pursuit. Neither of the elevators were moving. George collected a pistol from the older crow's shoulder holster, a snub-nosed revolver from the young one's pocket. Then he dragged the young one's body to the elevator, elbowed the button to open the door, and set the body to serve as a doorstop. He looked at the other elevator. No, if he disabled both, someone had to come looking. Better to get Daniels, burn his files and get out. George turned and padded down the hall.

64

Taken

Raymond told himself to be patient, not to prompt her again. It was her struggle, and a difficult one. The air in his small office seemed heavy with the problems and sorrows of today's patients. Thank goodness Maggie was his last. Loosening his tie, he leaned back in the swivel chair he'd brought out from behind his desk so that he could sit face to face with her. Finally, she glanced up from staring at her jeans, but she quickly pushed her mouth and chin into the high collar of her white fisherman's sweater.

"I'm not going," she said, her voice barely audible.

Raymond tried to keep his tone neutral. "To the Ethics Committee hearing? Why's that?"

"Not worth it," she mumbled.

"Who's not worth it? You? Nancy?"

She brought her mouth and voice out of hiding. "My testimony's not worth it. Nancy's out of there, I'm out of there – I just want to forget it."

"And what about the other young women that doctor will do things to?"

"Let them look after themselves. I had to, didn't I? Why do I have to get pulled through the mud again?" She turned her head and spoke to the wall. "No, sir, I'm not crazy and no, I am not a whore — that doctor is a pervert. No, I'm not a liar or a lesbian. Was I ever molested in the past?" She turned back to Raymond. "I can't deal with all that. Even if I could, with my history, no one's going to believe me."

"For whatever good it does, I be – " His head swiveled toward the door. A thump? "Did you hear something out there?"

"I wasn't listening. I was thinking about what that pervert doctor would tell them about me. You worried Tex and Fritz are making it in the waiting room?"

"No," said Raymond. Fremmer and his buddy could handle whatever came up.

"They told me they'd see we weren't interrupted," she said. "I think you're wiggy if you think Doctor Taylor would send people to follow me or spy on you."

"Wiggy?" Let her notion stand, he thought. Not fair to involve her in his fears. "I believe we were discussing your decision not to go to that hearing." Was his own decision to report Cruber shooting his daughter wise? He was jumping at every sound, every shadow.

"I don't want to feel like a piece of rotten meat laid out for inspection."

He grimaced. "Is that how you've felt with me?"

"Sometimes. That's why I still haven't told you some things. Even though I've trusted you more than anyone."

"Your trust is a true gift." Not like the geode, he thought. "I appreciate that." Maybe now was the right time. He reached back to his desk and picked up the stone he'd used as a paperweight. The geode's exterior was pitted and rough, but the amethyst crystals sparkled within. "Look, I want to give this back to you." He held it out to her. "It does not – I repeat, does not – mean that I appreciate or care for you any less."

She made no move to take it. "Why?"

He heard her hurt and suspicion. He reached over, gently took her hand and put the stone in it. "Because as long as I have it, you'll always be waiting for me to cast it at — "

The door slammed back against the wall. Raymond recoiled. He heard Maggie gasp. An ape was pointing a gun at them. Where was Fremmer? Oh, God!

"Holy Virgin!" Maggie cackled. "A gorilla – I thought you were acting strange, Raymond." She waved her empty hand at the ape. "You scared the hell out of me, you know that? He's terrific, Raymond. I love it!"

"Tell her it's not a joke," said the ape.

Cruber! Raymond felt nauseated; his heart pounded. "It's – it's not a joke, Maggie."

"It's not?" She smiled. "Sure it is. This four-hundred pound gorilla comes into the psychiatrist's office and he says – well, tell me the punch line." She laughed and shook her head. "Is that you, Tex?"

"She's in shock," said Raymond. "Why don't you let her go home? She doesn't know who you are."

"Don't be an idiot," said Cruber.

"I tell him that all the time," said Maggie. She looked at Raymond. Her face was pale. "No joke?"

"No." Raymond clutched his knees to keep his hands from trembling. Maybe Fremmer was just injured; maybe he'd called the police. Play for time!

"Get up." said Cruber.

"We need to talk."

"How many grubsuckers are downstairs?"

"Grubsuckers?" asked Maggie.

Cruber stepped closer. Raymond kept his eyes on the gun, didn't see the mittened hand until it whacked the side of his face, jolting his head. He saw pinpoints of light, felt a sharp pain in his ear.

"He knows what I mean," said Cruber. "Guards, cops, crows in and out of uniform. How many?"

"I don't know."

Cruber hit him again. Raymond grunted, fought back the tears.

"Stop!" yelled Maggie.

Rubbing his cheek, Raymond shook his head in an effort to clear it. "There were two up here. That's all I know about. I don't think there were any more."

"Tell me the truth!" Cruber raised his hand.

"That is the truth, God damn you."

"Then get up. Both of you."

"In a second. My head's spinning." Fight back? With the desk lamp? Cruber could kill them both in two seconds. The stone? In Maggie's fist. "You shouldn't have hit me," he said. "It's in the Bible. Let he who feels sinful cast his – fist into the waters," he ad-libbed. Would Maggie understand? "Help me up," he said, extending his hand to divert Cruber's attention.

"Get up, yourself."

Raymond made a show of staggering to his feet.

"I'm glad I got you to read the New Testament," Maggie said, getting up. "You ever read it?" she asked Cruber.

"It doesn't mean crow-crap to me. Put your hands behind your heads and back away from the desk." As they did, Cruber went behind the desk, slipped off his mitten and dropped it in the plastic bag lining the waste basket.

"Too bad," said Maggie. "From the Bible, we draw our salvation."

"Amen," said Raymond. The stone must be in her sweater; the code was in the Bible.

Cruber picked up Raymond's appointment book and desk calendar and dropped them in the waste basket. Then he pulled the plastic liner from the basket and moved toward the door. "Come outside!"

Slowly, Raymond lowered his arms and walked toward the door. With eyes and gun focused on Raymond, Cruber backed into the corridor. Raymond heard Maggie right behind him.

"You okay?" she whispered.

Okay? How could he be okay? But he lowered his head a fraction, hoping she would see that as a yes.

"I want everything you wrote about me," said Cruber. "If I don't get it all, your crow-bitch'll pay for it. Understand?"

"Crow-bitch?" said Maggie.

"You can have your clinic record. No problem. Your chart's in the file room, up the hall." Where the hell was Fremmer? "But let Ms. Saxe go. You've no quarrel with her."

"I'll think about it. Meanwhile, let's get my record. The bitch goes first, then you."

"I have a name. It's Mary Margaret Saxe."

"Walk, bitch!"

She did, muttering "That may be my diagnosis, jerko, but it's not my name."

Cruber would take his file and then kill them, thought Raymond. Maybe there was a chance he'd let Maggie go. He paused before unlocking the door to the file room. "Let her stay outside, so she doesn't see what drawer I pull your file from."

"So she can run off? Open it up."

The lock clicked open. Raymond entered and flipped the light switch. Cruber shoved Maggie in. The room had no windows. File cabinets lined every wall.

"I don't want her to see your name," said Raymond. "Let her turn her back and close her eyes."

"Get my record," said Cruber.

Raymond walked to the file cabinet marked C–D. Behind him, he heard Cruber say, "Look right at me, bitch. Do you know who I am?"

"Yes. You're a big, stupid gorilla."

Shit! thought Raymond. She's into 'go ahead and abuse me, you bastard' mode. "Your file is in here," he called out. His hands trembled as they flipped through the manila folders.

"I guess this grubsucker didn't introduce us properly. My name is George Elton Cruber."

Raymond glanced over his shoulder. Cruber had pulled off the mask. His face was flushed and sweaty. "I'm not a gorilla. I'm a toll collector," the man said.

Oh, fuck! thought Raymond.

Maggie shook her head. "You got the wrong person, George. I don't own a car."

"You can pay for something else, then. Get over there with the crow-turd."

"Here's your file." Raymond pulled the manila folder from the drawer. As he turned, Maggie was backing up in front of him.

"Why doesn't he like you, Raymond? Couldn't you cure his impotence?"

"Don't stand in front of him! And don't call me impotent. Not unless you want me to prove otherwise. Give me the file."

"Be quiet, Maggie," said Raymond, stepping around her to hand Cruber the file.

"Look," said Maggie. "If you don't call me bitch, I won't call you impotent. How's that?"

Why won't she shut her mouth? thought Raymond.

"Good," said Cruber as he looked at the name on the file. "Now each of you take as many of those folders as you can carry out to the waiting room. And fast."

Thankful to have a few more minutes to live, Raymond went to pull case records from another drawer.

"Can I get my file?" said Maggie, as she opened the drawer labeled 'SA-SM'. "I'd love to see what this crow-turd's written about me. Maybe I'll kill him for you."

"Not a bad idea," said Cruber. "But this isn't the library. Get some from the C's, the rest from all different drawers."

When their arms were laden with files, Cruber said, "Enough! Let's go. The bitch first."

Maggie froze. "Do you need a big gun because your little prick won't fire?"

"Move!" snarled Cruber.

"Calm down, we're going." said Raymond.

Maggie didn't budge. "My name is Mary Margaret."

"I'll kill you, you bitch."

"I got news for you, sir. I never gave a fuck about living. You're just saving me from the mortal sin of suicide."

"Bullshit."

Clutching the files against her chest, Maggie walked toward him until his gun was inches away.

"You don't believe me? Look in my file. Look in my eyes. One dead person can see it in another."

"I only see shit."

"That's our reflection – yours and mine. My name's Mary Margaret. If you don't like that, call me Maggie."

"Well, move your big mouth out to the waiting room — Maggie. Or stand here and watch your friend die. I have no problem adding his body to the two out there. Then you'll really wish you were dead."

Fremmer dead? Raymond felt like he'd been punched in the gut. All of them would die because of his stupidity. "I'm sorry, Maggie, but let's do as he says."

With a scornful look at Raymond, she brushed past him and walked to the waiting room. "Jesus, Mary and Joseph!"

Raymond saw the bodies two steps after she did. Vomit rose to the back of his throat, but his muscles clamped down and he continued forward, his body sagging, his mind overwhelmed by grief and guilt. Brain tissue was spattered on what was left of Fremmer's head; the back of his jacket was bloody. The elevator doors were recoiling again and again from another torso. Oh God! This was worse than any death he'd witnessed as an intern, any autopsy he'd ever done. He'd talked and laughed with these men earlier in the day, and they'd given their lives to help him. Fucking Cruber.

"Put those folders down on that desk."

Raymond dropped his armload of medical records onto the receptionist's desk. Maggie placed her pile next to his. "Sweet Jesus," she whispered. "I've never seen a dead person before."

"Go empty their pockets," said Cruber. "I want everything from their pockets, and then your pockets too, out on this desk."

Taking Fremmer's silver cigarette case from the man's pocket brought tears to Raymond's eyes. How stupid they'd both been. He should never have gotten Fremmer into this. Fremmer should've refused. He could've smoked as much as he'd wanted.

With Maggie still bent over the body half-in, half-out of the elevator, Raymond placed Fremmer's cigarette case, wallet, and other personal effects on the desk, then proceeded to empty his own pockets. What had he missed out on or postponed for later because of studying, working, meeting other people's needs? Stop it! This wasn't the time to feel sorry for himself; he had to find a way for them to live.

"Back away," said Cruber. "Now you," he said to Maggie.

She came back and put a wallet, a comb, a fingernail clipper, a key case and some loose change on the desk. "Robbing the dead is low-class, George."

"Is that all?" Cruber asked.

"No," she said. "You killed two people. I think you owe God a major apology."

Cruber smiled, took two steps forward and smacked her across the face. Maggie grunted as her head jerked away. Raymond bit his lip.

"Don't get wise with me, anymore," said Cruber. "Just answer my question. Is that all he had in his pockets?"

Maggie smiled. "Hit me again, big fella. I get off on it. The answer is yes, like in the Gospel according to Mattathias. *'For there is nothing covered, that shall not be revealed; nor hidden, that shall not be known'.*"
"

Raymond stared at her. Mattathias? Matthew. No, she meant Mattathias, the Jew who began the rebellion against the Syrians. She was out of the New Testament, but still into code – she'd found something.

"Empty your pockets on the desk," Cruber told her.

Raymond watched her extract tissues, a rubber band, bobby pins, a University ID, two keys and several dollars from her jeans. What had she hidden away?

"Turn your pockets inside out," said Cruber.

She did. They held nothing.

"Your sweater," said Cruber.

"It doesn't have pockets. Neither do my panties. You want to search them, too? How about my asshole and my vagina? I have a greenish discharge but I don't think it's from gonorrhea."

"Shut up!" yelled Cruber. "You yak more than my wife. Get over there with him and keep your trap shut." After she'd complied, he began extracting himself from the gorilla costume.

Raymond forced himself to take a deep breath. Maggie'd bluffed her way through, still had the stone and whatever else she'd discovered. And it looked like they'd been given a stay of execution. He watched Cruber carefully, but the man's eyes and gun never wavered for more than a second. Out of costume, he wore a black windbreaker, a dark blue body shirt and jeans, and another gun in a shoulder holster. A flat canteen and two leather sheaths – one holding a large knife, the other, a cleaver – hung from his garrison belt. Why a cleaver? Oh, God! That's how he planned to dispose of their bodies.

"Okay," said Cruber, "break's over. Now you're going to work for your keep."

Cruber supervised them closely as they followed his orders to gather wooden furniture — chairs, tables, magazine racks – from the waiting room and nearby offices. They made two piles, one in the dead man's elevator, the other in the stairwell outside the exit door, leaving enough space for a person to squeeze by. Cruber had them dump some of the medical records on the pile in the stairwell, but his file and many others, plus the contents of Raymond's wastebasket liner, the gorilla costume, and all personal items except for Raymond's keys and handkerchief and Fremmer's cigarette lighter were tossed into the dead man's elevator. Then he ordered them to drag the bodies onto that pyre, leaving a couple of metal chairs as a door stop.

Maggie hesitated. "I've never touched a dead person."

"Better to touch one than be one," said Cruber.

"Help me out here," said Raymond, bending to grab Fremmer's feet.

"I'm not so sure," Maggie took a step toward Cruber. "Raymond thinks people are basically good and the world can be a nice place. You and I know better, George. Raymond's the lunatic. But he hasn't hurt anyone, so let him go. Just kill me, then kill yourself – you'd be doing the right thing for all of us."

Cruber unsheathed his knife. "I won't kill you. I'll cut out your tongue – how's that? Now help him with the bodies."

Maggie blanched and went to help Raymond. After that was done, Cruber made them locate the fire extinguishers and carry them into the file room. He locked the door, pocketed the keys and marched them back to the glass panel containing the fire hose. He had them sit on their hands while he broke the glass and slit the hose.

Finally, back in the waiting room, Cruber unhooked the canteen from his belt and tossed it to Raymond. "Sprinkle this on the pile and give me back the canteen – and don't pour it out in one place."

"Lighter fluid?" asked Raymond.

"Gasoline," said Cruber. "You don't have a lighter, so don't get any funny ideas. I'd be wet, but you'd be dead."

"I know better than to do something like that." Raymond unscrewed the cap. Sorry, Fremmer. Probably be joining you soon.

The gasoline gurgled out and splattered over the pyre. The task and the fumes were sickening, but Raymond focused on avoiding contact with the liquid. Still, a few drops spattered his trousers and shoes. Cruber tossed him the handkerchief to wipe the canteen clean of fingerprints, then directed him to come out of the elevator, toss the handkerchief across the room, and give the canteen to Maggie.

She took the canteen from Raymond but looked at Cruber. "What am I supposed to do with this?"

"Put it down on the carpet and go push the button for the other elevator," said Cruber.

"Why give it to me, then?" Maggie tossed the canteen onto the carpet.

"He wants our fingerprints on everything," said Raymond.

Maggie pushed the elevator button. "It's all going to burn and he's going to kill us, anyway. What difference does it make?"

"The sprinklers won't let things burn out here. That's why he used the elevator and the stairwell."

They heard the elevator rising. Cruber had them stand in front of it, using them as a shield and threatening that if one misbehaved, the other would die first. Raymond doubted there'd be any help coming from the elevator. The clinics were closed. If a security man was coming to make his rounds, he was as good as dead. Perhaps he could knock Maggie aside and fall back against Cruber at the first glimpse of a passenger. But suddenly Cruber's forearm was around his neck, Cruber's breath hot on his ear. "Stand up tall, Doc." The doors of the elevator slid open. Empty!

Cruber had them disable the second elevator with two more metal chairs. "Time to go," he said.

Raymond eyed the distance between them. His muscles tensed.

"Don't try it," said Cruber. "We're all going to walk out of here, unless you do something stupid. See that piece of paper? Roll it up tight and hold it at arm's length."

Walk out? No choice but to believe it. Keeping his eyes on the gun, Raymond bent to pick up a piece of paper that had fallen from one of the files. Relief at being spared didn't change the fact that Cruber planned to kill them eventually. He just wanted hostages until he was sure he'd gotten away.

Raymond held out the paper. Using Fremmer's lighter, Cruber set the end of the paper on fire, then backed away. "Toss it into the elevator!" As Raymond moved toward the elevator, Cruber fitted the plastic wastebasket liner over his gunhand.

The small whoosh and a burst of flame made them all take a step back. The smoke alarm buzzed ferociously as they went out the door to the stairwell, where Cruber had them shove some of the furniture against the door and set the medical charts on fire.

"Let's go," said Cruber. "Hold hands going down. I'm right behind you. If we meet a crow, you smile and say 'Hello', that's all. Anything more, you'll all die."

As they descended, they heard the shriek of the hospital's fire alarm. "Faster!" shouted Cruber.

"What going on up there?" yelled a security guard charging up the steps.

A bullet ripped through the plastic bag and the man's right eye before Raymond could say a word. The man toppled backward, cracked his head on the steps.

Maggie's face contorted in anger. "Impotent shithead!"

"You bastard," Raymond shouted.

"Move it!" yelled Cruber

They burst out onto the street and heard sirens coming, but the only flashing lights belonged to two parked ambulances. Raymond spotted a policeman frantically trying to get visitors and gawkers to clear the area as patients in wheelchairs and on stretchers, some half clad, others covered by sheets, were being evacuated from the Emergency Room exit, only to be left to fend for themselves as nurses, attendants and paramedics rushed back inside to bring out others. Raymond's hopes sank. Who would notice three people leaving the Clinic building?

"Turn left and walk away," said Cruber, poking Raymond's back with the gun. "And put your arm around her."

Raymond did. Maggie was shivering. She leaned into him. "Why'd you wait so long?" she murmured.

She was as afraid as he was —what an actress. "I'm sorry."

Sirens screaming, two fire trucks roared by. Raymond used the diversion to mouth the word "what?"

"I said I didn't know you cared so much," Maggie said loudly. "You must've discovered my Swiss bank account." She extended her hand a few inches in front of her and rubbed her wrist.

"Shut your mouth," said Cruber.

Not a Swiss bank account, thought Raymond. She'd showed him her wrist. Scarred from past cuts. Knife? Swiss Army knife! She had the stone and a knife. He felt a glimmer of hope.

65

Let Her Pray

Dear God, let it hurt! thought Maggie. *Let the pain cleanse me as it did your Son. Lord, let me be your loving daughter.*

Eyes closed, Maggie sat hunched over in the back seat of Cruber's car, her thigh raised to minimize the pressure on her wrists, which Cruber had handcuffed under her left knee. Pain and prayer had been her antidotes for fearful thoughts. Why had this monster seated next to her let them live a bit longer? Where was he taking them? What would he do to them before ending their lives? Raymond was driving, but he was helpless with her held hostage, and no physical match for Cruber. Only God could save them, if not in this life, then in the next.

"Wake up!" said Cruber, poking her with an elbow.

She jerked away from him, the sudden movement partially dislodging the geode from her bra. It was coming out! She opened her eyes. Cruber edged closer, his weight on the seat tipping her toward him. He stank like a garbage pit.

"I wasn't sleeping. Keep your hands off me. You smell like shit."

"You still don't get it," said Cruber. He grabbed the back of her neck and slowly forced her face against his jacket. "I give the orders. You keep your mouth shut."

As she tried to twist away, the geode came loose inside her sweater. She gave a muffled cry and butted her head back against his chest to distract him as the geode tumbled off her lap, hit her toes and dropped onto the carpet.

Cruber grunted but his grip tightened. "Stop struggling or I'll break your neck."

The car swerved. "Leave her alone!" shouted Raymond.

"Tell the bitch to sit still."

She heard Raymond's fear, his desperation, so she let her body go limp. The geode was at her feet. She could put a foot on it, but she'd never be able to retrieve it. Down and done with – like life itself. Stupid to resist the inevitable. She hadn't been able to stop F. Dexter, or the boys on the beach or any of her nightmares. All she could do now was pray. She closed her eyes. *Lord, I am sorry for all my sins. I have offended in thought as well as in word and deed.*

"That's better," said Cruber. He slowly released his grip. "Take the next left."

"The Stafford Reservation?" Raymond said. "What's that?"

I ask for your merciful forgiveness. I never meant –

"You ever been out here, Maggie?" asked Raymond.

Her eyes flicked open. "Shut up, I'm trying to pray."

Cruber chuckled. "Yeah, let her pray."

"Sorry," said Raymond. "I just wondered if you've ever been out here.'

God, help me rise above these assholes! "It's conservation land," she said. No, not fair – shouldn't blame Raymond for asking, for not giving up. He knew he was driving them to some kind of Hell. "I came here once with my geology class." He'd never do anything to save himself while she was trussed up like a sacrificial lamb. She'd have to find the right moment to provoke Cruber so that Raymond could escape. Maybe her death would have more purpose than her life. If she bent all the way over, could she reach the stone? Fucking handcuffs!

"Sit still," muttered Cruber.

"You try sitting on your wrists for an hour. Can't you loosen the handcuffs a little?"

"No. I'll take care of your hands later," said Cruber. "Take the next right," he told Raymond.

The car slowed and turned onto a dirt road. Each bounce of the tires over a rock or into a pot hole made the handcuffs stab harder at her wrists. Maggie hiked herself up enough to look out at the trees retreating from the headlights into darkness. Nothing to save them out here — they were going to die. Mother of God, why this way? With this maniac. "I feel sick," she said.

Raymond glanced over his shoulder. "Hang in there... You won't get away with this," he told Cruber. "Even though you burned the records, my supervisor knows I've been treating you and Protective Services has my letter. They'll track you down."

"The grubsuckers already have. You haven't stopped the crows from coming — or the spells. So we have to do it this way. And I'm not planning to go home. Everything I need is already out in those woods. Clothes, money, my bike – and her. Once we take care of her, she won't be able to send any more crows. And if you and your bitch act nice and tell me the truth, I may even give you this car to go home."

"The truth?" asked Raymond. "Are *you* telling us the truth?"

"He wouldn't know the truth if it bit him in the balls," said Maggie. "He's going to chop up our bodies and bury the pieces." Is that what he meant by taking care of her hands? This monster couldn't be God's instrument. "I feel sick to my stomach." She hunched over and let out a burp.

"You want the truth?" said Cruber. "You know what the grubsuckers do with truth, Doc? They peck at it until they're sure it's dead, then they suck it up and turn it into shit."

"Look – "

"No, you look!" said Cruber. "The truth is I died a long time ago. But I won't let the grubsuckers bury me as if I didn't exist. That's what the crow-bitch always wanted; that's why she's sending them. You're my witness, Doc. I'm going to show you something and maybe you'll die tonight, maybe you won't. The truth is that once you do your job, I don't really care. The truth is that death is easier than life."

"Amen," said Maggie.

"You think your mother is sending the crows?" asked Raymond.

"Take the next turn-off and go down to the end," said Cruber. "Park and hand back the keys."

"What then?" asked Raymond.

"We walk."

"I can't walk like this," said Maggie.

"I'll fix it. And don't try to yell. Nobody'll hear you, and you won't get a second chance."

"Where was my first one?" she said. F. Dexter? She should have screamed then. Turned a deaf ear to his lies, a dead heart to his promises. Screamed herself out of her family. "I feel sick. I think I'm going to puke." She bent all the way over and vomited up sounds. Where the fuck was the stone?

The Toll

66

Resistance

Raymond stepped carefully through the underbrush. His arms felt heavy, his hands cramped from carrying two five-gallon cans of gasoline. With tall pines blocking out moonlight, the only light came from the large flashlight with which Cruber pointed the way from a few steps behind. Maggie brought up the rear, wrists handcuffed in front of her, the rope around her neck tied to Raymond's waist. He knew escape was impossible and that a fall would bring her down, perhaps break her neck, so he focused on making every step a safe one.

"Stop!" Cruber swung a shovel down from his shoulder and planted the blade in the earth. The beam of his flashlight danced in a wide circle.

"It's about time," said Maggie. "I have to go pee."

Raymond lowered the cans to the ground and flexed his hands.

"We're almost there," said Cruber. His flashlight's beam flitted from tree to tree.

"You don't have a clue as to where we are," said Maggie. "Which tree is your mother?"

"Shut up!" said Cruber.

"This asshole is lost, Raymond. He doesn't know where the fuck we are."

"She's right around here, somewhere," said Cruber.

Play on his fears, thought Raymond. "So are the crows. We can protect you from them."

"Don't try to fuck with my head. I'm not stupid. I know what you two are up to."

"You don't know shit," said Maggie. "You're fucking lost."

Cruber pulled the shovel from the dirt and stuck the butt under her chin. "You shut your mouth. You two are slowing me down, trying to confuse me." He took a step backward. "Pick up the cans." His beam darted toward a thicket of prickly bushes. "Up around those bushes!"

Tackle him, hit him? Shovel and flashlight in Cruber's hands, gun in his holster, cleaver and knife sheathed at his belt. Raymond took a deep breath, picked up the cans and trudged uphill.

It took another ten minutes for Cruber to find the right place: a clearing beside a tall pine split by lightning. Cruber tossed the shovel into the clearing and drew his pistol. "Put the cans over here and untie your end of the rope," he told Raymond.

"How about untying my end," said Maggie.

"You're staying with me," said Cruber. "If he runs, I kill you."

"You run, Raymond. I'd much rather be dead than a rag doll for this mother-fucking maniac."

Cruber whirled around; his beam jumped to her face.

"George!" shouted Raymond. "I won't try to run." He saw Maggie's eyes close, her lips tighten – she was waiting to be hit. His cramped fingers fumbled with the knot. "Here! Here's the rope!" He tossed his end forward.

The light swung back. "You'd better get her to shut her garbage mouth," said Cruber softly. "Or I'll cut out her tongue."

"Maggie, please!" said Raymond. "Do us both a favor."

"Wimp, asshole," she said.

He kept his gaze on Cruber. "You said you were going to show us something."

"If you cooperate. Step away from the gasoline and lie down on your face."

"Yeah, lie down and roll over," said Maggie. "You're fired, Raymond. I don't want you to be my shrink, anymore."

Her way of releasing him? She probably thought him a coward. He grit his teeth but lay down in the weeds.

Cruber picked up Raymond's end of the rope, coiled it and tossed it over a strong branch. "Now for you," he told Maggie. "You're going to stay right here and watch old Raymond dig."

"You stupid bastard. That shithead couldn't dig his way out of a Dixie cup."

"I'm going to tie you to this tree so you don't fly away. I want you to meet my mother."

Raymond's hands explored the ground within reach. There were no rocks bigger than a grape.

"You never had a mother, you scumbag," said Maggie. "If you did, she must've mated with a giant cockroach, you larval – Raymond, run! Ray — "

Scrambling upward, he saw the flashlight smash against her face, heard his name die in her cry of pain. He barreled into Cruber's legs, driving them out from under the huge torso that crashed down on him and crushed all breath from his body.

"Stupid crow-turd," said Cruber, raising the flashlight.

Raymond tried to twist his head away, but it imploded with pain and a flash of red.

67

Is She A Crow?

Raymond didn't want to wake up, didn't want to move. He felt as if pain was ripping open his head and turning his stomach inside out, but his head rested on his mother's lap and she was caressing his forehead to comfort him. A couple of tears hit his face before he heard her muted sobs. Were the ambulance men taking her back to the hospital? She was crying about leaving him, afraid she wasn't coming back. This time he'd fight them, he wouldn't let them out the door. He opened his eyes to a blurred face hovering over him. He tried to reach up to her, but his wrist was restrained.

She stopped crying and withdrew her hand. "Wimp, asshole," she murmured.

Maggie Saxe. Cruber. Raymond groaned and shut his eyes again.

"Raymond, don't pass out on me." Her words were slurred, barely audible. "You hear me?"

"Uh-huh. My head, it's awful."

"I told you to run."

He heard his own raspy breathing, the chirping of crickets, a clink of metal against rock. Someone was digging. "I remember Cruber getting us out of the car, tying us together. And those gasoline cans — " His head felt ready to burst. "You told me to run?"

"Shhh! Not so loud," she whispered. "Don't you remember going after him?"

"No. It hurts to think."

"How well I know."

He opened his eyes and tried to lift his head off her lap, giving up the effort as a wave of nausea hit him. "I need to remember," he whispered.

"First I want to thank you – your wife's never going to forgive me anyway." She pressed her lips to his, then pulled away. "Ouch!" she said. "I need a new face."

"Just tell me what happened."

"Shhh! I got Cruber after me so you could run, but you, you lovely idiot, you ran right at him. He's twice your weight and waving a gun around, but you brought him down, so he clobbered you."

He tried to touch his head but his hand was stopped short by a metal band.

"Hey, take it easy — that's my ankle," she whispered sharply. "He handcuffed your wrist to my ankle."

"Where is he?" This time, he managed to raise his head for all of five seconds before nausea overpowered him.

"In the clearing, where the light is. He's been digging for a long time. You saved yourself a dirty job by getting bashed."

"Wasn't worth it. How much time do we have before he comes back?"

"Who knows. He's been back twice to check on us. I think he's dug up her body and he's looking for her hands."

"Her hands? I have to get up. Move your ankle with me, here." His head whirled and throbbed as he struggled to a sitting position.

"I'm gonna throw up." He sucked in a deep breath, held it, held everything in until the unbearable headache and nausea eased a bit and he dared to exhale. Oh God, what a way to die. "He buried her hands separately?"

"Maybe he cut her up into pieces and buried each piece separately." Maggie gripped his arm. "That's what he's going to do to us."

"No, he won't." Not with ten gallons of gasoline in those cans, he thought. "We have to find a way out of here."

"I don't see how. I don't mind dying; it's the foreplay that scares me. Mr. Hyde isn't going to make it easy."

"Listen! He's stopped digging. We need a weapon." He turned his head to look for one, saw the ground spinning and tasted bile.

"You okay?"

He didn't trust himself to nod. "It'll pass," he whispered, hoping it was true.

"I'm sorry I burdened you with all my shit. Thank you for believing in me."

"We're not finished yet. Where's that rock you stuffed away? Feel around you for a bigger one."

"It's no use, Raymond. We're in God's hands now."

He saw the beam of the flashlight move. "Bullshit. We're in a maniac's hands. Give me the rock."

She reached down her free leg and extracted the geode from her sock. "Mr. Hyde – Cruber – is part of God's plan."

"Then God's a maniac, too."

She handed him the geode. "Don't be sacrilegious — it's a bad time. Do you want the knife, too?"

"The knife?" Shit! How could he have forgotten? "Yes."

She reached beneath her sweater and brought forth the Swiss Army knife. He saw the light moving toward them.

"Open the biggest blade, then give me the knife. With one hand, I'm better off using that, so you get the stone." He put the geode on her lap, then took the knife from her. "When I stab him, you smash him as hard as you can. Go for the knees if he's standing, then the head or the Adam's Apple if you can, but keep hitting him hard and don't let up."

She tucked the geode into her sock. "I'm no good at this. I've never fought back physically."

"Neither have I, but there's a first time for everything." He put the open knife in his pocket.

"Then pray with conviction," she said.

The beam lit up her battered face. "What are you whispering about?" Cruber demanded.

"Praying," said Maggie. "'*He that is without sin among you, let him first cast a stone at her.*' That means you had no right to hit either of us."

"Get up," said Cruber.

"How? Raymond's handcuffed to my ankle. And you bashed him so hard, he can't even sit up. Why don't you just kill us here? Hey!" she said as Raymond suddenly yanked his manacled wrist.

"Get this off," said Raymond. "I can get up."

"If you do what I say, I'll let you both live," said Cruber. "I want you to see something, that's all."

"Sure," said Maggie sarcastically.

Cruber tossed a key down onto Raymond's lap. "Unlock the handcuffs and put them on her wrists again."

"If you're not going to kill us, then we don't need them anymore," said Raymond. "Shine your light down here." He found the little hole in the gleaming metal. Vision's improving, he thought. They'd have a better chance once they stood up. "We'll walk over without any trouble."

"You bet you will. As long as I have this crow-bitch, I have you. Stay down there and cuff her hands behind her back. And don't do anything stupid with the key – I have another one."

Despite Maggie's protests, Raymond complied. The fact that they were still alive meant that Cruber needed them for some purpose. At least he now had both hands free. But trying to get up brought forth a geyser of puke that made Cruber jump aside with a muttered curse. Raymond sprawled forward on his hands and knees as his stomach heaved again. His limbs shook, his mouth burned.

"Let him be!" Maggie cried.

Cruber yanked Maggie to her feet, then stepped behind Raymond, grabbed his collar, twisted it and lifted. Raymond gagged and fought for air as Cruber hoisted him up and propelled him forward. "You want your puke-face to live, you'd better follow us."

Maggie cackled. "Right to Hell, Mr. Hyde. '*For this I was born, and for this I came into the world'*."

Raymond forced one foot in front of the other, following the lightbeam over uneven ground. Each time he stumbled or his knees buckled, the noose of clothing tightened and righted him again. He tried to focus all his pain, all his hate, on Cruber.

"See that?" Cruber asked. His beam skipped half-way across a clearing pocked with recently excavated holes to a huge mound of earth and a large plastic bag, its misshapen load sealed in by a knot up top. Next to the bag were the two gasoline cans and an unlit fluorescent lantern.

Raymond grunted.

"She's in there, isn't she," said Maggie.

"You'll tell me what you see," replied Cruber.

Doesn't he know? thought Raymond.

"I see a cuckoo," said Maggie.

"Shut your mouth!" Cruber pushed Raymond forward until they stood beside the mound of earth. "Far enough! Watch out for the grave." His flashlight illuminated a deep pit behind the garbage bag. "Take a seat over there, Doc." A sudden push sent Raymond sprawling away from the grave. Thorns from a bush raked his hands and pierced his pants as he fell, but the earth was soft and forgiving. Maggie's scream stopped abruptly. By the time Raymond could turn himself around, Cruber was looking into the grave. "Maybe now you'll keep your mouth shut."

"Maggie!" Raymond struggled to his feet.

Cruber pulled out his gun. "She's okay. Come see for yourself, but nice and slow."

The flashlight beam half-blinded him as he hobbled forward. He resisted the urge to touch his pocket. Was the knife still there? He was almost to the grave when he heard her sobbing. "Maggie?"

"Didn't I tell you she was okay?"

"Yes, but you're a lying bastard," said Raymond. He looked down into the grave. Maggie was on her knees at the far end.

"You think the crows don't lie?" said Cruber. "And there are millions of them. I have to protect myself any way I can. But I have no reason to lie now. I won't kill you if you cooperate. This doesn't have to be your grave."

"Or Maggie's?" As if all his attention was focused on her, Raymond edged alongside the grave toward Cruber.

"If she'll shut her mouth, I'll let her live, how's that? I think you should go down there to make sure she cooperates."

"Don't do it, Raymond," Maggie said from below. "He'll kill us no matter what."

"Take another step and you'll get a bullet in your knee, Doc," warned Cruber. "Get into the grave right there."

Raymond's muscles tensed. Too far! He'd never make it. He *was* a wimp's asshole. What wouldn't he do to survive? Slowly, he sat down in the dirt, squirmed forward and put his feet over the edge. Cruber dipped the light so Raymond could see the bottom. Not as deep as he'd thought. Five, maybe five and a half feet. Probably close to seven feet in length. Certainly big enough for more than one body. Maggie, her hands manacled behind her, half-sat, half-sagged against the dirt wall opposite him. Her sweater was filthy, her hair a mess. Even worse, she looked defeated.

"Remember the first time we met," he said, "you asked me if I'd jump in to save you?" He lowered himself gingerly into the pit and moved toward her. "I'm afraid jumping in isn't my style."

Before the light disappeared, he saw her smile. "Asshole."

Cruber moved away for a few seconds, then clicked on the fluorescent lantern at the head of the grave. Raymond blinked and put a hand to his head. The grimy and tattered plastic bag now sat above them. Cruber had cut a large slit down the front. "Move back!" As they did, he lifted the bag and poured its load of bone and maggot infested flesh right in front of them.

"Don't look!" Raymond shouted, thrusting his hand in front of Maggie's face. He heard her shriek, smelled the rot of death and recoiled as if branded by it. "God damn you!" he screamed.

"God who?" said Cruber.

"He's the Antichrist!" Maggie fell to her knees.

"What came out of the bag?" asked Cruber.

"What?" said Raymond.

"Don't listen to him! He's the Antichrist!" She grabbed his thigh.

"For God's sake, Maggie." He reached down and tried to help her up. "It doesn't matter who the hell he is. Calm down."

"Yes it does. You don't believe!" She came up struggling, jerked out of his grasp and lurched toward the far end of the grave. "He's the Antichrist. Let him kill us, but don't do what he says."

The five-gallon can in Cruber's hands gurgled as he doused the mutilated, rotting corpse with gasoline that splattered in all directions. "What was in the bag?" he asked.

"You know. You put it there," said Raymond.

"Tell me!" Cruber kept pouring gasoline. "If you want to live, you'd better tell me."

Raymond stepped back. Cruber wasn't sure. That's why he needed them. "Maybe that wasn't your mother, George. Did you kill your mother?"

"Is it real?" asked Cruber.

"What the fuck is he talking about?" said Maggie.

"Shh! Stay out of this," said Raymond.

"Fine time to tell me," she muttered.

Cruber emptied the can and tossed it aside. "Is it real?"

Say yes? No? Either way, Cruber'd kill them. "Is what real?"

"Is that pile of shit really my mother?"

"I never met your mother."

"You're a doctor. Is it a human body?"

"What else could it be?"

"A crow. They disguise themselves as human. Ask the one next to you."

"Maggie's not a crow. She's human."

Cruber struck a match. "You see this? I'll roast you both. You'd better tell me the truth – is that a human body."

Raymond peered across the pit. "If crows look human, I'd need a closer look to be sure."

"So go do it."

"No. The gasoline – and that match. Uh-uh."

"Grubsucker." Cruber blew out the match. "Go look now."

"I'd still get gasoline all over my shoes."

"I have another can I'll dump on your head!" screamed Cruber.

Raymond forced his shoulders to shrug, his voice to stay even. "Then I wouldn't be able to tell you anything, would I."

"You grubsucking bastard!" Cruber stepped backward and bent over.

"I'm sorry I freaked out on you," whispered Maggie.

"Forget it. We have to keep him – "

"Catch!" said Cruber. Raymond looked up, saw Cruber with the lantern, then felt a soft blow on his shoulder. A small plastic bag dropped to his feet.

"Pick it up and open it," Cruber ordered.

As Raymond squatted to pick up the bag, he turned his head toward Maggie. "Keep him guessing," he whispered. "No certainties." Something had poked through the bag. A finger! Oh, God. Holding the bag at arm's length, Raymond stood up and undid the knot. He tried not to breathe as he looked into the bag of rotted hands. Like an autopsy, nothing more, he told himself. He'd never puked doing those.

"Take 'em out," said Cruber. "Are they human?"

"Are you?" asked Maggie. "How do we know you're not a crow?"

"You grubsucking bitch." Cruber set the lantern down and reached into his pocket.

Matches! Raymond shoved Maggie back toward the far end of the pit, away from Cruber and the decomposed body. "She's not sure, George, that's all. That's all!"

Cruber set the whole matchbook ablaze. "I'll make her sure." He tossed the burning matchbook into the grave and stepped back. With a whoosh, flame burst over the body and across the width of the pit. Raymond dropped the bag and tried to protect his face. The odor of burning flesh poisoned the air. Cruber picked up the second can of gasoline and came around the pit.

"Oh, dear God, please forgive all my sins," whispered Maggie. "Holy Mother of God – "

"Don't do it!" yelled Raymond. "I saw the hands. They're human."

"And this is all real, right? It's not one of my spells."

"If you say so," said Maggie.

"I'm not talking to you. I want it from the shrink."

His knees felt weak, his body was trembling. If he said yes, Cruber would kill them; if he said no, Cruber would go berserk. "I – I'll say whatever you want me to say, George. I'm too afraid to tell you the truth."

"You son-of-a-bitch," screamed Cruber. "I'm going to let you go if you tell me the truth. Look, I'll take the crow-bitch up here with me. I'll ask a question and if I get the truth from you, I take off her handcuffs. Give me a second straight answer, I'll let her go. And I'll let you go after you answer the last question – if it's the truth."

Raymond tucked his hands in his pockets and took hold of the knife. There'd only be one question, then Cruber'd throw Maggie back in. "Let us both come up, so we'll believe you mean it."

"Oh, I mean it." Cruber slopped gasoline down the earth wall. "Either she comes up here or gets torched down there." He put the can aside and lit a match. "Give her a boost up, Doc."

"Give Raymond the key to take off these handcuffs," said Maggie.

Bastard's out of reach, thought Raymond as he looked for a foothold halfway up the dirt wall.

Cruber dropped the match. A blast of flame and heat drove Raymond and Maggie back against the opposite wall. While they stood penned in by the fire, Cruber came around behind them, swooped down and grabbed Maggie by the neck. She gasped, but he dragged her backward, then up by her armpits. Raymond jumped forward; Maggie's wild kick knocked him back. She was out of the grave and in Cruber's arms before he could pull the knife from his pocket.

"Change of plan," Cruber said, then grunted as Maggie stamped down on his foot. He locked his forearm around her throat. She tried to twist away, but her mouth and eyes opened wide as she struggled for air. He saw Raymond step forward. "Take another step, doc, and I'll break her neck." He glanced down at the top of Maggie's head. "Stop fighting me and I'll let you breathe." Maggie went limp in his grasp. "Now, doc, you'll tell me the truth because you don't want her dead. First question, is she a crow?"

Raymond didn't hesitate. "No! She's human."

"Good," said Cruber. "I wouldn't fuck a crow. If she fucks good, I'll believe you." He smiled as Maggie's body stiffened.

"Second question," said Cruber. "Who sent those grubsuckers I killed in the hospital?"

"You said you'd take off her handcuffs."

"I said the plan changed."

"I'm holding you to your promise." Yes, Cruber's view would be cut off by the edge of the pit. Raymond stepped forward and took out the knife.

"You can't even hold your own puke. You give me my answer or you're going to watch me rape her."

505

Maggie coughed. "It doesn't matter," she croaked. "It's not real. It's a nightmare."

"No, a spell," said Raymond. He found a toe-hold in the dirt wall.

"You're lying!" Cruber grabbed Maggie's breast. "Look, I can feel you, I can touch you anywhere!"

"Stupid bastard," she said. "You can touch whatever you want. It's not real. I'm not real unless I touch you."

Cruber's head jerked. "You are going to touch me." He forced her to the ground in front of him. "Your hands are going to touch me everywhere, or else they'll come off." He tore off his shoulder holster and tossed it behind him. "Back up, doc, or I'll kill the bitch now." He watched Raymond take two steps back, then bent down to undo Maggie's handcuffs. "I'm going to teach you to touch me, you grubsucking bitch. You're going to beg to touch me so you won't lose you're fucking hands." He tossed the handcuffs aside, went to unsheathe his cleaver.

Maggie lunged for the pit, gasped as Cruber came down on her back.

Now! Raymond sprang for the toehold and clambered over the top.

Cruber looked up. "Grubsucker!" He struggled up on his haunches; one arm flew up to block Raymond's knife; his other hand went for his cleaver. Raymond felt jarring impact as his blade pierced Cruber's forearm and the handle was whipped from Raymond's grasp. Cruber yelped. Raymond looked at his empty hand, at Maggie struggling up, at Cruber fumbling for his cleaver. "Run!" He kicked at Cruber's face, but his foot was grabbed and twisted and the ground reached up and whacked him from behind. Then Cruber's knees were upon him, driving all breath from his body.

"You filthy crow-turd!" Cruber looked at the knife protruding from his forearm. "You really stabbed me." He wrestled the cleaver from its sheath. "I'm going to chop off your dick and cram it down her throat. Then we'll all know it's – " He grunted as Maggie smashed the geode against his temple. Cruber's head pivoted, his body sagged.

"You bastard!" Maggie yelled. She smashed the rock into his head again. "You bastard, F. Dexter, you bastard!" Cruber toppled to the earth. Maggie stood over him and raised the rock again. Her body jerked. "Mother of God! Mother of God." She doubled over.

"Hit him again!" Raymond, struggled to his feet. His chest ached. The world seemed to be spinning. "Hit him again."

Maggie shook her head. "Come on! We can run; we can hide."

Cruber's legs moved.

"We'll never be safe. Hit him again, God damn it!"

"No." She jammed the stone into her pocket.

Cruber's hand twitched on the cleaver.

"Are you crazy?" yelled Raymond as he staggered forward. His head felt like it was bursting. He stomped on Cruber's hand, but his leg had little power. Cruber didn't let go of the cleaver. "Find the gun!" He kicked Cruber's hand as hard as he could. The hand jumped, the cleaver flew into the pit. Cruber clawed at the earth. "Find the gun!" Raymond kicked Cruber's head. Cruber grunted. "The bastard won't stay down! Give me the gun!" He kicked Cruber again.

"Stop!" She held the gun.

"Give it to me!"

"No." She hurled it into the woods.

His pain and fury exploded. "Are you crazy? What the fuck did you do?" He looked for another weapon. He grabbed up the lantern and lunged over to Cruber. Had he moved?

Maggie grabbed his arm. "Don't kill him!"

"Let go!" He tried to shake free. "He'll come after us."

Her fingers dug in. "Then murder me with him. Please! If you want me to live, leave me the first commandment."

"Hypocrite!" he yelled. "You tried to kill yourself."

"That's different. I don't count."

"And Cruber does?"

"You do."

He put a hand to his head. Push her out of the way?

"Anyway, we need the light to get out of here," she added.

"Oh – then take it! Watch him!" He shoved the lantern into her arms, then lurched away. He had to pull twice to free a shovel from the dirt. His head throbbed, his body felt broken. Even half-empty, the gasoline can was almost too heavy to lift.

"What are you going to do?" She moved in front of Cruber. "We'll never sleep if you kill him."

"I'd sleep a lot better." He set the can down at her feet, took the shovel in both hands and brandished it over Cruber's head. "Roll him over."

She didn't move. "I won't let you murder him!"

"I won't, okay? This is just for protection. We need his car keys."

She set the lantern down, grabbed Cruber's arm and tried to pull him onto his back. "Holy mother, he's heavy. Why don't you help me?" She moved down to Cruber's hips.

"Because I don't trust him and you won't hit him."

"I did — uggh – " She lifted and pushed.

Cruber groaned as his body flopped over.

"Hurry!" said Raymond. "Get the keys. And get his matches."

She patted Cruber's pockets. "The keys are in here. And a cigarette lighter."

"Take them both. But he has matches, too."

508

She fumbled in another pocket, brought forth two books of matches and noticed the knife sheathed at his belt. "I'd better take his knife, right?"

"Unless you'd rather bury it in his heart."

She stood up holding all she'd confiscated. "I don't like you like this, Raymond."

"Well, I've had a bad day." He tossed the shovel away, got the gasoline can and started pouring gasoline on Cruber.

"You lying asshole!" she yelled. "You're just like every other fucking man."

"No, I'm me. I'm not lying. I'm not going to kill him." He emptied the can, then dropped it on the dirt. "I wouldn't lie to you. Do you have the matches?"

"I won't give them to you."

"Okay. If he tries to follow us, I'll ask for them. You'll give them to me then, okay?"

"Alright."

"Then let's get out of here." He stepped unsteadily toward the line of trees.

They both heard the sharp cry and looked up. The treetops were silhouetted against the dawn sky.

"Oh, shit," said Raymond. "A crow."

"Mother of God… Raymond, give me your hand, okay? I don't want you to fall."

He extended his hand. "Fucking crows."

68

Another Day

Raymond was just dozing off again when someone knocked on the door. His eyes snapped open. Cruber! He jerked upright in the hospital bed, one arm flailing at the bedclothes, the other reaching blindly for a weapon. No! He was in the hospital, guarded by police. From beneath the drawn window shades, enough daylight leaked into the room to take the edge off his panic. "Who's there?" he called. His voice echoed his fear.

"Officer Thurmond."

That sounded like Thurmond. And Cruber wouldn't have knocked. Raymond took a deep breath. His body ached; his head felt bloated under the gauze dressing. He pulled the sheet and blanket over his thighs. "Come in!"

Thurmond opened the door and stepped into the room. "You up for another visitor?" Light from the corridor highlighted his badge, spilled over his jowls and mustache; his eyes were overshadowed by his cap.

No, Thurmond couldn't stop Cruber. Poor Fremmer. Had Lisa

finished the packing?" Are there still two of you out there?" asked Raymond.

"Still two," said Thurmond. "You want to see this Miss Saxe?"

"Of course he does!" said Maggie, breezing through the doorway in sunglasses, a black turtleneck sweater, jeans and a shoulder bag; she held a cellophane-wrapped bouquet of scarlet and yellow tulips in one hand, a stack of newspapers in the other. "How're you doing, hero? We're famous!" Her tone was exuberant; an angry bruise distorted her smile.

That's not right, he thought. He gripped the lowered bedrail; his lips twitched into a tight line. Fremmer was dead, Lisa and Taylor were ripshit, and Maggie just waltzed in like she was on a drug high. "I could be better. I'm glad to see you up and around. Do they have any leads on Cruber?"

"Not as far as I know," she said. "I keep looking over my shoulder. It's been the longest two days of my life…Would you close the door, please?" she asked Thurmond as he was leaving. "Thanks." The door clicked shut. She dropped the newspapers and shoulder bag on a chair, jerked her head toward the door. "To serve and protect, I love it. My bodyguard's named Paul; you think that's my karma?" She glanced around the room. "Damn it's dark in here. How do you see anything?" Still holding the bouquet, she walked around the foot of the bed to the nearest window.

"You might want to take off your sunglasses." Raymond pulled the sheet up to his waist. God, he must look scruffy. He touched the stubble on his chin.

"Not for a while," said Maggie. "I look awful in puffed purple." Her hand reached for the window shade. "Will light hurt your eyes?"

"No." He pressed the button to raise the head of the bed. The motor whined. "At least, I don't think so."

She raised the shade. Sunlight streamed in; the tulips dazzled. "It's spring, Raymond. It's glorious out there." She moved to the second window and reached for the shade. "So are you dying or what?" The shade pulled from her hand, snapped against the roller. He started and ducked, saw her recoil from the window, shielding her face. Cruber! he thought, then heard a nervous laugh from her. "Sorry," she said.

Raymond sat up straight again. "It's like that now, isn't it…"

She shrugged. "A small price when you consider — " She shook her head. "I really don't like to think about it. What's happening with you? Is your brain going to be okay?"

"Just a concussion. I'm getting discharged tomorrow. My head feels like stuffed cabbage." He tried to smile. "I know. To you, it's no different."

"No way." As she approached, the tension in her face eased. The bruise made her look vulnerable; her expression seemed tender. "If you hadn't of — well, I don't — what I'm trying to say is that I'm alive because of you. And I don't mean only physically." She offered him the tulips. "These are for you, for — for caring and being there for me, so many times."

He felt a soft ache in his throat, wanted to reach out and hug her. No, she'd misunderstand, misinterpret. He took the bouquet. "Thank you." The cellophane crackled in his hand.

"You're not allergic, are you?" she asked.

"No. They're beautiful." He heard a double knock and turned his head toward the door. "God, it's been like a parade." He raised his voice. "Come in!" He glanced back at Maggie. "There's probably a plastic thing for flowers in the night table. Would you — "

"I'll get it," said Maggie, stooping to open the compartment under the drawer.

"Raymond, I — " Lisa stopped in the doorway. Her cheeks were flushed, the lapels of her denim jacket gaped open over a tee shirt.

Oh, shit, thought Raymond.

Maggie grunted. She grasped the lowered bedrail as she straightened. "Sorry. No vase." She smiled at Lisa. "Hello, Mrs. Daniels. I was just — looking for a vase."

"Hi, Lisa." The bouquet drooped from his hand, was touching the blanket. Damn, there was no reason to feel guilty. He raised the tulips. "Maggie was kind enough to bring these."

Lisa's face darkened. She came toward the bed. "I — yes, I see. Very pretty." She looked across the bed to Maggie. "Raymond said that you saved his life."

Maggie glanced down at him. "Well, we kind of saved each other. We fought back, didn't we?"

"Yes," he said, "we fought back hard." For the first time, he thought.

Maggie's smile faded as she looked at Lisa. "Neither one of us could have beaten off that fucking monster alone."

"Then thank you," said Lisa. "I don't know what I would have done had I lost my husband."

Christ! he thought. "Well, I'm glad to — "

"I didn't kidnap your baby," said Maggie. "I want you to know that. I'd never steal — anyone."

"I'd like to believe that," replied Lisa.

"For cryin' out loud!" Raymond snapped. "Will you two stop! I'm not anyone's baby or anyone's prize, got that? And my head didn't get smashed hard enough to make me lose my boundaries."

Lisa glared at him. "Good thing." Then she winked and her expression softened.

Awesome! thought Raymond — she hasn't done that in ages. He

winked back, then looked quickly at Maggie. Her smile was bittersweet.

"You're right. You're certainly not anyone's prize," said Maggie. "Anyway, I was talking about your son, not you. How's the little breast-biter doing?"

She's hurting, he thought. "I think it's important that we all — "

"Raymond!" said Lisa, taking the bouquet from his hand, "She's asking about Joshua, not what you think." She looked at the flowers, then at Maggie. "The tumor's gotten much smaller. The doctor thinks he'll see fine out of that eye. Are yours okay?"

Maggie looked puzzled. "Oh." Touching her sunglasses, she smiled in understanding. "Just purple, like my face. And my vanity. A couple of cracked teeth, that's the biggest thing, but they can't keep me down... Now Paul, on the other hand — well, I have to be running along." She came around the bed to collect her things. "How long will they serve and protect us?"

"I don't know," he said. "We're going to get out of town, go stay with Lisa's sister for a couple of weeks. I'll call you when we come back. It may be a short visit back here if they don't catch him. And we won't stay in our apartment."

"They'll get him," said Lisa. "The officers who went with me to the apartment were very confident of that."

He saw Maggie's skeptical frown. Well, Lisa hadn't met Cruber. Not face to face, thank God. "Maybe you should get out for a while, too," he suggested to Maggie.

She shook her head. "Mister Hyde's everywhere."

"Mister Hyde?" asked Lisa.

"George Cruber's not Mister Hyde," said Raymond.

Air puffed from Maggie's lips; her hand flicked toward the

window. "Then why wasn't he there when I went back with the police? Why haven't they caught him?"

"Because he's strong and he's smart and he's paranoid," said Raymond.

"Well — " Maggie picked up her bag. "George Cruber doesn't know where I live, and I have an unlisted number. If he's not Mister Hyde, I have nothing to worry about." She put her arm through the loop and adjusted the bag on her hip. "It's you he wants, anyway."

"No," said Raymond. "He knows he can hurt me by hurting you. So go to Petro's for a while."

"I'll see. Meanwhile, maybe you can refer me to a less dangerous psychiatrist."

Raymond smiled. "We'll talk about that after I come back," he said. "In the meantime, Professor Bergstrom agreed to cover for me. You can ask him, too. He knows the psychiatrists out in practice a lot better than I do."

"Doctor Bergstrom came?" asked Lisa.

Raymond nodded. "With Doctor Taylor. They're going to give me credit for this year, provided I stay out on sick leave. I'll only be allowed one day back — under police protection if Cruber's not caught — for final meetings with my patients. I have to transfer them. And I have to say nothing detrimental about Taylor or his department. The good news is that he's arranged for me to get a fourth year fellowship in a hospital in New York. But if I violate the agreement again, he'll fire me and see that the fellowship offer is withdrawn."

"He won't fire you," said Maggie. "Read the newspapers." She tossed a few onto the bed. "He's after a new hospital building just for psychiatry. He says he wants 'state-of-the-art security,' whatever that is. And you're a fu — ferocious hero. One idiot even labeled us `the Psychodynamic Duo'."

Damn! She must have built up the story for the reporters, exaggerated his heroism. "No — Taylor wants me gone, but he wants us silent. You think you can keep from saying anything about him or John?"

"Another secret for my collection?" Maggie grinned. "Anyway what could I say? I've never met either one of those fuckers." She glanced at Lisa. "Excuse my language. Your husband hasn't cured me of that."

"He hasn't cured me of that either," said Lisa.

"Well, no doctor is perfect — and damn few men are good. So you're a lucky woman." Maggie turned back to Raymond. "It's time for me to try something different. Get me the name of a good female psychiatrist." She headed for the door.

"Will you go to Petro's?"

"Don't worry about me. I'll be okay." With a dismissive wave of her hand, she left the room.

"Damn," said Raymond "She did it again."

"Did what?" asked Lisa

"Walked out on — " His lips tightened; he rubbed his forehead. No, not on him. "Walked out like that," he said. To end it for them? To get him to pursue?

Lisa put her hand on his shoulder. "She has a lot of pride. She's giving you an out."

Her touch was warm. He looked up at her. "You want me to take it? Not stay in touch with her?"

"Yes," said Lisa. "I wish I could be more generous, but I can't. The risks are too great."

Never to hear from Maggie, to know anything more about her

life? Sadness enveloped him. "Imagine if everyone felt that. What then? Do we let the Crubers determine how we live?"

"They do anyway," she said. "You don't have to look for more trouble."

"No," he said. "I don't have to look for it."

THE END

Made in the USA
Columbia, SC
03 October 2018